KENAI

BY DAVE DOBSON

Copyright © 2023 by Dave Dobson.

All rights reserved.

No portion of this book may be reproduced in any form without written permission from the publisher or author, except as permitted by U.S. copyright law.

— *First published edition, June 2023* —

Cover art by Kara Dahlheimer:
https://www.facebook.com/frecklef0x

Cover design by Olivia Pro Design:
https://www.fiverr.com/oliviaprodesign

To Christina, with love.

Contents

A Note on Future History

If you are the kind of reader who likes to know background information on the setting of the book before diving in, you might want to make a first stop at the appendix located at the end of the text. This appendix gives you a brief review of how the human civilization imagined in the story came to exist, or rather, will come to exist, over the next millennium or so.

If you are the kind of reader who likes discovering all that from context as you read and imagine, then read on and enjoy.

1

BIRD WATCHING

Everything was fine on Kenai until that bird died all over Welk.

I mean, mostly fine. And it wasn't the bird's fault. It got a raw deal, too, same as us. It wasn't even a bird, although with xenobio, you kind of go with whatever's close. It's just human nature to lump things into familiar categories. But that bird marked the time the whole thing turned from a peaceful jaunt on a world full of feathery red and gray plants and trees, fun little animals, and crumbling ruins, to a pile of skog. A big pile.

Welk had gotten up like he always did, eager to dig. I'd been awake for a couple hours, of course. Sleep comes hard, especially on planet, although there wasn't supposed to be anything dangerous on Kenai. The megafauna were all herbivores, and there weren't many of them. The sentients were long dead, and Kenai itself was at the ass-end of Council space. That's why I took the job. Distance, peace, and isolation. All recommended, after what I had been through. Doctor's orders.

Anyway, Welk had gotten up, like I said. Drank some of the coldbrew I'd set brewing the day before. Thanked me. All polite and proper, these scientists. Ate a biscuit left over from last night, then went to pee and shower. The shower I still thought was funny. I couldn't count the number of worlds I'd been to, often for months at a time, with nothing but a couple of ZestiWipes to keep the grime at bay. But Welk used the water condenser and shower every day, all before just going to dig in the dirt. At least he smelled nice. Better than my usual gang of grunts, that's for sure.

He came back from the shower, running his blue and white towel over his curly black hair. "Better get to it," he said. Always cheerful. That was nice. The guy wasn't stressed about anything, and he was at home out here in the field. Maybe it had something to do with the showers. "Did I tell you? I saw a couple lizardoids yesterday getting some sun on the stones of the wall. They kind of matched the shapes we saw carved in the big stones over at the first site I visited. I think the carvings might be representational."

"Great, chief." Unlike some of what he said, I followed this.

"I told you, you don't have to call me chief."

"Proper respect for ranks and titles is kind of a thing for me, sir. And you're running this show, right?"

He sighed. "Yeah, well. Such as it is." I wasn't sure what he meant by that. The whole operation seemed pretty elaborate. Eight dig sites, ten paid staff, plus a healthy bankroll for transport, bots, provisions, nanites. And me and a few others like me. Security. Which was kind of a joke, because I hadn't even met a biting insect on Kenai yet, much less something to shoot. Somebody was paying a lot of credits to get us way out here. We'd gotten a ride with a long-range Patrol ship, one outfitted with Hlojeng coils, because the Kenai system didn't have a jump gate. On account of nobody lived here. Or hadn't, not for a couple dozen millennia.

"You going to excavate today, chief? Finally?" Over chili last night, he'd said he thought he was ready to set the bots and nanos up for the first dig. The seismics, LIDAR, and diffraction beams had revealed the foundations of the structure we were here to unearth. It was all scanned and mapped and reconfirmed. He'd shown me on his personal console – his "con" – a fancy model with a big holo and lots of add-ons. He wanted to hit the main chamber of the sunken building. Do the most interesting spot first.

Welk smiled. "You excited?"

I snorted. "Excited is bad in my line of work, sir. When things are exciting, people are generally shooting at you. Or bleeding on you."

"Well, Jess, we'll just try to keep it tedious." He poked me in the arm of my mechsuit. "You're not the least bit curious about what's down there? I mean, a major structure, built of stone and mortar? When the bigger cities are all complex alloys and synthetics? This might well have been built by the ancestors of the folks who built the cities. A precursor culture to the Kenai empire. Their Stone Age, as it were."

"Not denying the importance, chief. And anybody's curious what's in a hole. That's how holes work. Human nature."

Welk laughed. "You play like you're a big tough warrior woman, but I can tell you're with me. This is going to be cool." I didn't reply. He was right. I was trying to be tough and detached, like I always did. That was stupid with Welk. He was a genuinely nice guy, and I had nobody to impress or scare off out here. And of course, I was out of the marines and out of the Razors, and past a bunch of other stuff I'd rather not talk about. But it was ingrained after five tours and then the merc work and what came after. Just a way of life.

Welk folded his towel and put it over the bar affixed to his tent. Next to the lounge chair. Say what you will about the guy, but Welk hit the field in style. He put on his sun hat, a big floppy mesh thing. Rodan Alpha, the local star, didn't put much hard stuff out, at least not much that didn't get stopped by the atmosphere, but I guess it was nice to keep the heat off. My suit kept me cool, or I'd have brought something similar. Maybe less floppy, though. A cool bandana, or a field cap, maybe. One had some dignity, after all. Welk adjusted the towel one last time, then pointed toward the dig site. "Shall we?"

"Sure, chief." The servos in my suit whined as I moved over to pick up my rifle. Although my pistol would have been enough. Heck, a sharp stick or even a firm expression of displeasure would probably be enough. There was nothing here. But better to be ready. That's what they were paying me for. "You need me to carry anything?"

"Not your job, Jess. I've got it. Or Wizzie will."

That set the bot going. "Please state your command, Joran."

"It's Jordan, you confounded gearbox." Welk was easygoing, but the name thing really set him off somehow.

"Yes, Joran. As I said, Joran. Please state your command." The bot's voice was exceedingly pleasant and well-mannered.

Welk bared his teeth. "Bring three packs of nanites and a C-class power cell and follow me to the dig site." He frowned. "And get some standard rations. The spicy chicken with the pepper relish. And the water cooler, and two beers. I don't want to come back for lunch."

"Right away, Joran." The bot rolled over to the supply dump and began rearranging things.

Welk looked after it for a bit, scowling. Then he turned to me. "Spicy chicken OK with you?"

"You know it, chief. I could live on that pepper relish." The meals here were a step up from Patrol rations. More like a few flights of steps. I had eaten something called *Protein, Brown* for a couple weeks straight back on Entan IV. You don't forget something like that.

Welk set out down the path, and I followed. We'd been here less than a week, so it was less a path and more a matted-down trail of weeds. Welk's operating procedure was to keep the camp away from the site, to avoid contamination, he said. And maybe to make it feel like you were able to go home from work, even if it was just forty meters or so. As we came around a wide tufted tree, the crumbly walls of the site emerged before us. A rough and incomplete square of stone blocks, most of them shaped into irregular rectangular chunks. Welk had shown me the tool marks. Funny to think of the Kenaians, whoever they were, using crude tools to bash things, just like the early humans did back on Earth. Nothing more universal than hard labor, I guess.

Some of the stones still sat on top of others with bits of mortar showing in between. Others had fallen or been moved out of place, but it was obvious they were part of the site. Toward the center, just outside the tallest surviving wall, was our big scanner console, about two meters wide by one high and one deep, covered with holo displays and control screens. Welk went over to it, but I couldn't help but check sightlines and do a perimeter walk, full circle, both directions. When you see grunts die in front of you, you get habits. Just rituals, maybe, but they help.

By the time I'd finished, Wizzie arrived, rolling up and converting to his standing mode, both sets of wheels close together. The bot laid everything out in a row next to Welk. That was stupid, both because a row of random items was silly, and because that's right where Welk wanted to dig. But Welk didn't notice. He was too busy flipping through information on the scanner unit. I saw his fingers flying over the console. His face was set in a frown. Bad news from the overnight data processing, maybe? Not my business, but I sort of hoped we'd still be able to dig. That would be more exciting than just watching him tap the console all day.

I stepped over the wall, moving towards Welk. "Wizzie, head back to camp. Notify me if there's anything out of the ordinary, as I defined yesterday."

"Yes, Jess." The bot converted to travel form and whined its way back along the path.

"Something not right, chief?"

Welk let out a sigh, then pointed at a holo display. "See that?"

I followed his finger. "Looks like the red line's got a bad attitude, sir."

Welk laughed. "It's an age estimate. And it's wrong. Or at least, I think it has to be."

"How so?"

Welk looked at me. "It's way too young. The stratigraphy model has to be wrong, but I can't figure out why."

"Come again?"

"Sorry. You know the ruined cities on the planet here?"

"Yeah. I saw a few up in the northern hemisphere as we were flying in. Looked like major urban centers, but weird. All built up on top of themselves, even though there was lots of room."

"That's right. You'd expect less building density for a place like that, one that had room to grow. At least, for human cities, with similar high-grade construction materials." Welk sounded like he was ready to rip up into a lecture. That was all right. He was paying the bills.

"The buildings are advanced?"

"Yes, a lot more advanced than what's here. They include complex metal alloys, processed materials, remnants of electronics and circuitry, although that's long corroded and useless. Even some bits of advanced self-propelled vehicles."

"Maybe they were just hypersocial and loved living all together. Like a happy commune or hive or something."

Welk smiled. "That's possible. We don't know much at all about their culture. We're the first research team, and study here has only just begun. The world was only surveyed less than a year ago." I knew that. It had all been in the briefing. Kenai, named by the survey team. The lead surveyor traced her cultural roots to Earth, to Alaska, and in her culture, Kenai meant flat land. That seemed accurate. The briefing said there wasn't a lot of volcanism or tectonics here, and it rained a lot, so not many significant mountains that weren't worn down and tree-covered. There was also another Class M planet in the system, which was really unusual. Hardly ever see two. The surveyor had called that one Ninilchik. Place of the lodge. Only it had no evidence of settlements, and this one did. That bugged me a little, but naming planets wasn't part of my operations order sheet.

Welk waved a finger. "I don't like the hive angle, though. Another idea, one I like maybe a little better, is that they just made most of their buildings out of biodegradable material. So the center of the city, the dense parts, are metal and stone, while the outlying buildings are of degradable materials that have vanished. We know there's lots of wood and resin here, although there hasn't been an official biological survey. Just the original scans."

"Advanced race, building out of wood? When better stuff is available? Not how it goes on most other planets."

Welk frowned. "Could be aesthetics or tradition that kept them using that stuff. Fashion. And biodegradable materials would explain the apparent concentration of the cities, if the wooden buildings rotted away."

"You sounded like the cities had something to do with the bad age estimate." Sometimes you had to get these intellectuals back on track. Mission focus first and foremost.

"Yes. So, the cities almost all date from about fifty thousand years ago, give or take."

"Isn't that weird? Seems like it would be spread out over longer."

"If you look at Earth history, people created nearly all the major industrial cities within a few centuries." He was sounding a little more pompous now. Or if I was generous, enthused. "So that's not so strange. When you get agriculture working well, and population can grow, you can have a population boom, accompanied by an urbanization boom. Then big cities pop up all at once."

"You sure of that, or making it up?"

Welk chuckled. "Making it up. We don't know much at all about these folks and their history, other than it seems like it may have been pretty short. That's why we're out here looking for older construction. Trying to figure out how the culture developed."

I knew that. He said it every couple of hours. "So what's wrong with the ages?"

"This skogging machine says this site is twenty-two thousand years old."

"That's way after the cities." Even I could do that math.

"Right. Which is why it's wrong, I think."

And that's when the bird showed up. Fell out of the sky, more like, in pieces. And it was a big bird, maybe a two-meter wingspan. One of the larger pieces hit Welk in the shoulder on the way down, leaving a trail of blood and hairy stuff down his freshly-showered body. Yeah, the birds here were hairy. Forgot to mention that part.

2

NUMB

"Amiko! Bring the ARP over here!" Juno's voice was tense. Understandably. We'd been told the rebels were disorganized, poorly funded, a rabble full of nature-loving free-spirit types. Now, we were down four from our squad. Only eight of us left, and the rebels had energy weapons. And a sniper. I still couldn't fathom that Kenzi was gone. Not possible.

"Set it there and get us some covering fire. Now, Jess." Juno's voice was tight. She fired a burst of four at the dirt mound across from us, in front of the mud building. The smoke from the building was starting to wrap around the mound. That kind of cover would help them, not us.

I set the ARP on the ground and pressed the deployment control. Its two squat feet popped out, and its holo sight came online. It wasn't seeing any heat, though. Not through the dirt mound. And the planet Vega was close to body temperature here, anyway, so no contrast. I hit the dirt behind the ARP and triggered the gunner shield. Not that it would stand up to a sniper rifle that cut through our body armor. But it might keep off some of the blasters.

Torqueda rolled over to give me more room. The ARP had a pretty wide swing. "We should just call down orbital fire." His mouth split into a grin under his stupid mustache.

"Cut the chatter, soldier." Juno didn't think Torq was funny. Of course we couldn't call down orbital fire. That was forbidden under Council law. Outbound only, for planetary weapons. Anybody could fire up, but nobody can fire down.

Not a bad rule, given humanity had almost offed itself entirely a few centuries ago. By doing things like firing on planets from orbit.

I let loose at the mound with a burst from the ARP. The energy bolts smacked into the dirt. I aimed at the top, so the hot melted soil would spill down on whoever was behind. Didn't want them popping up to fire at us. I knew from experience that incoming ARP fire was scary, and I wanted to be scary.

"We could use a tac drone right now." Torq was bitter this time.

"Didn't bring any, dumbass." Juno looked through her sight. She had it digitally periscoping so she could maintain cover. "This was supposed to be a growler."

Growler. Where we show up and act scary, and then everybody agrees that we could kill anybody we wanted to, and dying wasn't really cool, so they'd give up on whatever they were fighting about. That was our usual mission. Fly in, growl, get paid, leave.

And now Kenzi was dead. I knew that was true. And in the abstract, I knew that my heart was on fire inside, so much that I might well be dying myself. I would become utterly devastated, shattered in ways that would never come back together. I knew this. But I couldn't feel it. The combat stims were keeping me from that reality. All I had was just a buzz of something not right, something that occasionally stirred to hint at the horror behind the chemical curtain.

"I've got the sniper." Juno adjusted the sight, flicked on the side mirror display so I could see. I spared a glance between bursts. Purple shape in the false color, lying flat on some kind of platform in a tree.

"So shoot him." Torq was getting on my nerves.

Juno made a hissing sound. "He knows we're here. Can't risk leaving cover."

"Skogol," swore Torq. "It will just take a second. He won't be ready." Torqueda pulled his legs up under him.

"No, Torq. Don't—"

But Torq did. And then he twitched. And a CHONK sound arrived from near the tree. And Torq crumpled down. His suit started beeping. Like Kenzi's had.

"Skogging..." Juno rolled over to Torqueda, but I knew there would be nothing to do. Not against what was probably a C99. Our helmets would be like paper to one of those. And the sniper was a good shot.

I slapped the periscope control on the ARP and spun it around to where I could see the tree on the holo sight. I couldn't risk getting up near the sight to aim properly. But trees are big, and they don't move. I emptied a full A-cell at the tree. On the holo sight, I could see the tree catch fire, then totter sideways, then fall down. I kept firing, even as incoming blaster fire smacked into my gunner shield. I assumed if the guy fell, he'd be about where I was firing. Maybe. I wanted him to have a bad day.

The cell screeched, then ran dry. I thumbed the eject and got another cell from my belt. Up, rotate, insert, click to lock. Just like in training, back in my early days in the Patrol.

Juno gave up on Torq. I couldn't grudge her making the effort despite the firefight, however token that effort was. I hoped I'd get at least the same attention if I went. She didn't say anything, just lay back down and got behind her weapon, focusing on the sight.

"Skogging... That's not good."

Not what I wanted to hear. "What is it?"

"The village is on fire. Lots of it. Bad. What did you shoot?"

"The tree." I thought. I mean, I didn't really know what exactly was behind it.

"It could have been Dice and Murr. They're over there. If they're still alive. They're the ones with the heavy stuff." There was a small blast from the direction of the tree. Something flammable going up, maybe? "A-team Juno. B-team, report status."

Dice's voice came over the comm. She had a broad, slow accent from a childhood spent on Minerva. It was so broad that almost all the words gained an extra half syllable, usually around the vowels. "B-team Dice. I am in cover, returning fire.

There have been explosions from within the compound." I didn't like the pronouns she was using. It should have been 'we,' not 'I.' "Murr is out. He took fire during an advancing maneuver. Servo controller hit, suit froze up. I pulled him to cover and rendered basic aid, but I did not have time to get him out of the suit."

"A-team Juno. Murr report status. Over."

Silence.

"B-team Dice. His suit comms might be down. He took a few more hits before I could get us back to cover. Over."

Or maybe he was down permanently. Gone forever. Like the others. I fired another few bursts at the mound, although the return fire had become much more sporadic.

"A-team Juno. Are tactical weapons secure? Report status of heavy muni. Urgent. Over."

"B-team Dice. I mean, they're on the ground next to Murr, if that's what you consider secure. Over."

"C-team Noor. Orders from CentCo are to take out the village. Tactical R22's authorized."

Juno looked at me. I kept firing. "A-team Juno. Cannot comply. That's a war crime."

"C-team Noor. CentCo says we're covered for that scenario."

"A-team Juno. With respect, we are not. We saw civilians, non-combatants, prior to engaging. Some of them were kids." Juno was smart. She knew all field comms were recorded. Getting those facts on the record would keep her safe if this went bad. Or, if it went worse. It was already bad.

"C-team Noor. CentCo says we're covered. Proceed with R22 deployment. Order B-team to comply."

Juno tapped her helmet control. That would cut the comm link. She wanted to talk to me. What the hell did I know? Juno was the squad leader, so her call. Noor, on tactical comms, was bringing down the big orders from orbit, but Juno was in charge of the operation.

I squeezed off a few more shots. Only an occasional bolt came our way now. Something was going down over there. Maybe the sniper had been a leader? I didn't know.

"Jess. We're not going to murder civilians."

"Yes, chief. I approve of not murdering civilians, chief."

"We're probably going to get fired." She was right. Disobeying Razor CentCo was a sure way to get canned. About the surest way.

"I am not enjoying my job today, chief. I would not mind finding other work." I thought of Torq, lying beside me. And Rapp and Fitzgerald, a few hundred meters back at the side of the road, and maybe Murr, now. And Kenzi. A flash of despair, rapidly quashed by the stims. I squeezed my eyes shut and tried to slow my breathing. Not really tactically advisable to close one's eyes under fire, but whatever.

There was an enormous flash from behind the mound. Or I thought it was there. I couldn't tell. It was so intense that my visor went black immediately, leaving weird afterimages in my vision. I flattened myself against the ground. When you don't know what the hell is going on, that's always a good option.

After a moment, I lifted my head, and the visor cleared. I saw a plume of fire and smoke rising up fast. It wasn't behind the mound. It was much farther away, back near the village. And that meant that it was really big if we could see it from here. The hot air in the middle rose fast, glowing orange from the heat, and causing the smoke and dust around it to coil into little spinning donuts round the main stem. The shockwave hit us first. Then the sound, impossibly loud. Like the orbital cannons firing, from back when I was doing drills in the Patrol, back on Glisson. Before the mustering out, before all this. Then the heat. I could feel it burn my cheeks, and the suit flashed warnings all over. All three of those – shockwave, sound, heat – meant that whatever had gone off was big. Really big.

Juno stopped talking. I did too. I didn't even think of firing now. Nothing was coming back our way. Juno scanned the area with her periscope sight. Nothing. But then she stopped on a figure staggering outward towards us. I could see on the mirror display on the side of her rifle. The figure fell to their knees, then toppled forward. Juno kept the sight fixed on the person, but they didn't move again.

Then something fell from the sky into our little depression. It hit Juno and rolled off, leaving a trail of red along the side of her suit. And in the trail of red, I saw some long brown hair.

3

AVIAN FLEW

"What the…?" Welk touched his shirt, then realized he'd just gotten bird on his hand. He held his hand up like it was poisoned or something.

I wasn't worried about his shirt. I was on the move, rifle up, alternating my view between the sky and the surrounding area. "Show me energy emissions, heat signatures, threat assessment."

"What?" said Welk. He didn't realize I was talking to my suit. The heads-up-display holo popped up in front of my face. I had left my helmet over by the console, preferring the fresh air. I'd thought maybe even the suit was overkill, but now I was glad to have it. It was comfortable, familiar, especially when things went bad. I looked at the holos on my way over to pick up my helmet.

The display showed very little yet other than its own readings, but it would take the suit a bit to make a data request of the ship in orbit and fill in the map. No obvious heat signatures, no energy emissions, no unusual radiation. What had killed the bird, then? A bigger bird?

I slapped the helmet on my head and the seals engaged. I waved a hand at Welk. Downward. Get into cover. He didn't know the hand signals, of course, having never served. He looked at me, eyes wide, but then he figured it out and got down behind his scanner console. "Stay put," I said.

I waited for the scans to resolve. They came in one at a time, the display shifting with each new report. The suit wasn't picking up anything, but its sensors weren't too long-range. We didn't have anything like a tactical scanner here. We shouldn't have needed one.

What I wanted was a situation report from orbit. That wasn't going as fast as I wanted. The suit should have no problem reaching the ship, which was in planet stationary orbit above. Not over us – over the biggest dig site north of us. But it still should have been online, and not taking this long.

Would the orbital scan even show anything? Probably not. "Dismiss holo, clear field." I went over to the bird. Pieces were spread out over maybe fifty square meters, and there might be more I couldn't see. Welk cowered there, staring up at me. He opened his mouth to speak, but I held up a hand. I gave the area one more 360 recon, and then I knelt next to the bird.

Not good. It was torn into fragments. Some of them had clean edges. That suggested something sharp. And hot. Some of the skin looked scorched. I'm no xenobio expert, but most normal animals don't cook their prey before eating. That meant maybe weapons fire. But there was no possible reason it should be. Was there something else that was hot enough to sear flesh?

The ship had finally responded to the data request. It wasn't showing anything, which was reassuring. But there was still the fried bird. "Open channel to orbit. Maximum priority, emergency comms, authorization Jess Amiko."

A voice crackled over the suit. "Support Vessel *Deimos* responding to emergency comms. Go ahead Amiko. Over."

"Amiko here. We have a potentially hazardous situation here. Local wildlife killed suddenly, perhaps by weapons fire, maybe three minutes ago. Evidence of intense heat. Over."

"Understood, Amiko. Checking logs, initiating search and overwatch of your vicinity. Will report. Over."

Well, that was good. They were taking it seriously, not laughing at me. Of course, if all it was was a dead bird, they'd probably have a grand time, and I'd look like a fool. I'd been around enough sailors and grunts to know they liked to laugh at stuff like this. I'd have a nickname, and it wouldn't be a cool one. Not at all. Seconds ticked by. Welk bent over to look at the bird, but he stayed in cover, so that was probably OK. I pressed the comms mute. "I'm going to walk the perimeter. Stay in cover, Welk."

He nodded. I started a perimeter patrol. I couldn't see much through the trees, but I turned on the HUD holo again. Nothing unusual. Little animals moving around, lots of waving plants. Tranquil. I made it about halfway around when the comms crackled.

"Amiko, this is *Deimos*. Over."

"Amiko here. Over."

"We're reading negative on ground-level energy discharge near you. Negative on unusual activity, in your vicinity or anywhere. Negative on anything in orbit. Repeat, no unusual activity, no threats detected. There is a persistent data glitch blocking some coverage near you, which is unusual, but the sensors officer thinks it's just routine meteorological interference. Sensor logs indicate high-altitude lightning discharge in the area. Maybe your wildlife got hit by that? Over."

I didn't like that answer. Would lightning tear something to shreds like that? I looked up at the sky. It was its usual daytime shade of copper green. There were some clouds up high, but nothing that looked stormy. And I hadn't heard anything before the bird fell. But I didn't really know what a lightning storm would look like here, or how long a bird would take to hit the ground. I'd only been in the system for ten days, on planet for six. "Amiko here. I copy. Do you know how high the birds here fly? Over."

The professionalism broke for a moment. "Amiko, negative on local bird height knowledge." The voice was amused. "But lightning is probably your best bet. No squads of marines or assault craft. Or enraged bird haters with energy weapons. Over."

"Amiko here. Very funny." I understood the ribbing. I was looking foolish. "Can lightning even hit birds? They're not grounded. Or whatever. Over."

There was a pause. "Database search indicates lightning can strike flying animals. Over." He was still amused.

"I bet that's the first time that's been asked of the Patrol database." I neared the end of my perimeter walk. Still nothing. "You're probably right about the lightning. Even so, request continued overwatch of our area, with reporting of anything suspicious. Over."

"Understood. Will continue overwatch. Science officer suggests you preserve specimen for analysis upon return to base camp if you want to know for sure. Your call. If not, enjoy your fried chicken, Amiko. *Deimos* out."

"Thank you, *Deimos*. Amiko out." I made my way back to the dig site. Welk was still crouched there. He looked up at me, questioning.

"Can't find anything unusual, either me on the ground, or the ship in orbit. They think it might be a lightning strike." I stopped in front of him. "I think you can get up, now, chief. Seems safe."

He got up. "I don't know what an alien avian that got hit by lightning should look like, but this doesn't seem like that. There's a lot of blood. I would think it would be cauterized, not bleeding."

"I defer to your superior knowledge of bird-lightning interactions, chief." But it bugged me too.

"Very funny." He looked down at his shirt again, then looked a little sad and wiped his hand on his chest.

"They said we could store it for analysis later, if you're curious."

Welk's eyes lit up at that. "Hey, good idea. Have Wizzie bring a sample container." He went back over to his console. "We know so little about the local wildlife. Maybe this would help – a chance event that might shed some light on the ecosystem and the meteorology here. Might get a paper out of it.

I decided not to point out that this would be the most boring paper I could imagine reading. And I'd been through a 20-pager on best practices for barracks cleanliness. "Gotcha, chief. I'll get Wizzie to bring one of the tubs." I looked him over again. "And maybe a new shirt."

4

DATING APPS

My thoughts were on birds and other dead things for a while. That was getting me nowhere, and it wasn't making me a good security officer. I needed to get my head clear, and Welk was my only option. He was looking happier with the new shirt, but I still saw him look around a lot more than he had before. Jumpy. Like me.

Before the bird, we'd been talking about the age of the site here. How it seemed younger than it should. That topic would get him going. I thought for a bit, just quiet like. I was starting to do that more, recently, now that I was out on my own. It was a little scary. "Hey, chief. About the site here being too young. Could they just have had some kind of cultural meltdown or something? One that sent them back to the stone age, long after the cities fell?" I did a little more math. My math was rusty. "If it's twenty-two thousand years ago here, that's not long before they died out, right?"

"Yes. At most, this place is a few thousand years before the youngest date we've gotten for other sites, but there's some uncertainty. Could be a lot closer than that, or the same age even. They may have died out then, or they may have persisted as a hunter-gatherer culture for a while after this, not building anymore. Maybe in small, distributed groups. That wouldn't leave much trace, especially if they don't have hard parts that fossilize, which seems to be true from the lack of any mineralized biological remains in the city sites."

Huh. "So, this thing could be the last place they built? Just before they went extinct?" That sounded kind of cool. But also morbid.

"Maybe, if the date's right, and they didn't live on in a more primitive state. But I still think the date's wrong."

"But if it is right, maybe they died out from disease, or famine, or something? Shortly after building this? After their society went down in flames, and the cities burned?" I thought of, but didn't mention, *The Bloodeaters*, a holo series I'd been watching, where humans catch a mutating virus and become maddened flesh-devouring predators, leading to the downfall of society. I didn't feel like Welk would like it if I proposed that ravenous undead took out the Kenaians. Probably because it was stupid. Besides, societies found ways to crumble even without a death virus.

"If the date is actually right, I suppose that sounds plausible. But there's a big gap between the cities and here. More than enough time for civilizations and technologies to rise and fall. Potentially." He shook his head. "But my gut says this place is much older than the cities. It just has the look of a more primitive society. I don't think you'd lose all that learning and knowledge so fast, and so completely, and go back to crude stone structures. The cities are in bad shape, but not that bad. There are some records preserved, some technology. And they'd have been in better shape back when this was built. These people wouldn't have needed to revert to something this simple, this primitive, not with what was left up there."

I set my rifle down and vented my helmet. I should change the cartridge. The air was getting stale in there, even after only a little bit of use. That meant a cartridge on its last legs. We actually had plenty of them, but frugality and stretching resources was still my standard mode. Maybe I should embrace the luxury and have myself a shower. But if I took a shower on planet, I might have to cash in my badass mercenary credentials.

I was still curious about the dating thing. "So, chief, do you trust your fancy machine, or your fancy gut?"

He laughed. "Neither, yet."

"What are you using to get ages for things?"

"Carbon dating, mostly. There are other isotopes we could use, but most of this world is covered in sediments, and there aren't a lot of volcanic eruptions to lay down ash layers we could date. The planet's magnetic field is weak but stable, and we don't see evidence of magnetic field reversals, which you can sometimes use for dating. Carbon-14 is the only radiometric tool we have that's got the right half-life."

"So the machine looks at the carbon and says this place was built twenty-two thousand years ago."

"It's not quite that simple, because the machine is dating soil profiles as it digs holes down into the structure, and carbon dating soils is tricky. But yeah, the oldest soils should have started accumulating after the building fell into disuse."

"You mean once they all died."

"Or left. But there could be a gap. Maybe it stood empty for a while and then started to fill with soil, or filled with soil and then got cleaned out and then filled again. Hard to say exactly."

I had an actual thought, one that I thought might be a good one. "So that could be your answer, then. It's a really old building, but it stayed open and undisturbed, no soils, until more recently. Maybe it was a tourist place or something, and they sold tickets and ran groups through it, and sold sausages, or fried bugs, or whatever the Kenaians ate."

"That might work as an explanation if they weren't so far apart in age, but the date here is so much younger than the cities that I don't think they could possibly be contemporaneously occupied. And if they weren't, then none of this makes much sense. I think there might be something else going on." He tapped a few buttons on the console. "To be honest, the carbon isotopic regime here is pretty strange, anyway. It might be that the signal is just messed up."

"How so?" This time I was asking more to be polite, less because I thought I would understand.

"Well, the process of decay and the half-life are the same everywhere, but each world has different amounts of carbon-14 available. And it can vary over time. This world seems to have had a weird event that made a lot of C-14, maybe 53,000 years ago, although that's plus or minus a couple thousand."

"That's not long before the cities went up, is it?"

"Yeah. That's also weird. You see that kind of signal sometimes, where there have been nuclear weapons used, or where there's a big change in solar activity or something like that. Earth had an event like that back when they were first using nukes, long ago, that changed all the radiocarbon signatures. But three thousand years before they built the cities, you'd think nobody would have that kind of technology. So maybe it was a natural event, a bump in sunspots or something."

I pondered. "Could they have been attacked from off-world?" As somebody who'd on occasion attacked people from off-world, I knew this was a thing that could happen.

"Maybe, but there's no other indication of extraplanetary contact or space travel."

"That might explain how the cities got built so fast, if benevolent aliens showed up and helped them. Maybe the aliens pooped out radioactive carbon."

"I told you, having a bunch of cities come along in that time frame is not necessarily unusual. You don't need aliens." He grimaced.

"How do you know there's this big carbon event, anyway?"

"Ice cores. There's some permanent glaciation here on Kenai at the poles. You can date the ice from CO_2 bubbles, but the ice sheets also lay down ice each year, so you can count the years, too, from the seasonal layers and dust. And when we check the ice layers against the carbon dates, once you go past 53,000 years, there's way too much radiocarbon produced for a short interval, and then it goes back to hardly any, like normal."

"How long a short interval?"

"Not long. A few hundred years, tops."

I tried to put all this together. "So, you're saying, your site here seems too young. But the planet has a history of messing with carbon, so maybe the carbon is just wrong here, too."

Welk looked appreciative. "You do better at this than some of my students. Have you thought about going to university?"

I laughed. "That's a negative. I tried some courses after… well, a while back, and I did OK. But I think I've just spent way too much time on extracurriculars." I thought of my last tour, and what came after, and suddenly I was no longer thinking about ages or dates. Other than the ones marking lives gone too soon, or the ones just marking time passing.

Welk didn't notice me go quiet. "I don't think I'm going to solve this question, at least not here and now. I'll compare dates with other sites and see what they've found. I think I'm going to start digging. Wizzie brought the nanites, so we can program them and set them going. Should get a good chunk of the soil cover removed by tomorrow morning."

Digging holes with tiny robots seemed pretty fancy to me. Especially since I'd had to dig latrines by hand more than once. Nanites were expensive. We didn't run into them much in the service, other than the medical ones. I'd operated those on occasion in the Patrol. The Razors, the mercs I worked for after mustering out, generally didn't supply medical nanites, because the Razors didn't usually take many injuries. And because nanites were expensive, and RazorCorp could always find more warm bodies. "You're OK having them dig overnight? Unsupervised?"

"They'll be OK. We have good scans of the area, and I can coordinate with their software. They won't overstep if I can calibrate them to be cautious." He raised his eyebrows. "I have done this before, you know."

"Right, chief. Sorry."

"No, it was a good question." He sounded a little embarrassed at my apology.

"It's OK. Not my department, chief." I turned and moved toward the edge of the site. "Going to walk the perimeter again." I passed the dead bird in the box. Well, all the parts I could get Wizzie to collect, which I thought was most of it. The box was sealed, and Wizzie had replaced the air inside with nitrogen to preserve the specimen. "I'll get Wizzie to bring this thing back to camp, too."

5

Unboxing

I hadn't slept well. I never really trusted a WatchBot, even though they were fairly standard operating procedure for one-person security details in non-hostile settings like this. And the business with the bird had me spooked. But neither the WatchBot, nor I, when I was awake, had noticed anything unusual. My eyes were scratchy, and my head throbbed, though. Always happened when my sleep got cut short. If I didn't have combat stims. On stims, everything throbbed, but in a good way.

I saw a little lizard critter at the edge of my tent. A visitor. He looked at me, cocked his head for a moment, opened his mouth a few times, then skittered away. I got up, dumped today's coldbrew into the pitcher, and prepared a new pot of coldbrew, water and grounds, chilled by my portable unit. I liked it rich, so I left it going a full day, which was about eighteen hours here. I could have just rehydrated some crystals, of course, but the fresh tasted better, and it was something I tried to do whenever I was on deployment. Gave me something to hold onto, said the unit psych officer back in the Patrol. A foundation, and a bit of normalcy and control. She might be right, but I thought I just liked good coffee.

Welk made a snorting noise, then shifted in his tent. The rotation on this world was short, and it was summer where we were, which made the nights even shorter. So, the local sun had been up for an hour or two. All of that made the sleep schedule pretty weird if you tried to keep anywhere near-Earth standard. I was long used to sleeping whenever I got free, on whatever schedule the situation offered. They beat a standard sleep schedule out of you in Patrol basic training, and since then, any pattern I needed to fit almost never caused a problem. The dreams were another matter.

I set the pot down to let the coffee steep. Probably time for a weapons and armor check, then some calisthenics. All of that was ingrained routine. I imagined I'd be some old geezer in a retirement place somewhere, still insisting on checking my weapon before doddering off to the chow line and a day full of card games and romance holos. If I made it to old age.

My weapons were fine. My suit was fine. Of course. I peeled back the suit's flaps, split the limb segments open, and got myself suited up. When the suit wrapped around me, it always felt like a good solid hug. Comfy, like a parent, or a lover. I had elected not to share that analogy with the psych officer. The servos whined up, and I was stronger, faster, thermally regulated, fluid-managed, surrounded by data sensors and holo readouts, and of course, protected from many dangers. I went through the standard diagnostic maneuvers. All joints and servos functioning, all data readouts green.

Probably time to scare up breakfast. The chili was gone, as were the biscuits. Time to see what other breakfast packs Welk had stowed away. Maybe there was something spicy. As I moved around toward the food section of the supply dump, I stopped. Something was wrong.

"Wizzie, did you mess with this?"

"With what, Jess?" The bot rolled over to me and pulled itself up to its full height. Of course, I could have talked to it if it were down in travel mode, but some engineer probably thought I'd be more comfortable talking to something human-shaped. That's probably why it used first names, too.

"With the sample box here, Wizzie."

"Please define 'mess with.'"

"Did you do anything to the bird?" I let an edge creep into my voice.

"I preserved the fragments with nitrogen, sealed the box, and delivered it here, as instructed." Wizzie almost sounded miffed.

"I know that, you glorified toaster. I mean after. Since then."

"Please explain, Jess. I'm sorry. I don't understand." Stupid, stupid machine.

I held up the box. "The bird is gone."

6

THERE'S NO B IN TEAM

"No, I didn't do it," said Welk. He was still groggy, his hair kind of lumpy. "Did it escape?"

"It was dead. It was in multiple pieces, lifeless, burnt to a crisp. Deader than most of us ever get."

"Maybe things here regenerate." He yawned. "Or they're colonial, like sponges or something, and they can rebuild when fragmented."

I just looked at him. "Chief. I know dead. It was dead."

"We have barely researched the biota here…"

"It had been bathed in nitrogen for hours. How's it going to come back to life when it can't breathe?"

Welk frowned. "That is a good point. But still, we don't understand how life here works. It could have hibernated." His mouth bent down. Even he wasn't believing his arguments at this point.

"The box is still latched and sealed."

"*Skogol.*" Welk rubbed his forehead. "All right, so it vanished. What does that mean?"

"Somebody was here. Somebody took it. I don't see any other option, other than teleportation."

Welk shook his head. "That's not a real thing."

"No."

He unbuttoned his shirt in preparation for his shower. "Could the nanites have gone rogue?"

"There are no unopened packs here, so it could only be the ones at the dig site. And you're the one who said they were trustworthy."

"They'd have timed out and self-destructed by now anyway."

"And the nanites wouldn't have let themselves in and then closed the latch on the way out."

"*Skogol*," swore Welk.

"You keep saying that."

"Oh, like you're not thinking it."

"Correct, chief."

Welk pondered. "Your robot watcher thing. It should have picked up any intruders to the campsite."

He was right about that. "Yes."

"Any way to disable it?"

"I checked. It showed a clear run of ten hours on its records, and those are hard to fake or disable, by design. No interruptions, no visitors." That part was bugging me, too.

"Wizzie. Did anybody come to the camp while we were sleeping?"

"Not that I detected, Joran." The WZ unit was the only one of us who was not stressed.

"It's Jordan, you skogging..." Welk ran his hands through his hair. "So, what do we do?"

"I could call the ship again. Ask them to repeat their scans, do a threat assessment."

"Because our bird is missing?"

He had a point. We'd look like complete fools. "Maybe we don't tell them that's the reason. They have nothing to do up there anyway. We could just say there were some abnormal readings from the WatchBot or something."

Welk shook his head. "Can I have some of your coffee?"

What. Now? I bit back a retort. "Sure, chief." Drink coffee while we discuss the invisible bird raiders further.

Welk poured himself a mug. "I'm an archeologist. Xenoculture specialist."

That was not what I expected him to say. "Is that relevant now, chief?"

"Yes. Because I am only leading one part of this expedition."

"There's another part?"

"Yes. And I think they're not telling me stuff that's important."

That was interesting. "What do you mean?"

"I met with the other team, back when this was in the planning stage. I went in all friendly, academic, collegial. They would only talk logistics. Food, security, transport, supplies, the basics of the early recon reports. Nothing about their side of the project or their focus." Welk's frown had grown deeper.

"You think it had anything to do with how birds get electrocuted and then vanish out of boxes when they're dead?"

"Very funny." Welk took another drink of coffee, then sat down in his camp chair. "But maybe. I don't know. I did hear two of them talking when I was coming down the hall to the dining room, back at the planning meeting. They shut up as soon as they saw me, but I caught a little. No details about the project, but I overheard some names of people they were recruiting as team members. I looked them up once I got home. Two xenobiology experts, three physicists, one high energy, two theoretical."

I considered. "That's weird, isn't it? I mean, seems weird. But what do I know?"

"Having biologists along isn't weird. They'd be a given for a new world with native biota as rich as this. Physicists, though, that seemed strange. These folks have never had anything to do with planetary exploration." He let out a breath through clenched teeth. "And the secrecy is very weird. You do an initial planetary survey like this, and I've done several, everybody's usually on the same side, excited to share data. The joy of exploration and all. Not this need-to-know spy stuff."

"Any reason you're telling me this now?" Earlier would have been nice. I did not like surprises.

"Just that there may be something, a lot of things, going on that we don't know about, and some of it might relate to the local biota. And maybe also weird physics."

"So, what you're saying is, you don't want me to lose my skog about this?"

Welk looked up at me. "I mean, that's up to you."

"Nice." I thought some more. "Who's behind all this? I mean, I know my credits are coming from the Kenai Expeditionary Corporation, but that's got to be a one-off, a front for something else. And it's weird that it's a private organization. I'd have expected a Council agency. Who's really pulling the strings? They have to have some serious gravity, or we would never have gotten access to a Patrol ship."

"Two Patrol ships."

"What?"

"The other team, the physics and xenobio team, got here two weeks ago. They've been on planet since then. Their ship left before ours got here."

Skogging... "Chief, I don't know how much you know about security, but getting fed fake intel about the situation on the ground is not a success-forward strategic model."

"I understand."

I was starting to understand a little more too. "Having me here, when there are no obvious threats, is probably also part of this Secret Ops business. And Franz, that other merc who I met at the city dig before we came out here." He had seemed like a decent guy. Retired Patrol commando, had his own freelance business. I thought some more. "Does the other team, the physicist-biologist team, have its own security?"

"There was a security consultant there, at the group meeting. From a big company, not individual contractors like you. SpearPoint was the company. Their guy was named Rivald. I think he was one of their higher-ups."

Great. This was getting worse. "And what would have happened if I'd just blundered into an armed SpearPoint fireteam, and we'd ended up killing each other?"

"I suspect the information deficit is not reciprocal."

"You mean…"

"We're the B team. The other team is the important one."

My dislike of the situation added another few layers of I-don't-like-this on top of what was already a pretty big pile of this-is-skogged.

"Does the Patrol know all of this?"

"I have no way to know that."

They might, I guessed. Or maybe not. If this was coming from deep inside Council government, or one of the shadowy bureaucracies, or even just some private somebody who was wealthy or powerful, they might be able to just pay enough credits to charter two Patrol ships, no questions asked. It wouldn't be the first time. But like Welk said, I had no way to know that. "So what do we do now?"

"We dig up an ancient ruin." He smiled. "Archeology, soldier. We can do that even on the B-team. And the thrill of discovery will never let you down." He stood up. "I'm going to go take a shower.

7

AFTERMATH

"Come on," said Juno. "Let's go in."

"Huh?" I looked at Torqueda's body next to me. "Chief, this is... This is over. I think." There hadn't been any fire from the village in over forty minutes. Or any noise, other than stuff burning or falling down.

"I know." Juno switched to squad comms. "A-team Juno. We are moving in to recon the village. Other teams stay in position. Respond affirmative. Over."

"B-team Dice affirmative. Murr is not responding to stims. Remains unconscious, but he's not dead. Yet. Administering further aid and waiting for evac. Over."

"C-team Noor affirmative. Juno, CentCo advises do not enter village. Repeat, do not enter. Over."

Juno scowled. "A-team Juno. B-team and C-team affirmative noted. CentCo advice received, but we need to recon to assess ongoing threat to personnel. Ground team prerogative. Switching comms off for silence during recon. Will reactivate in ten minutes. Over."

That wasn't standard. I wanted to ask what she was doing, but I thought I knew. 'CentCo advises' was probably about to turn into 'CentCo orders,' and she'd headed that off. If I asked her about it, the recording would show me questioning, and I didn't want to get her in trouble.

She signed for me to move first, to cover to the right. Then she'd advance. I left the ARP in place and picked up Torqueda's rifle. Safety off, muzzle clear. Cell at three quarters. Ready to go. I took a deep breath, then hopped up and sprinted to the tree she'd indicated. 'I'm up, they see me, I'm down.' The phrase they made you learn in training. Three seconds, the time it takes an enemy to aim and fire once you're exposed. My skin itched, waiting for fire, but my training kept me moving, and I got behind the tree. Scan with rifle sight. No sound, no movement. I held up a hand and motioned Juno forward. I could hear her moving behind me.

We advanced in turns like this, but there was no need. The rebels we'd been fighting were gone, except for a few bodies. I found the sniper in the ruins of the tree. He did have a C99, like I thought. I wasn't sure if the fall killed him, or the holes from the ARP fire that I could see in him, but he was gone. He was probably the one who killed Kenzi. And definitely Torq, but Torq wasn't the one I cared as much about. Kenzi hurt. I hated this dead guy in that moment, even if he didn't really deserve it. We were the aggressors. We came to his home.

And we had destroyed it. Well, not us, specifically. We weren't carrying anything like what hit the village. Not us, not B-Team with the R22s, not C-team, unless somebody was hiding something. It had to come from somewhere else. There wasn't a whole building still standing, just a few walls, with bodies and blood everywhere. Some of them little bodies. And that was only at the edge of the village. In the center, it was just a big crater, nothing recognizable. Still hot enough to burn your cheeks and eyes if you got too close. I slid my helmet visor down.

"Cover me, Jess. I need to document this."

"Yes, chief." I already had my rifle up, but I got my back to a wall and started surveying the area. I was surprised when Juno pulled out a mini-con from her front suit pocket. That wasn't standard issue. We had tactical cons that fit in a back slot, full of map and terrain data, weather, satellite links, sensors, all that. But this was a little personal one. She held it

up and moved around the village. Recording. Narrating what she saw.

I was on guard, and thus not thinking about stuff, because thinking about stuff and guarding in a high-risk zone were incompatible. But later, once we had recovered the bodies of our team and reached the extraction point, I tried to figure out what she'd been up to. I decided she was either covering our asses, which a good commander would, or she was building a case against whoever had actually destroyed the village. Or maybe both. Either way, I don't think either of us could have anticipated the entirety of what happened next.

8

THE HOLE DAY

"They did a pretty good job." Welk was looking down into the hole the nanites had made. "Nothing seems harmed, sides stable, dirt removed and disposed. Good job, little nanites."

The nanites in question had worked for a few hours and then died according to their programming. It was part of the law governing nanites – except for highly-regulated special cases, it wasn't legal to allow them to operate for more than a couple hours. I doubted Welk invoking praise over a pile of their corpses was doing anything for them. Not that a microscopic robot had a personality, or an ego, or a well-developed sense of positive reinforcement.

They had done a remarkable job, though. These must be pretty high-end nanites. Any nanites were expensive, and getting access to enough of them to do hard work like this was worth more than my contract, I guessed. Maybe several times more. He'd used six packs, and we had nine more packs, industrial sized, back in our supply dump, plus the one Welk had brought this morning. He seemed oblivious, or maybe indifferent, to the money he was blowing on digging holes.

Welk set himself to programming another batch. I had my itch again, the one I get when I think people might be ready to shoot at me. The thing with the bird wasn't sitting well. I walked the perimeter again, but there wasn't anything to see, either by eye or by sensor. Maybe Welk was right, and we should just do our jobs and not worry about disappearing birds or secretive physicists or shadowy corporations.

When I returned to the dig, Welk was done programming, and the nanites were at work. It was weird to see the dirt moving itself up and out of the hole and over to the growing waste pile, a kind of a weird brown stream that violated both gravity and logic. I looked down into the hole. They'd reached the stone floor below, and they were starting to widen out the dig, exposing more of the shaped blocks that we'd seen in the walls. The blocks got picked pretty clean by the nanites, whose orders were to remove everything that wasn't part of the facility. I imagined Welk must have had to program them using his scanner results in order to avoid a chance of damaging anything or removing support that might leave things unstable. But that was beyond me, and presumably part of what the big console was for.

I saw a little lizard-like animal sunning itself on an exposed bit of wall. Mostly brown, with big eyes and some frills at his neck. About ten centimeters long, four of that being a narrow forked tail with green stripes on top. I checked the suit sensors again for any risks, then went over to take a look. I wasn't much of a wildlife person. If it wasn't trying to kill me, I didn't much care. But after the bird had vanished, and after Welk said the xenobio scientists were part of the secret important part of this, the A-team, I was curious about what lived here. I realized that I hadn't considered that maybe the dead bird had just turned transparent or invisible, although that would be just as weird as the reasons I had considered.

The lizard raised his head and put out a forked tongue. His big eyes rotated to focus on me, four of them, with complex lenses in a symmetric pattern. I wondered if he was totally brave, or just acting tough while terrified. If it was the latter, he was putting on a good performance. Maybe he just didn't have any natural predators. Or maybe the prey here were just stupid or didn't mind being eaten.

I held out my hand next to him, wondering if he'd run away. He didn't. He came up and darted his proboscis over the suit glove covering my finger. I realized that what I was doing now would probably be the scene near the beginning of the horror holo, the one where the lizard punctured my suit with his laser tongue, laid eggs in my flesh, and mind-controlled me into lumbering around eating other humans until I exploded, releasing a new crop of tiny ravenous lizards. But that didn't happen. Instead, he crawled up onto my glove. Brave little guy.

Suddenly, I had a flashback to the *Silver Saber,* the Razors' main assault transport. My bunk, across from Kenzi's in our quarters, although we were together in Kenzi's bunk as often as not. That cat, Chewie. Orange with deeper orange stripes. She liked me, but she loved Kenzi. Always ran over when Kenzi came in, purring and rubbing against legs, and always slept on the gray fuzzy blanket at the foot of Kenzi's bed. Chewie was long gone, I figured. I wished I knew what happened to her. I wished I hadn't had to leave her, after, on the ship. Seemed like a betrayal of Kenzi. Not that I had a choice. And not that Kenzi knew. Kenzi was gone too. My eyes went wet. The lizard looked up at me, then took a couple quick steps up to my wrist, still exploring the air with his elongated nose.

I carried him over to Welk. "I found a friend."

Welk looked at my lizard. That was probably him being polite, because I was being silly and definitely one hundred percent not being a good security guard right now. Because good security guards don't play with cute little animals. Welk smirked. "There are a lot of little scaled animals like that here. A bunch of varieties, different sizes. They seem to be a big part of the zoology." He looked up at me. "The bird ones are another big group, probably related. And then there are worms, and the fishy things, and the insectoids and beetle-ish ones with exoskeletons, and little shelled guys, coated with slightly-mineralized protein sleeves. There's a whole different set of marine organisms if you get out toward the coasts and oceans. We really haven't catalogued very many of them, because the first scouting mission didn't spend that much time here.   It didn't include a real xenobiologist because planets with complex ecosystems like this are pretty rare. The notes aren't very detailed."

The lizard ran farther up my arm, then stopped, looking out over the dig site. "Well, they must have found something, or they wouldn't have sent all those biologists and physicists. Or you archeologists."

"Well, a planet with non-human ruins is always going to require an archeological survey. Depending on what we find on this initial survey, there could be teams here for decades trying to puzzle all this out, but I doubt it. It seems pretty minor, and pretty unremarkable." I couldn't tell if he wanted to stay for decades or not. I wondered if he had a spouse and kids. And if they knew they were maybe a distant second place in his priorities.

I thought about what he'd said. "I think you're right. They aren't focusing on the ruins. You're not on the top secret super important team, right? That's the biologists and physicists. That's the real prize here. There's got to be something special going on." The lizard ran up to my shoulder, then settled himself there, looking out over the dig site like he was the king of everything.

"Maybe." Welk shrugged. "Probably. But I get to do what I love, with somebody else's credits, so I'm not going to worry about it."

"Worrying about it is my job," I grumbled. I looked over at the lizard. His eyes had narrowed to slits, and it looked like he might be going to sleep. I felt a wave of warmth, like I was a goofy kid or something. Look at me, bridging the gap between worlds, befriending alien life. I had a thought. "This lizard seems to be taking a shine to me. Is that OK? Can I leave him here, see what he does? Maybe see if I can feed him?"

Welk squinted at me. "You want an alien lizard as a pet?"

I realized I was sounding foolish. No, being foolish. "I mean, if it's against regs..."

Welk laughed. "I don't care. Do what you want. But we can't take anything off planet. That is against regs. And the sterilization protocol would kill it anyway."

"Yeah, I'll just leave it here when we're done with the dig."

"You're not going to go all weird on me and start talking to it or making it little lizard clothes, are you?" I got the idea he'd seen some horror holos too.

I laughed. "No, chief. Nothing creepy. Just doing some science, right? Exploring the local biota."

"Right." He smirked back at me. "Time for some lunch?"

9

THE KITCHEN SKINK

The sun was going down. We'd stayed up late, which meant the short night probably wouldn't give us enough rest. But I was enjoying the down time. Even if I'd pay for it in the morning.

"He likes salsa," I said.

"What?"

"Look." The lizard was sitting on my knee, chewing on some gooey tomato blobs from my meal pack. He'd started with some hesitation, just tasting, but now he was really putting them away. I spooned a few more tomato bits onto my knee next to him.

Welk shook his head. "You better hope their proteins are compatible, and they're not allergic to beta carotene or something."

I felt a surge of panic. "*Skogol.* I hadn't thought of that. You should have said something."

"Too late now. Let him enjoy it before he dies."

I thought that was kind of twisted, but I didn't say anything. "I was going to name him, but that would be sad if I killed him right after."

Welk laughed. "Yeah, maybe hold off on naming him until sunrise. The moment of truth."

I watched the lizard eat some more. "What's on the schedule for tomorrow?"

"I think we'll be able to get down there. I set a few more packs of nanites running tonight, and I programmed them to carve us some dirt steps down to the floor as they clear out the space."

"Smart."

"Not my first time, I said." Welk smiled. "And ladders are annoying."

"What do you expect to find down there?"

"So far, with the ornamentation, it looks maybe like a ceremonial building, but that's a wild guess, probably rife with anthropocentric bias. Who knows if the Kenaians even had ceremonies? Maybe they decorated their storage lockers or warehouses, and that's all this is. We haven't seen a lot of other buildings to compare. The cities we've seen are exposed to the elements now and in a lot worse shape."

"Because they're older?"

"I still don't think so. The more I see of this, the more it looks like it's from an earlier time, an earlier phase of culture, although that could totally be anthropocentric on my part too. But I really think the dates must be off. If we're lucky, we might find some remains or some artifacts that we can analyze and date. Then we might get a better idea of the age of this place than the soil profiles provide."

"You think we will find stuff like that?"

"There's almost always something around with a building this big and this well-preserved. Remains, garbage, tools, decorations. If we have a chance to dig any of it up. Ideally, we'd have a month or more to excavate a place this big, really tease everything out of the site, but we're due back in only a few more days."

That might explain the big nanite budget, I supposed. I looked at the lizard. "I'm going to set up the WatchBot and try to get some sleep. I don't know if he'll stick around. Do you suppose animals here sleep? He looked sleepy earlier."

"Hard to say. Nearly all planets have some kind of daily cycle, and these guys are ectothermic poikilotherms, I think, if I remember the briefing."

"Huh?"

"Dependent on the environment for heat, and heat is usually correlated to metabolic rate for animal-like organisms. So, I'd guess he goes dormant at night, or at least gets less active." Welk yawned. "He's small, too, so he'll lose heat fast."

"Maybe that's what he likes about me. I'm warm."

"There have been long-lasting relationships built on far less." Welk grinned. "I'm going to turn in, too. Tomorrow's going to be a big day."

He was right. Not in the way he thought.

10

HEARING THINGS

"Let's get started," said the man in the white suit. "Council Commission on Interplanetary Conflict, Matter Number 8-43522, Hearing Number 16. Jessalyn Amiko, Respondent. Blaise Chesterfield, Administrator. Begin formal transcript."

"It wasn't an interplanetary conflict. The government was attacking its own people. On one planet." I was done with this process before it started. I was confident that being held alone in a cell for ten days was the likely cause of my bad attitude. Well, the worsening of what was admittedly an already bad attitude. "Juno should be here. Where is she? The contract I signed says all after-action hearings are to include all parties participating, including officers senior to those accused."

The legal AI assigned to me, a little console built into the table beside me, blinked his little yellow light, then interrupted. "Client should not engage in direct conversation with the hearing administrator. Recommend silence. Recommend only direct and truthful answers to specific questions."

The man in white ignored my robotic counsel's interruption. "That language is in a private contract between you and RazorCorp Security Service. This hearing supersedes that language, which does not apply to Council commissions, laws, or courts. Lieutenant Juno is having a separate hearing, as are the other members of your squad."

"The surviving members, you mean."

The light on the console blinked again. "Repeat. Recommend—"

"Shut up, counsel." I was angry.

"Yes, of course, the surviving ones." Chesterfield placed his palms flat on the table in front of him. "Citizen Amiko, this is not yet a criminal proceeding."

"Not yet? Then why was I transported here against my will and confined to a locked room? Sure feels like a criminal proceeding."

The AI's yellow light came on again. "Advise not—"

"Not now, counsel." The AI shut up.

The man in white paused a moment before speaking. "Those are standard procedures for matters of this severity." He nodded. At what, I didn't know. "If you will allow it, I will explain the nature of the hearing and the possible outcomes for you based on what happens here today."

"I'm supposed to have a human counsel, top notch, paid for by RazorCorp. It's in my contract. A ten-thousand credit retainer, up to a million guaranteed if needed. I request a stay, or a delay, or whatever you call it, until that counsel is provided."

The man looked at me. Deadpan. The guy was probably a good poker player. "We have already explored that with Citizens Juno, Noor, and Dice, whose hearings have already concluded. Although that contractual clause exists, RazorCorp provided no funds to make good on its promise of counsel."

The yellow light went on. "In 68% of major and minor crimes trial proceedings studied, AI counsel has been found to be as effective or more effective—"

"Shut up." I stared at the man. Blaise, he'd said. "Then I will file suit against them to force them to fulfill the contract."

"That will not be possible."

"I don't have rights?"

"You have rights. We permitted your fellow Respondents to explore this option in previous hearings. However, they failed. There is no effective corporate presence remaining for RazorCorp."

"What does that mean?"

"The company's offices are empty, and the ships we have not impounded are missing along with the owners and senior management. We have not been able to determine where they are." He looked at me. Seeing how I would react, I bet. I denied him the pleasure of revealing my innermost thoughts, which at that point were in the neighborhood of SKOG SKOGGING SKOG SKOGGITY SKOGGGG.

"Do they have assets you can seize?"

"The accounts we froze were already drained. The impounded ships and materiel have some value, but they must go through a waiting period and then a complex process to be liquidated. The company's debts are significant, which means any proceeds would be dedicated to unpaid wages and debt service prior to incurring new contractual expenses."

"They didn't have insurance for this? They were supposed to have legal insurance. Liability insurance. They had us sign the policy documents."

Blaise looked at me again. "In my experience, companies that reach the financial state that RazorCorp now seems to inhabit begin to cut corners. Insurance is generally among the first to be cut."

The yellow light came on again. I didn't know what to say, so I let it talk. "Advise tabling this discussion until a future time should the situation change. Request the right to note, record, and cite this evidence of corporate malfeasance as a defense against charges."

"Request granted. Transcriber note request and grant." Blaise was still looking at me.

"I'm screwed, aren't I?"

"Advise against characterizing—"

"Shut up, counsel." I stared at Blaise. I was a good poker player too.

Blaise held my gaze for a moment, then looked down. "That was a conclusion reached by many of your RazorCorp colleagues." He tapped a control on his con. "Are you ready to begin questioning regarding the incident at Treyna?"

11

NAP TIME

It was just getting light out. My eyes didn't want to open, but I have a hard time going back to sleep when I wake up on mission. I start to imagine all the things that could go wrong, all the threats I could face, and then sleep just jets on me, never to return.

The lizard was gone. I figured he might be. The little hollow he'd squished into my sack mattress was still there, though, right next to my arm. That had been kind of adorable. If it was still there, that meant he hadn't been gone long, or the foam would have adjusted to fill in the hole. I felt the spot to see if it was still warm, but then I remembered he was an ecto-poiki-whatever, and he wouldn't leave a warm spot.

I looked around, but I didn't find him. No sign. *Run free, little guy,* I thought. *I hope the tomatoes don't kill you.* I could hear Welk snoring. I slid out of my sack and checked the WatchBot. A high-elevation flock of birdoids had passed during the night. Various small animal movements. The AI hadn't thought those worth mentioning, and I concurred with its decision. I got a stim pill from my field kit. Unlike when I was back in the Razors, when I ate them like candy, I didn't use them much these days, but the short days and nights were taking a toll on me, and I thought I needed more than the coffee today. I dumped the fresh coldbrew from the steeping pot into the pitcher and set the pot up to brew tomorrow's batch. Quick look around the camp, then I used the head. Awkward, in the woods, but Welk or his minders had sprung for a self-cleaning travel toilet, so that beat most of my deployments. Five stars for Kenai's amenities.

I wandered back to camp. Still quiet. I took a deep breath. The dawn air was cooler than during the day and less humid. It felt good. I closed my eyes, tipped my head back, pulled in another deep breath. I was a little nervous still about the vanishing bird corpse and the intrigues Welk had mentioned with the research teams. But this was a better gig than I thought I'd have after getting out. I'd worried I'd end up with no business at all, that the conviction would scare everyone away, and I'd end up in mining or construction or something menial, but this was working, at least with my first client.

Welk was still snoring, soft breathy hisses. I found I was curious what the dig site looked like now, especially after more nanites had done their thing. Leaving Welk wasn't 100% secure, but I could leave the WatchBot on, and the dig site wasn't far. I tore an oatmeal pouch open, stuck the opening in my mouth, and flattened the pouch with two fingers sliding them up to my mouth to expel the pouch's contents. Kenzi always thought that was disgusting, but it was fast, and I didn't mind the cold oatmeal. Got me calories fast, and I could swallow a standard pack in two gulps without chewing. I said it provided enhanced readiness and efficiency. Kenzi said I was repulsive, but said it cute, so I knew I was actually endearing. Or so I thought. Dammit, Kenzi. Miss you.

I slipped into my suit, checked the load and safety on my rifle and sidearm, and signaled to the WatchBot to ping me if it saw anything. I went off down the path, servos turned off so as not to wake Welk. That made the suit heavy, but it also was good exercise. I didn't want to get soft here.

Even at the edge of the site, I could see the nanites had done a lot of work. I saw the beginning of a set of dirt stairs over the lip of the hole, all polished and compacted. As I neared the hole, I could see down to the floor, although with the sun at an angle, and coming through trees, it was hard to see much of the bottom. But I saw lots of exposed stone, some of it carved. Not the big art like we'd seen on the wall blocks, but little carvings. Almost like writing, maybe? It was hard to see. Welk was going to be jumping up and down. Or shouting "Huzzah!" or whatever academic types did when they were excited. I knew they'd found bits of preserved written material in the remains of the city, but if this place were older, like Welk said, then this might be more interesting than the random street signs and tax files and junk the cities held. This might be important. Sacred or ceremonial or something.

The stone the nanites had exposed seemed pretty well preserved despite spending a long time underground. And there, at the bottom, off to the side, was something – a rectangular shape. A bench, or an altar, or something else? I clicked my tac light on and held my arm over the hole. It was deep, so there wasn't a lot of light, but it almost looked like a cabinet or something. It had carvings all around it. I really wanted to go down there and have a look, but I held off. This was Welk's game, not mine, and it would be rude if I went down before he did. Plus, I might screw something up. I was security, and I had a job to do, not a hole to explore.

I did a perimeter walk, not because I thought I'd find anything, but because I wanted to get some exercise. I left the servos off. That gave me an extra 25 kilos of inert suit to lug around, but that was all right. I got my heart rate up, got some muscles tired, and felt good doing it.

As I rounded the halfway of the perimeter, I looked up at the sky. Most of the stars had faded, although one of the nearby planets was still bright. Maybe Ninilchik, the one similar to Kenai. I wouldn't know any of the constellations, of course. My sky and my stars were on Ramine, and most of those would look different from here, even though they were the same stars.

There was something bright in the sky to the south. Could have been a cloud catching the dawn light, but it didn't quite look like that. Weird, bigger than a star, kind of a glowing ring. I didn't remember anything like that from other nights, but maybe I hadn't looked. Might be some kind of meteorologic thing, an aurora or something. It didn't look quite like what I'd seen on Genua when we were stationed there at Stoking Patrol Base. There, the whole night sky had lit up with shimmering blue and green. But Kenai was a new world, and maybe it had new mysteries. Assuredly it did.

I turned back toward camp. Time to check on Welk, and get him coffeed up and moving, so we could see what was down in the dig site. Anybody's curious what's in a hole. I realized I was liking this a little, more than I thought I might.

There was a noise above me. Unmistakable, as I'd heard it so many times on different worlds. Air thrusters, the whine of a fusion engine. LCOA. Light craft operating in atmosphere. There were too many trees to make it out, but I could hear it. Passed northeast to southwest, then circled back. My suit pinged, and I engaged the tracking sensors. It was making a circuit of camp. The thing was fast. Not some lumbering transport. Closer to fighter speed, although there'd be no reason for fighters on this world. More likely a scouting ship. But why hadn't they notified us?

"Open channel to *Deimos* in orbit. Authorization Jess Amiko."

Silence.

"Repeat. Open channel to orbit. Authorization Jess Amiko. *Deimos*, do you read?"

Still nothing. I checked the comms status for flags. Nothing out of the ordinary. Our camp antenna was powered and functioning fine.

I raised my wrist and tapped the controls. Getting the WatchBot to wake up Welk. Just a precaution. It's possible he'd know something about this. He'd not told me about the other team, after all. He wasn't 100% reliable. Maybe it was nothing, just a scouting run, or a delivery. But still, seems like they'd have announced it over comms. I checked my rifle again. Safety off this time. My internal alerts were pinging too.

The ship was banking again, and then I heard the thrusters whine higher. Landing. I could see dust and scraps of leaves and debris kick up through the trees. It was setting down by the camp.

There were two ways I thought this could go. One was maybe the likeliest. There was a mission problem, one that came with a communications breakdown, and somebody was coming to tell us what was happening. That fit with the *Deimos* being offline. The final outcome there could be anywhere from all right, if it were just an informational thing, to less good, if *Deimos* were having issues.

The other way was less likely, but much worse. That was, this ship was hostile, and we were under attack, and I was going to earn my security officer credits. Or not, if I didn't get back to camp. But I didn't see how that could be it. Our mission should be the only people here. And we shouldn't attack ourselves. Unless the A team had decided the B team was a liability.

I turned back towards the camp. I had to get there, and fast. I heard blaster fire coming from camp. Infantry rifles, not ship weapons. Then the little *zzzip zzzip* of pistol fire. That was weird, switching weapons. I didn't think Welk was armed, but maybe he had a sidearm I didn't know about. Then the massive *whump* of heavy muni, two blasts. Oh, hell. I set off at a tactical sprint back towards the camp. With the help of the suit, my strides were well over two meters. Until they weren't.

Without warning, my suit seized up. All joints locked, then the limbs extended to full length. The motors and gears were stronger than I was, and there was no resisting them. The holoscreen lit up with messages. CRYOSLEEP MODE AUTHORIZED. STANDARD COMFORT POSITION ADOPTED FOR LONG-TERM TRANSIT. PREPARE FOR ADMINISTRATION OF SEDATIVES.

Except I wasn't in a cryoberth, and there were no sedatives, and I certainly wasn't part of a cold sleep transit to a planetary assault. Those barely ever happened now that the jump gate system was up and running around most Council worlds. Instead, as my arms fell to my sides and the gyros pushed my legs straight, I toppled forward. I shouted

"Abort! Abort cryosleep mode!" as I went down, but the suit was being administered externally.

Which shouldn't be possible. Not remotely. This was my suit, that I bought with my own credits. I wasn't assigned to a unit. There were no external administrators. It should answer only to me. And cryo mode was disabled, by me, along with all the other military subroutines I had turned off, when I'd taken the suit out of the shipping crate and set it up.

That was all technically true, but none of it helped. My face smashed into the dirt of the forest floor.

12

SHRINKAGE

"You some kind of church person?" The office door said this was Counselor Otieno, but she had some churchy-looking books on her shelf.

She shook her head. Her glossy black hair reflected the harsh light of the little meeting room here. "No, my title is counselor. If you're religious, I'm versed in most faith traditions, but I'm only ordained with the Universalists." She wrote something on her con with her finger. She had her other hand resting in front of the con's display, so I couldn't see from across the table. I was pretty sure that was intentional. The security AI watching me wouldn't let me get closer.

"So why am I here?"

She nodded. "Good question. I'm here to help you transition into custody. I can serve as a confidential discussion partner, or a source of information and advice about life here, or in some cases as an advocate if you have needs that are going unmet. Mostly, I'm here to help you maintain a healthy, balanced life during your stay."

"I don't need counseling. I need an appeal. I need an actual advocate, not an AI. I need to get out of here. I'm innocent. We all are. Or, Juno and Dice are, and obviously Murr is. He was down before it even happened." I put my hand around the edge of the table and squeezed pretty hard. "Can't speak for the others. Definitely can't speak for RazorCorp. They sold us out, big time."

She looked at me some more, then wrote some more. "There's not going to be an appeal."

"I'm guaranteed an appeal. It's in the Codicil of Rights."

"That's for a regular criminal case." *She stopped writing.* "This isn't that."

I glowered at her. I'd been working on that look. "I had kind of put that together."

"Do you know what you're in here for?"

I snorted. "I was supposedly convicted of orbital assault on a Council planet and murder of civilians. But that's a skogging lie. And they all know it."

She looked at me some more. It was kind of maddening. "Did you assault a village on Treyna?"

I didn't say anything.

"I know you did."

"Then why ask?" *I kicked the desk, just to see what she'd do. She flinched. That was satisfying, although she recovered quickly. The security panel beeped a warning at me, but I didn't care.* "We were hired guns, paid by the Treyna government. That's legal. We were sent to help contain a rebellion. That's legal. We were fired on, and we fired back. That's legal. That is the limit of what I did."

"Commander Juno made that clear."

That I didn't know. "Is Juno here?"

"No."

"How come?" *Could she be free? I didn't think Juno would dodge the rap if I didn't. Except she had the recording. But that should have helped me too.*

"She was convicted of a more serious charge, which means she got sent to a longer-term facility."

I was thrown by this. "How long term?"

The woman looked at me some more. "Life."

That was sobering. "What? Why? We were together. She didn't kill any civilians, and I didn't either. And we sure as hell didn't firebomb a village."

"Are you sure?"

"What? I was there. Of course I'm sure." *Well, sure I didn't bomb the village. Less sure about the civilians, what with all* the ARP fire, and that part was eating at me. But I wasn't going to tell her that. "They should know all that. Just have them check the suit recordings."

"Those weren't recovered."

"I know." I was getting angry again. "I was at my trial, you know. There's no way they could be deleted under standard practice. That's even more evidence that this whole thing stinks like a rotten corpipod."

"Sergeant Noor—"

"Is a lying sack of vomit." If I ever saw the guy again, I was going to kill him. Then I could go to prison for something real.

"Sergeant Noor testified that you and Commander Juno carried out the orders he relayed."

"Noor was nowhere near us. Noor is making it up. I'm sure he's nursing a pile of credits from RazorCorp, or maybe from the Treyna government, in exchange for setting us up for this." I slapped the table. "And Noor knows Juno and I didn't have any R22s with us. Murr had those. He was heavy muni. And he was down, out of action before the village got lit up."

I'd been through all of this at the trial, but it felt good to shout it all at somebody again. "And if you watch Juno's recording of the village, after, which I know still exists, because they showed it at that farce of a trial, you can see the damage done is much bigger than a couple of R22s. Whatever hit the village came from somewhere else, and it was a hell of a lot stronger than what we had with us."

The woman flipped through some displays on her con. "Investigators confirmed that it likely came from orbit or at least from a high elevation craft not of Treyna origin. Both of those are a serious violation of Council Law."

"Yeah, that's what they said. Turns out, though, I wasn't in orbit. I was on the ground."

"According to the court documents, you were part of an effort that included illegal use of weapons, and also murder of civilians. An accessory."

I looked at her, long and hard. "You're a counselor, you said? I don't feel very counseled right now." She didn't say anything. "Why did Juno get life? That's not right. If anybody *was going to get life, it should have been CentCo. And that's Jamison. Odd, isn't it, that the RazorCorp CEO is somehow presently unaccounted for."*

She looked at me for a bit and took some more notes. "Everything we say here is confidential."

"Yippie."

"I'm saying that because I'd like it if that applies both ways, although you're obviously not obliged. Regardless, I hear you, and I believe you. I've studied your case some. It's a good deal more messed up and irregular than most of what goes through this system."

"Which is what?"

"The worst cases are crimes against humanity. That's what your Commander Juno got hit with."

"Why?"

"Because somebody needed to. She got to where she could see it coming. Smart. But not of much help to her, in the end."

"So, what, she pled guilty?"

"Acceded to a directed verdict, but more or less the same thing. But in doing so, as part of what she negotiated and testified to, she got you and Officer Dice much lesser sentences as unwitting accessories."

This I didn't know. "She took the heat for us?"

"Yes, and her testimony and bootleg audio logs got Noor sent to Vylos with her."

Vylos. Wow. Maximum security prison camp world, barely livable, on a rocky planet in the same system as Glisson, the heart of the Council. If it was even half as bad as the news holos said, that was going to be an ordeal. Juno, what did you do to yourself?

"What about Murr?"

"Didn't make it off Treyna. Died of his wounds. I'm sorry. I don't know if you were close." She flipped through some more displays. "Noor and Juno are serving life terms on Vylos. You and Officers Dice and Coble here, with five-year terms. Imani was an unarmed field medic and was able to use that status to escape charges, also with the help of Juno's testimony."

One of us free. Five of us in prison. Two of those for life.

That left six more. Six of our twelve. Torqueda with his bravado. Jahns, the quiet one, but good at poker. Wigg, who liked to draw. Murr, with a wife back on Metis. Ennis with her big ears and goofy smile. And my Kenzi.

My eyes went wet. I hated that. Hated showing weakness. I got a snarl face going, so that maybe the counselor wouldn't see. "If you believe this is all a set-up, then what are you going to do about it?"

She flattened her lips into a line. "Nothing. Not my role, and I don't have any pull regardless. And I don't know much. I just watch the holos. But others are working on it. There are some journalists on Treyna digging into the case. And the holo channels are awash with rumors and speculation, and even some high-quality reporting. A violation of the planetary assault codes is a big deal. Really big."

I felt a glimmer of something. "So we might get out of this?"

She tapped the holo screen on her con once more. "No. Not going to happen. Not in five years, anyway. There's maybe a shot that Juno could get out after that, or at least get pardoned, if there's enough of an outcry, and if the people who are digging keep digging. But that would take years, and the system would resist it, hard. The more likely outcome is that this buzzes for a while, and then something else happens – a holoceleb gets married, or divorced, or cloned, or another conflict erupts somewhere. Then this will all fade."

"And RazorCorp goes unpunished? And the government on Treyna that put us up to this?"

She looked at me some more, her brown eyes focused on mine. "There were some high-profile resignations in the Treyna government, and a pretty intense independent Council inquiry is still ongoing. There will likely be trials that run through the Treyna legal system. The Supreme Oligarch Yusse, who hired RazorCorp, looks pretty likely to lose the next election, even though his side rigs the vote pretty hard." She paused, watching my face for a reaction. "There's no sign of RazorCorp leadership anywhere in Council systems. Some people think they left Council space, maybe to outlying unincorporated worlds. Some even think they went inward to hide out somewhere in the remnants of the Trade Union, although that seems like a stupid idea to me. Others think they just assumed new identities somewhere."

"Great. While we rot in prison, they get to spend their credits."

"How does that make you feel?"

"What?"

Finally, she smiled. "Counselors have to ask that at least once a session. Union rules."

13

FOG OF WAR

The suit's cryosleep mode took a while to spin up and engage, what with all the temperature regulation, power reallocation, and biometrics it had to sort through. After a minute or two, it became clear to the suit that I was not, in fact, entering cryosleep, maybe on account of the constant stream of profanity I directed toward it. And also at the suit's engineers, coders, designers, and contractors. Eventually, the cycle entered an error-induced failed state, and I got control back. The first thing I did was roll over onto my back and spit out dirt. The second was to grab my rifle, and the third was to get up and start running.

There was smoke rising from the camp. That was bad. I pinged the WatchBot for status, but it was offline. Maybe destroyed. I checked the suit's sensors. They showed some heat but no motion, and with the planet being as warm as it was, the hot points were vague.

Time to head in. I set the suit servos to stealth mode, where they'd assist less but stay much quieter. If I started running, they'd kick in and assist as normal. I crept around the bend in the path. I could see the supply dump, and Welk's tent. Then mine as I took a few more steps. The tents had been hit hard, covered with black scorch marks.

Then I saw an armored figure in a suit like mine. Well, nicer than mine. Way nicer. I wasn't sure of the model, but I could see an embedded thruster pack and a beam weapon mounted on the shoulder. There was a launch tube set in one arm for heavy muni, probably R13s, with a magazine of maybe six shells. That was a lot of firepower, the kind that stood a chance even against armored vehicles. A heavy airborne assault suit. Better than we had in the Razors, and much better than we had in the Patrol. Top of the line, and very expensive.

And also very skogged up. The suit was face down, limbs splayed, helmet dome lowered like you'd expect for a flying suit. There was a massive hole in the back of the torso armor. Much bigger than a regular infantry weapon could make. Whoever was inside was definitely not living through that. Had one of their shells gone off inside? I couldn't think how else that would happen. Maybe I wasn't the only one dealing with a suit malfunction.

But then I saw the other body. Same kind of suit. This one was on its back, helmet cracked with a jagged hole, and another massive blast wound, this one mid-chest. Not a suit malfunction, then. Instead, somebody or something armed with heavy muni, and a pretty good shot at that.

Welk? No, couldn't be. I wasn't sure of everything that was packed in our gear, but I was pretty sure he wouldn't have any regulated heavy munitions or explosives. And if he was this good with those, he certainly wouldn't have needed to hire me.

If there were two of these guys, both better armed and armored than I was, there might be more. And of course there was whoever shot them. This was not a great situation. My drill instructor would have called it a real rectal clencher. He was not much of a poet.

I took a few slow steps into the camp, rifle raised. My weapon was reasonably powerful, a Rebus C38, but I'd need to get a really lucky shot in to take out somebody wearing this kind of gear. Or maybe three or four such shots. I didn't really have any business taking them on, but I'd been hired and paid, and I'd given my word, and that was my standard. Welk could be in danger, or in need of medical help. Or dead. I needed to do what I could.

Still nothing on the suit sensors. I saw the orb of the WatchBot lying on the ground next to its collapsible stand. It was fried, probably from blaster fire. Would have been helpful to have that because it had better sensors than my suit. I saw some scorch marks elsewhere – a smoldering tree branch, some crates slagged, and a big, blackened hole in Welk's tent that was still red around the edges. Mine was in even worse shape, the tent down and my sleep sack destroyed. But there was nothing moving, other than the wisps of smoke and vapor rising from the fragged assault troops.

Then my suit pinged. Movement, 300 meters south southwest. I spun in time to see another figure in one of the assault suits rising up fast into the sky, suspended on thrusters. I hit the deck behind the supply crates, although those wouldn't do much against an R13 or whatever the suits had. But being out of sight and behind something hard would help. Or at least it felt better. I got the rifle up, hit the periscope sight, and scanned the sky until I found them, then zoomed in 10x. Same suit model, same armaments, except this grunt also had a rifle, maybe a Durning X19. They rose up to about 50 meters, looking down at the camp.

And then they did something I absolutely didn't expect. They let the rifle drop to a casual one-handed grip, then waved at me. Then, they rotated away to the left, bent a little at the waist, and jetted off away from the camp, vanishing behind the trees.

14

GET WELK SOON

"Don't you come near me!" Welk was agitated. "I'm armed."

His voice came from over by the shower. "You brought a weapon to the shower?"

"Jess. It's you. Thank everything." I could hear the tension releasing as he spoke.

"You decent? Can I come around?"

"Are they gone?"

Delicate point, and still kind of an open question. "In a manner of speaking."

"What?"

"We're safe. I think. For now."

"Let me get my pants back on." I heard him moving. "Thank you so much. I'll put in for a bonus for you. Above and beyond."

"Wasn't me, I'm sorry to say." I gave him a minute, and then he came back around into view. His shirt and pants were matted with water spots, and his skin was glistening. He clutched a small pistol in one hand, and his eyes were still wide, taking in everything.

I chuckled. "Did you just take part in a significant infantry action in the nude? With that gun, against assault troops? I might need to write up an after-action report on this one."

Welk's cheeks went darker. "I mean. They were firing at me. They took out the tents first."

"You haven't taken a weapon to the shower before. What changed?" I didn't mention that I didn't know about him having the pistol. That was maybe going to turn into a sore point.

He looked at me. "I was getting a bad feeling. I lost comms last night, during my check-in with the team at the city. I got nervous."

Understandable. "You want to explain why you have a gun out here? Did you expect to be attacked by assault troops?"

He looked down. "I... Like I said, the mission was putting off some bad energy. I didn't fully trust the people I was working with. I didn't think they were telling me everything." He held up the pistol. "I got nervous when I lost comms. I have this for peace of mind. Have had it for years. I work on a lot of low-population worlds, or zero-pop, often in wilderness. Never know what you're going to run into. Or who. And I don't usually have a security detail with me."

"You telling me everything now?" I put an edge into the question. He was fragile, near breaking. I could tell. Maybe my best chance to cut through the halo of crap surrounding all of this. If he knew anything.

His eyes went wider. "Yes. Like I said. I don't know what the main purpose of this is, but I know we're not it. It's the law – when you find a world with any xenoarcheology, you have to shut down and have it surveyed before you can make a claim or take any further action. That's why I'm here, and the others on my team. Probably just to get it done, and fast, so they can move on with whatever they really want here."

I had a thought. "A full survey on a world with this many ruins, this many sites, that would take what, years?" With cities, advanced tech, it would be a big project, I reasoned. At least a few tens of millennia of culture to explore.

His eyebrows took a dip. "Well, if you wanted to be thorough. Over thorough. That's not technically—"

"You're here because you work fast." I thought I had it now. "Maybe too fast. That's what makes you the right guy for the job here."

He bristled at that. "I do good work. I've led the surveying on a dozen worlds, worked on maybe 30 more projects. My reports have never been questioned or sanctioned." He was angry now. "I'm good at this. The work doesn't suffer."

"What's the timeline you were given?" I was getting angry too.

"I make the calls on how long it takes. It lasts however long I decide."

"They have an expectation, though. And I bet your compensation is tied up in that. What is it, six weeks?" That was the initial term of my contract. They had an extension clause with a bonus, but I doubted I'd be seeing that now.

He didn't say anything.

"Tell me I'm wrong." I'd been in the service, and around mercs, long enough to know when I was being fed a line. It had taken me a while to realize it here, but I recognized this smell now, and it didn't smell good. "Tell me I'm wrong, or I walk, and leave you here."

"No!" His shoulders sagged. "We're supposed to have the survey done in five weeks. That's usually enough. There's virtually never anything on this kind of world to merit an archeological lockdown."

"Not when you're in charge, at least." He gave me an ugly look. "Enough of that. Tell me about the attack."

"There were two of them at first. I heard this big noise, a ship maybe, and then they appeared over the trees. They shot up the tents. One of them turned to head for the dig site, maybe to go after you, I don't know. The other started after me, and I ran away from the shower site and tried to fire back. But then the third one of them appeared, and whoever that was shot the other two. Two shots, one at each. They came out of the arm of the suit. Big shells or shots or whatever, maybe fist sized, trailing smoke, moving fast. Big explosions, one right after the other. The one shot went down towards the ground, maybe at the first attacker, and the other shot hit the one in the air. They fell, spinning." Welk had been agitated at the start, but his voice got quieter as he spoke. He was going to remember this forever, I knew. You always remember your first action. "I've never seen anything like that. It was like something out of an action holo."

"I bet." I chewed on my lip. "Why would someone want to kill you? Or us?"

He shook his head. "I have no idea. Honestly. This site isn't very important. None of what we've seen is. A small population, not very technologically advanced, less than a hundred thousand years in total with any recognizable culture, and maybe less than a thousand with any kind of sophistication. The cities are sort of impressive, but there aren't that many, and there are no survivors that we can see anywhere. They've been dead for far longer than our culture has existed, at least in any form more complex than hunter-gatherer societies. The genetics on this planet aren't found anywhere else that we know about, and there are no signs of any kind of space presence – nothing in orbit, no satellites, no debris, even. So we are pretty sure they never got beyond a pretty rudimentary technical civilization, and frankly, after this much time, there's not much left in the cities that would be of interest even to hardcore researchers."

"Sounds like you're already writing your report. This planet is ripe for exploitation, says Jordan Welk. Nothing to see here but dead unimportant alien savages." I felt a twinge of guilt for ripping into him. Not that he didn't deserve the scorn, but I was hardly a paragon of virtue. Pot, kettle, all that.

He glowered at me. "The archeologic resources here are minor and primitive. Any xeno culture is fascinating, but what's here is no reason to slow the settlement of the planet. The sites can be preserved while development takes place elsewhere. Reaching that conclusion on an expedited, efficient timeline doesn't change the facts."

"Something had to have changed, though." I was puzzled by this. "You were already doing what they wanted, on the schedule they wanted, right? What they paid you to do. So why the attack? Did their plans change? Is SpearPoint working for a third party? A competitor?" I chewed my lip some more.

I thought of something else. "You said the ground comms were down? I couldn't reach the *Deimos*, either." I suddenly thought of the glow I'd seen in the sky in a whole new way. "Oh, *skogol*."

"What?"

I turned back to the camp. "Come on." I made my way to the antenna, to the display mounted on the stem. The one showing active connections. I linked it into the con built into my suit. Once it connected, I hit it with a bunch of queries.

-- How many active links on network?

Three.

The three dig sites. I realized Welk's mystery other team, the A-team, must have had separate comms.

-- When was last contact with orbital vessel?

Contact with Deimos was lost at 0.73 hours past midnight local area time.

-- Scan area for vessel signatures or other comms in orbit on visual and all other standard frequencies. Search width 0.3 radians in all directions.

No vessels in search area.

The antenna had more than enough juice to do a limited sweep. Not picking anything up didn't mean there was nothing up there, but it meant there was nothing up there that was sending out signals.

-- Scan area for non-standard emissions.

Significant electromagnetic emissions above background in search area. Significant ionization of upper atmosphere underneath last known position of Deimos.

There was no good reason for that. But there was a very bad reason. I suspected now that whoever wished us ill had a lot more going for them than heavy assault suits. They'd apparently taken out a Patrol vessel, albeit a light supply cruiser. Even so, that put them squarely in one of two realms. Realm one was bad – they were too twitchy or maniacal to understand the massive response they were bound to bring down on them for such a blatant and serious crime. Realm two was worse – they were too strong and confident to care.

15

BAD BEHAVIOR

"So, how've you been?" Counselor Otieno had her usual emotional mask on. I was starting to hate it. I was hating a lot of things.

"I was in solitary confinement for forty-two days. How do you think I've been?"

"You're out now, though. And Inmate Urtenga didn't die, so that's probably the end of it." Otieno waved a finger through a holo control over her con. "She's in solitary now too, now that she's off life support."

"Would the universe have cared if she died?" I realized I was primed to pick a fight.

Otieno didn't take the bait. "Well, you'd be heading to Vylos now if she did, for a much longer sentence. So you'd have cared."

I wasn't sure she was right about that. "It was self-defense."

"Yes, that's what the recording showed. A very vigorous self-defense."

"She was out to kill me."

"I'm fairly certain that she regretted that decision early in the process, perhaps when her head was hitting the table, or later when her arm broke."

"Shouldn't have come at a marine."

"She is cognizant of that now, I'm sure."

I thought about pointing out that if I hadn't taken her out in that way that I'd probably have been in a few more fights, *and given the population and layout of the prison, I might not have won all of those. But Otieno probably didn't see it my way, and even if she did, she likely didn't care.*

I was quiet for a while. My thoughts were dark. "Would the universe care if I died?"

I regretted saying that immediately. It was chum in the water for somebody like Otieno. And it would get me written up, classified as a head case, probably subject to remedial treatment. I knew how big organizations worked. I'd get flagged, maybe have to do a stint in a psych facility after I got out. If I got out. Stupid, stupid.

Otieno didn't write anything down. She often made notes, so it was a little weird that she didn't when I went to full-on pathetic self-pity. But maybe that was in her guidelines, too. I wasn't good at second guessing her. She was craftier that way than my noncoms had been. Them, I could usually read, unless they went ragey. But ragey wasn't a color on Otieno's palette. I didn't even know what she was painting.

She looked at me, then said, "You really want me to answer that?"

"No. Sorry. That was stupid. I didn't mean it."

"Solitary gets its claws into you, doesn't it?" She shoved her con a little way away, like she was done with it. "I wish they wouldn't do that. Tons of research says it's not healthy."

"Yes, it is very much out of keeping with this facility, which is otherwise a model of nurturing support."

Otieno didn't respond to that. She seldom did when I was being sarcastic. Instead, she said, "You know, you can do your time angry and come out angry, or you can get a grip, and come out in a better place."

"'Get a grip' doesn't sound like sanctioned psychiatric treatment."

She laughed at that. That was rare. "There are pretty much two ways people handle this, although of course there are variations and a wide spectrum between. But angry and accepting are pretty much the end members."

"I'm supposed to accept all this? That a corporation sent me on a job that went bad, not because of anything I did, and

then they made it worse, and I'm in here because of the worse, and they're out there living it up?"

"So you're not guilty? Is that it?"

"No. I'm not guilty."

"Not at all?"

"No."

That was hasty, and a lie. Otieno knew that. She kept pushing. "So if you could go back in time and start over, you'd do everything the same?"

I mean, no. Of course not. I'd spot the snipers. I'd save Kenzi. I'd not get ambushed in that hole and start ARPing the village blindly. If I'd known what was going to happen, I could have made it come out a lot better. Hell, if I went back far enough, I could never have signed on to the Razors, never gone there, never seen the village burn. Never met Kenzi, and not be left like this, imprisoned and only half alive.

That wasn't useful. More self-pity. I thought bigger picture. Was there anything I could have done to prevent what we were actually accused of? I still didn't know fully what had gone down. Inmates didn't get unregulated access to the news network. We barely got access to anything at all, except to old books. Anything on the prison net was only the happiest or blandest of holos, comedy and romance and education and home decorating and dancing and kid shows.

But I knew the general sequence of events, both from being there and from the inquiry and trial afterward. I supposed, if I had it to do over, I could have asked more questions about the mission. That one, or any of them. We were routinely hired to intimidate. I knew that. Was the bombing just an extension of that function? Probably, but that was totally illegal. What we were doing wasn't illegal. The law had to mean something, right? And we hadn't done the bombing, hadn't known about it. I mean, we were ordered to do something similar, pretty much just as illegal, but we refused. That counted. That meant we were just wrong place, wrong time, and paying the price now. Some of us a much higher price than others.

Except. We were there, and we knew our role. It was one we'd accepted, even grown comfortable in. Scaring folks who were taking political action. Political action that had turned violent, but against a repressive regime. The regime that was paying us. The regime we represented. And those regular folks paid a higher price than any of us. We were soldiers. We were ready to die. Our lives were cheap, and we'd put them on the line in exchange for credits. We weren't kids playing in a town square. Not families sharing a meal.

Otieno was looking at me. I needed to say something. Otherwise she'd know I was thinking, and I didn't want to give her the satisfaction. "I would like some new clothes. These got worn out in solitary."

"Not surprising. You did a lot of exercising."

"You watched me? That's creepy."

"No. But the AI sentry made notes."

"That's creepier."

Her mouth twisted. "Prison is sort of creepy by nature, you know."

"I'm familiar."

"I can get you some new clothes." *Otieno pulled her con back and made some notes.* "Is it just new prison scrubs you're asking for, or is this a broader metaphor?"

I snorted. "You think you're hot stuff, don't you?"

She smiled.

16

SHIP OUT

"You think the Patrol ship is destroyed?" Welk seemed to be grasping a little of what that would mean.

"Yes. I mean, it could also be disabled, or departed, or captured. But none of that is good for you and me. Not with a heavily-armed third party around." I checked the two downed assault troopers. There was a small logo on the breastplates of their suits with the word SpearPoint under it. The A-team's hired security, then. Well, not security. Murderers. I hadn't heard of this SpearPoint outfit, but there were hundreds of mercenary groups, and I was fairly fresh out of a long stretch in prison. The suits were blue and red and silver, not subtle, which suggested they focused on intimidation and other showy jobs. If they were strictly a combat unit, they'd have planet-appropriate camouflage. Another puzzle. They were very well equipped, overequipped really, out here in the middle of nowhere, and not at all stealthy about what they were doing.

Well, you couldn't blame them. Armed like that, they didn't need stealth. It would have been easy as anything if one of their own hadn't taken them out. My suit was nice, best I could afford, and that was pretty good, because I hadn't spent money on anything else in seven years and my accounts had been doing pretty well. But it wasn't the equivalent of something like this. Not close. A hit from their shells would have done worse to me than it did to them, and it did plenty to them.

So who was this mystery third person? A defector? A spy? Somebody who'd found a hint of conscience in mid-mission? But the wave they'd given me was pretty casual, which suggested this was planned, not something dreamed up in the heat of the moment.

I had to know more. We weren't safe, not until I figured this out. Knew how many they were, whether there were more on the ground, or more coming, or what they wanted, other than to make sure we got turned into high-temperature mulch.

"They flew over the site first. In the ship." Welk had been thinking too. "Hovered for a little bit. Could they have wanted something there?"

"Could have just been checking it out. They might have known I was there from sensors." I didn't add that, if they did, that maybe made him the primary target of their operation, since they'd left me alone to attack the camp.

"What are we going to do?" There was an edge to Welk's voice. Not anger. Stress. He hadn't been in this situation, hadn't trained for it. He'd just been fired on, seen people get killed, seen the results. He'd break, sometime soon, probably, and go to jelly for a bit. Unless he was stronger than I thought. Some people were.

But he needed me now. This was what I was supposed to be good at, although none of this was in the job description. And I had almost no information. At least none that made sense.

Time to half-ass something, then. "I'm going to go check on their ship. It's bugging me that the third one didn't go to the ship when they were finished killing their friends. I mean, it's also bugging me that they killed their friends. Not that I am objecting." I was rambling. "So, I'm going to the ship. You should get to cover. Hide somewhere, preferably under something solid so they can't see you from orbit. Get a headset, pair it with the field antenna, and use it to contact me if you see anything. You know how to do that?"

He nodded.

"Don't move around, and don't make noise. If you need to tell me something, keep your voice low. The headset mic will pick up even whispers."

His face told me he didn't want me to leave him alone. Understandable. But not what I needed now. "I'll be back. Just a quick recon. If I took you with me, you would be an easy target." His frown deepened. "If they had more troops in the area, stands to reason they'd have attacked with more. So I think they don't. I think they're neutralized. I just don't know who the other person is, and I need to get the lay of the land. There might be answers with their ship."

He nodded again, then swallowed. "OK. I'll lie low."

"Good man." I checked my scans. Nothing unusual except the heat from the smoldering suits, but the range was limited by the trees around us. "I'm off. I'll check in with you in ten minutes." I could have given him instructions beyond that, for if I didn't check in, or if he heard explosions or me dying or whatever, but I didn't want to plan for that, and he'd be screwed anyway.

He nodded once more and gripped his pistol tighter. I moved off toward where I'd heard the ship setting down. I wanted to check out where the other assault trooper had gone, too, but they could be nearly anywhere within twenty kilometers by now, traveling by air. I didn't know the range of those suits, but I figured they had to have at least an hour of thrust. The Patrol flight suits could go for an hour, and these were similar. Probably.

So, our mysterious ally would have to wait. I'd need more than the limited gear I had on the ground to track them. The *Deimos* could do it, but I had a feeling they were not interested in my problems right at the moment. I hoped they weren't an expanding cloud of gas, debris, and jump plasma. Not least because they were my ride out of here.

17

See An Enemy

The ship was a two-seat scout, although it had a big enough bay in the rear to transport a couple more people or cargo if needed. I wondered if they flew in with the assault suits on. That would be uncomfortable, but they must have, because they appeared so quickly after landing, and it took a little time to mount a suit like that. Likely the ship interfaced with the suits, and they could fly mounted up.

The rear door was down, lowered to the floor of the clearing, but I didn't have a clear view. The ramp was on the far side from where I approached. The jet wash had cleared away the forest detritus, leaving bare red-brown dirt below. Most of the trees I'd seen on Kenai had big, sideways-growing leaves that sprung directly from the trunk. The leaves were mostly yellow or red, but once they fell to the ground, they turned brown and more fibrous-looking as they dried and decomposed.

I approached with caution, although my suit said nothing was moving. There was nobody in the cockpit, just two empty seats behind a transparent dome. I circled around to the left. Same logo on the ship, SpearPoint. Same red-blue-silver color scheme. I came around the wing to where the ramp angled down from the rear. I slowed, listening, and letting the suit listen as well. Nothing.

Rifle raised, I cut to the left, away from the ship, then came around behind the ship, using some trees as cover. Nothing inside, at least as far as I could tell. I could see trees and sky out the dome in front, so it looked like there was only a single room in the ship. Not much place to hide. If there was somebody in there, they could only be crouched down in front. And, importantly, they couldn't be wearing an assault suit. Those were too bulky. I'd have seen them from here. I waited for a while anyway. People tended to get twitchy when you waited, especially if two of their friends had blown up. Let them make the first move. I took the time to study the area around the ship. Some potential spots for ambush, but no sign of people breaking through trees. The leaves were undisturbed. Still, I watched for a while. Three minutes. Five.

If there was somebody on the ship, I probably had superior gear, and superior arms. Not necessarily, but probably. If there was even anybody there. I came out from behind the tree, the broad blade of a leaf scraping on my leg armor. I took a few steps up the ramp, conscious of the clank of my boots. No response. I got high enough to see into the bay. Stacked crates and gear around an aisle, with the aisle wide enough to allow somebody in an assault suit to pass, although it would be a little tight. My suit wasn't nearly as big, so I had no trouble.

I popped between the front seats, using the suit to boost my speed. Nobody there. The ship was empty. Well, except for me. Everything I was seeing said the ship had carried two people in assault suits. There would maybe have been room for a third, but it would be tight and awkward. I was thinking the third person had come from somewhere else. That could mean a second ship somewhere, although suits like that would have pretty good range – a few hundred kilometers on a full charge, or so I guessed.

I needed to poke around, but I couldn't risk somebody sneaking up on me. I backed out of the cockpit and found the rear door control. There was a mechanical growl as the ramp raised up, sealing the ship. That made me feel safer. I went back up to the front and sat in the left seat, setting my rifle in the right within easy reach.

The displays and controls were pretty standard. I wasn't much of a pilot, but I was qualified for AI-assisted flights, and this looked like what I had used before. I flipped through displays, trying to find anything useful.

Flight time: 3.54 hours. Total distance over ground: 904.6km. Huh. Long flight, unless they'd spent time circling or shuttling back and forth.

I brought up the telemetry. They'd come from a location south of us, but there was no detail of what was there. Not anywhere I was familiar with. The ruined cities and the other archeology teams were north.

I found the menu for comms. That might tell me something, if they weren't encrypted or locked to the pilot's genetics. I hit the History control, and a set of recordings appeared on the holo display. It looked like I could poke each one and have it play back, but that would take a while. I saw a control marked Transcription and hit that. A set of time-stamped entries filled the screen.

01:52 Ground Control: Operation is a go. All teams begin maneuvers according to existing orders. Repeat, operation is a go. Check stealth settings, engage signal jamming, and begin maneuvers.

02:31 Ground Control: Is Phase One behind schedule? Eagle, could you please report? Waiting on your go.

02:32 Eagle: Rivald here. Slight delay in weapon arming required recalculation of orbital intercept trajectory. Weapon was released on track, ballistic path verified. We have lost tracking with distance as expected, but no problems anticipated. Intercept expected in approximately one hour, 12 minutes.

02:33 Ground Control: Other teams take note and delay action as needed. Do not act until Phase One complete. We must avoid outgoing fleet comms. Repeat, delay action as needed.

02:33 Fox Squad: Acknowledged.

02:33 Viper Squad: Acknowledged.

02:33 Wolf Squad: Acknowledged.

03:44 Wolf Squad: Holy hell, it worked.

03:45 Eagle: Verifying, warheads detached as designed in close proximity, target evasive maneuvers taken too late to avoid impact. Impact from 86% of warheads with others detonating in proximity. Target is down.

03:45 Ground Control: Nice work, Eagle. Other teams proceed as planned.

03:45 Fox Squad: Acknowledged.

03:45 Viper Squad: Acknowledged.

03:46 Wolf Squad: Yee haw!

03:46 Ground Control: Wolf Squad, please respond with designated communications.

03:46 Wolf Squad: Such a tightass. Acknowledged.

04:01 Fox Squad: First city dig site neutralized. 100% casualties on archeo team. Moving to second dig site.

04:15 Ground Control: Viper Squad, we are not showing you moving as planned. Is there an issue?

04:15 Wolf Squad: What's the matter, Wigg? Hit another bird? [Laughter] You really put the stealth in stealth flyover. You should take some flying lessons.

04:16 Ground Control: Viper Squad, please respond.

04:17 Ground Control: Viper Squad, report status.

04:18 Ground Control: Viper Squad, we show you immobile where you were parked yesterday. You should be airborne by now. Please respond. You acknowledged orders earlier, just a . . . a half hour ago. What is the problem?

04:19 Ground Control: Fox Squad, when you've completed operations at second dig site, can you redirect to Viper Squad's location? We show them at 45.233, -40.441.

04:19 Fox Squad: We can head that way, but we will have to refuel first. It's too far for the suits, and the ship is low. Estimate one hour to terminate second dig site, another hour to reach fuel, three more to reach Viper Squad.

04:19 Wolf Squad: We could check on them if you want, boss. We're not far.

04:20 Ground Control: Negative, Wolf Squad. Carry out orders as planned. We need your target down. Viper Squad's goals can be delayed without much cost. Fox Squad, proceed with orders, then refuel and then check on Viper Squad.

04:20 Fox Squad: Acknowledged.

04:20 Wolf Squad: Acknowledged, boss. Permission to say Yee Haw?

04:20 Ground Control: Shut up, Morowitz.

06:11 Wolf Squad: Approaching destination. Will do a flyover to recon, then assault camp.

06:11 Ground Control: Acknowledged. Note there is a security detail at site.

06:11 Wolf Squad: I read the brief. One person, right? Light arms? Won't be a problem.

06:11 Ground Control: Take care, Morowitz. Don't screw this up.

06:11 Wolf Squad: If we screw up, it's Han's fault. She's the unlucky one.

06:12 Wolf Squad: Visual contact on campsite. Going in.

Well, that answered some questions. And raised new ones. Viper Squad had gone silent, maybe rogue, and they were near me. Sounded like they were maybe the ones who'd taken out Wolf Squad, the ones assigned to kill me and Welk. And the *Deimos* was down, which was huge. That would elicit a response from the Patrol, although it was hard to know how soon they would send anyone out here, well beyond Council space. If *Deimos* had managed to report the attack, it might be only a day or two, and the Patrol would come in force. But it sounded like the attack was stealthy. If *Deimos* hadn't sounded an alarm, it could be weeks. Probably not longer than that, but still. Patrol might just think it was a comms interruption, which was routine on long range missions to places with no jump gate to relay messages back. Like Kenai.

Why kill the archeologists? That question still hung over me. And the *Deimos*, of course. SpearPoint was up to something. They'd betrayed their employers on A-Team, or maybe they were following separate orders? No, SpearPoint had to have gone rogue. Kenai Expeditionary Corporation certainly wouldn't want the loss of a Patrol vessel on their accounts. So, whatever Welk's A-Team was investigating, SpearPoint had seen an opportunity for something bigger than just a class-M world to settle. That, and the high-end equipment and arms, meant SpearPoint was wealthy, violent, and not big on common courtesy or obeying laws.

But that made it weird that whoever this SpearPoint group might be, they were showing logos. This situation was going to be radioactive. When word got out, SpearPoint would be in serious trouble. Which, I realized, had not stopped RazorCorp from setting us up for war crimes convictions. Maybe SpearPoint management didn't care and was just soaking up credits, or maybe they were supremely confident that they'd handle the situation with no survivors. They probably had handled it, too. With the Patrol ship gone, they'd control the skies and anything in orbit. And they had the most significant military force on the planet. Because, probably, the second-most-significant military force on the planet was me.

Welk's A-Team, the biologists and physicists, weren't mentioned as targets in the transcripts. Unless they were what Viper Squad was supposed to take out. That made sense. If so, SpearPoint had just gone completely feral, killing both A-Team and B-Team, and getting rid of prying Patrol eyes while they did whatever they'd come here to do. This take was growing on me. It held together some. But I still wasn't sure of anything, and obviously Viper Squad wasn't following orders. For which I was grateful.

I poked around the ships' controls some more, but there wasn't much of interest. If the ruined assault suits had deployment recorders, which they probably did, there was a chance I might be able to recover those and maybe see farther back than the transcript went. But that would take time, and we needed to get the hell out of here before Fox Squad or whoever came for us.

I realized I hadn't radioed Welk, and he was probably going bananas. Good on him for not breaking radio silence, as I'd requested. "Welk, this is Jess. Sorry for the delay. What's your status?"

He sounded relieved. "I am all right. No sign of any more attackers."

"Where are you?"

"I took cover like you said. I'm in the hole."

"What hole?"

"The hole we dug. The site."

I was going to have to have a talk with Welk about what constituted a defensible position. But if he'd covered up like I said, then maybe it was all right. For now.

He spoke again. "Jess, there's something here you should see."

"This is no time for archeology, Welk."

"No, I know that. I'm not stupid. But this is different. Weird. Somebody left you a message."

18

CHOICES

Kenzi's breath was warm on my cheek. Big brown eyes, glowing in the gloom like embers. I felt a pull. A longing. Familiar, now.

I pulled away. It was so hard. "We're going to get caught."

"No, we're not." Confident, measured. Like Kenzi always was. "It shouldn't be forbidden, anyway. I'm not in your direct chain."

"Fleet Command doesn't care about shouldn't. You were in my chain, and you outrank me, and that's all that matters. And we will get caught. I know some of them suspect already. And when we do, you'll get sent to the brig. Court-martialed. You'll lose your rank, your pension, everything you've earned." I couldn't reconcile that with what I was feeling.

"So you want to stop? Break it off?" Kenzi's voice was neutral. Not mad. Just asking.

"No, I..." I swallowed. "But I can't be the reason your career dies. I can't."

"I could get transferred to another unit. We could file the paperwork. Declare everything. Go above board." Kenzi smiled. "Get married, even."

No. That could well mean we'd be assigned to different ships, different planets. That would hurt even worse. "I don't want that either."

"What do you want?"

"This." I put my head back on Kenzi's shoulder. "But not at the cost I think we'll pay."

Kenzi's hand found mine. It was so warm. Always warm. "What if we muster out? Your term's almost up, and I've got five years in, so I can leave anytime."

"But the Patrol is your life. All you've ever wanted." And all I've wanted too. There were no good options.

"I'd give it up for you, Jess. In a heartbeat."

"I can't ask that." Did I want it?

"I've got a friend in a mercenary squad. They do private security. The pay's better, and you get regular vacation, benefits. And they wouldn't care about us being us. We'd live together, work together. Nothing in our way."

That sounded like a dream. I thought for a while. "But it's not Patrol. Not service, not the honor and the uniform. I know that's what you wanted." What I wanted.

Kenzi squeezed my hand. "I did. And I've enjoyed it. Needed it. But I don't need it like I used to. I've found something better." Warm breath, then a kiss on my cheek. I felt a shiver radiate from the touch and run down my side. The good kind of shiver. "Something worth a lot more than bars on my shoulders."

The sun would be up soon. That meant we had to get out of this storage shack and sneak our way back, Kenzi to barracks, me to mess. This posting on Delvar, with a thin garrison, staggered shifts, and solo billets, had offered so much opportunity for us. More than I had thought possible. And more danger, and more potential heartbreak. Our time here was almost done. Or probably, anyway. We'd get orders next week, and I doubted we'd stay. Could I go back to a group billet, guard stations, eyes everywhere? Retreat back to shared glances, stolen kisses, stifled longing? I didn't think I could.

I swallowed. "Maybe... Maybe we can think about it. But you have to think, too. You've got more at stake."

"I don't." Kenzi stroked my arm, then pulled me into an embrace. So warm. "Your career is as important as mine. But I don't need to think any more. I want to be with you forever."

19

Pit Stop

Welk looked up at me. His eyes were white in the gloom of the pit, in contrast with his dark skin. He'd dragged what was left of his tent over and spread it over part of the hole. That had to be a lot of work. The result was not terrible, and it was in keeping with what I'd told him to do. I made my way down the dirt stairs. I didn't like the tactical setting, but it was probably OK for now.

"Are there any others? Are we safe?"

"It was a two-seater, so there aren't any more." I could see his shoulders relax. "But I think there are more on the way. And whoever killed those two could come back."

He sounded doubtful. "They helped us."

"No guarantee they would again." I reached the bottom of the pit. "There's some serious stuff going on here, stuff I don't understand. We need to get the hell out of here and lie low until we figure it out. Very low. Like, turning invisible is not low enough." I saw he was holding a black box. It looked like stone or metal, but it had a kind of a wood grain texture to it. "What is that? The message you mentioned?"

"No," he said. "This is weirder."

"We're under attack by unknown enemies and you're doing archeology?"

He looked embarrassed. "I actually do love this stuff, you know. And I figured if I was down here, I might as well poke around. Kept my mind off..."

"Off bad guys trying to murder you?" Welk didn't look like he appreciated that much. "So why is that thing weird?"

"It's a living organism."

"What?" I took another look at it. "It's a box."

"It's both. I contacted the scanner and had it do a detailed workup. The box is actually a living organism. One with impossibly slow metabolism. But the whole thing is made up of cells and a genetic code. But not the same as the other organisms on the planet." He looked proud.

"But you found it down here?" I was struggling to keep up. "It's been buried for a hundred thousand years or something?"

"No. Twenty-two thousand, I think. At least. I can't date it, because it's still alive and exchanging carbon with the environment, which itself is just tremendously exciting, after all this time. But it's that old if the dates we were getting from the soil profiles were right." Welk was almost bouncing up and down. "It's like it's an immortal being or something."

"Did you open it?" I didn't see an obvious way to do that.

"I couldn't figure out how. But there's a cavity inside, and something solid sliding around in it." He was really digging the mystery. I could tell.

"So, if the soil dates are right, this place really is younger than the cities?"

"Yes, much younger. Which I don't understand, but that's what the data are saying." He started talking really quickly. "I found some mineralized skeletal material down here in that alcove. One of the lizard creatures." He pointed at a gap in the stone wall. The cabinet I'd seen, now opened. He'd removed the stone cover and set it on the altar. Or what I thought of as the altar. "The box was in there, just sitting in the hole. The nanites cleaned it off, and I saw there was a door that could come off. We were lucky they didn't get inside. I bet they would just have torn it apart, like they did the roots and such. Or maybe they did get inside, but the box triggered the artifact algorithms and got preserved that way. The nanites are pretty cautious."

"Sure." I had no idea what an artifact algorithm was.

"It was in a cavity built into the wall, one fitted to its size, which must mean the builders put it there, intentionally. It was probably put in there for ceremonial purposes, and then sat here until today. Oh! And I found some other materials to date. Calcite concretions on the rock faces, probably from just after it was buried. They can precipitate from groundwater through a process—"

"Keep it simple, Welk."

"Right. The bottom line is, they prove this place is young, much younger than the cities. That means the culture regressed from city building, and maybe even nuclear technology, to simple stone tools and basic construction. But at the same time they were in this kind of stone age, they were making boxes out of living beings. That's all super interesting, and super weird."

"Maybe they had an apocalypse and their society collapsed, and then they built new living box technology later."

"Possible. Probably something like that. But they'd still have the cities to loot, technology to recover, so it's odd they'd be that limited to primitive construction. And the only indication of a major war or something like that is the radiocarbon anomaly, but that's from just before the cities, fifty, fifty-five thousand years ago. It doesn't make sense. I need to look at this harder. Get more data."

I snorted. "You know somebody tried to kill you not three hours ago. Maybe not the time to worry about this." I realized I hadn't told him about the rest of his team. "I think they took out the teams in the city and the other sites. The reports I saw..."

"They're dead?" His manic edge was gone now, and his voice was quiet. "All of them?"

"I think so." I needed him not to go too dark. "I'm sorry. But they didn't get us, and we are still alive. We need to get out of here. Go on living."

He stared for a moment. Not at me, just into space. Then his eyes met mine. "The message. For you. I told you. It might be relevant to getting out of here."

"Yeah, what was that?" He pointed over to the other side of the hole, over past the stairs. It was a con – a personal console. What was something like that doing here? It was human tech, and current, so it had to have gotten into the hole after it had been dug, which meant today or yesterday. And I hadn't seen it down here this morning.

I heard Welk let out a sigh, then a groan. He was losing it, I thought. But I didn't have time to comfort him. I had to think. He'd deal with it in his own way. Death could be hard to swallow, and he wasn't accustomed to being attacked. Maybe he'd known some of the people well. His team. Probably needed a minute, and I knew myself well enough to know I wasn't great at emotional support. Not anymore.

I bent over to get a better look at the con lying on the floor. Ordinarily, I'd have said it had to be mine or Welk's, but it was an unfamiliar model – not mine, and nothing I'd seen Welk using. Somewhere behind me, Welk sat down heavily. I reached out a finger and tapped the screen. It sprung to life, and a message floated on the holo display.

Jess Amiko. Things are skogging bent, as you know by now, and they're getting worse. You need to come to these coordinates: 67.181, -43.993. There's somebody you need to meet. He has some answers. I'm not setting you up, even though I know that's exactly what somebody setting you up would say. But this is for real, and I'm a friend. Yomo Code.

The whole message was surprising, but by far the most surprising part was the last two words. In the Patrol, I'd been stationed for a while on a base on a lifeless world called Yomo. It was a desolate, boring place, and there was a tradition that anybody who'd also been stuck on Yomo was an official friend for life. There were all kinds of rules. You had to be on Yomo for at least five rotations, and Yomo rotated slowly, so that was about 78 standard days. They had an induction ceremony, sometimes for an individual, but usually for a whole group or squadron, because they'd all arrive on Yomo at the same time. Each person got assigned some stupid task, like measuring the base's perimeter with a curry ration pack or delivering nonsense rhyming messages, which you had to memorize perfectly, back and forth across the base to various NCOs. But eventually you were sworn in, and everybody got sloshed and ate tons of curry, and you then were part of the Yomo Society, loud and proud, bound to help out any other member as needed, for life. The Yomo Code.

The author of the note must know I'd been on Yomo. That meant they had my deployment history, which was weird. That information was not generally available outside the Patrol. Could the assault trooper who'd helped us be a member of the Yomo Society? And knew I was too? That seemed like a ridiculous explanation. The Yomo Code was a joke. At best, it meant you bought somebody a drink when you met them somewhere, or you got them a better billet or extra rations on a transport vessel. It wouldn't extend to fragging two allies on a deployment on a remote world, unless you were some kind of Yomo Society zealot, but I'd never heard of that.

I pondered whether we should go to the place they indicated. I didn't have a lot of other options. It might be a lure for an ambush, but I suspected that it had to be the trooper who'd helped us who had left the message. They seemed to be our only ally, and maybe our only chance if the whole situation had gone vacc leak on us. Which it looked like it had. And I didn't have any better plan. I hoped Welk would be willing to go. I supposed at some point the situation might get so bad that I'd have to ditch him and save myself, but I wasn't there yet. I'd signed on to protect him, taken his money, and I'd keep my word. I warmed up my official competent-soldier-giving-orders-voice and turned back toward him.

He was on the ground, back against the wall of the hole, one hand on his chest, eyes staring upward.

20

PRISON

Otieno had her can't-read-me face on, but I was used to it. I smiled, big and fake, to see if I could get her to crack a smile, or show any reaction, really. No dice.

"You're down to one year left, as of today," she said.

"Yup."

"How do you feel about that?"

"So sad to be leaving. Don't worry, I'll give you a great review in The Council's 100 Best Prisons."

Still no reaction. "A lot of inmates start to worry about how life is going to be outside. Especially those who've experienced loss of career, loss of status, or loss of loved ones."

She was messing with me again. She often did. Sometimes it even worked. "I haven't been worried." That was a lie. But I didn't want to get into it.

"Sometimes, inmates facing release even pursue actions that might extend their sentences or complicate their release."

"Are you talking about that weaselly hairball Freja? She had it coming."

"No doubt." She tapped a button on her con's display. "The dental reconstruction is scheduled for tomorrow."

"Can they take out her tongue while they're at it? That would be kind of a public service."

Otieno pursed her lips. "Jess, we'd been making progress. This is a step back."

I didn't like that. Because it was true. "Freja went at me first. It was on the cameras."

"You sat at her table."

"She doesn't own the cafeteria. Or the tables."

"I think you did it to provoke her."

Well, give the counselor a prize. I didn't say anything.

She sighed. "Jess, you might think you're special or unique, but you're a textbook case. As in, I could show you the chapter describing what you're doing, and why."

"Is that supposed to make me feel better, or worse?"

"It's supposed to make you feel boring. And you're not boring."

"Well, sure, I'm a war criminal, right? They aren't boring. Everybody knows that. Check out my maniacally evil grin." I gave it my best shot.

She raised an eyebrow. Finally, I'd gotten a response. She was quiet for a while, long enough for me to feel stupid and awkward. A trick she often pulled. "What are you going to do when you get out?"

That was something I'd given a lot of thought, as I'm sure she knew. That must be in the textbooks too. I wasn't qualified for much other than killing people. There was the training in related skills that helped me kill people. Map-reading. Weapons systems design and function. Basic vehicle operation and piloting. Weapon and suit maintenance. Recon and scouting.

All of that pointed to re-upping with a mercenary team, or a security firm, or maybe some kind of training facility. But anything like that would be next to impossible for somebody with a Class-L conviction on their record. I figured I'd likely end up on some end-of-the-line world doing mining or security or something. Or maybe I could be a bar bouncer. That might be fun.

"Have you thought about going to school? You've done well in the courses you've taken here. You've got probably two years' credit towards a degree if you combine it with the military certificates."

"What kind of degree? Mayhem Science? With a minor in violating laws and morals?" I snorted. "Not like any school is going to admit me."

"We have some programs that can help make that possible."

I thought about it. Gave her that, at least. "I think I took the courses only because everything else here is so soul-crushingly boring. I don't see myself wanting more of that outside."

"Well, what do you want?"

"I want my old life back. My old status. Respect. A sense of self-worth." A lump filled my throat. I wasn't getting any of that. And there was something – someone – I wanted back more than anything. But Kenzi was five years gone now.

"You can't have that." Otieno studied me.

I was tired of being studied. "Thanks. Brilliant analysis. Whatever they're paying you, it's too little."

"You're right." Otieno pushed her con aside. "I think what you want, what you've always wanted, is a life that meant something. Where what you do matters. I think that's why you signed up for the Patrol. From what you've said, I think you were happiest there."

No. I was happiest with Kenzi. And that couldn't happen in the Patrol.

Otieno continued. "You need your life to matter. That's not at all uncommon. That's why I'm here, dishing up platitudes to violent miscreants like yourself. You want to be someone who helps. Who other people look up to."

I laughed at that. "Hey, Counselor. I'm a convicted war criminal. Nobody's looking up to me, other than wanna-be war criminals."

Otieno sighed. "You're not a war criminal. That's not what the conviction means. But you know that. It will follow you around, for sure, but not in the way you're carrying on about. Not with the press coverage after, and the reporting about your case."

"Haven't you been trying to get me to accept that what I did was wrong? I thought that was the whole point of our sessions."

"Not the whole point." Otieno looked at me.

"You want to hear it again? What I did was wrong. I signed on with a corrupt corporation. They exploited me, but I also took their money. What we did got innocent people killed. A lot of them. Not because we set out to kill them, but because we were there. And we chose to be there." And we got our friends killed, too. The lump was back.

Otieno reached out and held my hand. That was weird. "You said nobody's going to look up to you. That might be true. At least, if it's to the person you were. But you can be somebody new, now. And the first person who needs to look up to that new person is you."

I stared at Otieno. "You know, Counselor, that was desperately cheesy, even by your standards."

"Whatever works."

21

Grave Matters

I sat by Welk. I'd closed his eyes, laid him down. The sensor pads for the medic kit were on his chest, but I'd turned off the machine. There was nothing for it to do. No heartbeat, brain activity flat. *Diagnosis: Major disruption of cardiac circulation. Cardiac vessel(s) likely ruptured. Probability 98%. Recommend immediate referral to surgery unit.* I'd tried chest compressions, and the machine had shocked him a couple of times, but he was gone even before I started. On a world infinitely far from wherever home was, in a hole of his own making.

I peeled off the sensor pads and adjusted his shirt, still wet from his aborted shower. What kind of luck is that, to survive an assault by an overwhelming force, only to keel over an hour later? Was it the stress of the attack? Or the thrill of discovery of the ancient culture? Or hearing that the rest of his team was dead? Didn't much matter.

The box he'd been so proud of, the one he'd pulled out of the wall, lay askew by his hand on the flagstone floor. I felt like I should take it with me, maybe so that at least something would survive of his final project. His work. That seemed noble.

It also seemed totally impractical and stupid. I didn't know what it was. Neither did he. Babysitting a weird box from a hole because I'd failed at keeping a guy from getting dead was no kind of plan. Not when a whole planet of bad guys were out to kill me. I needed to leave, and fast.

I looked at the cavity in the wall that Welk had said he found the box in. It was box-shaped, to be sure. The stones making up the door, the ones that he'd removed, lay on the floor nearby. I put the box back in the cavity and put the stones back up in place over it. They were cut into regular blocks by hands long dead, so it wasn't hard to restore the cabinet to how it had been when we found it. If I made it through this, which was looking increasingly unlikely, I could carry the news of this place to people who'd actually use it. Who cared about these ancient aliens. That would do something for Welk's legacy. Maybe they'd even name something after him. Best I could do.

I took a last look around the pit, at the rough-hewn walls with the strange carvings, the windows and doorways still filled with dirt. They must once have stood open to light and air. I wondered what kind of people had wandered these hallways and rooms. Welk's map showed that there was even more to this complex than what we'd dug up. There were probably whole families here, a whole village, living, working, praying, or whatever these people did. They were gone, but what they'd built had lasted for an improbable twenty-two thousand years. Nothing I did would have that kind of impact. Well, not in a good way.

I picked up the con, its mysterious message still visible. No sense leaving behind a trail to where I was going. I made my way over to the dirt steps the nanites had carved. I had some coordinates to visit and a ship to get me there. I took the steps three at a time with the help of my suit.

22

YOMO SAPIENS

The ship whooshed away above me. I picked myself up off the ground and brushed some mud from my elbow joint. Not a good deployment, Amiko. Glad nobody was watching. Or so I hoped. I'd programmed the ship to fly low to drop me off in motion, then take a course up north toward the camp near the xeno city sites. I figured that would look like what Wolf Squad might have done after killing Welk and me, although the lack of comms would still look fishy. I had the ship's autopilot set to return to a location west of here tomorrow, although I doubted it would make the trip. Surely somebody from SpearPoint, or their client, or whoever was behind this, would check out the ship before then. But hopefully that inspection would take place far from me, and my drop here would go unnoticed.

I didn't have much of a plan. I'd taken some basics from our campsite. A week's food, the broadcast antenna, the medic kit. A few packs of the custom nanites. I couldn't carry Welk's big field console, obviously, but I should be able to get the nanites to do something basic and useful through my con's interface if I needed to. Or if I could figure out anything useful to do. Maybe I could have them carve HELP in big letters over a couple hectares of forest for when the Patrol arrived. Whenever that might be. I might well be able to live off the land until then. Just keep hidden, then use the antenna to contact whoever came. Unless they had really specialized equipment up in orbit, I might well be able to keep out of sight.

Except. There was almost always an except to any improvised plan that sounded good at first blush. In this case, it was a workable plan, except that they were still looking for me, and wanted to kill me, and I didn't want to die. And except that I'd gotten the message directing me to a meeting. Yomo Code. That was too interesting to ignore, and it might give me either somewhere safer to hide out, or some way to fight back against these people who were murdering innocent archeologists, and who'd blown up a Patrol vessel, presumably with all hands. I wasn't in the service anymore, but that kind of transgression couldn't stand.

Not that an ex-marine Class-L convict with two light weapons and a few meal packs was going to avenge anybody. Not yet, anyway. I checked the rest of the equipment I dropped, made sure everything was powered down, then stowed it under some of the big fleshy trees.

I checked the load on my rifle and my pistol. Full charge, and some spare cells for each. The suit was charged, too, topped off from the ship's batteries before I dropped out. The holo display in front of my face said 20.4 klicks to the coordinates, north by northeast. With the suit's augments, I could cover that in a couple hours. Unless assault troops showed up and finished blowing me to bits.

23

COORDINATED EFFORT

Low, bushy plants. The same red and yellow leaves I'd seen on the trees, but these were more like groundcover. A squat quadruped loped past, pausing to graze. Probably a couple hundred kilos. Bigger than I was, but the dental plates were flat, not pointed, and it looked docile. The suit had it marked yellow on the HUD, but that was probably just because of the size.

I was close to the coordinates listed on the con Welk found in the hole by the dig site. From my maybe-ally, who had claimed not to be setting me up. Yomo Code, and all. I was crouched low under the broad leaves jutting from the trunk of one of the many trees. Had been for 32 minutes, said the suit timer. But I was happy to wait and watch. Trusting people came hard, even if I hadn't been targeted for death that morning on a planet maybe swarming with hostile mercs.

I wasn't positive who had put the con in the hole, but I had a good guess. There weren't many candidates. Not Welk – he'd been as surprised by it as I was. Not the assault troopers. They'd just wanted to kill us, not leave us cryptic messages. That left the mysterious savior. Not a lot of other options, although it could have been yet another party, maybe. Whoever it was knew a good bit about me, enough to invoke Yomo.

The coordinates were pretty precise, and they indicated a small hill nearby, covered with some of the tallest trees I'd seen yet. Some of them got to maybe 30 or 40 meters, trunks three meters across at the base, with broad leaves all around, narrowing upward with ever smaller leaves. There was an impressive grove on the hill, maybe a few hundred trees around it, and they were dense enough I couldn't see through them to the exact location specified. Which was probably why that was the exact location specified. Great place to hide, and also great place to ambush a stupid former marine short on friends.

A yellow box flickered on the display. Movement, behind one of the trees. Then it disappeared. Maybe another of the herbivores. The suit wasn't worried. That probably meant no unusual energy signatures, no humans, and certainly no flying assault suits. I played back the tactical recording, but all I saw was a hint of motion, nothing I could identify.

The short day was moving on towards afternoon, the shadows getting longer, the copper green noon sky taking on a little extra color at the horizon. Pretty. Once settlers came, as inevitably they would, they would be able to earn some tourist credits for that view alone.

I should probably do this if I was going to. Shoot or shove off, my drill instructor used to say. Whoever had left the message wouldn't wait around forever. Still, I didn't want to wander in there with no information. Tactical dark, for sure, and I had precious little in the way of illumination.

There was a crunching noise from the hill. One of the big trees wavered, then toppled. It was wedged up against a bunch of others, but once it got going, it fell pretty fast and found a way to the ground, knocking against the others, leaves flying off. I heard a shrill shriek. Not human. Maybe an animal, or maybe the trees here could scream. Wouldn't be the weirdest thing I'd seen.

The tree might have gone down on its own, or maybe there was somebody there trying to signal to me. Or fighting someone or something, or just hating on the vegetation for some reason. I saw it as a sign, though. I should go check this out. No other good options anyway, other than slowly starving to death on an alien world. I watched for a few seconds more, then checked my loads and headed out towards the hill, and towards where my ally had pointed me. Yomo Code. I hoped that wasn't a lie.

I made it about 30 meters toward the hill when my suit picked up the sound. Audio, not transmitted. Just a guy yelling. Raspy voice. "Help. Please, help."

24

T HE P INNED IN THE W ILLOWS

Help. Please help. I stopped. Two divergent possibilities. A person hurt and in need of assistance, or somebody lying in wait, playing upon my humanity, such as it was. This cursed planet, and this cursed situation. No tactical clarity.

The best answer to no tactical clarity was to have the biggest guns. I wasn't sure of that in this case, but the people trying to kill me before had much bigger guns, and they could fly. Their side had taken out a Patrol ship, for that matter. A grunt with no friends shouldn't be a challenge. They wouldn't need a ruse.

So, somebody genuinely needing help. Let's go with that. I took another few steps, big ones with the suit's help. Kept trees between me and the center of the hill. It looked like there was a depression at the top of the hill. Maybe a crater? No, narrower, more like a slot canyon. I circled sideways, trying to see in.

The fallen tree was there, one of the tallest, a massive log. It lay nearly horizontal, low to the ground. Nearby trees were snapped off, destroyed as their larger neighbor fell, jagged splintery stumps pointed skyward. Other trees had their broad red and yellow leaves shorn off. The tree that had fallen had a jagged scar down the side, a groove with blackened edges. A lightning scar, I realized. But not a recent one. The tree had healed after being struck. But maybe not enough. It was down now.

I checked the suit display. No hazards nearby. A marine who trusted suit scans blindly was a dead marine, but in this case, I thought it might be accurate. No sign of movement, no sign of heat, although the animals on this world generally weren't too much hotter than the surrounding air. Maybe there was something big out there. The thought of coming all this way to get eaten by a giant space lizard was kind of funny, actually.

But somebody was calling for help. I heard it again, fainter. "Help. Please."

Screw it. I bounded up the hill towards the slot canyon, towards the fallen tree, towards the voice. I kept my movements erratic, pausing at times behind cover, but I went fast. The base of the fallen tree, where it was widest, was the best cover I could see. I rounded that and came to the stump. It swarmed with little blue worms. The wood at the base was shot through with holes and slender tunnels, enough to rot the whole thing through. Tiny soldiers bringing down a big enemy. No enemy, actually. Just an innocent victim.

I made my way along the fallen tree trunk toward the canyon. The voice was coming from somewhere near here, I thought, but I couldn't see anyone. A thick chunk of vine extended out from under the tree trunk. Not a type of plant I'd seen before, which caught my eye. It was coated with scaly bark, knotty, with multiple threads of growth wound together. The surface was covered with little diamond-shaped scales, and the vine ended not with fronds and leaves but with a sharp angle leading to a round, flat blob, also scaly with diamonds. No time for xenobotany, though. I kept moving, quick glances in all directions.

As I stepped over it, the vine moved, bending sharply at the angle. The flat blob thrashed up and down. I stopped and looked more closely. Some of the knotted threads of vine were pulling, like tendons, and others were contracting, like muscles. The flat blob at the end flexed, the fringe rippling upward. Then it came to me. This was not a vine. It was a leg.

The fallen tree lay across it, pinning it to the ground. I used the suit assist to jump and clamber over the tree trunk, nearly three meters thick here, narrowing going up the trunk. As I came down on the other side, I saw the rest of something, or somebody, sticking out the other side of the tree, but broken leaves obscured my view. My suit didn't register a heat source, but there was definitely something there. I slid down to the right and pushed the leaves aside.

Below me on the forest floor was a humanoid shape, more or less, composed of a network of the gray scaly vines, all coated with the little diamond patterns. What must have been the torso was a rounded brown mass, with no clear shoulders or neck. The fallen tree lay across the width of the body, so I could not make out a waist or any other legs. Three arms, or maybe tentacles, lay splayed around the figure, each ending in a ring of vines and a broad pad, like a miniature version of the foot I'd seen on the other side of the tree. I could not figure out the creature's construction. There might be another arm lying under the body – it was hard to see in the clutter of leaves and detritus. I did see, lying next to one arm, what looked like a rectangular satchel with a strap.

Above the main body was a rounded lump, like a head, but with no clear face. It had glistening, wet-looking blobs set at regular intervals about halfway up. My brain classed them as eyes, but I really didn't know. There was a fleshy gray tube protruding from the top of its head. The tube was not covered with the diamond-shaped scales like the rest of the body, and it seemed to be made of a different material.

As I watched, the network of vines making up the head convulsed, and more of the eyes shifted around to look at me, or sense me, or whatever they were doing. They were milky white with red centers, no pupils, but covered with countless small facets that caught the light. The fleshy tube retracted back into the creature's head. I wondered if that was good or not, or if I should try to stop it, but I had no idea what I should be doing here.

The whole experience was giving me the zavvies, but that was to be expected. I took a breath to clear them out, going through the triggers and accommodation we'd learned back in basic training. Those of us who'd grown up on worlds that were near 100% human, like my home planet, Ramine, had to be brought up to speed with the diverse group of people and non-human cultures present in the broader society of the Council worlds. The instructors said that for a lot of humans, it was part of our innate wiring to get weird about people who looked different from us, and it took some work to overcome this tendency, especially when it was triggered by non-humans. For people who grew up on worlds with a lot more diversity and exposure, this was no big deal – they got used to interacting with all sorts of folks, human and not, from a young age, so they just saw everybody as people, regardless of how they looked. But people like me who grew up more isolated could adopt all sorts of stupid behavior, from going up to strangers and touching them, or saying offensive things, or making bad assumptions about how they lived, acted, or carried themselves.

The zavvies – xenobiologic aversion - was a common reaction for some folks. Your brain sees people different from you, with skin not at all like yours, or with parts you don't have, or voices that don't sound normal, and your mind and body go into fight or flight. You usually control that, but something down in your brainstem still thinks it's seeing monsters that want to kill you. The training was actually kind of neat. Rubes like me got to interact with a lot of new non-human people, ask them questions, get a close look at their skin, faces, and anatomy in a way that would normally be rude. The non-human instructors were actually some of the coolest, most relaxed people I've ever met.

But I still had that tendency. The zavvies. You know, like some people are scared of heights, or confined places, or snakes, or bugs. It wasn't rational, and because what you were scared of was just regular people, it was really offensive. If you didn't keep it under control, you'd make a real ass of yourself, or worse – shoot somebody just because they walked out of an alley and looked different.

The fleshy tube came out again, but not out of the top of the head. Instead, it came out pointed at me. There seemed maybe to be a different kind of tissue inside the creature, mobile and flexible, hidden under the vine exterior. I didn't know, though. This was coming at me pretty fast.

The edges of the tube vibrated, and I heard the voice again. Clearer and louder now, but still raspy and weird with almost harmonic undertones, like it was being made by different kinds of organs than vocal cords.

"Hello, Jess, my old friend. When the tree fell, I knew this must be the day we meet. I suspected it was coming. I am so honored to be your *lajaret.*" The voice was deep, male sounding, but of course I had no idea what gender this person might be, or if they had a gender at all.

But the bigger question pressing on my mind was, how in flaming fire did they know my name?

25

PLANT LIFE

I left that question alone for the moment. I struggled with the tree, trying to pull it off the fallen being, but it was too heavy, even with the suit assist. If I'd had a regular toolkit, I could have cut the tree into sections, but it might have taken a long time. Didn't matter, though. The rifle and pistol wouldn't work for that at all.

"Hold tight, uh, friend. I'm trying to get this off you."

The being's head tipped to the side, and it spoke again through the little tube. "That will avail you little, I am afraid, and me even less. I can feel my inner sac leaking. I fear I am to die. But it is a good death, better than most. Do not worry. These things happen."

It didn't seem like a good death to me. Not even top fifty. I picked up a log and tried to slide it under the tree to lever it up, but the older wood of the log was rotten, fibrous and soft, and it bent rather than lifting anything. I looked for something else. My rifle was solid, but it was far too slim a piece of metal to do anything here. I drew my pistol and started firing at the fallen tree, trying to score a line across it, but I didn't accomplish much. Maybe I should keep him talking. "Are you a resident of this world?"

"I am. I sprouted here, and here I have lived all my days." The speaking tube bent and fell to one side, then extended out again. "And what days they have been. I am truly blessed."

"Don't talk like that. We'll figure something out." They'd said in training that being positive around somebody wounded could help them cling to life. I wasn't sure if that applied to smashed hose-mouthed wooden people, but it was worth a try. I figured I'd want some encouragement if our situations were reversed.

"Perhaps you will, but not today." The tube bent over once more, and when the melodic voice came again, it was softer. "Best of luck, and may the dawn find you whole."

The tube slid back inside the being's head. I got my leg under the tree a bit and tried again to lift. I heard the suit's servos straining. It seemed like the tree flexed a hair upward, but I just couldn't move it. I saw thick green liquid coming out from under the trunk, staining the vine-like limbs. Perhaps those were the contents of the inner sac. I knelt and put a hand on the side of the head, trying to avoid the glistening eye blobs. "Hey. Don't let go. Tell me how to help." I nudged the wooden body. I took hold of the textured, vine-like arm and shook gently, but there was no response.

For the second time in two days, somebody lay suddenly dead before me. Well, really the fourth time, if you counted the assault troopers. But I only cared about two of them. Welk, who'd been a friend, of sorts, even if he'd been lying to me some. He was still basically a decent guy, though. And then there was this person, who seemed pleasant, and called me friend, but whose words, and speech, and presence here at all, made no sense to me.

I wondered if I should dig the body out and bury it, but that seemed hard, and it might not be what their culture did. I had no way to know, and any action, or inaction, might as likely be an affront as a comfort. But it seemed like maybe digging a grave for a person I'd just met on a hostile world full of people who wanted to kill me might not be good tactics.

I checked the satchel, but it just had a few thin wooden sheets with weird writing on them. Hardly anything for such a large bag. Weird. I had no room to carry anything, and no time to figure out what it meant. I could come back if I needed to.

I stood, resolving to leave the unfortunate person where they lay. A thought occurred to me. If this was the person who left me the note in the pit, the person I was supposed to meet, it was fair to say that it had gone exceedingly poorly, and I was almost definitely MSTBFO. That was an acronym popular among grunts, particularly those who'd seen action. More screwed than before following orders.

26

SELF-DESTRUCT SEQUENCE

Otieno's face barely ever revealed emotion, but this time I was pretty sure she was projecting disgust. "Why the frowny face, Counselor? They've cleaned up all the blood."

"Yours, or theirs?"

"Lot of both, I would think. But I was unconscious for the ending part, so I can't be sure."

Otieno sat in the chair next to my bed. It was bolted to the floor like much of the furniture here, and it didn't look comfortable. She pulled out her con and tapped a few controls. "You're fighting again. Why?"

"It's who I am. A grunt. You know."

Otieno frowned. "The marines I know don't pick stupid fights. You're lucky to be alive."

"Didn't pick anything. They ambushed me. Not my fault they couldn't execute."

Otieno frowned. "Don't play stupid. It's insulting, and it's not helpful."

Maybe I wanted to insult her. She deserved it. But she was right. I'd gone to the rec area near D block, and everybody knew that was run by the Yenekani gang. I knew that, and I knew they'd respond. So did Otieno, so did everybody else here. Suddenly my glib attitude, probably supported by the pain meds, shrank away. "Don't know what you're talking about." But I did.

She looked at me for a moment, then fiddled with her con. "Lacerated kidney. Five broken ribs. Fractured vertebra, now replaced, at government expense. Broken leg, shattered knee, significant ankle sprain with bone chips. Spleen almost damaged beyond recovery." She paused. "You're a disaster."

"You should see the other guy."

Otieno pursed her lips. "No. That's the difference here, a bit. You didn't fight back this time. Not as hard, anyway. Why?"

"You win some, you lose some. I tried."

Otieno shook her head. "No, I watched the video, and I watched the video from the earlier fight. You were holding back this time."

"I wasn't."

"You were. Remember, don't play stupid with me." She shifted her display and pointed to a still from the video. "You saw the shiv here, and then you did nothing to avoid it. Just punched at his head. You're better than that. These guys have nothing on you."

"I was—"

"No." The word was strong and sudden. "You were trying to die."

I felt heat rush up my cheeks. "I wasn't."

"You were."

"If I wanted to die, I wouldn't have fought back." I felt my eyes get wet. "I could just have walked up and insulted one of their parents or something, then sat there."

"I think it's not in you not to fight back, at least a little. But you held back. You have three expert ratings in hand-to-hand martial arts. You should have taken them apart."

"But I won the fight." My voice was doing something I didn't want it to. And I was suddenly itchy inside the immobilization splints.

"No, you lost your nerve." I didn't know what she meant, and I think she picked up on that. "You couldn't go through with being beaten to death. You chickened out. Or maybe this was a dry run, just to see how it would feel."

I felt hot again. "That's ridiculous. I'm not some kind of head case."

Otieno laughed. "That's rich."

I felt a surge of anger. "What's it to you, anyway? And aren't you supposed to be all supportive? Help me find my feelings again?"

"Not my job."

"What the hell is your job?"

Otieno was quiet, studying my face. "Why did you want to die?"

"You just said I didn't." I felt like I scored a point, but her face didn't change.

She stared at me for a moment, then grimaced. "Fine. Why did you go in wanting to die, and then change your mind?"

"That's your narrative." She just looked at me. It was infuriating. I felt anger well up. "You think you're hot stuff, you know? But this isn't helping me. Or helping anybody else."

"Answer the question."

I wanted to scream. I clenched my teeth. "What am I worth, at this point?" It felt like a confession. I thought Otieno might respond, or look smug, but she just sat there. My neck was all knotted up. I wanted to throw something, or hit something, but the splints kept my arms and legs immobilized, and the security restraints kept me lashed tight to my bed. "What am I worth?"

"What do you think you're worth?"

I didn't answer. But the answer was nothing. I was hated, as a matter of public record. A war criminal. Career ruined. Life ruined. No family left alive except my sister, and she'd made it clear she wanted no part of me now, after all the bad press. Too toxic for her company and brand. My time here was growing shorter, although it still passed agonizingly slowly. But then what? What was the point? Yeah, I wanted to die. Or I thought I did. I could think of nothing to live for. No purpose. No point.

Otieno was quiet for a time, watching me. I held her gaze, not blinking, mostly just because I didn't want her to feel smug, even if she wouldn't show it. Finally, after enough time had gone by, I turned my head away. Maybe she'd get the hint.

"They're adding two years to your sentence. For inflicting bodily injury, aggravated by a second fighting incident."

My breath came in fast and cold.

27

Dead Ahead

I wasn't sure the dead tree guy was who I was supposed to meet. I wasn't sure of anything. But I had no other options or ideas, so I figured I'd explore the site further. I moved past the fallen tree. In front of me, the little canyon wound down into a depression in the rocky hill, often obscured by the spiky, colorful vegetation. It was pretty, but I found I had little time or interest in appreciating the scenery. It was too hot for sightseeing. And I had a lot on my mind. Pretty much zero had gone right in the last two days. And a lot had gone wrong. A whole lot.

Maintain high ground. Make the other guy suck dirt. That was in the grunt rules somewhere near the top. I kept to the rim of the canyon and walked along it, pausing occasionally to watch and listen for movement. There was normal stuff – wind through the leaves, little lizardoids scurrying through the brush, a couple of what passed for birds chasing each other overhead, occasionally taking roost amid the upper leaves of the trees. Bland, normal stuff. My grunt instincts told me the more boring something was, the more I was probably screwed, but even after a hundred yards along the rim, everything seemed tranquil and peaceful. Bucolic, even.

Then I saw a gleam of blue metal down in the canyon. That didn't belong. I crouched to the ground, stopping still. I gave it a good twenty-count, watching my suit scanner, waiting, keeping my breath under control, everything still. I let the suit support my knees – that helped prevent cramping and fatigue, although I hadn't done that much today and was still pretty fresh. Nothing happened.

I took a few waddling steps over to the canyon rim, careful to keep my motion slow and quiet. I clicked up the periscope sight on the rifle and used it to peer over the edge of the canyon rim. I found the blue shiny thing fast. It was the bottom of a boot lying on the ground. It extended to a leg, also horizontal, wearing tight gray pants. Somebody was down there, but they weren't moving.

The colors matched the SpearPoint assault suits, more or less, but this wasn't powered armor. Just regular clothes. That might be a lucky break. I might not be able to take on an assault trooper, even with surprise, unless I got off a solid shot from cover. I wished I had a grenade, or an ARP, but those were hard to come by (at least legally) and not really appropriate for this kind of job, on a supposedly abandoned planet with nothing more dangerous than grazing lizard-cows.

The scope would only show me so much, and the angle downward was hard to work with the scope and the long rifle while keeping in cover. I wanted to get a better look, and that would require my actual eyes. Still crouching, I took a last scan of the area around me. All clear. I got down on my stomach and commando-crawled over to the edge. I retracted my helmet dome the rest of the way to give my head more freedom to move, and then got my head over the edge for a quick look, pulling it back to avoid making myself a target from below.

The person down there was dead. Yet another corpse. They were really piling up, reminding me of a time I thought I left behind long ago. One might wonder how I was so sure the person was dead. My response would be that, so far, 100% of the people I've seen who are missing the left half of their heads are dead, so it seemed like a safe assumption.

28

SHELL GAME

I wasn't sure what had hit the woman down there, but it looked like it involved high energy. A beam rather than an explosion. A nearly perfect circular arc cut from the top of her head down her neck and out below her left armpit, or what would have been if she'd still had an arm to make a pit. It was a little uncanny, like a kid's paper doll cut carelessly. She was wearing a jumpsuit, shiny gray cloth. SpearPoint logo on the chest. Brown curly hair, shaved close on the side of her head.

Part of me wanted to shout obscenities, and part of me wanted to run like hell. Those were both reasonable responses, but my training took hold of those two parts and shook sense into them, as it always did. I thought about the tactical situation.

SpearPoint meant enemy. They were the ones trying to kill Welk and me. They were up to something bad, and I didn't know what. Somebody was acting against them, maybe from their own side. Maybe this woman was my Yomo buddy, and she'd been killed for helping me. But I didn't think so. It looked like she'd been dead a while. The blood was congealed where it wasn't dry, and her skin had gone purplish. So, let's say, for the sake of argument, this is another one of the bad guys. If she's dead, that's good.

If the person who'd killed the assault troopers was the one who'd left me the note directing me here, then it made sense that they would maybe also have killed this

SpearPoint woman, since they were already in the business of killing bad guys. That was all speculation, but it fit together in a nice resonant way. The thing that didn't fit, that was distinctly messed up, was the friendly dead tree person. The person who seemed to know who I was, and who spoke fluent Tradespeak despite living on a planet the Council had hypothetically just discovered and marked devoid of sentient life. Nothing about that resonated with any scenario I could come up with.

I had two options. The safest path, at least short term: Get out of here and go hide. Wait for the Patrol with head between my knees. That had a lot of merit. Then there was the trickier path: Investigate further. I'd been sent here, and I hadn't figured out why or by whom yet. Knowing either of those facts would help, and learning something might give me some better action to pursue. This path had potential, both good and bad. Couldn't know which without taking the gamble.

Screw it. I was more curious than I was scared to die, and hiding didn't guarantee that I'd survive anyway. I seemed to have an ally, and they seemed to be proficient in killing these SpearPoint weasels. That was good, and it buoyed my spirits a bit. All right. I needed to find a way down there. I was going to be the one sucking dirt at the bottom of the canyon. But sometimes you had to do that to get where you needed to go, or to kill the guy who needed killing. And killing somebody like that sounded satisfying.

I made my way back along the canyon rim. The canyon got shallower, and its flat bottom rose up to where I could jump down without breaking anything. I landed in an impressive combat crouch, rifle out, and for a moment I wished somebody could see how badass I was, despite really being too old for all of this. I rose up and made my way down the canyon towards the body. A stream trickled along beside me, the water seeping from the hillside and finding its way down, like water did everywhere. Comforting, that. It would be nice if other things worked everywhere, like common decency and business contracts.

I went slowly, cautiously, with rifle up, but I needn't have bothered. Eventually, I got back to the site I'd seen from above. On the negative side, as far as tactics went, the woman I'd seen from the rim was not alone. She was accompanied by two of the assault troopers in heavy suits, plus another assistant dressed like her. On the positive side, as far as tactics went, they were all dead, with similar sharp-edged circular holes blown through them. That was weird, because usually when people get disarticulated, it's a lot messier. At least, in my personal experience. What was also weird was that there was no sign of the parts they were missing. It was almost like they'd been hit by some massively powerful beam that cut through them, obliterating whatever got in its way. But there was no indication of where the beam came from, or where it went to, or what caused it. They just had big, half-meter-wide holes cut through them - flesh, bone, armored, suit, whatever was there. One of them had a hole covering most of his torso and a second one that had removed his feet, while the rest had been hit only once each, seemingly at random positions around their bodies, but always taking enough of them away to kill them. More than kill them.

The bodies were stretched over an area of about five or six meters. There looked to be a small campsite here along with a well-appointed supply dump. There were boxes, crates, a couple chairs, a comms unit on a table, and other equipment. That suggested they'd been up to something here that was going to take at least a few days. There was a fabric structure stretched over collapsible struts over to one side of the canyon, and when I poked my rifle inside, I saw bedding enough for three. I figured that was maybe the two in regular clothing, plus one more who either wasn't here or had died elsewhere. I wondered if they were the physicists or xenobiologists from Welk's A Team. I knew they were operating with SpearPoint security, so that might explain the jumpsuits and the troopers. The assault troopers I figured were here as guards, not permanent, maybe rotating positions with the others, or perhaps just arriving today. In time to be made holey by whatever didn't want them messing around.

I realized that I, too, might be construed as messing around, and that I really didn't want to end up like them, valuing, as I do, nearly all of my body parts. That argued for leaving, and not getting whoever had the hole cannon angry. But I also wanted to know what these people were up to, out here in the middle of nowhere, far from the dig sites in the cities, at a place just as remote as where Welk and I had been working. That might be a key to the mystery of SpearPoint's transgressions, something that would help me know what to do, or information that might be valuable to the Patrol when they came. Information that might make me look less bad.

There were three hoverbikes next to the supply dump. Nice models, too. Reffington 180s. That was really appealing. A hoverbike like that could do 150 kilometers an hour in open terrain, which would be great for covering distance, and especially for putting distance between me and all these corpses. But the bikes would likely be obvious from orbit, streaking across the surface, and the light ships they were using were faster anyway. Couldn't outrun them. I'd be painting a target on myself for not much gain. Stealth was probably a better bet, even if I were less mobile. A lot less.

I saw that the canyon floor ahead of me was covered with footprints and little ruts where equipment had been rolled along through the mud. My answers lay deeper in, if they lay anywhere. I followed the ruts down the canyon to where it bent around to the right. The canyon walls were about five meters high here, riotous with colorful vegetation and vines, and the canyon itself was only maybe six meters across. The whole thing felt like a cage. Or like a trap. I had only one way out now, back where I'd come from, and I wasn't confident I could outrun whatever had taken two assault troopers by surprise. But the scene was quiet, serene almost, and it seemed hard to believe it could erupt into violence.

I pressed my back against the inside canyon wall and approached the bend. I used the periscope sight to look around the corner, but the view was obstructed by plants and vines. It looked like there might be a piece of equipment there, and maybe a metal structure in the side of the canyon, but I couldn't get a better view without waving the rifle all around, and that would be all kinds of obvious. I pulled the rifle back, holding it straight up and down, took a breath, and rounded the corner fast, bringing the rifle down to where I could shoot anybody disagreeable.

There was a whine, and a bolt of energy came at me from the right. It smacked into the breastplate on my suit, sending up a shower of sparks and knocking me back. I didn't have time to look where it was coming from. I fell back into cover, aided by the suit's servos, my mind and body suddenly alive with energy. Combat energy. Something was shooting at me. Something I hadn't seen. I heard five more shots in quick succession, all of them smacking into the canyon wall. Then a downward whine. I'd heard that sound before. A field turret, set on auto, probably with friend or foe detection enabled. I felt my breastplate with my glove. Hot, and scorched, but it had held up all right, just a little burn and melt. I was lucky. The armor wasn't rated for that kind of fire. I couldn't afford any more hits.

But the turret also meant that whatever was there was important. So important that they were defending it rather than the camp. It was good that my assailant wasn't a person, because automated systems were more predictable, but bad that it was there and shooting at me. Unmanned turrets were expensive and hard to come by, but that fit with an operation as well-funded as this one, I supposed. This was definitely a lot higher grade than the WatchBot I'd requisitioned for our camp. The WatchBot could only yell for help, while the turret could do something about any intruders. Something really unpleasant. And it was trying to, for sure.

I stuck the tip of the rifle barrel around the corner, then stretched my arms out to move the barrel of the gun until the periscope sight had a good enough angle. The whine sounded again, rising, ready to fire at the rifle tip. Through the scope, I caught some motion at the edge of where I could see and pulled the rifle back. The wine changed pitch, winding down, its target no longer visible.

It took me a few more tries, and some fire directed my way, to get a good sense of where the turret was set up. It was placed high up on the far wall, the outside wall of the canyon, maybe ten meters past the bend where I'd found cover. A good spot, able to see anyone approaching from either direction, and with a good field of fire. Again, I wished I had a grenade or some other heavy muni. Those would make short work of it. I had a thought worth pursuing. I retreated back down the canyon and found one of the assault troopers, the one who still had most of his arm. They'd had R13s, or something similar, back at our camp.

I knelt beside the man. His torso looked really weird where it was cut through, almost like an educational cross-sectional model of a person, except that this was really him. He'd lost a bunch of blood after getting hit, and some of his inner contents had sloshed out. All in all, not a pretty sight. But I was focused on the launcher on the arm of his suit. I wouldn't be able to fire the weapon – the suit's electronics had to be fried from the massive damage it had taken. I could hardly put on what was left of the suit, even if I wanted to evict what was left of its current tenant, which I didn't. But the ammo might still be useful. I found the release for the magazine set into the arm of the suit and slid it out of its slot. Six shells, light heavy muni, R13's like I thought. The little shells, each only a little bigger than an egg, lay all in a row, ready to be fed one by one into the launcher. They didn't look that impressive, but they had a tiny speck of Thuringer compound as part of their load, and each of them could put a hole the size of a pumpkin through twenty centimeters of steel, easy.

For most folks, a find like this would be useless. But not for somebody who'd done a few rotations as a heavy muni officer back in the Patrol, and more importantly, somebody who'd gotten drunk with Sergeant Flinz on Genua more than once. Flinz, or Flinty as he insisted people call him, knew everything there was to know about R13s. One of his favorite stories, one he usually forgot he'd told you before, was about a pirate attack on a Patrol base they were trying to establish on Kelvin, a sand planet with a small mining facility. The pirates had killed the sentries and gotten into the base, looking for weapons, and Flinty had been stuck at the end of a hall with an injured squadmate bleeding out next to him and a jammed R13 launcher his only weapon.

In Flinty's telling, that should have been the end of him, but he'd read the specs on R13s backwards and forwards, and he figured that if you were careful, you could crack the outer shell without setting them off. The failsafes should keep the shell from triggering if it didn't detect that it had been launched. You just needed to take it slow and keep the shell still. If you didn't, then you'd basically be setting the shell off in your hands, which was counterindicated for people who enjoyed having hands. He'd cracked it, though, and used his knife blade to loosen the screw on the failsafe far enough that he thought it would allow the damaged shell still to go off. The trick would be getting it to go off when it landed rather than when it was thrown. If it worked, it would turn the R13 into a crude but high-yield grenade, one that no munitions officer anywhere would suggest using, but which Flinty thought might work.

And work it did, or so Flinty said. He'd brought the corridor ceiling down on the heads of the pirate invaders, killing five of them, and hit them a few more times for good measure. He liked to show off the medal. I hadn't checked up on it, and I had no real way of knowing that Flinty wasn't lying, but he didn't seem the type to inflate a story (beyond the standard inflation that all grunt stories were understood to include), and he did have the medal. But I had a look at the R13 manual afterward, and it all looked potentially possible.

"Potentially possible" isn't the best standard to use when messing around with high explosives, but if you've been in the service for long enough, you start to get a sense, almost an uncanny perception, of what will kill you or not. Or at least, you tell yourself that, because the alternative is that you've only survived so far through dumb luck, and your number could be up tomorrow, because you're not special at all. So, yeah, uncanny perception. I thought this might work.

I took one of the R13s and set it down on a supply crate. The grip assist servos in my suits' gloves should give me more than enough force to crack the outer shell, and if I just held the R13 steady, everything would be fine. Right? Yeah. Just fine. I pushed on the base of the shell, away from the tip where it normally hit targets, gradually applying more pressure. That led to some unpleasant tingling action running around along the back of my neck, and a suspicion that this might be the stupidest way a grunt would ever die, but I kept at it. Finally, the outer shell gave a crack and a pop and slid up a centimeter or so, leaving only a thin, jagged line of white where it was fused with the metal of the shell's propulsion engine.

The actual explosive shell underneath looked a lot clunkier than the smooth exterior, with asymmetric pieces, tubes, and bits of circuitry. But it didn't need to be pretty. I found the screw that Flinty had described. It was painted red, which probably stood for Don't Mess With This, which was probably good advice. My suit had a knife sheath in the leg, and although the blade was pretty long, it was easy enough to get the knife tip into the screw head and turn. After about ten turns, the shell gave a beep. Flinty had made the sound seem a lot more dramatic, more of a clang and a buzz of impending danger, but in reality, it was pretty innocuous. I'd have to call him out when I saw him again.

With the motion failsafe disabled, the thing was live, all day, all the time. I needed to throw it, but I needed to make sure that I didn't accelerate it too fast, or it would go off in my hand. That was one area where the suit's assistance might not be the biggest help, because it was hard to know what your strength was with the suit helping. If you trained enough, it became second nature, but this suit was still new to me, purchased just before this job, and I didn't want to risk it. I tapped the releases and pulled off my right glove and then the right bracer and upper arm piece, freeing my arm. That felt more natural. I knew how hard and how far I could throw, and I'd have more control. Or so I hoped.

I picked the shell up with a lot of care, getting my hand under it and lifting slowly. Nothing sudden, nothing jerky. I wondered if I should prepare a second shell, but maybe one would do, and preparing them felt risky. I could use one or two to gauge my throw, though. I took two of the intact shells over to the edge of the canyon wall, just out of sight of the turret. I played back my suit video, checking locations and angles. I had a pretty good idea where the turret was. Now to get a shell there without getting shot. I used the periscope sight once more, found my target, got shot at a few times. I read the distance off it - twenty-two meters, give or take. A tough throw to hit a target on a side wall, but I'd played a lot of rillball as a kid, and I had a reasonable bit of grenade training, including five years of annual weapons requalification. And a little real-world experience, under fire, too. Also, grenade weapons were fairly forgiving, one of their most useful features, and the R13 would have a reasonable blast radius. I pulled up my suit's tactical interface and had it construct a map of the canyon around the bend from video, making manual adjustments as I went. It marked an idea of where the turret was, and I thought it was pretty close.

I took one of the unaltered shells, hefted it in my bare hand, and thought. I was going to have to throw for distance, but not accelerate too fast, or I could find myself minus a right arm. That meant I should probably avoid the snap I usually threw with, and instead do something with a steadier wind-up, with the full arm extended. Maybe even a spinning throw, like with the discus. That was a little less familiar and less comfortable for me, but it was sometimes how you got a grenade over an obstacle.

I stopped for a minute. This was kind of stupid. I could just walk away. But I wanted to know what was going on here. And it was a tactical challenge, which was always interesting. And given that seven of the last eight people I'd met on this skogging planet had died horribly, that was probably where I was headed anyway. Might as well go out with a bang.

I extended my arm, feeling the weight of the shell. It was small but pretty heavy. Not bad for throwing. I took a breath, went over the trajectory in my mind. I stuck my arm out behind me, down low, then practiced getting it moving at a steady pace. I did eight or ten warm-ups, until I got the feel for it. This might even work. I switched back to the suit's tactical interface and had it identify and mark the shell, hoping it could calculate the trajectory and tell me how close I was.

This felt comfortable. Reassuring, even. The kind of problem I liked solving, the kind I'd trained for, but unique. And with stakes. I was good at this. Or at least, I used to be. I did another couple practice wind-ups, then I let the shell fly in an upward, side-arm throw, careful to spin into it smoothly. My hand was exposed as I released the shell, but that was unavoidable, and the turret didn't respond immediately. I snapped my hand back behind cover and waited. I heard the shell crack through some leaves and then thump into the ground with a wet splat. It sounded like I might have hit the general area, but maybe low if I was on the ground rather than the wall. I checked the suit's tactical display. It showed a weighted range of potential landing spots, a shaded circle draped on its terrain map. The edge of the circle covered the turret's location, which was good, but I was probably a bit short.

I got out the second intact shell. Another practice run would help. A few warm-up swings, then marking the shell with the suit's tactical interface, then a throw. I heard the turret whine this time. It had probably seen my hand, but I pulled back before it could lock and fire. I heard two thumps this time. I hoped the first was turret fire into the wall, and the second from when the shell fell to the ground. The suit's map showed a better target circle for the second throw, but without being able to look, I had no way to tell exactly what I'd accomplished.

I felt like it was time to try the real thing. Worst case, I'd miss, and then I could decide whether it was worth continuing this exercise. Well, actually, worst case, I blew my arm off before I even released. But let's assume that Flinty wasn't lying and that this was possible. I went back over to the crate where I'd left the shell I'd tampered with. Picked it up gingerly, carried it over to the canyon wall slowly and carefully, like it was one of my mother's thin blown-glass sculptures she used to decorate the table at the harvest dinner.

No warm-up swings this time. Too risky. I thought my way through the throw, trying to connect with my muscle memory. This would work. Famous last words. I took a few deep breaths, in through my nose, out through my mouth, the tang of dampness and rotting plants filling my nostrils. I was ready, or as ready as I'd be.

Slide my arm back and down. Cradle the shell, feeling the rough angles of its inner structure against my hand, a contrast with the smooth surface of the others. A dip down, then a swing out and around and up, releasing at the fastest point, then snapping my hand back.

No immediate kaboom. That was good. I still had a hand, which was also welcome. The turret whined again but didn't fire. Time was slow, now. It would take a second for the shell to get there, and then there'd either be another wet thump, or I'd succeed in altering the terrain, at least.

The kaboom was louder even than I thought it would be. My ears rang. Might have been better to wear the helmet with its sound dampening, but you always realize stuff like that after the fact. Bits of soil sprayed from the hidden part of the canyon around the bend. If I hadn't taken out the turret, I'd at least made my mark here. Flinty would be proud. If he were sober and paying attention.

I waited a moment, then stuck my rifle barrel out around the corner. No whine, no shots. I might have actually done this. I pulled it back, then stuck it out again, waving it around. Still nothing. I didn't think the turret could be playing games with me. Turret control was usually just a set of simple algorithms, not a full-fledged AI, and it had shown no sign of complex behavior so far. I used the periscope sight to view around the edge, risking more of the gun now to get a better view. The turret was down, on the canyon floor, smoke rising from the assembly. There was a significant crater in the canyon wall. Didn't look like I'd scored a direct hit, but close enough. *Close enough*, the motto of heavy muni grunts everywhere.

I waited a bit. Not because I thought the turret was live. I was reasonably certain I'd taken it out. Because I'd made a loud sound, one that would be of interest to anybody listening nearby. That might include whoever had cut holes in my fellow humans behind me, or allies of the humans nearby, or even more of the viny tree people like my unfortunate apparent friend. Any of those parties, I'd rather not meet. Any other parties at all, really. But I heard nothing.

I went back to my improvised workbench and got my sleeve and glove back on. I returned to my spot of cover, then waved my arm around the corner. Nothing. Stuck it out and left it there for a moment. No whine, nothing. All right, time to commit. I moved around the corner. As I did, a little part of my brain decided to mention the concept of "second turret." I didn't like that part of my brain very much.

But it was fine. The turret was down, the barrel bent by the fall, the mechanism and stand broken into several jagged pieces, twisted by the blast. It showed no signs of life. That was interesting, but far more interesting was what was across from the turret, on the near side of the canyon wall, a little closer to the corner. Another person lay on the ground, the same meter-size circular hole cut through her. From her outstretched arms extended a bulky gray metal box with a protruding barrel. This I guessed was an industrial laser drill, not least because it said *Ronson Industries Laser Drill*

Unit on the side. It was pointed towards what looked like a doorway, about eight feet wide, set into the side of the canyon wall. The doorway was surrounded by a series of rounded bricks of silver metal, each with a character engraved on it. The whole thing looked like a set decoration from a cheap sci-fi holo, except that such a thing had no reason to be on this planet.

The bricks around the edge were obviously placed there on purpose, fourteen of them, forming a rim around the doorway. They were etched with brilliant silvery white lines, some kind of writing or decoration, unblemished despite all the dirt and mud around the site. The doorway they surrounded was a rounded opening, maybe three meters tall in the middle. I couldn't see anything inside, but not because there was a door or barrier in the way. Instead, the opening was filled with an opaque fog.

I thought at first the whole thing might be some kind of clever holo display, so out of place it seemed, but as I walked around the edge and saw it from different angles, it looked real. I could see traces of metal in the canyon wall behind the brick, which suggested that there was maybe a chamber or dwelling set into the side of the canyon. It looked too strange, too alien to be something the humans had built. If it were an alien site, that would explain their interest and some of the secrecy surrounding the world, and maybe even the attack on the *Deimos*, if it had something of value they were trying to protect or steal. If this were what was important, though, I would think they'd have sent more than a team of five, two troopers and three apparent technicians. All five of them deceased, likely all at once, or they'd have dispersed after the first went down. Maybe it had been more than five, but I saw no sign of any other campsites, beds, or equipment, and there weren't many footprints in the mud between their campsite and this place, so I figured it had to be a small crew.

Could it be a house? Maybe where the vine person lived? That could be. They had been in the area too, and they said they were from here. That might be a good working hypothesis. Maybe the vine guy was just trying to get away from the humans drilling at his door. Maybe the vine guy set off whatever killed all of them. I saw no place a weapon capable of inflicting those injuries could launch from. The turret I'd disabled wouldn't make nearly as large holes as that.

Too many threats, too many variables. I should probably not stay here, and definitely not do anything, although of course I was tempted. Human nature is to mess with things, although in this place, that seemed to have gotten five people killed, five people defended by an automated turret. At the least, I reasoned, anybody who lived inside the doorway would probably be grateful not to have a turret outside. Maybe that would earn me some points.

So, no touching, just like my dad said when we went into fancy shops when I was a kid. But that didn't mean no looking. I knelt next to the laser drill. It was on standby, ready to drill, but given that drilling seemed to be the last thing the unfortunate woman at my feet had done, I wasn't about to do that. I had a look at the screen. It was set to maximum power, with an overheat warning symbol glowing on the display. *Maximum output limited to 8 seconds for operator safety,* it said. Under *Target Material* it said *Norodium (experimental).* I hadn't heard of that material, but I was no chemist. Under that, it said. *Danger: Material's response to drilling not documented.*

I asked my suit what it knew. The suit had a library module installed that included basic reference materials. It updated whenever the suit got connected to a public network, similar to what was included with most personal consoles, although unlike the suit, cons often required an active network connection and didn't store anything themselves. I'd paid a little extra for the reference module feature in case I was deployed somewhere without a net connection. Like Kenai.

I tapped a few holo controls on my forearm plate and accessed the library.

Norodium (Chemistry). An exceedingly rare superheavy metal element with no naturally occurring deposits. Derived only from experimental processes in high-energy reactors and particle collision facilities. Atomic number 154. Unstable isotopes include atomic masses 460, 459, 454, 463, and 468. Stable isotopes include atomic mass 462. The small quantities produced, with their unpredictable atomic masses, make calculation of half-lives somewhat challenging, but initial mass spectrometry results suggest Norodium-462 may be permanently stable or at least metastable for long periods. This potentially stable isotope does not appear prone to reactivity. However, this isotope has been reported (perhaps apocryphally) to have become undetectable (or vanished) within minutes to hours after generation (see Norodium mysteries). Only tiny quantities of the persistent isotope are thought to exist within the facilities where they were generated.

Economic importance and applications: None known. The metal has never been manufactured in enough quantity to determine its properties or to make applications feasible at any scale.

Research potential: very high, due to unusual properties, rarity, and difficulty of manufacture and storage. Ongoing synthesis efforts continue at several facilities (see entries for physicists Amachi Mabaso and Marta Turner).

Financial value: Synthesis of Norodium continues, but with limited and transient success. Any stable source of Norodium would be of tremendous interest. The market value of such a

source is incalculable, but it would be
exceedingly high.

29

ELEMENTARY

Norodium.

I was no chemist, but if the material were that rare, and what I was looking at here was fourteen bricks of the stuff, that started to explain the secrecy and the murders. This was probably unique in all of Council space. I had to say the attempt to drill it looked like a major blunder, however. Either the material itself, or whoever had designed this place, didn't want people messing with it. I wasn't sure of the mechanism by which these people had been provided with significant internal ventilation, but it was pretty clear that drilling the archway was the last thing this woman had done. Odd, though, that the others in the camp had died in the same way. There was no sight line from the doorway to the camp, so if it were a weapon, it was not clear how it worked. Perhaps something in orbit, a beam weapon, although I figured something up there should have been obvious to the Patrol ships or earlier visitors.

I took a closer look at the doorway, being careful not to get too close. Fourteen stones. Characters or carvings I didn't understand. A slow-moving mist obscuring whatever was inside. I was sure Welk would be able to say more, but I didn't get much beyond (1) this is weird and (2) I should not go in. Maybe there was a (3), somebody wants me to see this, but I couldn't be sure that was the goal of whoever had left me the coordinates. They might have wanted me to meet the vine person, although that seemed to accomplish nothing. Or maybe I was supposed to meet the researchers, but they were also dead. So maybe it was this. Or all three, or something else entirely.

This was skogging useless, and it was becoming more dangerous. I needed to put some distance between this and me. Somebody was sure to check up on the five dead humans, or the one dead vine person. People checking up on people who turned out to be dead were hardly ever friendly. And I didn't know enough to do anything with the site, other than not to drill it. So, I should leave. But I had nowhere else to go.

Wait for further orders. A grunt could get behind that. It was what we spent most of our time doing, except when we were trying not to die, or trying to get the other guy to die instead. But really, waiting was most of service. And I was all right with that.

I went back around the bend to the campsite. These folks weren't going to need their supplies, and I was hungry. And sleepy, too. The short day on Kenai was still playing havoc on my daily rhythm, and I hadn't thought to bring my stims from our camp. I could tough it out, I resolved. Maybe. But I was tired.

I found a box of rations. They were fancier than what Welk had brought, although it was hard to do better than good old chicken with pepper relish. I chose a couple bags and some vitamin drinks. There was a spare bedroll in one of the tents, so I picked that up too, lengthened its strap to accommodate the bulk of my suit, and slung it over my shoulder.

I took a last look around. Lots of dead people. Lots of gear. I hadn't left much evidence of being here, other than blowing up their turret and stealing a few supplies. The ship I'd flown in had left. All that was good. If I got clear of this place, I could find a hiding spot and wait to see if anybody came back around, maybe somebody who'd know more. Or somebody who needed killing. I wouldn't mind that at this point. The situation had turned into a massive vacc leak all up in my face, and sometimes there was nothing to do but start killing the folks who were making it worse. Otieno might not agree, but she was gone. Like Kenzi, like my family. Like everybody here.

I shrugged the bedroll strap up onto my shoulder, then started off through the weird spiky trees and other plants, letting the suit assist stretch out my stride. If I were lucky, I'd live to see the sunrise, and then I might come back. Maybe the author of the note in the pit in the ancient temple would be back and sort all this out.

And maybe I'd sprout wings and fly away.

The air dropped a few degrees as it got darker, and the sun vanished, leaving the sky clear. The night was black. Kenai didn't have a moon, and there wasn't any other light source. As I walked, looking for a suitable hiding spot, I could see a thousand stars above, maybe more. The bright one low in the sky would probably be the companion planet to Kenai, Ninilchik. The sky here was pretty, especially as it faded from green to pink to red, then to a deep blue, and finally to black.

Two hours after sunset, give or take, something weird happened. The noises around me – insects, animals, birds calling – all of them glitched. Or something like that. Animals I'd been hearing went silent in a flash, and others started up immediately in full song, and the buzz of the insects (or whatever they were) shifted in tone and rhythm. I stopped, and a wave of discomfort swept over me. It was kind of like when you're sick and you get a chill, but there was nothing wrong with me. I hoped. Well, nothing bacterial. Just the usual personality flaws and bad luck.

The night sounds came back unabated and continued without any further interruptions. Maybe it had just been a hiccup with the suit's audio. Sure. That sounded like a nice, comfy answer, like some rear-echelon prick would come up with to avoid having to deal with something potentially unpleasant.

30

CLOSE ENCOUNTERS OF THE WOODEN KIND

It was raining on me as I woke. Not hard, just a gentle tick, tick against the surface of my face shield. Sleeping in the suit wasn't the most comfortable, but it wasn't horrible, and given the number of people both murderous and dead I'd encountered recently, it seemed prudent. It kept the temperature regulated, too, although Kenai nights weren't cold. The planet's distance from the sun and relatively high atmospheric CO_2 content made it balmy, and the short day-night cycle kept things from cooling off too much between sunset and sunrise.

I woke up the suit and checked the suit's sensors for anything interesting nearby. The suit filtered its many sensors before flagging threats, checking for things like mass, velocity, toxicity, and being-on-fire-ness. I had it on silent mode, so it couldn't use all of its active detection. I didn't want to be a big fat EM source if anybody was looking for me.

There was nothing out there, at least as far as the suit could see. That made it maybe safe to get up. I'd still be covered by tree canopy, and therefore probably safe from overhead visual inspection. I wouldn't think there'd be much of a satellite network over a just-discovered planet, but I wasn't counting on anything given my current predicament. Had to assume people were watching, and that those people wanted more holes in me than I preferred.

I'd found a hollow under some trees as a campsite. It seemed like a pretty solid spot, hidden, sheltered, and I hadn't died during the night, which was a definite plus as campsites go. I left my pilfered rations and bedroll and got up. I considered taking the suit off and airing myself out a bit, but that felt awkward and vulnerable. To a seasoned grunt like me, a suit was almost like a second skin, and I'd be OK wearing it for a few days straight if needed. I popped the codpiece flap and squatted, remembering Lars, a perennial private who, despite an undistinguished career, had been dedicated to peeing on as many worlds as he could manage. A million years of humans peed on only one world their whole lives, he said. Time to celebrate progress. He even volunteered on courier and guard missions to add to his total, and as far as I knew, his record of sixty-five stood. He'd probably added to it since. But he hadn't peed here. I was one up on him.

I raised my visor and ate a DuraBiscuit. Familiar, sweet, a hint of lemon. Good stuff. But it was time to stop messing around. I was about five hundred meters from the strange doorway. That place was by far the most interesting spot nearby, but also the most dangerous. Still, it's where I'd been told to go, by an ally, maybe. I was worried I would miss out on a chance to get off this rock and back somewhere safer, far away from murderous mercenaries and people with giant holes in them.

I pulled the bedroll up and over the rations and took off towards the doorway. Slow, steady, pausing in cover for tactical scans. I wasn't in a rush, and I wasn't in the mood for surprises. Well, more surprises. I kept the face shield retracted. Kenai was a place of interesting smells, and I always felt I could hear better somehow, even though the suits' electronics and audio pickups were fine. This place had a dense, loamy smell, wet and damp, with an underlying sweetness that I assumed came from the plants. Or maybe when things rotted here, they smelled good. I didn't know.

The microbiota here were supposedly diverse, but I had stopped reading the briefing after "non-infectious" and "unlikely to cause harm."

Gradually, I came up on the ridge overlooking the narrow canyon. Things looked mostly as I'd left them, aside from some new puddles and moving water from the rain. I noticed one of the bodies was barefoot. I didn't remember that, but maybe I'd missed that detail before. Weird thing for somebody to steal with all the other stuff around. The doorway was unchanged – still gray and swirly, but nothing, not even the swirls, coming in or out. Mysterious. Wait, one of the hoverbikes was gone. There were only two there now. I hadn't heard it go, but maybe I'd been too far away, or whoever took it kept it on low. The bikes were reasonably quiet at low speed. Much more important to me was who had taken it. That was bugging me because it meant there was an unknown independent actor. Nobody here yesterday had been alive. Maybe the bikes could be remotely operated, from orbit, or maybe they could be summoned for a pickup. I didn't remember that from riding them before, but I wasn't that familiar with them.

The suit pinged. Something moving behind me, something big, moderate distance. Maybe whoever took the bike. Not going fast, though. I scuttled over to one of the trees and got in cover behind the conical tree's broad base. Still moving, now thirty meters and closing. Coming towards me, or towards the door. No clear shape yet – the suit was just picking up vibrations and sounds, not visual. But it was out there. I leveled my rifle and looked along the barrel. Whatever it was, it was too close for the sight. I saw some leaves on one of the trees jump and thrash, and then a shape came into view. One of the beings like I'd seen yesterday. Like the bark-covered guy who'd gotten crushed under the tree. A barrel-like torso with three arms, a knotty protrusion at the top for a head, and three flexible legs below. All covered with a network of fibrous vines.

I considered hiding, but they were going to come too close for comfort, and if they found me lying in wait, they might get hostile. The one yesterday had seemed friendly. Even spoken our language. Maybe best not to surprise it. Maybe these people were the ones I was supposed to meet here.

"Hold up," I called out. "Stop." I held out a hand, palm out. If this one didn't speak my language, maybe the gesture would convey my meaning. Unless an open hand meant "please kill me now" or something offensive to them. You never knew with xenos.

"Jess. It is good to see you. I am no threat. I am a friend."

Skogol. "How do all of you know my name?"

"It is written on your suit." That was true, on the left breast ID plate, but it was small. The guy must have keen vision to read it from there. And be able to read Tradespeak, which itself was weird. But I wasn't sure I believed him about seeing the tag. The other one I'd met yesterday seemed to have recognized my face immediately.

The creature spoke again. "Have you met... others like me?"

A dead one. That might not look good. But better not to lie. "Yes. One. Yesterday."

The little mouth-trumpet vibrated. "I see. But I should not have asked. I apologize for my rudeness."

Huh? "What do you mean?"

"I'm sorry. I should explain. In my culture, it can be a great affront to speak of past conversations."

There were all kinds of logistics issues with that statement, but it was actually not a bad bit of relationship advice. Best not to get into it now. "OK. I understand. Why are you here?"

"I came to meet you."

"They told you to come here too?" Skog it. "I mean, if that's not a rude question."

"I was told someone was coming. An e*tivar.* I hoped to make contact."

"I am an etivar?"

"Most assuredly. I can smell you from here."

"The other one, who I met yesterday. They were here to meet me too?"

"Please don't speak of that. I told you."

Right. Great affront. "Sorry."

"You have seen the doorway?"

"That thing behind me? In the wall?"

"Yes."

"Where's it go?"

"That is a complex question."

I heard a whine. A ship drive laboring in atmosphere. I turned my gaze upward. High above, a ship was making a slow transit. "That's not good."

"Your people?" I saw the creature's head incline, rocking back. Looking up, maybe?

I snorted. "Well, my species. Decidedly not my friends. They've been trying to kill me." I thought about Welk. "Already lost one of my friends, probably because of them." I thought about the other dig sites and the *Deimos* and felt a little guilty. It wasn't all about me. "And a lot of other innocent people are dead too."

Overhead, the ship made a broad turn. Maybe surveying the site. Seeing a bunch of people not moving, with holes in them. That wasn't likely to make them any friendlier. I hoped we weren't visible under the leaves. I was glad the suit was on silent. From the gear I'd seen in the camp, it would have an active beacon and comms, so hopefully whatever I was putting out might be masked.

I'd had enough, though. "I think we should get out of here."

The creature tipped its head back to level, and its speaking tube sprouted towards me and vibrated. "Agreed. I can hide easily among the trees, but you are perhaps more obvious."

I couldn't tell if that was a 'stay away from me so you don't get me killed' kind of statement or just a practical observation. I wasn't picking up much from the inflection. "I've got a place to hide, too. Can we meet later, though? I need to know more about you and what's going on."

"I'd like that. But there is no need to go back to your spot. Your distance units are 'klicks,' yes?"

How did this person know that? This was unnerving. Maybe this species had already encountered humans, lived among us, but I'd never seen or heard of anybody like them, with their anatomy, and I'd been to some crowded, diverse worlds. "Yes. Kilometers. But we call them klicks."

"I believe we should meet at a spot away from here, where we are less likely to be observed."

"Good plan."

"Are you able to travel to a spot 30.445 klicks north, 24.822 klicks west?"

That was highly specific. The suit was listening, and it picked up the coordinates and automatically plotted the location with stored map data on the display. About 40 klicks total over ground, to a spot near what passed for a mountain on Kenai, with a stream meeting a river nearby. Maybe five hours travel with the suit assist, longer if the terrain were rough. Doable. "Uh, sure. I can get there."

"There is rock there, with cover. I have some supplies. It would make a good spot to camp, and it is sheltered from the sky."

"Sounds good. Can you get there?"

"That will not be a problem."

OK then. "I'll see you there. Stay safe. These people are dangerous."

"Thank you." If I was right about the blobs on the head being eyes, they seemed to be studying me, but I might just be anthropomorphizing. "It is my culture's tradition that when we first meet, we tell others of our selves. What is your full name?"

I saw no harm in sharing. He knew the Jess part anyway. "Jess. Family name Amiko."

The creature inclined their head. "I am Elihar. Of the Weynik people."

The ship was making another pass. "Pleased to meet you, Elihar. I'll see you tomorrow?"

"I hope so. We have much to discuss." Elihar turned, rotating the entire vine-covered body. "Farewell, new friend." Elihar ambled off into the trees, the three solid legs lurching underneath. Elihar's viny arms reached out to trees and rocks and pulled the rest of the body along, greatly increasing the speed and grace of the whole endeavor. After he got going, he picked up speed, really moving, maybe 30 or 40 klicks an hour. Pretty good for a tree. It was mesmerizing. Elihar disappeared, leaving only a rustle and a receding twitch of distant leaves.

I took a last look up at the ship, still moving above me along another slow path. Getting to Elihar's hideout might risk leaving me exposed, but it seemed like the risk was worth it. I didn't want to be here when they came back and found their dead companions. It was bad enough being held responsible for the people I actually had killed.

31

FRIENDS

"You don't make friends easily, do you?" Otieno's hands were folded across her con. She hardly ever wrote on it anymore, not after six years.

I laughed. "What brought that on?"

"Well, you've been in here a long time. Most inmates have a lover, or three or four, or a gang, or at least a circle of friends."

"I have that. I ate lunch with Jinny just an hour ago."

"She was trying to sell you hooch."

"I mean, friendship takes lots of forms."

Otieno looked at me. "I'm just wondering, I suppose."

"Wondering what?"

"Whether you haven't made friends because it's the way you've found to navigate this place." She shifted in her chair, then looked at me again. Even after all this time, I never knew when she was baiting me to talk, or just being exasperatingly slow. She was kind of infuriating. "Or is it because you don't ever make friends? But that can't be it, because you were close with some of your fellow mercenaries, and with your squadmates in the Patrol."

Closer than you know, I thought. Dammit, Kenzi. "Does it matter?"

"Well, sure. People are social beings. Going without close friendships is isolating. Leads to bad outcomes on re-entry into society." She smirked. "Plus, I want you to be happy, and well-adjusted, and ready to go on with your life."

"So what do you think it is, counselor? Why don't I make friends with the other kids?" Light, sassy. I knew she didn't like when I did that.

"Maybe you'll go out and start over. Find a place to settle down. A new job, maybe, and a new life. A new community."

I snorted. "Not too many communities looking to welcome a war criminal, are there? Oh, hello, tell me again who you murdered? Was it a big village, or just a few choice homicides?"

Otieno didn't laugh. "I think you'll find that all of that doesn't matter as much as you think it will. The galaxy is a big place. Lots of people all over, living lives big and small."

"If you say so, Counselor."

"So what do you think?"

"About what?"

"Why you're not making friends."

I frowned, staring back at Otieno. But I knew from experience she wouldn't let it lie. And I wanted to go back to my unit and keep reading the new book I'd found in the library. It was a combat memoir from a Patrol sergeant who'd fought on and around Porcus V, against a pirate fleet with delusions of being something more than criminals. Exciting stuff. "Well, Counselor, I think part of it is that everybody here is a violent reprobate. And even though I am too, I'd rather not associate with people like that. Like myself."

Otieno nodded. "OK, that's the glib answer. You get one of those. Now tell me the real one."

She was infuriating, all right. "Everybody I make friends with ends up in trouble, in pain, or dead, Counselor. Keeping to myself seems kind of like community service."

32

Hidden Agenda

On my way toward Elihar's coordinates, I had my suit read me the planetary briefing again. I would pay closer attention this time. The geology notes were pretty extensive, but the biology notes were strangely sketchy. Kenai had enough rain that the mountains didn't last long, weathering and eroding quickly. There were some fresh ranges on the large eastern continent, and evidence of continental collisions, rifts, and subduction zones. Like other tectonically active worlds, there were two varieties of crust, one old and less dense, one younger, denser, and constantly recycling. Because the denser type sat lower, Kenai's surface water found its way down there, making oceans that covered about 80% of the surface.

I flashed back for a moment to happier times. Back in the Patrol, I always liked reading the geology notes before a mission. I had an aptitude for the subject, or so my Patrol intake exams had indicated. When the test said I might be good at it, I'd read up a little. My thinking was that if I could get into a technical or engineering corps, I might be less likely to die, but that strategy hadn't worked out. Front line infantry for me. Just a grunt. But even so, I hadn't died.

There were lots of silicates here, but also a high aluminum content, which led to rocks that were easier to weather chemically than on other such worlds, with water plentiful enough to push it even faster. Or so the report said. Don't get the idea that I could come up with all that. I'm good at remembering and repeating phrases that make me sound smart. Anyway, the end result of all this was that the planet's mountain ranges were generally soft and rolling, covered with the unusual vegetation. The rocks here were all folded, some of them intruded by volcanic dikes and sills.

At the place Elihar had sent me, where I was now, there was a slot canyon cut in the rocks, narrower and with higher sides than the place I'd just been, the one with the weird doorway. All of it was very different from the soil-covered site where Welk and I had set up our dig. Elihar was right. It was a good spot, and it was sheltered. And there was water nearby, a necessity if we were going to be here for a while. Tactically sound, too. Cover from the sky, thick enough to shield from ground-penetrating sensors.

I figured Elihar was in there somewhere, hiding out in the canyon. The plants grew over the slopes to either side, but the canyon floor was shaded, with a little stream running along it, spilling over blocks and fallen rocks as it went. There was room to walk alongside, though, sometimes on muddy banks, sometimes on gravel, sometimes clambering over boulders, although the suit made that easier. Once I was deep in the shade of the canyon, I took a look around, but there seemed to be nothing out of place. The cooler temperature and the mist made it a little more comfortable than my cross-country trek, just concluded.

"Elihar!" I shouted. That gave away my position, but I hadn't seen any ships near here, and there was no sign of anyone. "You here?" I called up the map. It looked like maybe the coordinates Elihar gave me were deeper in, but the map data resolution wasn't detailed enough to give me a good 3D render on the canyon here. I struggled to hear a response, but I couldn't pick up anything. I kept moving upstream, deeper into the canyon. At times, it opened up and let more light in, but it was mostly a crevice with steep sides, often with smaller plants clinging to the walls, digging into whatever little crack they could find, soaking up the water that sometimes seeped out of the rocks above. There were insects about, and I occasionally saw some of the hairy lizard-bird things, although these were smaller than the ones I'd seen in the forest with Welk. They made little squawks to each other, and it was actually kind of nice walking along the rushing water, into and out of little patches of sun that sent the mist into prismatic hues.

The map thought I might be close to where Elihar had told me to go. "Elihar!" I shouted again. "It's Jess. You here?"

This time, I heard a response. Elihar's musical voice, echoing around the rock walls. "Jess. I am here. Good to see you again." It sounded like Elihar was just a little farther on, so I pressed further into the canyon, uphill. I rounded a bend, and Elihar was there, standing in a wide spot in the stream, three arms buried in the riverbed. As I approached, one of the arms emerged with a wriggling scaly creature wrapped in the viny hand. Elihar pulled another hand out, dripping with water and mud, and quickly twisted the creature between both hands. It went limp.

"You fishing?" I asked. "Nice catch." That was a bit of generosity on my part. The animal he'd recovered had an oily-looking body, long and narrow, covered with scales that gave off an iridescent sheen. It had no visible eyes, but it did have three antennae sticking out of one side. I had a little glitch of the zavvies.

"Collecting lunch, as you call it." Elihar held out the animal for me to examine.

"The short days here mess up our meals," I said. "Kind of too short for three, too long for two. I find myself snacking a lot." Why had I said that? Jess Amiko, you have no small talk game, especially for a first-contact situation. Except that this couldn't be first contact, because Elihar spoke Tradespeak almost as well as I did.

Elihar just looked at me. Long enough that I felt uncomfortable, which meant I wanted to talk again. "How'd you find this place?"

"A friend recommended it." Elihar tucked the scaly eel into a crevice between vines on the side of their torso. It stuck there, kind of wedged in. I wondered if that was how they carried things, kind of like a whole alien species covered with tape or something, just sticking their stuff to their bodies. Elihar studied me a bit longer. "This is your first time here?"

An odd question. "Yes. You just told me about it this morning, remember?"

Elihar's head twitched. "Yes. But do not speak of past conversations, I implore you."

Oh yeah. "Sorry. I meant no offense. I will try to remember." I was blowing the first contact thing even harder. If that's what this was.

"You should come to our camp." Elihar pulled the third hand out of the river. "My camp, I mean."

I felt a twinge of unease. I was not at all sure I wanted to go camping with an unknown xenoperson in the middle of a campaign by hostile forces to murder me and everybody else, but my lack of other viable options weighed on me. If Elihar was planning on eating me, they would probably be sneakier about it. I imagined choice cuts of myself stuck on Elihar's torso alongside the eel, then shook my head. "Lead on, sir. Or madam. Or something else. Do you have a gender preference? Our language has issues. Sorry." I realized I had been tending to think of Elihar as male, maybe, because of the deep voice, but of course that was silly.

"Yes, your language is odd in that regard, and complex in other ways as well. It took me a while to master it, although I had a good teacher." He made a little wheezy noise here, but I didn't know what that was about. "I donated gametes to my mate in our relationship, so I chose a male gender construct for myself in your speech."

"Sir it is, then." And married, I guess, or whatever passed for shacking up on Kenai. Elihar moved along the river, keeping to the right side, and after a few turns, it opened up into a wide flat space. I saw crates and boxes there – human gear, with words I could read. Provisions, mostly, along with some medical supplies. A lot of it looked like the same kind of supplies Welk and I had brought to our dig site. "Wow. Where'd all this come from?"

"Stolen from the alien invaders. Sorry, I mean, you people."

That sounded a little hostile, or maybe he was joking. I couldn't quite tell yet. I left it for now. "That's a lot of stuff. But if you're planning on cooking your fish, it would be rude of me not to sample the local cuisine."

Elihar swiveled his head around. "You could eat it if you wish, but you would gain little sustenance from it." Weird. "It would be better if you ate your people's food." Not rude, just practical, at least as far as I could tell.

I thought a little. "Are the proteins incompatible with my digestion or something?" I'd heard about that on some alien worlds, where you could eat until you were full and then gain nothing at all from what you ate, starving to death with a full belly. Which was sort of better than the worlds where everything came with a neurotoxin, or radioactivity, or that kind of thing.

"Something like that." Elihar pointed at the cliff wall. "You can set up your bedroll there. It is a flat spot, and the ground is not stony. There is an enclosure – a tent. I endeavored to set it up for you."

Elihar seemed to know a lot about sleep and comfortable digs, especially for an alien plant person. I looked around for a bunk for him but found nothing. "Do you sleep?"

"We go mostly dormant during the dark hours, although sometimes we wander. But it is more refreshing just to meditate." Otieno would like this guy. Plenty of time for self-indulgent navel gazing. His head lump rotated around, with the little wet blobs twitching at me as they passed.

I wanted to ask about the person who'd rescued me, and why I'd been told to go to the gateway, and who Elihar was, and who his people were, and how the hell he'd gotten involved, but all of that seemed daunting. I figured maybe I could ask a simpler question, like an ice breaker or something. But how to ask? "Hey, uh, Elihar. I don't want to offend you, but I'm curious how you, uh, experience the world. I have these two organs here and here that perceive light—"

"You mean, eyes?" His inflection changed a bit, a little more musical. I could swear he was being sarcastic.

"Yes. OK, wise guy. How does your body work? Other than that trumpet thing you talk out of."

Elihar grunted several times. "You aren't the most tactful emissary for humanity, you know. Perhaps they should have sent someone else."

I laughed. "I wish they had."

Elihar gestured at his head with one of the snake-like arms. The pad at the end flapped open as it approached, and I could see him flex it into a sharp point. "This is my head, or as close to one as I have. The round objects are light sensors, like your eyes, but they're arrayed all around, giving me vision on all sides." He spun his head lump, and I could see the little blobs in a row all around. "My eyes perceive a broader spectral range than yours, probably because a wider range of wavelengths reaches the surface of my homeworld than on your home planet. But my vision is monochromatic, and I cannot see colors. I don't even understand them, really, although people have tried to explain them. So if you tell me things are green or blue or orange, you will just be tormenting me for my limitations, which is unspeakably cruel." He started quivering.

Was that emotion? Was this something he was sensitive about? "Er..."

He made the grunting noise again, then pointed an arm at me. It twitched. I frowned. He grunted some more.

"Are you laughing at me?" The grunting continued. He slapped his torso with the other two arms and bent over a little. "OK, buddy. At least the world is pretty to me. Rainbows and flowers and stuff."

"You should have seen your face."

"At least I have a face. All the aliens in all the outer worlds, and I have to get stuck with a comedian."

"You're the alien. I live here." He grunted some more.

"Good point." I looked at him more closely. The diamond scales across his vines were pretty, actually, and when he moved, all the vines and fibers covering his exterior shifted in mesmerizing patterns. "Do you eat through that speaking tube? Like, where are you going to put that fish?"

"Kind of personal, wouldn't you say?" He grunted some more. "No, we don't share your repulsive re-use of bodily openings. I can't imagine breathing, eating, and vomiting through the same hole." He pointed at the little gray fleshy trumpet. "This is only for sound. There's a set of vibrating membranes inside, and the cone amplifies it." With another arm, he pulled the fish off his body. "That goes here." He gestured toward his head, and then he popped his head lump up, and it separated from his torso, suspended on another viny arm, a thicker, shorter one. Where his head had sat on the top of his torso, there was a circular hole around the arm, or neck, or whatever it was, exposed now where it had been covered by the head. The hole contained a ring of fleshy pink ridges radiating out from the neck, each with bumps at the top. The gaps between the ridges looked pretty deep. Involuntarily, I took a step back. Zavvies.

"What's the matter, never seen a digestive opening before?"

I swallowed. "Uh, no. Well, not with a neck sticking out of it."

He tossed the fish into the hole around his neck, and the ridges started roiling, pulling at the fish. His head popped down. "You do know you look as weird to me as I look to you, right?"

"I'm sure."

"Maybe weirder. That hair stuff you grow is seriously creepy, you know." He grunted again. "Are you hungry? I've heard it's rude in your culture to eat in front of somebody else when you haven't given them any food. In my culture, it's only rude to eat somebody else." He grunted again.

I was hungry, I realized. It had been a long walk here, even with the suit's help. "Yeah. I'll go get something, if that's all right?"

"Be my guest. It's here for your use exclusively. I wouldn't touch that stuff." He made a low, gravelly noise, kind of an 'eeugh.'

Whatever. Sheesh. I went over to the boxes. Some standard rations, basic carbs and proteins, but there were some better meals there too, like the higher end stuff Welk and I had enjoyed. I found a few packs of the spicy chicken with pepper relish, and my mouth started watering. Even here, stuck with an alien would-be comic in the middle of nowhere, surrounded by hostile forces gunning for me, things were looking up. Just a little.

I tugged the opening strip on the spicy chicken. That would trigger the chemical reaction in the container and warm the whole thing up, although it would take a minute or two. I pulled the chopsticks out of the slot in the side. This was going to be nice.

Then I looked down at the ground and noticed something, something that led me around the side of the supply crates, toward the rock wall. There, pressed into the mud, was a set of unmistakable shapes. Tread marks. Boot prints. Human ones.

33

FACE PLANT

I stuck my finger into the chicken. Hot, but not enough to burn my mouth. I set the chopsticks up and ate a few pieces. They were hot and tangy and good and familiar, and I stuffed my face and didn't chew much. I might eat a second pack. Like most grunts I knew, I wasn't above a little therapeutic eating. Not hardly.

At length, I took a break to swallow and catch my breath. I looked at Elihar. His head was vibrating a little, moving up and down. I wondered if that was because of the fish in his neck getting chewed or scraped or cut up or whatever, but that seemed like maybe a rude question, at least for someone you'd just met. And I had something more pressing to ask.

"So, Elihar."

His speaking trumpet popped out towards me from a crevice. That was still kind of uncanny. "Yes?"

"Another human has been here. I saw the footprints."

The trumpet went a little limp, then withdrew back behind his vines. Elihar's head spun around, back and forth a few times, although given the radial distribution of his eyes, he always kept me in view. The silence went on long enough to be awkward. But I wanted an answer.

Finally, the trumpet reemerged. "Yes."

I waited a bit more. "That's all you're giving me? Yes?"

"Yes."

"Oh, come on." I didn't know if he could interpret inflection, but if so, he was getting a good example of irate.

"Look, I can't say more."

"Why not?"

"I can't say why."

I frowned. He continued. "There's . . . danger. It's delicate." He made a hissing sound. "There's a lot you don't know. Can't know, at least not yet."

"You have some kind of plans for me?" I grimaced. "Why did you meet me? What's the point of bringing me out here?" I pointed at him with my chopsticks. "I need some answers, my herbaceous friend."

"Herbaceous? I do not know this word."

Interesting. "Uh, I'm probably not using it right. Plant-based, I think. Or plant-related. Which you look like, sort of." I could feel my cheeks heat up. Making assumptions about alien sentients and shooting your ignorant mouth off about them was just about the opposite of protocol.

"So in your expert xenobiological estimation, I'm a talking tree?" I could swear he was being snippy. Whoever had taught him human speech had taught him well.

Double down, I guess. "Also walking. Although on my world, trees don't eat fish."

"You're not entirely wrong," he said. "My people are related to the sessile photosynthesizers, although not much like the ones that grow around here. These aren't able to uproot and move to get to better habitat or to find more prey."

I found myself just as happy that we were far from the home of his wandering homicidal tree ancestors. "You can photosynthesize? Then why do you bother to eat fish? Or eels, or whatever that was."

"Have you ever photosynthesized? It's so boring." He grunted. "I like fish. They're tasty."

This was interesting, but he'd dodged my question. "So, what do you want from me? Why am I here?"

"So the other humans don't murder you. Isn't that good enough?"

Well, it wasn't a drawback. "It's nice, sure, but they'll find me eventually. And that puts you at risk. Why not just go hide wherever you were hiding before? You should stay away from me completely. I'm trouble."

"I can't go where I was before. That's part of the problem." He hissed again. "Look. Like I said. Talking about this stuff is dangerous, and it's only going to frustrate you. I'm here because I want to work with you, but I'm going to have to let you learn some things on your own before we can get to that part."

Holy vacc leak. "So in the middle of a planetary invasion by murderous well-armed criminals, your plan is that I go on some kind of vision quest, having a discovery-based learning experience in the woods? Communing with nature, or something?" Now, I figured, he was learning sarcasm.

"Yes. That's exactly it." Apparently, sarcasm was lost on him. Or he chose to ignore it.

"This is a terrible plan."

"Worse than you know."

"What?"

"Nothing."

"That wasn't nothing."

"Shouldn't have said anything."

I glowered at him for a while.

"When your mouth hole curves down, and your nose makes that hissy breathing noise, that means you're angry, right?" His tone was light, but not quite mocking.

"Yes."

"Just checking." He popped his head up again, revealing the ridged chamber under his neck. His upper body convulsed a few times, his head going up and down on the neck stalk in little spasms. Finally, a shower of thin white bones launched out of his neck grooves, landing on the forest floor. The fish, or at least the mineral parts of it.

I stood looking at him for a moment, not really sure what I was seeing, and definitely sure I had nothing coherent to say about it.

"What?" He raised two of his arms, almost like a shrug. "Not like I can digest those. And seriously, I mean, it's no worse than what you do with your indigestibles. Now THAT is ridiculous. And messy. Imagine, having a tube all the way through you. So weird. And awkward." He stuck one of his hand pads into his neck hole. The little ridges massaged the hand as he felt around. It was unsettling. Eventually, he pulled out what looked like a fish head, still with some of the fleshy bits attached. He examined it, then tossed it away into the underbrush. "That reminds me. Why do you wear pants, anyway? Seems like they just get in the way of all that messy stuff. It would be easier just to go around bare naked and proud, like we do. Pants seem like such a waste of time."

I had no good answer.

34

MYTH, TREE? NOVEL!

The muggy day cooled, and the sun moved behind the ridge under which we sheltered. I began to hear sounds of animals moving about, rustling in the brush, and calling to each other. Elihar and I had talked, but he'd been remarkably evasive about anything real or useful. He'd tell me about his biology (weird), his family (spouse and twelve offspring, although I wasn't clear where they were or what parenting involved for him), his career (scientific research, from the sound of it, with a focus on archeology). I mentioned the site Welk and I had worked on, and the cities our other teams were exploring, at least before they were all murdered, and he went quiet. I wasn't sure if that was out of respect for my dead coworkers, or if it was a topic he got edgy about.

He asked only basic questions about me. He didn't seem too interested, more like he was being polite. I told him about my military service, but I left out the part about my time in prison. He was more interested in how our society worked, and what role the military played, and he steered me away from talking about my own past. Gently, with questions. But I could tell he didn't want me talking about me. Especially about how I'd arrived on Kenai and what I was doing here. Maybe that was part of the whole taboo against revealing past conversations he'd mentioned. I still didn't get that part.

I took off the suit, airing out both it and myself, and when the conversation dried up, I found a deeper spot in the river, got naked, let down my hair, and washed up. I'd found some extra clothes in the pile of crates, and some of them were my size, or close. And I could put the suit on again if I got cold. I made my way over to Elihar. He was seated on the ground, or resting, his legs bent. He didn't really seem to have a butt, so I don't know exactly what sitting was for his anatomy. He was making little scratches with a stylus on what looked like a board of deep black wood. I wrung out my hair and then ran my fingers through it, pulling out some tangles. He spun his head and looked at me with nearly all his eyes, a few at a time.

"Hair gets to you, eh?"

"It's weird."

"You should talk." I moved over to him and looked at his board. "Is this your written language?" It looked a little like the markings I'd seen at our dig site, with pictures and geometric shapes along with marks that were more like runes. We'd had very little time to explore the buried building before everything went to hell, but it looked like he was maybe from the same culture, at least.

"Some of it is our language. Some of it is mathematical notation. I'm working on some notes I took earlier." He pointed out some marks and glyphs on his plank and told me their meaning. I wasn't a polyglot, by any means, but I could usually pick up the important parts of new languages pretty easily. Like how to get to the bar, and what the penalty was for fighting. He gave me more than that, though. Some of their writing seemed to be symbolic. Those marks were simple little pictures representing common objects, like the sun, trees, mountains, different animals. He said that's how their language had started – more like art. Now, though, most of the letters had come to correspond to sounds, most of them related to the objects the letters originally represented.

He reached down to a bag on the ground beside him and took out another plank. He wrote out their alphabet for me.

It had what looked like over a hundred different letters, and he walked me through them, although of course I couldn't remember them all. It was fun. Some of the sounds I just couldn't make, like weird buzzing sounds, or percussive throbbing, or frequencies I couldn't hear – but I got some of it down. And he showed me how to write my name, which is always fun when you're somewhere new, and how to write his.

When we were done, he took some water from a jug nearby and rubbed it over the plank. The plank swelled up, and the letters we'd written filled in. After a moment, it was clean and ready to use again. "That's pretty neat!"

"We have a lot of natural technology like this." He suddenly sounded guarded again. "It's our way." He set the plank aside. "Are you cold?" he asked. "We could probably ignite something if you are."

"I'm fine." I chuckled. "I would have thought burning stuff would be off the table for a guy made of wood."

He grunted. "Just don't throw me on the fire." He grunted some more. "I would come back as a *zeethrit* and plague you and your offspring."

"A zeethrit?"

"A vengeful spirit of the dead." He raised his head out of his neck groove a little, and his voice got low. "They rise from the ground, howling like the storm winds, grasping at those who did them wrong. If they catch their enemies, they shred them to little pieces until their only remaining function is to feed the soil."

I laughed. Hard.

"What?" he asked. "Most find that scary." He waggled his three arms at me. "Evil spirits, right? I thought your culture invented such monsters as well."

I laughed some more. "We do. It just figures that the nightmare scenario for you people would be being turned into mulch."

"Mulch?"

I explained the term, and he did some more of his grunty laughs. I was relieved not to have caused offense. He seemed like a decent guy, even if he would absolutely not tell me what the hell was going on. I left him to get some more food, and then I returned, eating in silence while he worked on his tablet. The sky turned pretty colors as the end of the day approached.

He tilted his head back, looking up at the sky, or maybe down at his torso. When somebody has eyes on all sides of their head, it's hard to tell where their focus is. But I thought it was the sky. It was dark now, nearly completely. He spent a few moments in silence, just observing. He straightened his supplies, tucking the wooden board he'd been writing on into a coarse woven sack. "I have to step away for a bit."

"The meditation you were talking about?"

He looked at me for a moment. "Yes." He got up higher on his legs, so that he stood a little taller than I did. Then he put one of his hand pads on my shoulder. It felt warm, which was a surprise. It was a little weird being touched. "I will be back in the morning, perhaps even earlier. Please don't leave. I am sorry this is confusing, but there is a good reason for what I'm doing. We need each other."

"Where are you going?"

"Not far. Just out into the woods for a bit. There is no danger."

I frowned. More delays, and more weird hidden stuff. I didn't like that, especially not on a hostile world. But I had nowhere to go, and zero friends other than Elihar, and maybe the trooper who'd shot the other troopers. It might be worth my while to see where this led. Not that I had much choice.

"Well, then, goodnight, I guess. Don't let the termites bite."

"What?"

"Never mind."

He turned away, and I watched him go, his movements fluid and deliberate, using all three legs and all three arms to make his way into the trees. A little after he left, I found the tent and set up my bedroll. He was right – the spot he recommended was great. As I sat in the tent, listening to the river rush by and the weird trill of the alien critters around me, I felt another wave of chills, like I had the previous night. I didn't notice anything going on with the surrounding sounds, just the constant rushing of the water in the river nearby. Maybe it was just that I was still damp from my bath.

35

RELEASE

"Congratulations." Otieno even sounded sincere.

"For what, exactly? Entertaining you with my misadventures for seven years?"

Otieno smiled. "Still sarcastic. I think I was supposed to counsel you out of that or something." She patted my shoulder, and her hand lingered there, small and warm. She'd barely ever touched me the whole time, really. Occasionally her hand had brushed mine when she gave me a con with forms or tests to fill out. And there was a hug once, a little under three years in, when she'd given me a homemade birthday cupcake like she did every year. That was the only birthday hug, though, and I'd been through six. Well, one of them I was comatose in the med ward after getting beat up, so that didn't really count. Five then. And almost no touching. But that rule seemed to be fading.

Along with the rule against her smiling. She seemed really, genuinely happy. She patted me again. "Congratulations on making it through all this intact, and reasonably healthy."

"And fulfilling my debt to society?"

She raised an eyebrow. "I don't see it that way. Do you?"

"I mean, isn't that the idea?" I was sorry I'd brought this up. I liked seeing her happy, and this was sending her back into counselor mode.

"Any debt you owe is to the people you hurt. The rest of this is just rules, and disincentives, and laws that don't really cover complicated real-life situations very well."

That was interesting, sort of. I hadn't heard her talk that way. But I wanted to change the subject. "I really want to thank you, Counselor. I've really appreciated you talking with me and looking out for me." *I tried to sound sincere, but it got weird, so I retreated a little.* "I mean, it would maybe have been better if I'd actually taken your advice."

She laughed, and I was relieved. "I like to think I got to you a little bit. I mean, you haven't beaten anyone to a pulp in 882 days."

"You have an alarmingly specific handle on that information, Counselor."

She laughed again. "I saw it in your file as I filled out the discharge forms." *Finally, she let her hand slide off my shoulder.* "You've done some real work here, and that's good. I mean, I'm sorry you ended up here. I don't think your sentence fit what happened." *She saw something in my face, something I probably didn't hide very well.* "But that's behind us now, right?"

"Yes, Counselor." *I tried to sound sure of that. It wasn't so hard.* "I'm an exceedingly reformed war criminal, ready to go out and do stuff like saving puppies and planting trees and baking cookies." *She snorted.* "I'm as penitent as they come, you know."

"You'll have an apartment in Delgos for up to a year, along with a stipend and tuition if you want to study something new."

"I know all that. You went over it like five times. Made me sign stuff."

She smiled. "Use the time. Some people don't, but I think it could really help you. Take some time to breathe, especially out there when you're not all tied up with the toxicity of this place. Study something. Look through jobs. Be picky. Think about what you'd enjoy doing. What would be fulfilling."

"Something important, right?" *I suddenly thought of the village and the fire.* "I mean, something worthy."

"Yes. For sure. Get yourself doing something you can believe in. Like you had with the Patrol." *When I was happy, she didn't say. But she knew.* "You want some advice?"

"That's maybe the first time you've asked permission."

Her laugh was almost musical. This was really fun, in a way I hadn't expected. I mean, release was exciting, and I'd been climbing the walls for weeks. But seeing her in this new way, with the formality dropping away, was refreshing. "All right, let me force one more thing on you." She took my hand in hers. "I think you'd be happier somewhere new, somewhere maybe far away. Maybe somewhere without a lot of people."

"Because I'm dangerous, antisocial, and poorly adjusted?"

She smiled. "No, because I think you get lost in people sometimes. From what you've said, your best times have been in small groups, removed a bit from others. Like the couple of years on the ranch in the Wissel territory, as a kid. And then in your squad in the Patrol, once you settled in. And especially on Yomo. You were happy there, part of a small team, handling important stuff at the edges of the Council worlds, far from the bustle and crowds. I think that's where you were happiest, at least from what you've said. Having an adventure, and not dealing with all kinds of people and their stupid little petty issues."

I tried to think of something witty to say, but nothing seemed right. I also didn't mention that I was doing something just like what she was recommending when I did what got me sent to prison. But I could see where she was coming from. "Thanks, Counselor. I'll keep that in mind. Something with a purpose, and something far from other people."

"Doesn't have to be a big grand purpose. Just something that matters to you." She opened her desk drawer and pulled out a cupcake. Blue frosting. My favorite color.

"Hey, it's not my birthday."

"Kind of is, though, isn't it? Start of a new life?"

I snorted. "You can be really corny, you know?"

"I know." She handed me the cupcake and pulled out another. "Let me know where you end up, what you end up doing. Write me anytime. I want to know. I enjoyed you."

"Aww, Counselor. I'm sure you say that to all the inmates."

"No, I don't." Her smile wavered, but only for a moment. "I'm really pulling for you, Jess. I want all the best for you." She *handed me a con. Not a great model, but not terrible. Totally contraband in prison, too, but the screen was dark. "Compliments of the Council Penitentiary System. It won't activate until you get out."*

"Thanks, Counselor."

"I left my personal contact information on there. Not the prison address. Really, contact me any time. Especially if you're struggling with something. I'll still listen, and I'll try to help."

I studied her face, trying to figure out where this was all coming from, but she had her Counselor mask up, and I never had been any good at reading that. "Will do, Counselor."

"Atich."

"What?"

"My first name's Atich." She unwrapped her cupcake and took a bite. "Come on, eat. I didn't stay up late baking for you to just leave it sitting there."

36

MULCH ADO ABOUT SOMETHING

"Hello, Jess." Elihar. He was already back in camp when I awoke and emerged from my tent. I assumed he would return, but it was reassuring to see him even so. He had a couple of eelfish stuck to his side.

"Want a breakfast bar to go with those?" I held up a shiny packet.

"I can't eat your food." His head spun, giving the rear eyes a chance to look at me.

"So, the food embargo goes both ways?"

"Yes."

"Poisonous to you? Should I worry about my crumbs?"

"No, it's just non-nutritious."

"Right, the protein thing."

"What?"

"Never mind."

He came in and squatted in the middle of camp. I wasn't sure of the protocol, but it seemed maybe like an invitation to talk. I peeled open the breakfast bar and took a bite. Redberry. Sweet, fake, and tasty. Just like I liked it.

He didn't say anything, so I figured I'd start. "Thanks for the tent. It was nice."

He looked at me for a bit. "You slept well?"

"Breaking in a new bivvy is never easy, but this is nice."

"Bivvy?"

"Sorry, bivouac." There were some words he didn't know. "Campsite."

He was quiet for a little more. When he spoke, he sounded off somehow. Hesitant. "So, your first night was acceptable?"

"Sure. I mean, for a remote wet camp on a world where everyone wants to kill me, it's pretty posh."

"Not everyone. I don't want to kill you. At least, most days." He grunted, but then he stopped, and his head popped up out of its slot a little. "Oh, wait. I should say. That was a joke. I do not desire to murder you."

"Might need to work on the delivery." I crumpled up my breakfast wrapper and tucked it into a storage slot on my suit. "You going to tell me why we're here today? Or am I still listening to the great oneness in the woods until it speaks wisdom to me?"

A beat. "What?"

"You said yesterday…" I stopped. "Sorry, no offense." No past conversations. "I understood I need to learn about something here before we can act. There wasn't a lot more to go on than that."

"That is true." He spun his head again. "I am sorry it is vague. More will become clear soon." He reached a viny arm over to his bag and pulled out one of his writing planks.

I had an unsettling thought. "Is that wood?"

"Yes. It's from a tree."

"You're a tree."

He stared at me, his little eye blobs glistening. "Not exactly. And it's not from me."

"Yeah."

"Or a relative or pet." His head rotated. "Is there some kind of taboo I don't know about with your culture? Are you forbidden to write on meat?"

"No. Sorry. Just getting the feel for this."

He paused. "You can ask questions about this world and how my people live. I will be able to answer some of them."

"Would that be a productive use of our time?"

"That's up to you."

That was an Otieno thing to say. I smiled. "You remind me of somebody I knew before, who was also annoying. But nice." I bit my lip. "Sorry, that was long before I got here, and she has nothing to do with this place."

"Still, I'd rather not hear. Not yet."

Yet? Weird. "You got it, Elihar."

There was a whine from above. I couldn't see through the tree canopy above us, but I knew the sound. Light craft pushing through atmosphere. It was high, though. Probably hadn't spotted us. But might be trying to. "You hear that sound?"

"Yes. One of your people's vessels."

"Yes. You're sure we're safe here?"

"You know their detection capabilities better than I do. But I believe so."

Even so, I powered down the suit, feeling it become heavy around me as the servos and movement assist relaxed. It didn't put out much EM, especially on stealth mode. But who knew what they were carrying for instruments up there? The whole expedition was pretty well funded. And they'd taken down a Patrol ship, for skogging out loud. I vented the helmet and opened the sleeves and legs.

Elihar grunted. His laughing. "You're smaller without that suit on. Scrawny even."

"It's functional. Protection, motors, padding, sensors, other gizmos." I stepped out of the suit and bent it over into storage mode. "But it's not a drawback that it bulks us up. Being big and scary is kind of a universal advantage. There are rodents on my homeworld that can puff themselves up to twice their normal size." The sound of the engines receded. Hopefully they were leaving, as opposed to summoning reinforcements, or starting on a bombing run.

"Rodents?"

"A group of animals that are generally small, often herbivores or scavengers. Furry. In this case, genetically modified a bunch of times over."

Elihar's speaking trumpet waggled. "What is furry?"

"Covered with hair on all their bodies."

His head jiggled and spun. "That's even worse than you."

I laughed. "You're going to need to get over this if you're going to spend time with humans. We like our hair." I unpinned my ponytail from the standard helmet coil I used for the suit and let it down. I ran my fingers through it. Damp from sweat, but still pretty clean from yesterday's bathing.

"Is your world the one where humans evolved?"

"No, that's Earth. I grew up on Ramine. We're not even sure Earth exists anymore."

Elihar made a gurgle. "What happened to it?"

I liked that he was curious, talking to me, but I thought I'd press a little on the part of this I didn't understand. "I thought we couldn't talk about the past."

"No," he said. "Just, your past on this world, with my people. That is forbidden. Your distant history is fine. Anything on other worlds is fine. Your people are fine." He paused. "Mostly."

I looked at him for a moment. He could tell I thought he was full of it. "It's complex," he mumbled. "Cultural."

He was sounding a lot like an officer justifying a bad decision after somebody called them on it. Like that time when Major Esperanza requisitioned a hundred crates of heat-reflective tape rather than a hundred rolls. "Supply lines were not secure," she said. "Better to stock up when we can." Never mind our quartermaster had no place to put it. We taped a lot of things that didn't need taping after that. Including taping a Duranian obscenity in five-meter-high letters on the outside of our drop shuttle. It stayed on there for a whole deployment cycle, although I think Niall touched it up sometimes. He said he didn't, though. But he must have. We certainly had enough tape for him to. Dammit, that was all a long time ago.

But Elihar wanted to know about Earth. I tried to explain. "There was a war, after we expanded to a lot of different worlds. A big war. Really big. It was bad. Most of the major human worlds and colonies were wiped out. Er, killed or destroyed. The humans that are left are all from worlds that were on the edges of human space, mostly minor backwater worlds, or recently settled. We haven't heard anything from the original worlds in a few hundred years." I wanted to go on, to say that we'd emerged from darkness into light, spirits triumphant, like the anthem lyrics say, but I figured he didn't need the whole history. The Council was at least trying to pick up the pieces after humanity's near-extinction and start over, and it had done pretty well. Or at least that's what I was taught in school.

Elihar was quiet for a time. "War. I have heard that term before. Were there many wars in your history?"

Well, that's embarrassing. "Countless wars, dating back to when the first guy took offense to something and went to sharpen a stick. But this last one was the biggest ever. Whole worlds died. Billions of people." And here I was, a marine, trained in combat. But the Patrol was supposed to prevent wars. That's why I signed up. And that's probably what most marines said to themselves throughout history, shortly before being told to go kill people.

Elihar was quiet again. I thought he was going to go all moralistic on me, all *our enlightened species does not believe in murder, unlike you violent, horrible, hairy savages.* But he didn't. "Our society seems destined for our first. Our first war." He said 'war' like he was trying out the word.

"I'm sorry to hear that." I thought for a moment. That wasn't squaring with what I thought I knew. Elihar must not be from here, then. The cities here were old, long since destroyed. We hadn't seen any evidence of the people here that wasn't long extinct. There certainly didn't seem to be enough tree people around to have a war. I suppose if they all just stood still, we'd mistake them for a forest. But it seemed like if they built cities once, they'd build them now. Or maybe the cities were from somebody else? A people who'd gone extinct long ago? Had Elihar's people emigrated offworld? Was the war he was talking about going on elsewhere? "Is this not your homeworld, then? Are your people from somewhere else?"

Elihar grunted. I wasn't sure if it was a laugh or not. "That is a complicated story. But I'm from here." He tilted his head down for a moment, then rose up on his legs, spreading his arms in what I thought passed for a polite gesture. "Should we get some food? The noises your midsection makes suggest you are hungry. Is your gut sentient separately from the rest of you? I have heard of a species of aquatic animal that has multiple nerve centers that can disagree with each other. Or perhaps your gut is a sentient symbiote?"

I could tell he was changing the subject, awkwardly, even, but I let it go. "No, my stomach doesn't have a brain, and it's not a parasitic organism living inside me. At least, not most days. The sound is just my internal plumbing. Gets noisy when empty. And also when full, I guess."

"Plumbing?"

"A series of pipes built into a structure, used to carry water and sewage around." I studied his face, although I couldn't read his expressions yet. There were some weird holes in his seemingly fluent language knowledge. "I was looking forward to breakfast. And you've got your eels."

"I do." He peeled an eel off his body, popped his head up, and tossed it in. There were some muffled squelching noises.

I tried not to stare. I wanted to try for some more information. "Can I ask about your people and how they live? In general? Or will that violate your code too?"

"You may ask." I wasn't sure of his inflection yet, but it sounded like he was hesitant.

"You talked about a war coming, maybe, but that takes a lot of people. I've only seen two of you so far. You, and one other. Where are you all hiding?"

"Please don't tell me about the other one you saw." He spun his head around and looked at me with another couple of eyes. "It is forbidden."

There was the taboo, in full force. "That's super weird, you know. I don't know how your society functions with that prohibition in place."

"There's a good cultural reason, believe me."

I didn't. "Anyway. Are there a lot of you here now? I'm surprised the first humans to come here didn't identify it as a populated planet and stay away or make first contact with you."

Elihar paused. "There were many people here once. Not very many now. Not enough for a war."

He seemed to be choosing his words carefully. "So the war is going to happen somewhere else? Some other world?"

"In a manner of speaking."

I frowned. "You're not very good at lying, you know."

"I've been told that. That's why I try not to speak when I will have to lie."

"Do your people not lie often?" That was something we humans could definitely teach them.

"No. Well, only to ourselves."

I smirked. Pop psychology from a tree person in the middle of nowhere. Great. "I suppose if you lied to somebody, they'd probably turn zeethrit and come back to kill you. And then there'd be mulch everywhere."

"Mulch? What is mulch?"

Now that was weird. I'd explained mulch just yesterday.

37

Broken Records

I looked at Elihar for a moment. It was impossible to read his weird, woody face. How could he have forgotten? Was it possible their memory didn't work like ours? But he seemed to pick up on other memories in a normal way, and of course he'd learned our language somehow, almost like a native speaker. He passed as pretty normal, all things considered. Not like the Mantu matriarch I'd met once, who could only speak through a device. Her voice had been mechanical and flat, but her words had been flowery and obscure, full of extra adjectives.

Was he a different person entirely? Maybe when he left at night, somebody else came on shift to watch me. Another Elihar. I wouldn't necessarily pick up on any physical differences, although he seemed like the same person, with the same voice and sense of humor, and as far as I knew, he looked the same.

It wasn't a big deal, I realized. It was no weirder that he'd forgotten about mulch than anything else in this whole bizarre and vacc-leaked situation. But it bugged me. Didn't fit.

Was there a way to test his memory about other topics? What we had talked about earlier? I tried to remember. "If this is all right to ask... before, when we were talking about gender, you said you had a spouse? A family? Some little sprouts?"

"It would be best not to speak of past conversations." His head spun to give another eye a look at me. Eventually, he answered. "I did. They're gone now." His voice was low, no inflection.

Oops. "I'm sorry. That must have been painful." If your family relationships are the same as ours. Maybe you just set them loose and lose track of them as their seed pods blow away on the wind.

"It was. But it is the way this world works."

Cryptic, I thought. But I could relate. "I've lost a lot of friends and family, too. Kind of why I ended up here." That and a host of other bad decisions, not to mention the associated criminal convictions.

Elihar studied me for a moment. "Of course."

Well, that was rude. "What do you mean?"

"I am sorry. That was the wrong thing to say. I sympathize and I grieve your losses."

I felt a flash of anger. "Look, buddy, I don't know what's going on here, but I'm getting fed up with this."

"Completely understandable. And unavoidable. I'm sorry." The same line as always. Still useless, and still frustrating.

I had a thought. I could ask him about something about which we'd never spoken. See if he'd know that. That would be a test, of sorts. "So, remember yesterday, when I was talking about music?"

I thought he might just tell me not to talk about past conversations. But I think he could maybe tell I was angry and wouldn't like that answer. Not at all. He was quiet for a moment, and then he just said, "Yes."

A lie. Test failed. We hadn't talked about music, ever. He looked at me, waiting for me to say something. I didn't help him out. After a moment he continued. "We don't have music the way you do, although we do create complex rhythms on tree trunks for celebrations, and sometimes we chant together."

"You said that yesterday." I tried to make the statement neutral.

"Please do not speak of past conversations." I was beginning to see why. You lying shrub.

"Sorry. I was wondering if you could show me more of the rhythms you played. I rather enjoyed them."

His head spun around, twice. "Certainly." He looked around the camp. "I shall collect some sticks."

More lies. "Elihar. We didn't talk about music yesterday. You didn't play anything."

He was quiet. "I see."

"I don't. What the hell is going on? Why don't you remember yesterday?"

"An important question."

"Why are you lying to me?"

"I wish I were not."

"Are you not the same guy who was here yesterday?"

"I assure you, I am." He made a snorting noise. "There are no others of my people anywhere near here."

"Like I can believe anything you say." And actually, what he'd just said was another lie. I'd told him about meeting the other one like him, the one who got crushed under the tree. Could the guy not say anything true? "Even assuming you are the same person, why don't you remember yesterday?"

"I can't answer that."

"Why not?"

"I can't answer that either."

A hot flash of rage. "Why? Why not?"

"It's dangerous. You don't understand."

"Obviously." I wanted to tear into him, to cuss at him, to smack him. I needed to cool my head. Otieno said I made bad decisions when angry. I felt like I made bad decisions all the time, but maybe the angry ones were worse. "I'm going to go away now for a bit. From you. Over there." So I don't kill something.

Elihar hunched down, his whole form compressing into something smaller. "Probably a good idea. I am sorry. This was always going to be hard. Take the time you need."

I walked over to the pile of supplies. I was seething, my face hot. Maybe I should just bug out. Go see if I could commandeer a ship, attack a base. Anything. That would almost assuredly result in my violent death. Which might not be a bad thing.

Can't think like that. Otieno would be angry with me.

Tactical assessment. That always helped. Except when you were totally skogged, no hope. But even then, at least you knew.

Situational Observations. SOs. That's where you start. I'd never made officer - never been interested - but I'd heard them talk.

SO 1: If Elihar wasn't lying, and he was the only one of his species around, then he was clearly forgetting stuff overnight. Stuff that happened, that he should know about. He'd admitted as much. Hadn't played it off or anything. Or tried to explain.

SO 2: He left at night. That might be related.

SO 3: He clearly wanted me to figure something out here, something he wouldn't tell me. That was probably related.

That was all true, but it added no clarity. My face felt hot again. Why was I screwing around with these stupid games while a patrol ship was being shot out of the sky? Skogging skog...

SO 4: Elihar wasn't the only one of his species around. There was the other guy, who got killed by the fallen tree. That guy was obviously another guy. Therefore, Elihar was lying, or Elihar was ignorant of the other guy. My money was on lying.

SO 5: I'd met the other tree guy, the dead guy, near the weird portal, where I'd been directed to go by the mysterious human soldier who'd saved my sorry behind. I'd also met Elihar there, at the portal. But he'd taken me here, instead. All of that had to be important, but it was hard to figure how. Had the soldier known Elihar and the other one would be there? Maybe. Probably. Either that, or they wanted me to go to the misty doorway. But that was dangerous. The bad guys were there, and they'd been killed pretty hard by something alien.

All that got me to thinking. The suit's cams would have recorded those events. A standard feature of this suit model, helpful for after-action reports or recon missions. I should be able to call up a holo of what I'd seen. Maybe I'd missed something. The recording memory was enough for 300 hours, and then it cycled and overwrote the oldest data, but all of this weird stuff was still well within that window. I could have another look at the attack on me and the soldier too. That might help. Or it might just leave me with more questions.

I went over to the suit. Main menu, archived recordings, select starting point, playback. The suit sent out a little holo from the wrist console. I stretched it with the controls until I could see better. It was a multi-cam recording, which the suit's processor combined with sensor data and stitched into a 3D representation with the suit (and therefore me) in the middle. There were occasional glitches as it played - pieces of the environment suddenly appearing or vanishing or twitching or relocating or changing scale - but that was usually at the periphery. In the area around the suit, it was all pretty stable.

I spun the timestamp back to when I'd found Elihar. The holo image wasn't large, but he seemed completely like the same guy I was with now – size, shape, limbs, even his manner of carrying himself - although maybe all of them looked alike to human eyes. I watched our meeting again. Odd to see it in the third person. I paused and rotated to get a look on all sides. Nothing out of order.

I backed up the recording, looking again at the mysterious portal and the dead SpearPoint techs strewn around it. Nothing weird there either. I mean, other than a cloudy doorway into a cliffside and a bunch of dead folks with holes blasted through them. Nothing newly weird, I should say.

I wasn't really getting anywhere. I spun the timestamp back farther, to where I'd found the dying tree guy under the fallen tree. I rotated the angles to try to get a better look, but the suit cameras couldn't see past the brush, so a lot of the wounded figure was hidden, grayed out in the replay. I wondered if I should show this to Elihar, ask him if he knew the guy.

I couldn't see the dying Kenaian well, but I did get a good look at the tree with its jagged lightning scar. Weird to think that lightning and trees were some sort of universal constant, but I guess growing towards the sunlight and atmospheric electrical physics work generally the same way lots of places. Then I stopped cold. I remembered something, something I'd just seen while tracking through the recording.

I pushed the recording forward in time, through the night I spent in the jungle near the portal, to where I returned and investigated again. The day I met Elihar. I saw what I remembered. I rotated the scene around, exploring it from all angles. It was there, unquestionably, in the background. A massive tree, surrounded by healthy trees, none of them broken or splintered or damaged. And the massive tree bore the same distinctive lightning scar. Unmistakable. The problem was, that tree had fallen down the day before. I'd seen it go down. It had killed a guy, a guy who inexplicably knew my name. What was it doing back upright a day later?

38

WAKE

The room was pretty bare. Just a podium up front, with rows of chairs. I was early, but I had nothing else to do on this world except come here. I hadn't ever wanted to come back, but I was drawn, much more than I'd thought I'd be. Felt like a betrayal if I didn't return.

As I made my way in, wondering where it would be appropriate for me to sit, or whether I should be there at all, a holo snapped on up front, and my throat clenched up. She was life size, maybe larger than life. Not how I knew her, all businesslike and comfort casual clothing, but in a fancy orange dress, swirling as she turned back toward the camera with a bright smile. Her hair was done up in braids with little flowers tucked in them. I wondered when it was from. She looked the same age as when I knew her, same hair and gentle creases on her forehead and around her eyes. I realized she must have smiled a lot more out of prison, which made sense. Everybody did.

I felt a hand on my arm. Gentle, but I flinched anyway. Felt guilty for flinching, thought for a moment it was a guard trying to haul me away. I really hadn't wanted to come back to this planet.

"It's all right. I'm glad you came." The voice was low, gentle. Not unlike Otieno's, but without the edge. Kinder, less probing.

"I'm sorry, I'm early. Didn't mean to bother you." I turned as I spoke, and I saw a small woman, compact and wiry, with

short graying hair. A little older than Otieno, maybe, although her skin was smooth. It was always hard to judge age when there were so many treatments available these days. I recognized her from one of the pictures in Otieno's office, where she was on a boat in the sun wrapped in a floral towel. Today, she wore a trim black dress with a gray woven shawl.

She squeezed my arm. "It's fine, Jess."

That blindsided me, and my manners dropped away. "Did she talk about me? How do you know my name?" My emotions tied themselves in knots.

"The prison gave me notice of all the former inmates who intended to come, so I could choose to block any I didn't want here." She smiled again. "Not that I would have. But only three of you are coming, and I was able to look up each of you. That's how I recognized you."

I felt my stomach drop. "I'm sorry, you probably don't want somebody like me here..." My cheeks felt hot.

"People like you were her life's work. Which she loved. She would be so grateful that you came."

My eyes went wet. "I don't think that's true."

The woman put an arm around me. "Nonsense. She followed all the people she counseled. Tracked where they went, what they did, what they were up to. Hoped beyond hope they would find their way." She smiled again. "Many of them did, which is to her credit, I think."

I felt hot again. "I haven't had time to..."

"I know. You're just out, what, five months? It takes a while to adjust, and to find something rewarding and worth your time. It was kind of you to use one of your free travel chits for this." She squeezed my arm again. "It's all right, really. Do you want to sit down?"

I realized I did. I nodded, and she guided me to one of the rows of seats. She sat next to me, which felt awkward. I needed to speak, to say something, but it came out rushed and weird. "I'm sorry. You shouldn't be spending your time with me. This has to be tremendously difficult for you. A sad day, and busy, I'm sure. I'm nobody important, and you don't even know me."

She put an arm around my shoulder. To my surprise, I relaxed. Usually contact with strangers got me edgy. I suspected that was a general tendency of mine, exacerbated in a big way by my prison experience. This felt different somehow. She put her other hand on mine, in my lap. "You're very important. You're her life's work. You, and everybody else she worked with." She looked me in the eye. "I loved her for who she was, but also for how much she cared. You came back for her, and that means the world to me."

I couldn't speak for a moment. "I'm sorry if this is the wrong thing to ask, but can you tell me how it happened? The notice I got didn't give any information." I swallowed. "I know the details probably don't matter, compared to losing her, but I really hope it wasn't related to her work." I had imagined all kinds of scenarios, some of them including people I'd need to find and kill.

"It wasn't." I felt the tension in my chest relax a bit. "She was headed out to a concert. The music department at the institute where we both teach invites groups in to perform every month, and she goes — went — to all of them." She sighed. "The music gets too weird and experimental for me. I prefer something I can dance to. We made a deal - I'd go with her to four a year, and this was one of her solo trips. The tram she took derailed, and she and four other people were killed in the crash. It was just an accident."

"I'm so sorry." Unbidden, my mind filled with terrible imagined scenes, twisted metal, and then it flashed to other such scenes I'd witnessed on other worlds long ago. I tried to put a lid on them. It didn't work very well.

"She was on the way to something she loved. I wouldn't have wanted her not to go." She sighed again. "And she'd be so happy I wasn't with her for this one."

I swallowed. "I'm sorry, I knew she was married, but I never learned your name." Then I regretted what I'd just asked. I had no claim on her time or her attention, much less her identity. She didn't need to be bonded to somebody like me.

"I'm Mariela. So pleased to meet you, Jess." She turned to me. "May I give you a hug? I know I could use one." Her eyes were wet too.

I opened my arms, and she wrapped herself around me and wept.

39

IMMORTALITREE

I was perplexed. The tree had come back to life. Had it healed? Maybe trees did that here. But the others around it showed no evidence of it falling on them. Maybe they'd healed too. Maybe everything just healed fast.

I thought back to the bird. Just a week ago, maybe. The bird that had fallen from the sky, splattered a newly-showered Welk with gore. Killed by lightning, said the *Deimos*. But I hadn't believed that. And then the next day, the dead bird bits were gone from its sealed tub full of nitrogen. It would have to not only come back to life but also break itself out of a sealed box. Leaving the nitrogen undisturbed. Eeesh. Was that related? It had to be related.

I could just ask Elihar. Maybe he'd talk now, that I had figured out what was weird. But I hadn't really figured it out. I knew what was happening, sort of, but not why or how. My head hurt.

OK, my insane hypothesis was that dead things came back to life, somehow. Even that profoundly stupid hypothesis was testable. I just needed to kill something. I couldn't help but cast a glance at Elihar, but he hadn't earned murder in the name of science. Not yet.

I moved past the stack of crates to a stand of smaller trees. They were the same kind, maybe the same species, as the big one struck by lightning, with conical trunks and colorful leaves sprouting out in all directions. So, maybe the same kind of tree would act the same way. I could cut them down and see what happened. If I was onto something, they'd grow back. If not, I'd know that my totally stupid idea was, in fact, totally stupid, and the only victims would be the local foliage. And my sanity.

I didn't think my knife would cut through them, but I had an energy weapon. That would work, and it would be a bit more satisfying to shoot something. I wandered into the stand of trees and found a set of four trees in a row, all small, all about the same size. I could go ahead and cut down all four. Better to repeat the experiment. Plus I got to shoot more things. Never underestimate the therapeutic potential of blowing stuff up. I went back to get my rifle, checked the charge, turned off the safety, wound my way back to the trees, stood a safe distance away. Took aim, looked down the sight. Then stopped cold.

Through the sight, I saw something carved on the tree trunk, right where I was going to shoot. Here on an alien world, on a tree I'd picked at random, at a place I'd never been, someone had carved a word into the tree trunk. My name. Jess.

40

TRUNK AND DISORDERLY

I swung my sight to the next tree, scanned up and down. Jess there too. Carved so that I'd see it from here, a position I'd chosen more or less at random. Skog. I had to be losing it. Was I just hallucinating this whole process? Maybe I was in a cryotank somewhere, dreaming. I shook my head.

Third tree. Jess. Same crude carving, a sharp implement leaving slices in the bark. Fourth tree. Same thing. Jess. I lowered the rifle. I was sweating. This wasn't right. Couldn't be real. Even if somebody wanted to leave me a message, this was a stupid way to do it. No message, just my name. And in a place nobody could know I'd be standing, on trees nobody could know I'd decide to shoot.

Shooting sounded pretty good. I turned my head to check for Elihar. He was still crouched over by his bag with his writing planks. Not downrange. Safe. I lined up a shot, fired straight through the 'Jess' on the first tree. The top half of the tree was knocked back by the blast, and it fell down next to the trunk, leaning on another nearby. Then I shot the second. Then a breath. Then the third and fourth.

On a whim, I spun the rifle and looked at another tree nearby. Maybe they all said Jess. No. No sign of anything. I realized my jaw was tight, my eyes wide. I needed to calm down.

I heard Elihar behind me. His gravelly voice broke the silence. "Is everything all right? Are you functioning normally?"

I didn't answer. Just closed my eyes. Popped the safety on the rifle. Set it down. Took a deep breath. Felt my heart pounding in my chest. "What . . . what is this place? Is it affecting me? Am I going insane?"

"It affects all of us. But it hasn't gotten to you yet."

I snorted. "Oh, it has."

He didn't say anything to that. After a moment, he spoke. "You had a reason to shoot the trees, right? An idea?"

"Yes. But then it got really weird."

"I see. Don't tell me how. It's important you don't. We have to be careful communicating."

"What? Why..." I didn't know how to finish. "Is something watching us?"

"After a fashion. You're almost there. You've almost got it." He came closer.

"I'm not sure I want it." I sighed. And felt alone, and vulnerable without my suit, and lost, and desolate, and attacked, and confused.

"If it is any consolation, all our young go through this. We cannot teach them, but they must learn."

"Your society is seriously screwed up, Elihar."

"I agree, more than you know. But we have found that our young must learn the nature of this place themselves. If we teach them, they succumb to the curse."

41

GEAR

The guy pressed a few buttons on the measuring chamber and the little scanners started swerving around. I had a set of measurements on file, included in my discharge papers, but that was years ago, before RazorCorp, before prison, before all of it. I knew I'd emerged from prison lighter and leaner, but also wirier and better on my feet. I'd lost a good bit of general muscle mass after going off the chems and hormones the service and RazorCorp provided, but I'd replaced some of it, or maybe redistributed it, through exercise and more care with my diet. I thought I was actually more fit now, with a more natural build. Less grunt, more me, if that makes any sense. In any case, I needed new scans if I wanted my new suit to fit right.

"I was in the Patrol, you know, up until eight years ago. That's where I learned everything I know about the suits." The guy was looking at my arm tattoo, a sword piercing a glowing sun.

Great, he was a talker. Just what I needed. But I humored him. Never piss off your supports. "What unit?"

"No unit, I was navy. The Joseph Grimm, then Antares." I didn't recognize the Grimm, but the Antares was a K-class battle cruiser with troop drop capacity. I'd never been aboard, but I knew plenty of marines who had. She was a big, big ship. I'd mostly flown on smaller craft.

"What section, then?"

"DL." *Deployment logistics. That meant the guy would know suits, and weapons too, but he'd likely never have deployed. The marines had ground engineering squads for that.*

"See any action?"

"A little. We were at Fistin and took part in some of the fighting. Raven too, although we got there after it was mostly over."

"We were at Raven from the start. Among the first units down."

The man's eyes went wide. "You were there for the action in Qualang?"

I didn't really want to talk about it, but I thought I could smell a discount in the air, and I was broke enough that I could use any spare credits I could wring out of this deal. "I was at Keeling Wharf."

"Holy..." The man stroked his mustache. "You lost what, two thirds?"

"Of all forces, including dead and wounded. My unit fared a little better." Except for Gus, Mirrum, Meese, and de Gouw. I missed Mirrum a lot.

"Gave them pirates a real hiding, didn't you?" He sounded genuinely appreciative.

"For sure."

He looked at my tattoo again. "Is that the 43rd Lancers?"

"They have a spear, not a sword. I was 12th Light."

He whistled. "You were in the thick of it. Got a bunch of medals, too, I bet."

I was reminded of Sargent Phillo, who said more than once that medals were for when some rear echelon dumbass screwed something up big time, and the poor front-line suckers left in the lurch did better than anybody expected they would in dealing with it, often at great personal sacrifice. Not a terrible assessment. "Distinguished Service Mark, and a Red Cluster. Plus the campaign medals." The brass had saved the Warbirds for the ones who died, which was typical, although in this particular scenario, ambushed at the warehouse, they'd gotten killed far too early to be of much use. But that's not something you point out after the fact. Everybody assumes it's the most noble thing ever to die for your cause, when actually it's a lot more useful to make the guys on the other side do the dying.

"You saved the day there. They had surface-to-orbit weapons I heard. Could have taken out fleet ships." He snapped to a salute. "Thank you for your service, marine."

I returned the salute, although I'd been out for a long time, and it felt a little wrong. "And yours, sailor." Didn't hurt to butter him up.

He made a face. "Psssh. I sprayed suits, charged batteries, and stayed in long enough for a pension. You were the real heroes."

If he knew about my post-enlistment conviction for war crimes, he might not have been so effusive, but I figured this wasn't the time to bring that up. "Just doing the job." I wondered if any of this could translate to some savings. "Any chance you could knock a few credits off for a fellow Patroller?" I gave him a big smile. Lots of teeth.

His face turned shrewd. "I could throw in some extras at a discounted rate. Just got a full camera array in salvage. Or a sensor upgrade? The suit's what keeps you alive, I always say." It sounded like he'd said that a thousand times. "Just a few hundred more."

Nuts.

42

TIME AFTER TIME

I'd found a collapsible field stool in the gear my mysterious benefactor had left for me, and I'd set it up next to the trees. Elihar crouched next to me, mute and useless, but at least he was a companion. I stared at the splintered stumps of the four trees I'd shot. I clutched my field torch, but I felt more comfortable sitting there in the dark. There was a breeze, and it carried a cold edge, unusual here. The humidity had turned from soaking warm to a chill damp after the sun went down. I shivered. Colder than I'd ever been on Kenai. It was well past nightfall now. I turned to Elihar. "Don't you need to leave to do whatever you usually do? Commune with nature?"

Elihar stirred. "I'll stay."

"Why?"

He didn't say anything.

"Right, can't tell me anything." My tone was more mocking and bitter than I intended, but I didn't care much.

We sat in silence for a few more moments. Then he stood. "Don't freak out."

"What?"

Then he vanished. Not got up and left, not flew away. Just gone. There, and then not. At the same time, the tingle I'd sometimes felt before, in the middle of the night, washed over me. As before, there was a small hitch in the chirring and buzzing of the nightlife around me.

I snapped on the field torch, looking for Elihar. He was nowhere. I got up and moved back toward the camp, walking softly out of habit, although the torch would make me obvious. He was not there either. The supplies sat there, dark silhouettes of crates and bags barely visible against the night.

Then I remembered the point of all this. The trees. I went back to them. It took me a moment to find them in the dark, even with the chair as a guide. Not because I am terrible at looking for things. I'm not. It was because they were whole and undamaged. Completely recovered from the rifle shots. And there was no sign of my name carved into them. Had I imagined that entirely? This was far too strange.

Don't freak out, he'd said. Sure, buddy.

43

DISTANCE

"She's not well."

"I know that, Dad." That came out harsher than I meant to be. I wanted to take it back. I tried again. "What's it like today? Are the meds working?"

There was a lag. Fifteen, twenty seconds. That was normal, as the message reached orbit, then went through the jump gate relay. A couple relays, actually. Still fast, though, for interplanetary. One of the perks of being at Benton Base. And one of the few perks available to raw recruits.

I had a chance to study his face while I waited. He was calm, but he seemed fleshy, saggy. "She stopped taking them."

"What? Why? We had to go to four appointments just to get qualified." I swallowed. "And they were expensive." But that didn't matter.

More delay. A hundred thoughts raced across my mind.

"She's going to go soon. She's tired, Jess."

"I can come home. I'll come home." I wanted to say that I could talk her out of it, but I knew that wasn't true. And it wasn't fair to put that on Dad, anyway. I knew he was coping as well as he could.

"You can't, Jess. It would mess up your enlistment. She doesn't want you to, anyway. You know that. She said so."

My throat hurt. "I know. But still. I can get compassionate leave."

It seemed to take even longer for an answer this time. I saw him turn. Looking into the next room. Perhaps she'd called to him, or perhaps one of the monitors had reported some change. Or, more likely, something staying the same.

"She doesn't want that. It's way too far to come back. Too expensive, too. She wants you to finish. She wants you to go out to the stars. To help people."

I started to speak, but I could see he had more to say. The delay made conversations tricky. But I was glad he'd called on video. This would have been harder in messages. He looked at me square in the camera. "This was always part of it, Jess. We knew going in. We were old when we had you. We weren't likely to make it too far into your adulthood." He paused. Squeezed his eyes shut. "I'm sorry. But you were our miracle. Our little blessing, when we thought we'd run out of time. I mean, who has a kid at seventy?"

I waited a bit more, and he kept going. "Mina knows you're doing what you want. What you're called to do. She wants you to succeed. She wanted to see you finish infantry training, enter service. But it's just her time." A beat. "That's all. She's so proud of you, you know."

I laughed at that, although it was a little ragged. "She wanted me to go into psychology, Dad. Be a researcher, like her." That's why she was so surprised at my fights at school, back when I was her sweet little girl. Well, her little girl. I doubted she'd ever been in a fight. I doubted she'd ever been bullied, either. She'd have been too popular. She and I weren't much alike. Not at all. I had to wipe my eyes. "Can I talk to her, Dad?"

An interminable delay. "She's not awake much. I've got her on the pain meds. She'll take those." He let out a harsh sigh. "And she doesn't always make a lot of sense. I don't think it'll be long. But she was OK when she was up last. If you want to record something, I can play it for her. And I'll see if she wants to do that for you."

"Thanks, Dad. It's..." My throat closed up. "It's all right if she doesn't." I thought about what to say. Dad was distracted again by whatever was going on in the other room.

"She'll want to, if she can." His voice got louder. "Jess, I have to go. It's nothing bad. Just need to talk to the nurse." He *pressed a button on his screen. "But I'll leave this on. Record anything. It doesn't matter what. Just tell her about your training, anything. You know she just likes to hear your voice. To hear you tell stories."*

Unlike gravity and light, sorrow's strength didn't fade with the square of distance. "I will dad. Give her a hug for me."

44

FROM BAD TO CURSE

I sat in the dark for a long time, finally returning to my tent. I had trouble sleeping. Eventually, as the light returned, I heard footsteps. Or vinesteps, or whatever. I unfastened the tent door.

Elihar was there, arms spread wide. "Greetings, Jess Amiko! How was your night? Pleasant, I hope?"

I was nearly speechless. "What? Are you kidding?"

"Ah," he said. "Sorry, I did not remember. So much happened. Yes." He sounded uncomfortable.

"Yes." I stared at him for a while. The silence got awkward.

"So." He came closer. "You have made some observations?"

"Listen, you..." I started over, because that sentence wasn't going to end friendly. "I shot the trees. But they're back. And you're acting weird. You—"

"Don't tell me, please." There was urgency in his voice.

"Why not?"

He didn't reply. Not directly. "Tell me what you've observed. But do not talk about anything I did or said." He pointed a hand at me. "That is very important."

"Why?" His head spun around, but he offered no reply. I growled with displeasure. But I could do this his way. For a little bit more. "I shot the trees. Yesterday. To test if..." I trailed off. I was getting close to talking about the lightning-scarred tree. I wasn't sure if that was allowed. I was starting to have a suspicion about that whole event, something I was worried about, but putting it into words would make me sound completely insane.

I started over. "I think things reset at night, somehow. I shot the trees yesterday. Destroyed them. But in the middle of the night, they were restored to how they were before. Or almost." And you were here, and then you vanished. "I think you leave every night before then because something happens to you, too. Something you don't want me to see." Except last night, you let me see. But I can't talk about you. Why? "I've been feeling this... shiver, or energy, or something. At night. I think that's related."

"Good. Anything else?"

I wanted to tell him about my name on the trees, but I wasn't even sure at this point it was real. There would be no reason for that to have happened. And now it wasn't there, anyway. But how to put that into words? "It fits with some other things I've seen. Something happened with a bird when I was first at our dig site. It died, and I stored the body, and then it was gone the next morning. Out of a sealed container." I rubbed my forehead. "But that doesn't make sense. Because why wouldn't the container reset, too? Or me? Or the hole we dug? It should have filled in. Or something." I thought some more. "The people who were killed – they stayed dead, too. The ones with the holes in them by that weird doorway."

"Keep going." He sounded comforting, almost like a teacher, but I thought I could hear tension underneath.

Hard to do without talking about you. "So... dead things come back to life here. The trees, definitely. And the bird."

And that means the guy who got crushed by the tree probably did too. And I think that guy was you. But I'm sure talking about that is forbidden.

I had a thought. "Wait a minute." I ran over to my suit. Accessed the recording. Went back two days, to when I'd gotten here. Before I shot the trees. I hoped I'd been close enough to them for it to record them. I looped through a few hours of video quickly, checking the times when I was over on that side of the camp and wearing the suit. There they were. All four, cut down. They'd been cut down, before I arrived. Before I cut them down. And now they were whole. And that meant...

"Is..." It sounded ridiculous in my head. "Is time running backwards here?" I shook my head. "No, it's not, or you would be... Wait." I shook my head again. The trees fell down when I shot them. And the fish. He'd eaten the fish, no question. "No, you ate the fish and spat out the bones. That was forwards. Lots of stuff has been forwards."

I was losing it. "You... you make sense, each day. We talk. You do things, they have consequences. It's not like you're running around backwards, undoing things. We're both moving the same way."

Elihar bowed his head, but he did not speak.

"You disappeared last night. And the trees appeared. Is there... a jump?" I didn't know quite what I was expecting. "You jumped backwards, by a day?"

Elihar took a step toward me. "Please don't talk about what I did."

Hold on. I latched onto that. "You never want me to talk about what you did. Or past conversations. But that's weird. Unless." I swallowed. "If you're going backwards in time each day, then if I tell you what you did, I'm telling you... what you will do."

Elihar bowed his head.

"Is that bad?"

Elihar put a pad hand on my shoulder. Weird. He hadn't touched me much before. "That is very bad."

"Why?" My mind was racing. "I could tell you what to do." I thought of the falling tree. "I could help you avoid . . . problems."

"If what you say is true, I could do the same for you. Tell your future. But I have not."

"Because you can't? So I'm wrong?" It was almost a comfort to retreat from my outlandish assertions.

"I didn't say that." He paused. "You have discovered enough, I think. Reached *sobalihem*. If that is so, some of the risks of speaking of these matters are lessened. But not all." That sounded like progress.

He continued. "You have noticed I do not wish you to speak of your past with me, and that I do not speak of your coming days. It is very bad to speak of someone's future with knowledge."

"Why?" I squeezed my eyes shut. "Please, tell me why." Pleading.

"I can tell you that, *sobaliharinika*, because it is a truth. A fact, and a warning. Not related to what has happened, or what will happen. It is just how this place is." He squatted down, sitting in the dirt. "We cannot discuss what will happen in the future because of the *renfit sharah*."

"The what?"

"The *renfit sharah*. The curse. It spreads its malady to all those who would bend time to their will, and to those who share knowledge they should not."

Curses were magic, and magic wasn't real. Except that dead birds were coming back to life, and somebody was carving my name into trees. "Curse?"

"To understand it, you need to figure out a little more about this world. About the phenomena you've observed. You're almost there. I am sorry, but I can't tell you all of it, or the *renfit sharah* may strike. Worse than it already has." He paused, and his head rotated just a fraction. A few eyes closed, and others rotated toward me. "You have reached *sobalihem*. The first understanding. That is good. That lessens the danger to you if I should speak of these things. But you still must get to full understanding on your own."

So infuriating. But I was beginning to see, just a little. "If you're . . . going backwards, then you know what I will do tomorrow, but you don't know what we did together yesterday. Which I know, and could tell you. Which is in your future, I guess. But you say it's bad for either of us to say anything about what we know. Is that because we might change what happens, what we do, with that knowledge?"

"We could create a paradox. It is hard not to do so, on such a world as this."

I pondered. "Am I going the opposite direction from you in time because I'm not from here?"

"Yes. But there's more to it."

"Right. Because if everything here went backwards, then it would just seem frontwards to you. Until we came, you'd have no inkling that there was a time reversal. So you must know about it. Have known about it."

He made his grunting sound. His laugh. "Do you think we do not observe the stars? The sun? The clouds? See them jump in the sky once a day? See the water and the rocks move and exist opposite the way we do?"

"Wait." This was making my head hurt. "So, not everything goes backwards. Of course it wouldn't. If your planet rotated or orbited backwards, it would just look like it was going the other way. And I know it jumps at night."

"Night here."

"What?"

"It happens once a day. It is not night everywhere then."

I stared at him for a moment before getting my brain around that concept. "Right. Because your planet rotates." I grimaced. "So the reset is at the same time everywhere on the planet. Some places it's at night, some during the day."

"Yes. We call this time *rakineru*."

"And that's when you see the stars jump, or the sun, or whatever. Because you're moving backwards, and they're going forwards. So whatever this effect is, it's localized to your planet." I squinted at him. "Wait. You're going forward now, with me, today. The whole planet is. So, there is a jump. It's discontinuous, or whatever you'd call it. You live in forward time, like normal, but with jumps backwards in time. In my time. That's why you vanished last night."

"Please, don't tell me what I will do."

"Right, sorry. The curse. But it's also why the trees came back. Because when they finished the day, they jumped back to the beginning of the day before. Their day before. Before I shot them. Which is why they were whole again." I thought about my name carved into them, now vanished. "But that doesn't explain it all. There's something else weird about them. Really weird. Other than me shooting them."

"Your discussion of shooting trees makes me somewhat uncomfortable."

"What?"

"Joking. I am a tree, or so you say."

"Oh, right." I laughed, and I felt the tension in me loosen, just a little. "If I shoot you, you'll just come back tonight, though, right?"

"But I'll have been dead yesterday. For you."

It took me a moment. "Right. But you weren't."

"Please don't tell me about my future." His tone was firm but gentle.

"Aagh." I put my head in my hands. "This is so hard." I thought for a moment. "So, I still have two questions. One is, if the whole planet doesn't go backwards, what parts do?"

"Which parts have you seen go backwards?"

"You. The animals. The trees." I thought some more. "But not water and rocks. You said that. Is it only living things?"

"Yes. More or less."

"More or less? What does that mean?"

"Dead things that were once alive also move backwards, for a time, until they lose their connection to the flow of life. Then they become as the rocks and soil, and they reverse and go as the rest of the world does. As you do. We call this *avishar*, and we think of it as a kind of second death. The first strips them of the functions of life, while the second fully detaches them from time." He paused. "Sorry, you probably do not want me to launch into a lecture."

"I absolutely want you to lecture. I've been asking for a lecture for days now."

His head spun around on its stalk. "What is your second question?"

"What is this curse you're talking about? The *renfit sharah*. What does it do? How does it work?"

"I cannot tell you, for fear of invoking it. But I think you can guess."

I thought for a moment more. "You are worried about me telling you the future. Giving you information you shouldn't have. Like, creating a situation where I know you do something in the future, but I tell you that you did it, and then you decide not to do it."

"A paradox, yes."

"And you must know my future. You've seen what I do tomorrow. But you don't want to talk about that either." I pondered this some more. "So is the curse just a spooky way to say you want to avoid paradoxes?"

"Unfortunately, no. It is a real and malicious effect."

"Malicious?"

He looked at me with a few eyes in turn. "What would you imagine the worst thing that could happen to a person might be? The thing that they would care most about? Short of dying, or the world ending."

"Um." I imagined a lot of bad things. Pain, suffering, loss. "I suppose it might be losing someone close to you. Someone you love." Kenzi. Otieno.

"Suppose something bad like that was the price to pay for forbidden knowledge."

"What?" I twisted up my mouth. "Forbidden by who? An evil god? Who kills your friends? That kind of thing?"

"I have not heard it described before in a manner so devoid of nuance, but yes. That kind of thing."

"You have an actual god who kills people out of spite? When you mess up the flow of destiny or something?"

"Not an actual god. A curse. We do not know how it happens, but we know it does. That is why we try to be careful."

I remembered something. "You said that you'd lost... I'm sorry, that you'd lost your spouse and your children. Was that to this curse?"

"It was."

I had a terrible feeling. "Was it... because of me? Something I did?" I tried to remember what I had told him.

"No, it is something I did, something I set in motion without meaning to. An accident, but one that has put my life on a different course."

"I'm sorry." I wanted to ask more, but I felt like that might be prying into something painful. And it might invoke the curse again, for all I knew. "Does the curse affect you if you just know the future? Or do you have to do something to change the future? Or does knowing the future always change it?" I was bewildering myself.

"Knowing the future and deliberately choosing a different path is the most dangerous. That most often results in the death of many loved ones, or even the death of oneself." He took a step closer to me. "Creating a simple paradox is less dangerous, but it sometimes triggers the curse if it has significant impact."

"A simple paradox?" I tried to imagine what that would be. "Wait. Like, I think you knew my name. When we first met." When you died, if it was you who died under the fallen tree. "I mean, when we first met in my experience, a few days ago."

"It was very dangerous of me to use your name then. I apologize. It is dangerous for you to tell me that I did. Please stop such discussions." He made a hissing noise. "But yes, that would be an example of a paradox. I had knowledge that you had not yet given me."

I did not want to explain that I now suspected it was him crushed under the tree, and that he was already dying when he'd said my name. But if he were the one who was struck by the tree, who died, should I tell him that? If I did, he could avoid his fate. And it seemed like that would invoke the curse in a big way. This was way too much responsibility for me, way too fast. I knew far too little about how this worked.

I looked across the camp, at the stack of boxes, at the rocky face, at the weird, alien trees, at the green sky. Elihar let me sit there in silence. Of course, I suddenly realized, he knew what I'd do, or at least what I'd be doing tomorrow. So maybe it wasn't stressing him out. Couldn't say the same for me.

Finally, I looked over at him. "OK, supposing I believe all of this stuff, which I hope you realize is utterly bonkers." Elihar inclined his round, spinny head at me. "You must have a purpose in bringing me out here and having me guess at all of it. Come to think of it, you must have a purpose yourself, especially if you're one of the only one of your people on the planet. That's pretty strange. Have you all gone somewhere? Or are you all dead?"

"No. We haven't yet been born."

45

DESTINY'S WILD

I stared at him. "What, now?"

"You found our cities. They're all in ruins. At least, the ones that were made of stone and metal."

"Right." I blinked, twice. "Wait, if you live backwards, then the cities haven't been built yet. They're not tens of thousands of years old. In your time, they will be built in tens of thousands of years."

"Correct."

"But then…" I paused. "Why are they here now? If you built them, wouldn't they go backwards too?" He looked at me. "No! They wouldn't. Because they're made of non-living objects. Whoa, that's super weird. You live backwards, but the things you build go forwards?"

"When we build with stone and metal, we do not do it as you do. It is problematic because stone and metal go opposite to us in time. This means we discover the things that we will later build, fully formed, or sometimes in decay. When someone discovers one of these sites, the *renfit sharah* normally strikes them immediately. This can exact a terrible price. But some of my people see these cities and buildings, these paradoxical discoveries, as a gift to us from our future. We can live in them and use them for a time, and then at the end of their lifespan, we must build them, day by day, to support our past selves. Yet every day we do this work is undone the following day, until there is nothing left."

I thought I was getting somewhere. "So, each city, each building, is a paradox – it is something you will later build. But if you find one, and then ignore it, and don't build it, then you'll be violating the rules, and you'll get cursed."

"Correct. Some of the worst curses come when we try to resist our destiny." He made a whistling sound, a noise I hadn't heard before. "Those who build the cities put all of us at terrible risk. The cities are full of paradox."

I thought some more. "Who's doing the cursing? Is there really an angry god?"

"There might as well be." Elihar sounded bitter. I had figured out his manner of expression by now, and I was amazed again that he'd learned human inflection so well. "You've gazed upon the face of this god already. At least, that is what I guess."

What did that mean? Oh, wait. It had to be. "The weird archway. Where I met you."

"Please, don't speak of my future. Although I might well have guessed."

"The archway hands out the curses?"

"I do not know. I did not know of it until recently. I know it is connected to the flow of time. If that is true, it seems possible the curses come from there as well. But perhaps not. Some of us believe that the curses are not intentional or malevolent, but instead just a natural result of our existence outside the normal flow of time. In this view, the ill effects are merely how time attempts to heal itself when it is violated."

That was weird. I didn't want to think about it too hard. Then I had more thoughts that were just as confusing. "Wait up. If your people aren't around now, and they haven't shown up yet, then you are . . . what, some kind of ancestor? Progenitor?"

He made his grunting noises. "No, I am hardly that. I'm just a simple scholar, who lived a normal life until it became disrupted. As a result of that disruption, I traveled here from my people's future. From your people's past."

"What? Why? How?" My cheeks felt hot again. "I mean, I guess that's no weirder than the rest of it. But why did you come?"

He looked at me but said nothing.

"You can't tell me, because it has to do with me." I swallowed. "Which means I'm involved. Which means you came here to meet me." Which was all kinds of bad. "Is the curse business really this literal? Like, if you don't speak it, but just sit there staring at me, that's somehow better?"

He grunted again. "Actually, yes, it is. Deliberate actions, such as the overt sharing of paradoxical information, are punished much more harshly than passive action, merely appearing and existing."

"Great, your unknowable evil god is picky and judgmental." I sighed. "I guess that's how they are supposed to be." I picked up a stone and threw it towards the water. "If you came here to meet me, then I'm supposed to do something here, something you know about, because you've seen my future." I grimaced. "But why would you come from long ago to do that?"

He stared at me for a long time.

I thought about the dying being's first words to me. The dying being who must be Elihar. He'd said my name. *Jess, my old friend.* He'd known me for a long time. "Oh, skogging…. Unless you knew I was involved somehow."

"I know some of your future, but not all of it. Not how it ends." He seemed to be picking his words carefully. "But before we go farther, before there is any more, I want you to consider what you wish to do."

"I don't understand. I don't know anything. How am I supposed to decide?" I sounded flat, petulant. I regretted that, but it was how I felt.

"I know of a path where we . . . continue to interact. I suspect the moment you choose that path is now, or close to now. But it is not the only path open to you."

"Didn't you just tell me that if I resist destiny, I'll curse everything I love? The worst curses?"

"That is true of my people. I have no idea if it applies to you. You are not of this world. The *renfit sharah* may not extend beyond this place, or the living things here."

"Can you tell me what I'm going to get involved with?"

He gestured with one of his vine arms. "I can't. That would invoke the full weight of the *renfit sharah* on me and anyone I care for." He paused. "And I do not think it would be fair to you, to urge you into something of which you only barely have knowledge."

I thought about what else was open to me. Alone on an alien world, low on supplies, with malicious and well-armed criminals hunting me down. I didn't like my odds there. And I didn't like the idea of incurring this *renfit sharah* thing, although I didn't know who it would apply to. I had barely anybody left I'd consider a friend, much less a loved one. Some of my service buddies, of course, but we didn't keep up too well, just on chat forums. And most of them didn't want much to do with me after the conviction. Juno – she was a good friend, at least within the confines of service and rank. But she was still in prison. Would it apply to Mariela, Otieno's wife? We'd written back and forth, sent messages and gifts, since the funeral. I couldn't bring harm to her.

Elihar seemed sincere, even if everything he said was bonkers. And the guy had died to find me. Or would die. Just to bring me here, to face this question. That had to count for something. And he had called me friend. Not many willing to do that. And calling me friend would be the last thing he did, I realized. That was sobering.

I remembered Otieno's advice. *I think you'd be happier somewhere new, somewhere maybe far away. Maybe somewhere without a lot of people.* That was part of why I'd taken this job in the first place. But palling around here with time-traveling trees didn't seem like exactly what she had in mind.

In the end, it wasn't hard. This adventure, whatever it would be, kind of fit what Otieno was describing. More or less. And I was out of options, and out of other causes to live for. In the human world, I was detested, friendless. Hunted. I took a breath. "All right. I'm in."

Elihar's head spun around three times, and his viny arms flailed. I suspected he might be pleased. Either that, or he was having a seizure. But then he spoke. "I am so glad." He inclined his head and body toward me. "So glad."

"Right. Er..." I didn't know what to say. I barely knew what I was getting into, and all of this was hard to process.

One of his hands whipped up, then tapped his head. "You raised an issue, one that may bear exploration."

"What's that?"

"You mentioned that there was something else puzzling about the trees." He was being vague again. Choosing his words carefully.

What did he mean? That they'd come back to life after I shot them? I had an explanation for that now, no matter how outlandish. Oh, wait. "They had my name on them." That still creeped me out.

"I see." I couldn't tell if he was surprised. I thought he should be. I skogging was.

I waited for him to say more, but he didn't. That probably meant he was trying to get me to realize something. Probably a paradox. I thought. Then I spoke, slowly, trying to roll all this up in my mind. "If yesterday is tomorrow, and the trees had my name on them then..."

"Yes."

"...and they don't now, then..." I squinted. "They have to get my name carved into them today, which is the last chance before tomorrow. Their tomorrow. Which is yesterday." My brain was tired.

"Yes." He sounded encouraging this time.

"So who does it, then?"

"One of us is a lot better at writing your name than the other."

I felt a flash of anger. "You want me to write it?"

"You must have."

"Why? Why would I do that?"

"I don't know. Perhaps you enjoy defacing other living entities."

Funny, tree man. I'll carve my initials in you someday. But the whole thing still bugged me. "What happens if I just don't? Do the letters vanish tomorrow? I mean, yesterday?" Dammit, this was hard. "Do our memories of them go away? Just vanish?"

"If you don't do it, then you won't have seen your name on the trees. That might have been the nudge it took for you to focus. Many young ones have such a nudge, a triggering event, for *sobalihem*. Without it, you might not have figured all this out." Elihar's gravelly voice grew more serious. "But there is more danger here. Changing a future event whose effect you have witnessed in the past – that is the worst kind of paradoxical transgression. The curse nearly always punishes such an action."

I bristled at that. Not really at Elihar, although the guy was being annoying. No, I was angry at the world, which was forcing me to do something foolish that made no sense, just to preserve a timeline full of inconsistencies. I was tempted to just refuse to be bullied in this way. To see if Elihar was right, or if I were immune to the curse. To see what happened if I resisted this oppressive invisible authority. I clenched my jaw and let my anger have its time in the sun. Then I let out a slow breath, and my tactical brain took over again. No point in screwing with fate here. This place had already killed a ton of people, a lot of them right in front of me. Best not to make the planet mad.

I powered off the replay console on my suit and turned to look at the trees again. Dammit. Dammit three or four times over. "Let me get my knife."

46

PAST TENSE

The day that followed came in a rush. I learned a lot of important details, although I still felt woefully unprepared. Most of what I learned was from me guessing at what had happened in Elihar's past and my future. He was pretty cagey about admitting any of it, but I got to where I could tell. It still seemed bonkers that speaking of the future mattered. It almost felt like I was back in the service, and there was an Investigative Branch officer watching over what we did and said, and I had to make nice. But Elihar took it much more seriously than that.

I figured out one key thing, one achievable goal, or at least the parameters of that effort. What was called for next was a small unit operation against a superior foe. A very small unit, i.e. me. But I could do that. Had done it. And I was pretty good at it, or at least I had the overconfidence you needed to take on any field operation that might get you killed. And the foe, these SpearPoint skogs, were unquestionably the bad guys. They were killing innocent people and seriously pissing me off. Time to dust off my field manual and my training and bring the fight to them.

One big thing I learned as I talked with Elihar was that he had been born (sprouted, more like) and had lived most of his life (albeit backwards) back in the days when the cities thrived and were full of people like him. Elihar wasn't entirely clear on how far through time he'd traveled to get to me, but if Welk's dating estimates had been correct, it was probably at least fifty thousand years ago.

Another big thing I figured out, maybe the biggest, was that Elihar had first met me back then. Or, rather in my timeline, I would meet him back then. So, somehow, I was going to jump back in time fifty thousand years, before humans built cities and societies. Back when we were at the mercy of the wilderness, simple hunters and gatherers. That was wild. Elihar wouldn't tell me how I did it, but I had a pretty good guess. It had to be related to that archway I'd found. Or rather, the one that I'd been directed to from the note at the dig site, when Welk died. I would need to get back there and try something, but the way this world worked, I was pretty confident that whatever I tried would work, because Elihar had met me. It was destiny. Or so I thought.

Another thing I began to suspect was that when I met Elihar in the past, I was going the same direction in time that he was. Not opposite directions, like we were now. The reason for my suspicion was that he seemed new at all this. Each day that I advanced, and he jumped back in time, he grew more awkward and more ignorant of how I would experience things, even as I got smarter. That didn't seem like he'd dealt with it for a long time. I figured that, if I switched directions, that must have something to do with the archway as well, although I was hardly confident in my understanding how any of it worked. Elihar must have used it to come to me, and when he got out, he was still going backwards through time. So maybe whatever way you went in, you came out aligned to the world. I figured I could sort that out later.

All of that was fine. I was hazy on the details, but they'd work out. Or not. And uncertainty is something a marine lives with in the field all the time. Now that I knew I had a destiny, it seemed reasonable to let it happen to me, at least the good parts, and at least as far as it went. I knew I would go to the past and meet Elihar, and that I must have become friends with him back then. That was about all I knew, but it was a start.

Elihar spent a lot of his time scribbling furiously on his wooden tablets. I wasn't sure what he'd been working on, but he'd been doing this a lot. It turned out he had a ton of room to write. The tablets could be flaked off much thinner than I'd anticipated, and he spent his days leaving sheets full of writing around him at the campsite, at least until he gathered them all up at night. Of course, each day, his stack of completed sheets shrunk, because he was moving backwards through time towards when he started the project. It was hardly the weirdest thing I'd run into here, but it was a little disconcerting.

I spent most of my time planning what to do and when, from the bare bones on up. I felt some time pressure, although I didn't know exactly what I was up against. I didn't know if I could take anything through the portal, and I was worried that all the humans who'd messed with the archway were dead, as far as I knew. I was coming up with a plan, though. I needed to get back to the archway, and I figured I shouldn't bring any human technology through it. The planet's odd relationship with time affected only living things. I was coming to the realization that I'd probably have to walk through it stark naked. I would feel a lot more comfortable going through in my suit, but I really didn't want to get a massive hole put through me, and it had reacted poorly to human tech before. It could get a little awkward if there were any other humans around when I went back.

I mused about that, and then another thought occurred to me. I went over to Elihar. "Hey, Elihar. Still writing, I see. Must be important."

"Yes." He paused in his task, his stylus still touching the current tablet.

"I have a question for you, one that's been bugging me." I paused. I couldn't think of how to ask in the indirect way he preferred, where I posed an answer to a question and he either challenged it or let it stand. "I am wondering how you learned my language."

He was quiet for a long moment. "I had a good teacher, one particularly suited to me. My people are gifted linguists, so it did not take too long to learn to make your words and sounds. Nearly every being on this world communicates through sounds and vibrations, and we are particularly sensitive to those emanations."

He'd dodged the question, but he had given me a little bit to go on. "If you were taught by a native speaker, odds are that speaker was probably me." He didn't say anything, which was usually his way of confirming what I'd just said. "But I can't figure out how I'd possibly teach you anything about my language without knowing any of yours. I mean, that would take forever."

He looked at me further. "I see no flaw in your analysis."

I grunted. "So I go back and meet you, and then we spend what, five years getting you fluent in Tradespeak? That's going to waste a ton of time. I'm not bad at picking up languages, with help, but teaching is different, and not something I know how to do."

He didn't say anything, but I supposed it made sense that he wouldn't. The curse and all. Instead, he started writing again, which seemed a bit rude. After a moment, he peeled off the top layer of his tablet and threw it on the ground. Not near the other sheets he'd been stacking up, but over near me. It seemed like that might be an invitation. I glanced down at it.

Unlike the first day, when he'd shown me their alphabet and how to write my name, the tablet here was a mix of his writing and mine, although mostly his. Sounds spelled out in letters I could read. His handwriting was crude, like a child's, but legible. There were little sketches. Parts of speech. Verbs, pronouns. I picked up some of the other tablets. Again, a mix of words I could read, in my language, some with pronunciations, and then a lot of his words, written out in the odd little pictorial characters.

It clicked. "*Skogol*, Elihar. You're making a dictionary."

47

FUTURE SHOCK

Two more short Kenai days passed. By then, I'd done all the planning I could think of, asked all the questions I wanted to, checked the maps and committed them to memory, studied the sites I'd visited on my suit's recordings. Made my plans, checked my ammo, and cleaned my weapon. I sealed up my bag. "I think I've done all I can do here. I'm headed out. Going to go to the archway, try to go in, and see what happens."

Elihar tossed an eel into his neck slot and lowered his head down to its normal position. I'd found him a good way away from the center of camp, over in the direction where he went at night. I saw that there was a firepit here, one I hadn't noticed when I arrived. It had no ashes, so it seemed like he hadn't used it yet. I wonder when he'd dug it. Maybe he'd gotten cold during the night and wanted to change things up, although he'd never seemed to care about temperature. Burning things seemed like the opposite of what a tree person would want, though. Weird. Elihar reached out and touched my arm. His hand-pad was gentle, but the texture was rough. "I wish you good fortune."

"Isn't that inviting paradox?" I laughed. Then I wondered for a moment how luck worked on a world with actual supernatural curses.

He grunted. "May the dawn leave you whole, *etivar*."

"What is an etivar? You called me that before."

"It means outsider. Literally, one who appears out of the rain."

I laughed. "That would do a number on my hair."

"Eugh." His whole body quivered. The guy really hated hair.

"Hey, before I go. I've been wondering about something. I'm not sure you can answer, or that you even know the answer. I was working at a structure here, a ruin, buried in the ground. For us, that means it was built in the past. But the way the world works, it should be built in the future. My question is, where are the people who are going to build it? I don't see any other organisms like you here now. Nothing sentient, no mobile trees, no trees that even look much like you. There were no reports of anything like you in the survey briefings, either."

"I don't understand."

"We should be deep in your species' past. According to my friend Welk, you built those cities something like fifty thousand years ago, except for you, that's fifty thousand years in the future. If your world is like ours, we should be seeing your ancestors here, the ones who eventually evolved into your society. But we don't." I paused. I'd been thinking a lot about this. "We assumed you'd all died out, because you were gone, and your cities were in ruins. But now I know you live backwards. You shouldn't be gone. If you die out, it should be in the past. Which is your future."

"Perhaps your people took longer to develop sentience than did mine, and my culture will develop between now and the time your structure was built. Or perhaps my ancestors are merely somewhere you have not yet looked."

I still didn't like it. "I don't think evolution works that fast, but I don't know for sure. And I think we'd see your people from orbit if they were hiding out elsewhere. We're pretty good at scanning whole planets."

I thought more about Elihar's people, and how we'd assumed they died out. I remembered something Welk had said. "My friend Welk was studying radioactive isotopes, using them to date things. We saw evidence of a radioactive burst, a little older than your cities, way older than the ruins we were exploring." I thought some more. "If you live backwards, then that means the radiation comes from after your cities were built." I couldn't read Elihar. He wasn't moving, and he was completely still. "Sorry, am I using words you don't know? Radiation?"

"I know what radiation is." He squatted down on the ground, something I'd come to realize he did when he was unhappy. "We had discovered the poison permeating our forests, becoming stronger with each passing day."

"That's not how it works. It weakens as time passes, as the harder isotopes burn off." I'd studied nukes in training, along with all other weapons we knew of. I didn't know too much, but I knew that part.

"Remember, we live backwards."

Right, backwards. "So, if you see more and more radiation, then you know you're approaching a release."

"Or an explosion."

"Had your people discovered chain reactions? Nuclear fission?" I found it hard to imagine trees with nuclear weapons.

"Not my people, the Weynik people. But our enemies did."

"Enemies?"

"The Nurikna. Another nation or tribe. Another people. I don't fully understand those words, so I may be using them incorrectly. But they are a separate group of us, who live apart from us and follow different ways. The Nurikna are the city builders. My people do not work much with stone and metal."

There was a problem with that. "I'm assuming radioactive isotopes don't go backwards in time like you do because they're not alive. Nor would the metal casings, the canisters, the reactors, or any of the technology needed to concentrate and detonate a critical mass of uranium or plutonium."

"I'm sorry, I don't follow all of that."

"I'm saying, I don't know how you build a bomb when all the materials you're using to build it are travelling the opposite way in time from you. How do you even start?"

"The same way we build stone buildings. We discover them complete, or sometimes in ruins. As days pass, we do any work required to get them into the shape we found them in. Eventually, we come to the point when they are being constructed, and we do any work each day needed to build them, as a duty to our past selves. And eventually, we progress beyond when they were begun, and they just cease to be."

I wasn't sure what it said about me that I almost followed all that. Maybe I was getting the hang of this. "So, you're saying the Nurikna just found some nuclear bombs already made?"

Elihar slumped down further. "Worse than that. They found the bombs, yes, but one of them also discovered the secret of their construction, delivered through metal and machines, so that the information would travel back to them. They got not only the bombs, but also the instructions to make them, and all the other technology they would need."

"I'm new at this, but isn't that a paradox?"

"Undoubtedly."

I was trying to follow all this. "Doesn't that mean the curse, the *renfit sharah* thing... Wouldn't it really not like that?"

"Correct. That was a very bad thing to do. I have no doubt that the Nurikna involved paid a high price. But perhaps they did not care about the price. The Nurikna live by a different code, a harsher one."

I was still struggling a bit. "But, if you're willing to pay that price, you get access to science like that?"

"The price in this case was higher still, I fear."

"What do you mean?"

"We discovered villages becoming sick, the soil and water poisoned with radiation. Our people sickened and died, and each day it became worse."

I was starting to figure it out. "You were living in the aftermath of a nuclear explosion, maybe a lot of them. And because your time runs backwards, you were getting closer and closer to it, not farther away."

"That is correct."

"That means you were... You were doomed." I finished putting on my suit. Almost ready to go. But I knew this conversation was important. I stopped my preparations and just listened.

Elihar spun his head, then grabbed it with his three arms. "That is how it seemed. We tried to figure a way around it. We traveled to other locations, hoping to avoid the poison, but everywhere we went was also radioactive. Whoever had assaulted us had destroyed everywhere we could think to go. When they sent the bombs, they knew where we were, where we had gone. There was nowhere we could go to escape."

What a terrible thing, to know your people were doomed. It seemed Welk's radioactive burst, the one he'd detected in the soils, was from a nuclear war, one that had probably taken out Elihar's people, the Weynik. But that meant the others – the Nurikna - had maybe won. If anybody ever really won a nuclear war.

I thought some more. "I'm sorry, Elihar. That sounds terrible. I don't mean to be selfish here, though, and I don't want to mess anything up, but I don't see... I don't see what I could possibly do to help you. I know you said I showed up back there, but I don't really..." I trailed off.

Elihar perked up. "You did something tremendously valuable. Or rather, you will do it. You will bring us hope."

48

HEY, BUDDY, OVERHEAR

"Control, this is Chief James, Fox Squad. The new set of researchers is here. The physician you sent has completed field inspection of the bodies and is requesting evac for shipboard autopsy. Over." The man's voice was firm, audible even over the thirty meters separating us.

"Roger, James. Evac authorized. Use the T126 on site." I was lucky this conversation was relaying over a field comms unit. That meant I could hear both sides. Normally, it would have gone direct to his suit, but he wasn't wearing his. He was wearing a standard suit undergarment, though, all smooth and shiny and body-contouring. I wondered why he'd taken the suit off. Suits like the assault suits these people used were too bulky and clumsy for detail work, and it sounded like he'd been helping with the camp's logistics. He might have taken it off for that, but that was a little careless in a hostile zone. I glanced over to the far side of the camp. His suit was in the field charger there, and the light was orange. That meant less than 10%. He'd needed a charge after a few days of deployment. That was an even better explanation. The voice from the comms unit continued. "Any initial findings about the bodies? Rivald wants to know. Over."

James fiddled with his pistol, lying on the table next to the comms unit. Nervous, maybe. "The physician reports massive unexplained trauma from energy discharge. From where they were positioned, it seems very likely it's related to the artifact. I don't see another option. Nobody here would have weapons that could do that. I mean, I don't even know what weapons those would be." I agreed with his assessment.

He continued. "My suit's on the fritz. Draining power way too fast. There's something wrong with it. Abadi is the only qualified pilot here. The civilian teams can't fly the transport. If Abadi goes, that will leave only two of us here. Over." Actually, it would leave only him, but he didn't know that yet. If he'd been wearing his suit, squad biotracking might have shown him that his subordinate had flatlined. Well-placed rifle fire to the face would do that to a guy. Lowering his helmet bubble had been a tactical mistake, and I was a good enough shot to take advantage.

There was a pause before a reply came. "James, your caution is understandable. There's no sign of anybody in the area, and it's been quiet for the last few days. We assess the risk is low. And we will send reinforcements with Abadi upon return. And a new suit for you. The two of you remaining are well-armed and experienced."

"Well-armed and experienced didn't help Viper Squad or Wolf Squad. There's something really wrong going on down here. There has to be a bigger force here somewhere. One security guard couldn't have done all this. Somebody shot the hell out of the sentry turret here, too. Looked like heavy weapons. We need more firepower down here." He sounded unhappy. I smiled. At least somebody appreciated my handiwork.

There was another pause, then a different voice came on. "James, this is Commander Rivald. I hear you. We're trying to piece it together up here. Viper and Wolf were likely hit by the same assailant. That's the unknown party. We think it might have been a field operative from the *Deimos*, sent down for some reason before we took it out. We haven't been able to track them, but we do have some good news. We found the suit they used, unoccupied, left behind. It was one of ours. They turned off the recording, but it's pretty clear they stole a suit from Viper and used it on

Wolf. But the good news is, they don't have it now. And there's been no sign of them for six days."

"Why would they give up a suit like that?" James sounded agitated. "That might just mean they have something better. And how do you know it's one person? Who is it who attacked the turret here? I really don't like this." He started pacing in front of the table where the comms unit sat. "Have you figured out what happened to Viper?"

"They were careless. Really careless. Rostik decided to take a nap while they waited, and Trabelsi got picked off outside while eating lunch. Those were stupid decisions in retrospect, but they weren't expecting any resistance. You are. You know what's up now. Just stay alert, and we'll get you reinforcements."

James snorted. "We don't have that many people left."

"We have enough." The voice turned serious. Rivald. I needed to remember that name. "Do I need to remind you that you're under contract, and that the pay rate is even higher now than initially promised? The loss risk clause kicked in when the others died, so everybody's getting one and a half, retroactive to the start of the op. That is, assuming you follow orders and accomplish the tasks assigned." His voice turned harsh at the end. I'd heard that kind of talk before. A promise and a demand. "James, I need to hear that you understand. If you don't follow orders and procedure, you'll get nothing, and we can drop you off with the Patrol." Ooh, a threat as well.

James sounded angry. "I understand, sir." I could see his face twist up. "Get me more people and more weapons. And a suit that holds a skogging charge. I'm not going to be responsible for any part of this disaster if you don't. Over."

"Understood, James. We will. It will be a few hours. Just hold the area. The two of you are well-equipped, even without the suit." A pause. "Do well here, and we can see that you get paid even more. There's a lot to go around for bonuses. A promotion is guaranteed as well. Just do the job

I know you can do. You're a good officer. You've got this. Control out."

James looked at the comms unit for a while. Then he pressed a button. "Abadi. You're cleared. Take the civilians up. Khatun and I will guard the site. Get back here as soon as you can. I mean it." He stabbed a finger at the console to turn it off, then slapped the table. Hard. Three times. He gritted his teeth.

I'd been where he was. Angry at higher-ups who'd screwed me over, in the middle of something that was going far worse than previously imagined. I almost felt sorry for the guy. Of course, he was a murderous criminal mercenary. Just like me. But on different sides. I brought my rifle up to my shoulder and centered his temple in the crosshairs. He was my last obstacle. Just needed to wait for the sound of the ship departing.

49

Arch Rivals

The cloudy archway stood before me, mist swirling. One of the bird things made a screamy sound not far off. I had stopped walking. Not frozen, just a gut check. This was almost definitely stupid. It was dangerous. I was walking into a hidden alien site on a distant world. And I was stark naked. At least I was guaranteed to look foolish no matter what happened next.

I might die here, a giant hole blasted through me, like the others I'd seen. Or I might just wink out of existence. Or I might be transported tens of thousands of years into the past, never to return. Or I might walk up there, smash myself against the mist, and not be able to go in. Then I'd have to get dressed and leave. That would be awkward as hell.

My weapon and suit were cached nearby. Not impossible to find, but hidden and powered down. I'd had a good meal from the camp supplies. And I'd thrown a tarp over the guy I'd shot. The second guy I'd shot, that is. I'd done all I could to stall this. There wasn't anything left to do.

I stepped up to the arch and put out my hand. The mist was cooler than the hot, humid air of Kenai. I pushed my hand through, and the mist allowed it to pass. It felt damp, but that might have just been the drop in temperature.

I was messing around. I needed to steel up and go. I took three steps forward, feeling the coolness wrap around me. And then I was through.

I don't know what I was expecting. A chamber with a backdrop of stars. Weird brain people in robes. That kind of thing. But it was just like the inside of a house. An artsy house, maybe. Smooth, curved walls like polished stone, but featureless and gray. Lit from glowing panels set at the top of the arched ceilings. Carvings set into the ceilings, strange symbols with lots of curving lines attached, threading through them. I was in a chamber, and a hallway led off to the left, a little narrower than the entry.

I cast a glance behind me. There was no doorway there, no mist. The room I was in had only one exit, forward. Had I been transported somewhere, or knocked out and carried? It didn't feel like I'd lost any time. I straightened up, hitting attention pose for a minute, because I'd always found it made me more confident. Time to meet my destiny. Or some aliens. Wish I weren't doing it with my ass hanging out.

The corridor opened into another round room, larger than the first. It had more of the strange writing, or decorations, or whatever it was. It also had a sheet of what looked like clouded blue glass set into the wall, following the concave surface, oval in shape. On either side of that were two small side arches, shorter than the height of the room. They looked like the one outside, through which I'd entered, surrounded by the norodium blocks. They had mist blocking the view through as well. In the center of the room was a pillar reaching from floor to ceiling, inlaid with more of the strange characters. Unlike the room's walls, it was metal. I thought it might be norodium, like the bricks. It had the same silvery sheen.

I stopped, unsure of myself. Two exits, two ways forward, presented themselves. I had no way to choose. I looked at the markings. They were intricate and varied, but I could see no pattern in the chaotic web of symbols connected by curving lines. And then there was the pillar. Should I do something with that? I thought not. You didn't go into somebody's house and touch all their stuff.

The blue glass illuminated, and a cube appeared, as if on a display screen. The cube rotated around several axes. It was a pale pink, and it had some more of the intricate markings, one on each face. I had no idea what it meant. Perhaps it was an image of whoever built this place. Perhaps it was about to offer me a great deal on life insurance.

Then it spoke to me. I couldn't tell where the sound was coming from – it seemed to permeate the room. But the cube twitched in time with the sounds. "Trial Erdion control algorithm present and active, status quiescent. Perturbing agent protocol activated. Perturbing agent present in control center. Intuiting outcomes. Probability matrix constructed."

"What?"

"Elucidate unclear concept, perturbing agent." The voice had no inflection or accent at all, just bland words.

"Uh... Who are you?"

"Control algorithm, Trial Erdion."

"That doesn't help."

"Elucidate unclear concept."

"What is this place?"

"Control center."

"For what?"

"Trial Erdion."

"What's Trial Erdion?"

"Present trial. 611 trials allocated. 487 completed, 53 in process, 71 awaiting initialization.

"And what is the trial? Can you describe it?"

"No further trial information permitted perturbing agents."

Even in space caves, there was a skogging need-to-know. Great. "How do you know my language?"

"Define language from your perspective."

"How you're talking to me."

"Subdimension of probability matrix indicates most probable interactions to produce intended meaning based on all temporal instances and external referents. Perturbing agent deemed likely to respond to vibrations based on compiled anatomical, electric, and historical data. Vibration spectral analysis indicates simple symbolic relations likely.

Failure probability 0.7787 times ten to the minus 64th power."

What. "You just make noises that you think will probably mean something?"

"Yes. All other sound combinations less likely to produce optimal results."

"And what's an optimal result?"

"Perturbing agent needs to continue to affect trial to ascertain impact and outcome. Interval spent here is of minimal value to that purpose."

"You're making the noises that make me leave faster?"

"Yes. Rapid departure minimizes divergence except in cases comprising probability 0.3345 times ten to the minus 44th power."

"What if I stay just to spite you?"

"Outcomes containing that fork were included in matrix. These outcomes are likely to range from unchanged to less optimal, even when cross-analyzed from perturbing agent perspective."

"Huh?"

"Also, your trial subject friend requires your assistance. And I will also say please. Please."

"Well, when you put it that way."

"Rapid departure is optimal. Resulting pattern inversion paradox becomes difficult to analyze if you do not go."

"And that's a bad thing?"

"Trial termination result possible. 0.0013 probability and growing."

"Trial termination? What's that?"

"Cessation of trial. Forced extirpation of trial subjects."

I was taken aback. "You mean, you're going to kill everyone?"

"I said please."

"Am I a trial subject?"

"Negative. You are classified as perturbing agent."

"How did I get to be classified that way?"

"Entering multiple paradox loops beyond stability threshold despite disincentivization feedback. Classification as perturbing agent was required to realign probability matrix and retain trial integrity. Trial Erdion reclassed from original isolated trial status to perturbation modulation status."

I didn't know what that meant, but it sure sounded like a message I'd heard a lot in my life –something had gotten screwed up, and I was to blame. "Look, I didn't ask for any of this."

"Your decision inputs brought you to this point despite significant disincentivization."

"What decision inputs?"

"Please, just go." The voice suddenly sounded mournful.

"Can't I ask more questions?" I wanted to know what I was getting into.

"I shan't answer, Jess." The voice was earnest now, anguished. "I can't. There's no time. You must go save your friends. It's the only way."

"How do I go? What do I do?" This was bewildering.

"Pick an exit."

"How do I know which one to pick?"

"Matrix indicates probability of suboptimal choice is 0.4857 times ten to the minus 13th power."

I looked at both archways. They seemed identical. I'm left-handed, I thought. I'll go left. I took a step forward.

"Good choice, Jess." The voice was happy now. Perky. "Participant notification protocol required. Please be advised parties classified as perturbing agents are subject to paradox disincentivization following normal practices."

"What?"

"Good luck! See you later, marine." The cube on the glass now started bouncing against the left side of the display over and over. After a few bounces, it started making a "boing, boing, boing" vocal noise with every bounce, like a little child at play.

I stood there with my mouth open, listening to the boinging, trying to understand all this. I wanted to ask more, to learn more. But I wasn't really getting anywhere. And the voice had said it wouldn't tell me anything else. And the boings were getting annoying.

"Fine. Whatever." I stepped up to the left arch, then pushed through. It was cold against my bare skin, just like the other, but it was dark inside.

50

THROWN FOR A LOOP

Dark   and   empty   and   backwards
andterribleandborninsideout—

The space I was in blasted into white hot illumination for an instant, and then my vision narrowed to a single point. I tried to take a step forward, but I no longer had legs or knew how to move at all. I merely was. A consciousness suspended. The point expanded back to whiteness, and then it faded, with shadows taking shape, fuzzy at first, then sharper outlines. Cones with… with fronds. The trees. I was on Kenai again.

I didn't recognize where I was. My mouth tasted funny, and my skin felt like it was either cold or burning or wet, but it was none of those. I realized that my perception of everything was heightened, like I was on field stims on a deployment, except my emotions weren't dulled. I could feel the Kenai organisms around me. The trees soaking in the damp air through their leaves and trunks. Tiny insectoids crawling among the decaying leaf litter. One of the bird-like beasts passing over, scanning for prey. A family of small lizardish weaseloids, parent and four cubs, making their way in a line across the roots and tangles of the forest floor. How could I know anything of these beings, these alien beasts? I had no clue.

Something felt as though it were missing. Like many absences, it was hard to pin down. But I felt disconnected from something important, as if these new connections I could feel had supplanted something else, something fundamental. I was abuzz with this world and my place in it, but there was loss, almost as if I were in a river being pulled along, and whenever I tried to fight the current, I was far too weak. But I could not tell what that river actually was, nor the current, nor my struggles. Maybe it was just a moment of panic born of disorientation.

I looked around me for a door, or any place from which I might have emerged. I saw none. Just the plain jungle landscape in which I'd lived for the past ten days. I realized there were scorch marks around my feet, burned into the leaves and soil below me. I must have come in hot. Or something. I was still naked. That suddenly bugged me, and I felt a twinge of shame, from a lifetime of habit and vulnerability learned a hundred suns away from here.

I heard something. The grinding snap of a weapon discharge. Rifle fire. Then a gasp, then a thump and crunch. Something heavy falling. My battle-born instincts threw me into a crouch before I even processed the noises. The analysis came later, and it lacked depth and useful detail. This was really not good. Not at all. I was hardly going to be able to defend myself. Other than maybe throwing myself at an armed opponent. Not likely to work, although I'd give them a good story to tell. That one time a naked lady popped out of the leaves and tried to tackle me. In my suit.

I got down on my belly, the forest litter scratchy and damp against my skin. I listened. Footsteps approached, distant at first, then closer, right up to the other side of the low rise against which I now lay. The footsteps continued, moving back and forth, but they weren't coming toward me anymore. This close, I could hear the subtle whine of mechsuit servos. They sounded similar to mine. Maybe the same manufacturer, although that didn't make much sense. Most of the Spearpoint gear had been Stellar Dynamics, pricier than what I could afford.

I heard some birds cry out above me. Jarring, given the tension. I flinched, then chided myself. I heard whoever it was doing something on the other side of the rise, but I couldn't tell what. Lots of steps interrupted by silence. I waited for some time. I didn't want to expose myself to the enemy, in any sense of that phrase. Then I heard two noises. One was the little chime of a rifle safety engaging. A tiny step in a positive direction. The other was the pop and hiss of a suit being disengaged, followed by the rip of the seam binding opening. Whoever it was, they were taking off the suit. Doing that after shooting something, or somebody, seemed like an odd choice.

Maybe this was my chance. Taking off a suit was a challenge, given how tight and bulky they were. The person would be busy, maybe disarmed. The suit sensors would be disengaged, probably. I might be able to take a peek and see what I was up against. It was either that or lie still, waiting for discovery. That didn't appeal to me. All it would take would be a few steps uphill and I'd be found out, face down on the ground. And my hiding spot wasn't great.

I put an elbow forward, cautious, and dug it into the ground in front of me. Pushed back with a foot. Slow, slow. There was a tiny rustle as I scraped forward. I could feel the leaves and twigs and clods digging into my front. I was going to be filthy, but that beat dead almost any day. And I was pretty quiet. Maybe it was enough. I rolled my hips, pulled up my other leg, put forward the other elbow, and pushed again. The sounds from the other side continued. Whoever it was, they were occupied with something. I moved forward again, painstaking, slow. Quiet.

I aimed my head towards a spot with some low plants. Their broad red leaves should give me some cover. I inched forward some more. Another quarter meter and I'd be able to see something, I guessed. I didn't rush it, but I got my head up there, crown of my head first. My black hair might be inconspicuous. I rolled my head to the side and lifted it off the forest floor, finding a window in the leaves through which to peer.

I saw a figure there. Dark hair, about my height, wearing bodysuit underwear. Like mine. Holy skogging...

It was me that I saw before me. I was stripping down to my skivvies. The dead Spearpoint merc lay face down on the table. James, his name had been.

I remembered all of this because I'd just done it. Before entering the portal. Before being talked at by the weird cube. I hadn't noticed somebody in the leaves watching. I hadn't expected anyone. Thought I knew the tactical situation. Thought I knew where my enemies were.

Well, I had. What I hadn't known then was that there was a copy of me, stalking me. Naked. Yikes.

What had the cube done? This wasn't good. Not good at all.

51

OUT OF BODY EXPERIENCE

I watched the other me gut check and head into the portal. I considered interacting with myself, but I thought that would create an instant paradox, and what the cube had said about disincentivization made me nervous. Also, I had nothing to say to myself at this point. I mean, I hadn't done anything in the last ten minutes that I could see a better way to do. Other than maybe "don't bother belly crawling naked in the mud."

One thing was a help, though. I could now be suited up and armed. I found some ZestiWipes in the camp supplies and wiped some of the jungle crud off my front, then put on the bodysuit and the mech suit. There I was. Same as I was a half hour ago, essentially. Except for taking out the mercenaries. And I was damp now and smelled of Zesti. What had I gained from going through the portal? Nothing, really. Re-experiencing ten minutes of time during which hidden naked me watched clothed me strip down. That had to be the most pointless and boring time loop ever. And also kind of creepy.

There was the confusing conversation with a cave-dwelling sentient cube, but I didn't know what that meant, really, other than that I was a perturbing agent now, which sounded kind of badass, actually. The only significant change seemed to be this weird sensory connection to the local flora and fauna. That was shifting to the background of my consciousness now, like a strong smell does after a while, but I could still pick it up.

There was not much else worth mentioning. Yet I'd been so sure this was the next step. Elihar had confirmed it. Or failed to not confirm it, which passed for confirming it with him. What to do next? I couldn't stay here. The ship would be back. And that would be bad because I'd killed two of their friends. I needed to go somewhere.

Nowhere to go, really. Same problem I'd had a few days back. No real change in the tactical situation. I resolved to do what I did then. Head for Elihar's retreat. Maybe he'd have answers. At least there was hot grub. I could be there in a few hours.

52

SOPHIST TREE

"You are back." Elihar spun his head and stared. I thought I detected a hint of surprise coming off him. No, not surprise. Something else. Sudden satisfaction, maybe. He continued. "And…"

"And what?"

"Nothing." I could still not read his expressions, but I had a strong feeling he was hiding something. That was new. I sampled my new sensory perceptions. I could feel some of the wildlife about, as at the other site. And Elihar was present, and warm. A big slab of consciousness in front of me. And he was nervous, I realized.

"I went through the house, or cave, or whatever it was."

"What cave?"

"The misty portal. Where we met. The one I told you I was going to. Come on, Elihar, you don't have to play that stupid."

"How was the experience?" He came closer to me and leaned against a tree. He pulled an eel bone off his shoulder and threw it into the woods. Trying to act casual.

"Disappointing, I have to tell you." I popped my suit seals. The suit's climate systems did a good job of keeping me dry, even when I went in kind of wet, but I still felt dirty. A swim would do me good. "I mean, it didn't seem to have any purpose. And I got naked and saw myself, but that was pointless too."

"I'm sure some purpose was achieved."

"The cube guy seemed to think I was up to something, but I really didn't understand all of that. Perturbing agent, he said." Still badass.

"I'm sorry, I don't know that term. Cube guy?"

"You know, the AI or whatever it was in the cave. On the screen. Who talked. And boinged."

A tang of fear. I could feel it coming off Elihar. That was new. He spoke after a moment. "I... I didn't see that."

"What did you see?"

"I..." More fear.

"You can talk about that. It's not a paradox, right? In the past for both of us. Neither of us were present, or will be, for the others' experience." I wasn't sure that was true, but I was tired of his evasions. "Which doorway did you choose?"

"There was only one. The one I entered, on the wall of the canyon." Confusion now.

"Right, that one, but once you were inside, there was right and left. I went left. After the cube guy got weird."

"I emerged on a hillside immediately after entering. My feet were on fire. It was painful, and it took some effort to extinguish them."

Now that was interesting. "No talking cube? What was inside the cave house for you?"

"I was never inside a cave. I was immediately transported." His head spun on its stalk. "Or rather, I moved in what seemed like an instant, although it brought me from what was apparently thousands of years in the past."

"No cave at all? No markings? No metal pillar? No chamber?" This was weird. But perhaps my status as perturbing agent made it different for me somehow.

"I do not have any idea what you mean." Confusion again, stronger, but with an edge of curiosity behind it.

I got the bodysuit off. "Well, that's strange, but I'm not sure what the point was. I came out a little before I went in, but otherwise not much seems different. Except that I can talk to squirrels. Ha ha. Not really. But I do seem to be better connected with nature or something." I ran my fingers through my hair. Revulsion from Elihar. I could feel it now.

And I noticed how his eyes got narrower at the same time. A tell? "Wow, you really don't like hair, do you."

"I'm sorry. I do not find most of your anatomy repulsive. This is boorish behavior on my part."

"It's fine. You're no Roman statue yourself. I'm going for a swim. And then I'm going to eat something. And then I'm going to take a nap. This has been a day." Even with the suit's help, going to the portal and back had been a long march, and combat, brief as it had been today, always left you a little spent.

"I see." He stayed still, pressed against the tree.

He was hiding something. I realized that now. I couldn't read his thoughts, but I was more aware of his attitudes, his emotions. Not strong, but a little hint. That could just be growing familiarity, I supposed, but I suspected it was related to whatever the cave had done to me. I gave him a long look, but I learned nothing from it. "Maybe tomorrow we can figure out something else to do, because your magic portal didn't work." He remained mute, guarded. "See you in a few."

The water was cool, at least by Kenai standards. It wasn't too comforting to know how many alien eels were in the water with me. I could feel them now. It was a lot more than I'd thought. I could pick them out with my mind, hiding in their little hollows on the riverbed, or as they darted away. They kept to themselves. I did too.

53

WOOD YOU CARE FOR DINNER

I came out of the water refreshed and a lot cleaner. I had tried not to think about this planet, this situation, this mess, but the tactical parts of my brain were worried. I'd had a good day by guerilla standards. Killed two, got to my objective, in and out, no tracking I was aware of. But that was sure to get their attention. I wasn't much of a threat before this, and now I was. I'd gone from target, from victim, to attacker. Before, they'd come for me. Now, I came for them. And their losses were mounting. Viper Squad and Wolf Squad, both flatlined, though by whom I didn't know. And now two more, thanks specifically to me. I was persona very non grata now, I bet.

I finally admitted to myself something I'd been sort of hoping or pretending wasn't true. They were probably watching the portal site from above. They might even have security cams on the site. I hadn't seen any, but they could have a WatchBot somewhere, or something even better. If they knew it was me, knew what my gear was, they might be able to figure some way to track me. My suit was in stealth mode, but I didn't know what kind of ship they had up there, or what kind of sensors. Probably nothing rivaling a Patrol ship, but on the other hand, it had taken out a Patrol ship. They'd had surprise on their side, though. Just like me, today. Their ship could be anything from a small, specialized bomber to a dreadnaught, although that would be hard for anybody but the Patrol to acquire. I had no real clue.

I pushed all that out of my mind. I was feeling all right, I thought, despite seeing action. I had been involved in enough firefights, endured enough training, that two justified battlefield kills weren't going to bug me. It had been a long while since I'd done it, though, and I didn't want to brood on that side of my work. Plenty of other more useful topics for brooding. I smelled something, something out of place. Tasty. Cooking meat? Why would that be here, in the middle of a rocky cleft in a jungle?

I got back to our camp beneath the trees. I was surprised to see that Elihar was off to one side of camp, the part where he often sat and wrote. The place where I'd talked with him this morning. In the firepit, he now had a small campfire going with a metal grate suspended above it. I hadn't seen him use anything metal before. He had a few of his eelfish critters on the grill, nicely trimmed, heads and tails removed. That's not how he ate them. He ate them whole and raw. But this smelled a lot better.

"What are you doing? I thought you people didn't cook?"

"You don't know that much about me or my culture." Smarminess. I felt it coming off him. "I figured I'd try something different. If humans like heat-altered proteins and fats, there must be a reason, right? Call it a cultural exchange." He was still guarded, underneath. Playing it light, but he was nervous.

I saw he had a little wooden cup with some leaves and little seeds inside, all mixed and crushed up. Could they be seasoning? "Wow, you going full gourmet on me? Do you digest the spices too, or do you just barf them out like you do with the bones?"

"Very funny." He picked up the eels one by one and flipped them, then sprinkled some of his mixture on them. They were a nice even brown. He was kind of good at this, and the heat didn't seem to affect the grabby hand pads at the end of his arms. Maybe he didn't have pain sensors like I did, or maybe he just didn't burn easily.

"I could try some, if you like. Tell you how you're doing."

"It's my first time. Maybe when I get better at it?" It sure didn't look like his first time. "Besides, eating food from the wrong world can be problematic, remember?" He spun his head a quarter turn and fixed an eye on me.

"Right." He had said that about food a couple times, but I didn't really get it.

"OK, I'll have some curry. Give me a minute and I'll join you." I went over to the supply crates and got some clean clothes. Then I found a nice lemon beef curry with rice. Well, it was all processed vat-grown protein and carbs, but they did a good job faking it. I pulled the heating tab, and the exothermic chemicals went to work. I missed real food, for sure, but I'd eaten field rations for long stretches before, and it was no big thing.

We ate, and we talked. He told me a little about his family. Their species were hermaphrodites, just like many plants I was used to. He and his partner – he referred to the partner as "she," probably for my benefit - had agreed that she would be the one to bear the seeds. It sounded like that was expected of her somehow, like a role she'd taken on. They'd gone through several seasons of reproduction – *eginfehr,* he called it. It was their tradition to create the seeds together and then plant them. They'd let them grow a bit, and then they'd pick a few who were thriving, doing the best, and weed out the rest. That seemed a little brutal, coming from my human perspective, but the whole business was alien and different, and I had no standing from which to judge. He and his partner, Miern, had raised their kids together over what sounded like a long time. He called it fifteen years, but I wasn't sure if it was local years or whether he was translating to human standard years for my benefit.

Apparently, his kids grew rooted for quite a while, a couple years, even. What was even weirder to me was that some of them just stayed that way. They never pulled up roots and started walking around, instead being just content to grow where they'd been planted. The *Dumisel*, the rooted ones, as opposed to *Renares*, the walking ones like Elihar. Nearly always, he said, these Dumisel wouldn't develop speech or even interact with the others, preferring instead to remain sedentary and still, just photosynthesizing. They grew thick and tall, without the viny arms and legs. Going Dumisel wasn't viewed as a failure, just a choice or a calling, a developmental turning point that all of their people went through as they matured.

I asked Elihar if he could recall his uprooting, and he said it was hazy – it all just kind of happened, and most of his consciousness of the world dawned at the same time, so there was a lot going on that he wasn't used to. It sounded a little terrifying, kind of like being thrust into consciousness plus undergoing instant puberty or something. He talked about seeing his kids uproot, and he sounded proud. He said that five of their twelve had uprooted, becoming Renares, with seven remaining as Dumisel.

I asked if the Dumisel ever reproduced, and he said they sometimes produced seeds, but they did it the passive way, just releasing and receiving windborne gametes. Like pollen, I supposed. They left it to chance. And their seeds were always Dumisel, no chance to go the other way. I asked if a Renares ever mated with a Dumisel, and I got an earful. It sounded like that was seriously taboo, something only degenerates did. Interesting to see some other examples of a moral code within their culture, along with the mysterious prohibition on talking about past conversations.

It grew late. I was tired, and full, and I'd had a hard day. I walked the camp perimeter out of habit, looking for anything out of place, and wanting to stretch my legs a bit before settling down, hoping they wouldn't cramp after the long walk that day. I was worried. If SpearPoint knew where we were, we were done for. So far, we'd escaped detection, and I hoped that would continue, but it seemed like we couldn't count on that.

As I returned, I noticed Elihar hadn't finished all his cooked eels. He'd barely touched them, actually. Maybe his culinary efforts had been a failure after all. He didn't throw them away, though. He set them aside, near his fire, still on the metal grate, close enough to stay warm.

I appreciated the fire's warmth. "I think maybe I'll sleep over here tonight. The fire's nice."

"Oh, good! I'm so glad." I could sense real enthusiasm in Elihar's voice. Relief, even. Weird. I went over to the other side of camp and got my sleeping bag, then moved it over to the fire. Elihar looked at me.

He was happy, I thought. Or that's what it felt like. "What?" I asked.

"Nothing." But it wasn't nothing. "Never mind."

I gave him a long look, but I was too tired to worry about it. Just a tree guy being weird. Nothing new. I scrunched down into my bag. As I drifted off, I realized Elihar hadn't gone away from camp like he usually did at night. Maybe he'd just go later.

After a few hours, I stirred in my sleep, drifting towards consciousness. I had this sense that something was coming. Maybe it was from a dream, but I thought I could feel that the other animals and birds, and maybe even trees, anticipated something as well. It was a strange sensation. I was still half asleep, but it was odd enough that I woke a bit more, feeling the jungle around me.

And then there was that tingling sensation that I'd experienced some nights. It was stronger this time. As it flowed through me, everything became cold. I was on the ground beside the ashes of the fire, which were dark and cold, where a moment ago they'd been warm. My sleeping bag had vanished. And so had my clothes. I was stark naked, lying on the forest floor.

54

A HARD DAY'S NIGHT

I had an instinct to shout, to give voice to my surprise, but my training kicked in. Don't draw attention. Assess, react, plan, act. The first thing I noticed was that my stomach hurt something awful. I thought I might have taken ill, but then I realized I was just famished. Tremendously hungry. My stomach gurgled something fierce.

Something was moving in the darkness. I tensed, but then I realized it was Elihar. He bent over me. "Jess. Speak very quietly, please." His voice was barely audible against the buzz of the insects around us.

"Is someone here?"

"No."

"Where's my sleeping bag? And my clothes?"

"They're over by your tent."

"What? Why?" I hissed a little from stress.

"Jess..."

"What is it?" I was really confused. "Why am I so hungry?"

"The food you ate was going the other direction."

"What? I threw up?" I couldn't taste anything. Especially not curry. He wasn't making sense.

"No, the other direction in time. You're going backwards now. Like me."

"What... what do you mean?"

"I assume your trip through the portal aligned you to the way this world functions." He was still speaking very softly.

I stayed silent for a moment, thinking. "So my clothes went to tomorrow, and I went to yesterday? Today is yesterday?"

"I don't have the facility with your language to evaluate that statement fully, but I think you've got the idea."

I thought some more. "My food – it's not from here either. So when the day shifted, it vanished?"

"Not vanished. Just went forward, while you went back. That's why you're hungry." I imagined a bunch of half-digested curry sitting on the forest floor. No, not on the forest floor, inside my empty clothing, which would be inside my sleeping bag. That would be a mess. So weird.

Elihar held out something in the darkness to me. It smelled good. I held out my hand to take it. It was warm, flexible. Food? I brought it closer to me. Smelled it. Barbecued meat, I thought. The eels he'd cooked. I looked up at him. "You knew. You knew this was happening."

"I suspected. You no longer smelled so much like an *etivar*. But I thought if I told you, I might invoke the *renfit sharah*. I wasn't sure. I've never seen anyone reverse before."

He'd known something important, and once again, he'd hidden it from me. I found I didn't like Elihar very much right then. I didn't know what to say that wasn't just a lot of cussing. I was very hungry, though, so I ate some of his food. It was smoky and a little tough, but he'd cooked it well. A little bland, with a hint of salt. Good texture. I gnawed away at it, pausing to pick out some bones. Elihar watched in silence.

As my hunger abated, a realization occurred to me. A really weird realization. "If it's yesterday, then... then I was in the camp then. I slept here."

Elihar pointed over to my tent. "Why do you think I'm speaking so quietly?" Oh skog. I was over there, too. Forwards me. "It would be best if you could get out of camp. As soon as possible."

I agreed. But I had issues. "I'm naked. This is weird." I'd spent far more of the last day naked than I wanted. "Is there something I can wear?"

"There's a second set of supplies north of here about an hour's walk. Look for a very tall tree with red leaves. Extra clothing, another sleeping bag and tent. You'll lose your clothes at night when the time shifts, but you can put them on again if you finish each day where you begin it."

I could follow that, I realized. Even though it was weird. Then something occurred to me. "Who left that there for me? The same person who left this equipment here?" My mysterious benefactor. I never had figured out who that was. I should have asked about that, but there had been a lot going on, and Elihar was terrible at answering questions.

Elihar just looked at me.

Oh, skogging skog. "It's me, isn't it? I left all this stuff here. Or I will."

55

REINTEGRATION

Mariela put her hand on my shoulder. "Are you ready to start working again?"

"I think so. I'm heading out to Reynos after classes wrap up, and I've got a couple of possibilities there that might turn into something. That part's all right. It's just..." I frowned. "I've had trouble making friends. Or keeping old ones. I think that's why I came here, to see you." I smiled. "How pathetic and obnoxious of me. Imposing myself on you."

"I'm glad you came. It's good to see you again. It makes me glad to hear what you're doing, how it's going." She picked up her mug and drank. "You remind me of Atich."

"Because I'm a sad-sack war criminal she tried her best to help, even when I made it hard?" I smiled.

"That's part of it. But you remind me of her as a person, too."

I could not fathom what she meant. "Otieno – Atich – she was kind, and peaceful, and smart, and calm. I'm not any of those things. I couldn't be more different from her."

"You're wrong. She cared about people. I think you do, too."

"You must not have read my prison file." I hoped she hadn't.

"I think you changed in there. Despite yourself. And Atich helped you become something different. Or at least, focus your instincts differently." She smiled again. "I like to think that's

the case, anyway. I think you do want to help people. I really do."

I gave a little laugh. "There's almost nobody in my life at the moment. The conviction and prison make me toxic to my old buddies, the ones that aren't in prison too."

I'd written to Juno, still serving her life term on Vylos. I apologized for my part in the mess, thanking her for looking out for me. Commiserated about the parts of the conviction that I was still angry about, which was a lot fewer parts than when I'd gotten sent away. Juno had written back. It was nice to hear from her, but her message was formal, bland. I thought the prison might be censoring her. It didn't seem like her voice. Or maybe her voice had changed.

I continued. "I've gotten over some of the twitchiness and distrust. That took a couple months. Outside, not everybody is looking to kill you or steal your things, it turns out. That's kind of refreshing." I sighed. "But the ex-inmates in my classes are all focused on other things, new things. And anybody else I meet eventually looks me up." And then came the staring, the silence, the uncomfortable shifting away. "I've thought about changing my name, just trying to vanish, but I don't want to." I didn't quite know why that was. I think I was too proud. I knew that I'd been part of something terrible with RazorCorp. I admitted that to myself now. But I also knew I was a tool for others. People who were more guilty than I was, than Juno was. Who hadn't paid any kind of price.

I was used to being a tool. That's what you are as a marine, and also as a mercenary. It's what you sign up for. But you're not exactly just a tool, because you can still make moral and ethical decisions, even if you don't have complete control or information. I hadn't stepped up in that area, and people had gotten hurt. I'd paid the price. And so had the village on Treyna. A much higher price. But even with all that, all the hushed tones, the wide eyes, the staring, the unanswered messages, the avoidance, I didn't want to give up my name. My identity. For one, it felt like dodging responsibility. Slinking away. That wasn't me. For another, it felt like I'd lose the only piece of myself I still had that mattered. Who I was, what I had been, what I had become. I didn't want to disavow that, even as hard as that choice was making my life.

Mariela was looking at me. "You said in your message you had something to show me."

I'd been brave when I wrote that. Wasn't so much now. "It's not... It's not necessary. I don't really know what I was thinking. It's not something you'd want to see."

"What is it?" Mariela's voice was kind. "I'm happy to see something important to you."

I twisted up my courage. This was a big ask. "It's a recording. My mom made it for me, back before she died." I could feel a lump in my throat. "Just as I was in the middle of basic training. She was so sick, but she took the time to let me know she was thinking of me, and of the life I'd have after she was gone." I swallowed. "It made me feel wonderful, and sad, of course. But mostly wonderful." I swallowed again. "I haven't watched it since I got out, but I want to. I thought that maybe I could watch it with somebody. With a friend."

"Why haven't you? It sounds like it would be nice for you." Mariela studied my face.

"It would be, I think." I felt my eyes get wet. "It's just... I think she and my dad would be so disappointed in me. So horrified by what I was part of, and of the conviction, and the prison. Even though it wasn't all my fault. But some of it was. It's just... the shame of it." I made a wet snorting noise, and Mariela put her arm around me.

"I never met them, but it's been my experience that people who love you deeply go on loving you unless you fundamentally change who you are. Especially your parents. If they're good people."

"But I did change. You said I did. I'm a war criminal. Convicted. Infamous. Reviled."

"Careful now, you're insulting my friend." She smiled. "Those are changes in status. In labels. They're not who you are." She looked at me for a moment. Her coffee let off a continuous strand of white steam, coiling upwards. "Those labels were put on you. They are how you started your sentence. The change I was talking about was after that.

Changing back to who I think you are. You've been through a lot, for sure, and it affected you. You're older, wiser, maybe. And damaged, but healing. But none of any of it changed who you are as a person. And that's good. I think you're a good person, and you always have been. You just got caught up in something bad." She put her mug down again. "I've read a lot about it, you know. The original reporting, the groups trying to investigate after, the conspiracy fringe, the RazorCorp sightings enthusiasts."

Huh. I hadn't expected that. "I haven't gone into that. Otieno said it would not lead to anything good for me. That I should move on, get it behind me, build something new."

"Oh, she's right. But I have a lot of time on my hands, and it's fascinating, watching something go so wrong for so many people and then echo around afterward, in dysfunctional and harmful ways. It's not unrelated to my research, you know. But that's not my point. The point is, you were there, and you were part of it, but you were doing what you'd been trained for, in the way you'd been trained. And you were you, through all of that. Still are. You had it rough in prison for a while. Almost became somebody else, almost gave up. But you came through it. With Atich's help. And I think you've atoned. And grown. And worked on yourself." She patted my arm. "I think your parents would recognize that. And they'd support you, unconditionally. And love you. The way they always did."

Tears ran down my cheeks. "I don't think you're right. But it's nice to think they might." I would never know.

"Let's watch your mom's recording. I think you deserve to hear her love you again."

56

PAST MUSTER

It wasn't just the supplies. A whole bunch of mysteries were now becoming much clearer. One was the note left in the pit. That had confused me, but now it made sense. *This is for real, and I'm a friend. Yomo Code.* Not quite accurate, unless one could be a friend to themselves. I didn't know. Didn't seem like I ever had been. But that's how the mysterious assault trooper knew Yomo Code. She was me.

And that meant I had to commandeer an assault suit and blow away two heavily armed troopers back at Welk's camp in a little under a week. And I'd have to get the assault suit the same day I used it, because even if I could get my hands on a suit, when I hit the witching hour, the suit would go into the future while I went into the past. I'd be naked again. This world had a thing for naked.

There was other stuff I realized I had to do. I figured I was also the one who took out Viper Squad. That might even be where I got the assault suit. One killed napping, the other eating lunch, Rivald had said over comms. That sounded like the kind of low-down weaselly stunt I'd pull. But that meant I had to get to their site, which seemed impossible.

But I knew the coordinates. It was in their message. Well, I didn't remember it, but my suit would. The suit that other me, forward-me, was wearing most days in the camp. I'd have to sneak in and check the recordings. But even if I could figure out where I needed to go, it was sure to be a long way away, and I couldn't use my suit to get there. I knew I wouldn't use it, because it hadn't left my side back when I was moving forward in time, sitting in the camp. Stealing it from myself now would create all kinds of paradoxes. Future me, living in the past, must have found another way, but I was drawing a blank.

Had I blown the massive holes in the SpearPoint technicians outside the portal? That possibility scared me a little because I didn't even know how to do that. Maybe they'd done that on their own. I had to hope so, or I had to invent a superweapon.

And I had to find a bunch of supplies and get them here. With no obvious means of transportation, and no idea where they came from.

It seemed maybe like I had at least one really big day ahead of me. A day that I'd need to plan with a lot of precision and without a lot of knowledge, although I had the strange advantage of knowing a few parts of what I'd do, because I'd seen them happen. Even so, this was a tall order for somebody who started each day naked and alone in a jungle on an alien world.

57

A COMMANDO PERFORMANCE

The next few days passed without much incident. I spent the days thinking through what I needed to do. And also handling basic subsistence. Elihar came each night and brought me eels to cook along with some other edible berries, tender shoots, and seeds. It wasn't great, but it was enough to get by on. I realized that's what he'd been doing when he left camp. Also, I figured he was making sure that forward-me didn't see him go through the time jump each evening, which would have no doubt led to awkward questions.

He did ask me how to describe the location of this camp. I knew why. In a few days, he'd need to tell forward-me how to get here. He was familiar with kilometers – klicks – which meant he'd learned them some other way, but he didn't know how to describe the location. I told him what he'd told me, precise distances north and west. I figured that had to be a paradox, but he'd asked, and he knew better than I did about all this.

I was tempted to go observe myself, interact with myself. I knew I hadn't done the latter, of course. I'd remember talking to myself. But there might be no harm in watching how I carried myself. No real benefit either, though. And Elihar was deathly afraid of paradoxes, so I figured I should be cautious and avoid any interaction. Forward-me didn't figure this all out until the business with shooting the trees, of course, so I couldn't give myself any hints. At least, not until I saved myself's ass and left myself the note in the pit.

Elihar came and found me one night, as he did most nights. Just for a visit. After having left forward-me in the main camp, sleeping, and figuring none of this world out. "How does your planning go?"

"All right, I think. Lots to consider, some problems to solve. But I'm getting there. Weirdly, I know that my plans work, or at least I think they do, because I have evidence that they did."

Elihar bowed his head. "Be careful. You know part, but not all. On this world, one can know the results, but not the costs paid." I could feel him grow suddenly sad.

"Elihar..." Probably good to distract him, I reasoned. "After I went through the portal, I could..." I didn't know how to describe it. "I can sense the presence of other beings, and for you and some of the others, I can read how you're feeling."

Elihar spun his head a few times. "You mentioned this upon your return. You could not do this before?"

"No. I'm about as bad at being sensitive to other people's emotions as it comes."

Elihar grunted. "I do not believe this. Not the Jess Amiko that I know." He reached out and put a hand pad on my back. "My people are connected in this way. The *moft storeni*. The speech without words. Perhaps you have joined us in this. I hope so. It is part of the richness of our lives."

"It's really interesting. Mind-blowing, kind of. And definitely weird."

"No weirder than your hair. Seriously. That stuff is so unpleasant."

I used some of Elihar's writing tablet sheets I borrowed to plan out my next few days. When I had a chance, I sneaked into camp a couple times while forward-me was swimming and got what I needed from the suit cams and data records. Small unit covert ops. Hit and run. What the 12th Light Infantry was made for, although there was usually more of the 12th Light than one grunt, unarmed and without tacops support. But the 12th Light had never had what I had now. After-action intel, but available before the action.

After those few days of planning and preparation, I was ready, I thought. Or at least, I had to be. Because I knew what I needed to do. I had a timeline to follow, even if it was a weird one. I knew that all of it would start to happen yesterday. Which was tomorrow. And tomorrow would mostly consist of a really long hike.

My feet hurt a little, and I was thirsty. But I'd made it. The area around the cloudy archway looked as it had when I'd seen it last. Turret destroyed, by me, and bodies of the SpearPoint technicians still lying around the portal. Still only two hoverbikes, but I was starting to understand that now. I suspected there would be three when I checked in after the time shift, when I jumped back a day in real time. That day, my tomorrow, the universe's yesterday, was the big day. The day I was planning to grab one of the three bikes and use it, leaving two here now. Today, that bike was wherever I would drive it to during my tomorrow, which was the bike's yesterday. Which was confusing, but I was starting to understand.

What had cemented that understanding for me, and confirmed that my planned timeline was ready to go, was that this morning, a full set of clothing had appeared at my little side camp along with a field locator for latitude and longitude. All of that gear hadn't been there when I went to sleep. It hadn't been there because it was moving forward in time, and I was moving backward, jump by jump. That meant that I was going to put it all on and carry the clothes and gear somewhere today, and then jump into the past. When my day ended, and I jumped back another day, the clothes would vanish from wherever I carried them today, because the clothes and I were going opposite directions at the jumps, and because I was planning on moving. We could only share the day together, and then we'd be parted as I jumped back and they progressed forward, sitting in a pile by the archway here, probably until they rotted away. That also meant that when I jumped back tonight, I'd be showing some serious skin. I hoped there were more clothes wherever I went. Jumping in time the opposite directions of ones' clothing made it a little hard to pack.

It was probably fine to lose the clothes. They'd be gross anyway. I was sweaty. It had been a long walk back to the portal. I'd left in the morning, shortly after the time shift. I'd brought some of Elihar's food with me, and at least that would go the same direction in time that I was – I wouldn't lose it at the jump. I'd be naked, but well fed.

But all of that was just details. The important part for today was Operation Kenai Freedom. Phase One. The Big Walk, which I had just completed. Tomorrow was Phase Two: Find Some Wheels, and then Phase Three (and likely Four, Five, and so on): Blaze of Glory. All of that was going to be hard. I had to complete a lot of work, all of it without revealing myself to myself or to SpearPoint, at least in any way that they could act on. Tomorrow, forward-me would be near here meeting Elihar, where Elihar would tell that version of me to go to the camp. I knew I would take the bike before that, because it was missing when forward-me met Elihar. I'd checked that on my suit's records.

So, the plan was, stay out of sight, wait for the jump, then start Phase Two. Steal a bike. Hopefully I'd find some clothes, but I needn't bother looking now. Anything I put on in my tomorrow was gone from here today, to wherever the third hoverbike was now. I'd have to find clothes tomorrow. Or not at all.

Phase Two. Find Some Wheels. The Kenai evening wasn't too cold, but I still shivered when my clothes bailed on me. I was confident now that there wasn't anybody at the archway site. I knew forward-me was camping a good distance away and wouldn't arrive until midmorning. Elihar was going to follow me here and meet forward-me today. And then tomorrow he'd get crushed by a tree. I still hadn't told him, but I'm sure he suspected. He was smarter about this stuff than I was. But he was on a mission, same as me, and he was taking risks, same as me. I didn't know for sure what tradeoffs he'd want to make. What this was worth to him.

Actually, I knew he anticipated something bad. When I'd found him dying, he'd said it was worth his life. Hello, Jess, my old friend. When the tree fell, I knew this must be the day we meet. I suspected it was coming. I am so honored to be your lajaret.

I hadn't asked what a *lajaret* was, because I figured if it had anything to do with his dying, I'd be invoking the curse, the *renfit sharah*, pretty hard. I still wasn't sure the curse applied to me. But I was probably going to find out today. I was messing with all kinds of paradoxes. Hopefully that would be for my benefit, to defeat my enemies. And for

Elihar's. So his sacrifice was worth something. But I wouldn't know that for a while yet.

It was still dark as I made my way into the narrow canyon, past the bodies, towards the bikes. I didn't worry about the turret. Forwards-me had blown it up already, after all. She would do that tomorrow. My tomorrow. Her yesterday. When I reached the campsite, I took a moment to rifle through the supplies. I gave the food a long, hard look. I almost ate some, but I knew from recent hard experience that eating forwards food as a backwards person wasn't pleasant, and it wouldn't help me long term.

I did manage one lucky find – a SpearPoint jumpsuit that more or less fit. A little roomy, but I rolled the cuffs at wrist and ankle, and it worked all right. I borrowed some boots and socks off one of the bodies that was about my size. Pretty macabre, but soldiers have been doing that for generations, or so I'm told. There were three bikes as I arrived, as I'd predicted. I was a little proud of myself for figuring that out. I hopped on a bike, put on the goggles hanging from the handlebars, set the hover to low and the speed on dead slow, and made my way out of camp, the turbines whining a little in the darkness, just enough to hold the bike off the ground fifteen or twenty centimeters. When I got a little farther out, out of earshot of forward-me, I could open it up, ride higher up, and make much better time. I had a lot to get done today, after all.

I wiped the blood from my hands and stowed the knife in the belt of my jumpsuit. A nasty business, killing somebody over breakfast. But you took what advantage you could, especially when it was one versus everybody. Well, two versus, if you count the sentient tree, but I figured Elihar didn't actually count as a field combat resource.

I didn't imagine the SpearPoint guy lying before me would have been proud dying while watching a Nemeian soap opera, but that part wasn't on me. He shouldn't have had the volume on so high, and he shouldn't have left his knife out when he cut up his DuraBiscuits.

The ship in front of me was another two-seat scout with a big cargo bay. In this one, though, the assault suits were sitting in the cargo area, folded into their storage configuration. There was a dent on the starboard side of the nose and some scratches heading from there backwards. Something was written in the center of the dent, scrawled in some kind of paint marker. Graffiti, with a pointy circle drawn around it like an explosion. *SpearPoint 1, Bird 0. Wigg flies like his daddy.*

Along the side, out of the sun, lay the remaining mercenary, sprawled on the deck, his head on a gear pack. Snoring. I cast a glance at the hazard monitor on the status holo by the door, but I didn't really need to. If I'd been categorized as a threat, the alarms would have gone off already, and I wouldn't have made it this far with him still asleep. If the system could read my identity, which was potentially possible, it meant I was still classified as mission personnel. Of course, they didn't expect to see me here. Especially because there were two of me. Forward-me was at my camp with Welk at this point, trying to reach the *Deimos,* which had just exploded. Forward-me was already working on what would be a long and harrowing day.

I glanced down at the remaining member of Viper Squad. Sleeping like a baby. Except the babies I knew didn't sleep this well. You'd think being part of the murder of the entire crew of a Patrol support vessel, forty-plus people, plus a bunch of innocent civilians, might make your sleep more troubled. Not this guy.

Well, he should have been more careful, too. And made better choices. Otieno often talked about how choices have consequences. I never much liked those parts of our meetings. I much preferred being the consequences to receiving them.

I pointed his partner's pistol at him and fired. Unpleasant, but over fast, and as merciful as I could afford to be under the circumstances.

Now, to get me an assault suit. Phase Four. Death from Above. This part was going to be more fun.

I saw the two heavy aerial assault troops take off, heading out from their ship, which had just streaked in with a flourish and landed not far from Welk's camp. Wolf Squad. I'd have to approach this carefully. Two of them versus me. I mean, I knew that in the timeline I'd experienced earlier, the one that forward-me was experiencing now, I'd won, but I didn't know if that was absolute destiny, written in stone, or whether it could change, and fork off a new reality or just mess up the timeline somehow. But if forward-me got fragged, then I wouldn't be here now, would I?

Too much metaphysics. Needed to anticipate. They were headed for the camp. Where Welk was. Forward-me was at the dig site, a little bit away, I remembered. And I needed to keep forward-me out of harm's way. I squeezed twice with finger and thumb, and the holomenu appeared projected in front of my gloved hand. I hadn't used one of these suits before, but the interface was pretty standard. I poked through the menus, speaking when necessary for a voice command.

Communications.

Targeted comms mode.

Target: nearby personnel.

Morowitz. No. *Han.* No. *Amiko.* Yes, that's the one. Bypass audio, engage suit OS directly.

NT384 Light Scout SuitOS 1.345. Jess Amiko piloting. Transmit command.

Engage cryosleep mode.

Remote cryo engage not permitted. Permission denied.

Override, code Amiko AU Beta 426. Kenzi's birthday.

Code accepted. Cryosleep mode engaged.

That would do. I lifted off. I'd turned off my assault suit's comms, which meant my suit wasn't broadcasting my ID or position info on the local network. That should buy me a little time. A little surprise.

The other suits streaked by, heading for Welk's camp, low at the treetops. Morowitz, then Han, my suit told me. I popped up and followed, my hand on the R13 cannon trigger. They lit into the tents, strafing the area. I'd seen grunts do that when they were overconfident. Just blowing stuff up for the sake of doing it. Not locking down situational tactics, not seeking out enemies first, firing without care for collateral damage. I was glad I served with better marines than these clowns. Probably wouldn't have survived what I did with them along. I saw some light arms fire coming from the edge of the camp, over near the shower. Welk. Brave, but stupid.

I saw them split from formation, scanning the area. One headed off toward Welk, the other toward the dig site, where forward-me had just faceplanted into the dirt in cryosleep mode. They were finally getting to what they'd come for, which was Welk and me. I'd have to take them both out quickly, or whoever I left for second could get a shot off at me. A shot my suit probably wouldn't survive.

I'd gotten enough height to gain elevation superiority. Not vital, but almost always recommended. Gave you more room to maneuver, with fewer obstacles, and of course it was harder to aim up over your head compared to down toward the ground. That was just basic human anatomy, unchanged no matter what kind of fancy armor we built for ourselves. I found the Friendly Fire override and turned it off.

I saw my chance. Lined up one bogey in the sights, waited a heartbeat for a lock, led the target, fired. Specialist Han, the targeting readout said. The R13 streaked toward her and slammed into the back of the suit. A billow of flame and plasma erupted – the thruster fuel going up – and the suit was pushed forward for a bit, then dropped, limbs and body spinning. Lifeless.

The other suit changed course, spun around. Looked up. A voice crackled over the comms. "Wigg? Skog it, man, what are you doing here? Who's skogging firing on us?"

Not a sharp one, was Specialist Morowitz. My lock indicator bleeped, and I launched the second of my six R13s towards him. I heard a yelp over comms, and he tried to dodge, but the shell's guidance bent its path to follow. The shell hit his helmet. The impact and resulting blast knocked him spinning, and he hit the ground hard. A moment later, the suit's thrusters shut off. Not because of anything Morowitz did. He wasn't in any shape to do anything. Just the suit realizing it wasn't accomplishing anything by pushing itself into the ground.

I returned my cannon hand to my rifle grip. Safer holding it with two hands. I took a loop over the camp, looking for movement, but I was sure there wouldn't be any. The two of them had fallen where I remembered they would, suffered the wounds I'd seen on their suits and bodies. They were gone, as I'd seen before. Strange to see it happen from this angle, though. Really strange.

A few moments later, I saw a suited figure coming from the dig site. Forward-me, pumped full of adrenaline and misgivings. She examined the bodies, then saw me. She dove for cover behind the supply crates and raised her rifle towards me. Taking aim. Brave, and understandable given training and instincts. Not a great tactical decision, though. The only good decision would have been to dive in the nearest hole and make very little noise. I let my rifle's muzzle fall, held up my arm. Waved. At me. Forward-me looked seriously confused. I sympathized.

I took off before it got weirder. Had to make it to the dig, leave the note that would set all this up. Yomo code. I thought about Welk dying. He was going to eat dirt soon. Very soon. A thought trickled into my head. Could it be Kenai's curse that killed him? But Elihar had said it was loved ones. I'm not sure Welk was even that much of a friend to me, just an employer with whom I'd gotten along. Weighing in on the not-a-curse side, this was probably as stressed out as he'd ever been, so a cardiac event wasn't that improbable. I thought some more. I was tempted to go try to intervene, to do something. To save him. But that wasn't the timeline I'd lived. And I survived in this version. At least until now.

Was it selfish not to try? Maybe. But Welk hadn't been straight with me, either. He was mostly a good guy, just a little bent. A fine upstanding citizen compared to the rest of these SpearPoint clowns. But he'd still hidden the truth about Kenai. And if I died, then Elihar died. And maybe his whole race died. Hope, he said. I was hope. That had to be more important than Welk, right? No guarantee Welk would live even if I intervened, or survive another day even if he lived. SpearPoint obviously wanted him dead.

No. Best to let it play out as it had. The results were not great, but they could be worse. I was still around, and able to resist, taking effective action. When faced with an overwhelming force, or when behind enemy lines, the guidelines were clear. Stay alive. Stay an asset. Take risks only when the reward was clear and the mission achievable. You were worth more alive with the potential to act effectively than dead trying something heroic that failed. That had to be the play here. What's more, if I tried to save Welk, I might well invoke the curse and screw something else up even worse.

I thumbed the thruster control down and descended toward the pit.

I saw the pit yawning in the jungle ahead of me. Just as I remembered it. I only had a little bit of time before Welk came here, and given that he hadn't mentioned seeing a heavy assault trooper, I figured I wasn't here when he arrived. So, five minutes, maybe ten, but I should be quick.

As I landed, I pulled the field con out of the utility slot in the suit's chest. It was the one Welk found, the one he'd handed to me. I had to write myself the note and leave it in the hole. I dictated the words. To my mind, I'd read them nearly two weeks ago, but in reality, I would read them in about fifteen minutes. Even though I'd acclimated to the bizarre conditions here, it still bent me in knots sometimes.

The note complete, I moved over toward the earthen stairs the nanites had dug. Just needed to head down there, and I'd be all set. Drop this, then get out. And figure out what to do next.

Which was hard. This, here in the pit, was almost the last thing I knew I'd done, short of leaving the supplies at the campsite. Elihar had told me I'd traveled to the past and met him, but I had no idea when that took place. Perhaps I lived here on Kenai, backwards in time, for many years before making the jump. Or perhaps Elihar was lying about that part. It was pretty outlandish to think I'd travel to the time of Kenai's long dead cities. But he'd made me the dictionary. That was consistent with meeting him again at an earlier time.

The suit pinged. Unknown movement within tactical radius. Skog. Another trooper? Or was Welk here already? I checked the readout. The signal was coming from the pit. Welk couldn't have beaten me here. Forward-me was talking to him now.

I was making a lot of noise, what with the thrusters and the servos. Whoever was in there knew I was here. On the plus side, I was wearing a heavy assault suit, and they were in a hole. I probably had the tactical advantage. Still, best to be cautious. I raised the rifle I'd taken from Viper Squad. It had a periscope sight. I thumbed it on and leashed it to the suit's HUD, so I could see what it saw. Carefully, I put the barrel of the rifle over the edge.

I needn't have been so cautious. There were no hostiles in the pit. Which isn't to say there were no people. Just one person. Well, a kind of a person. Cringing, huddled in a corner. Clutching a rectangular black wooden box, one I had seen before on my last visit here. One about which Welk was about to get really excited, when he got here in a few minutes.

It was Elihar.

58

WATCH OUT FOR THAT TREE

"What are you doing here?" It came out a little angrier than I meant.

"Please don't kill me." Elihar's head spun in a circle, twice around, and his body shuddered. Then he froze. "Wait, Jess?"

The suit. I popped the visor control, and it retracted. "Yes, it's me."

"What are you wearing?"

"Not important. We have to get out of here. Why are you here? How did you get here?"

"We can move very quickly when the need arises, especially through forest. I need to leave this object here." He held up the box.

"What? Why?"

His head slid into his body. "I... I would rather not say. It's dangerous."

Skogging…. "All right. Just do what you need to do. Someone's coming, and we need to be out of here."

"I understand." He went over to the stone alcove on the wall and placed the box inside. It fit exactly, like the hole had been built for it. No wonder Welk thought it was placed by the builders. But Welk was wrong. Very wrong. It was placed by Elihar. It hadn't been sitting there for twenty-two thousand years when he discovered it. It had been there about four minutes. Which would be funny, except that Welk was going to die shortly after finding it, so laughing at him seemed cruel.

I made my way down the stairs, worrying that the weight of the suit would make them crumble, but they held up. The nanites were good geotechnical engineers, apparently. I left the con with my note on the shelf next to the alcove, then turned to Elihar. "We have to get out of here."

"Yes. I can go now." He looked around at the walls. "It is fascinating, this place. I have been here before, but this building was not here then. They must have built it when they discovered what was here. To honor it, perhaps. And out of stone! Fascinating."

"No time." I looked up at the sky. "Are you up for a ride?" It was maybe the only way.

"What?"

"Hold onto my front. Keep your limbs way from the thruster openings back here. I'm going to fly us out of here."

"How... exciting." He didn't sound excited, but he came over and wrapped himself around me. It would have been almost intimate, except the suit kind of killed the mood. I extended the visor back down.

"Hold on. Here we go." I thumbed the thrusters up, slow at first, then higher. We rose out of the hole. When we were clear of the trees, I hit it hard, and we shot up.

Elihar's head was twitching back and forth, his eyes squeezing. Taking it all in, I supposed.

I got us on a course away from the camp, moving about 80kph. He clenched his limbs tighter around me. "You good?"

"This is remarkable." His head was still flailing back and forth. "Thrilling." I could feel the emotion coming off him.

"Trees don't fly much, do they?"

"No, they don't." He was happy, I thought. Taking it all in.

When we got far enough away, I set down in a small clearing. We were out of the way of forward-me, of Welk, of

SpearPoint. I realized Welk was probably dying right now, and a pang of sorrow went through me. Elihar unwrapped himself from me and stepped back.

"Are you all right?" I could feel Elihar's concern. It pulsed at me.

"I'm all right. Just losing a... a friend. Back there. He died. Is dying now. Again." I felt a sudden cold chill. Elihar was about to die, too. Today was the day, the day he'd get crushed by the tree, right when forward-me met him. I squeezed my eyes shut. He only had a few hours. I hadn't expected to be with him again. Knew I hadn't been, or so I thought. This was hard.

"You're in distress."

"Yes." Should I tell him? I couldn't think what else to say.

He was quiet for a moment. Did he know? He'd said he suspected, when he died. Had I tipped my hand? Could he read my emotions? Could he read my mind? It stood to reason he was better at whatever this was than I was.

"I need to get back to the portal. The other you is going to head there soon. You will meet me."

"I will." I couldn't say the other part.

"We have to let that play out. Our meeting is important." He paused. "Extremely important."

Was it, though? Did it have to be this way? What if he didn't die? I could just meet him tomorrow. Forward-me's tomorrow. His yesterday. And then he could go on living today. "I meet you tomorrow. That's when you tell me about the camp. That's when we go there."

"I remember. It was yesterday for me." He was quiet for a moment. "But the forward-moving you meets a Weynik today, first. You said so." He didn't say more, but I could tell he had added my distress and my silence together to reach something like the truth.

"Elihar..."

"It is all right, Jess." He held two viny arms up and placed his pad hands on my suit's shoulders. "This world is cruel. We are given things to know that no person should. That is the test that his place sets for us. And still it makes us pay a greater cost, even, than this." He shifted one arm to the side of my helmet. "We should not speak of this. It is dangerous. But know that I want to go. I need this. My people need a chance to break free. To save ourselves. The chance only you can give them. That chance lies on this path. We cannot put it at risk."

I had trouble finding my voice. "Does it work? What I do?" Would it be worth all this?

"If I knew, I wouldn't tell you." He grunted. His way of laughing. "But I don't know. I don't know how it ends. Nobody does." He pulled his arms away. "But we can try." He spun his head around and looked at me with five or six different eyes. "It's time to go, marine."

I stood for a moment. Full of doubt. Full of regret. Or pre-regret. Or something. But he'd given me an order, I decided. And I was pretty good at following those.

"All right. Hold on, you." I flipped the visor down again. Hated showing emotion. Even to a tree.

We rose above the canopy of weird, pointy trees, above the thicket of red and yellow leaves, and flew north.

I said my goodbyes. I suspected from what Elihar had said that I would meet him again. But it would be an earlier version. Not this Elihar, the one I knew best, who knew me best. That one, I would never see again.

He pressed something into my gloved hand. It was a torn flap from a box. I could see part of the DuraBiscuit logo on it. I flipped it over, and I could see that the back side had some scrawled characters from his language, but faint, almost as if they'd been written with a stick dipped in muddy water. "Could you leave this where we came out of the portal. I'll need it."

"What is it?" I looked at the scrap, trying to puzzle out what it meant.

"I suppose there's no real harm in telling you. Any price has already been paid." He spun his head around, looking at me. "It's the coordinates for the campsite by the river and for your second site nearby. I found this when I emerged from the archway, and it is how I knew where to meet you, when I first did. Of course I could not keep it, as it is of your world. It left me when the night fell and I jumped back in time. But I recognized my writing, and I suspected I would later write it and leave it for myself, dangerous as that might be. My suspicions were confirmed when I found the exact scrap near the place we have just been. The site my ancestors built. All that was needed was to write upon it, and I have done so."

"I'll get it to where it needs to go." This kind of paradox wasn't even weird for me anymore. That was weird in itself.

"One last thing." He pulled his satchel off his shoulder, or where his shoulder would be if he had a regular body. "Take this. It's ready now." He flipped through the set of wooden sheets in the satchel and pulled out most of them, leaving only a few behind. The ones he handed me were covered with writing. The dictionary he'd been making. I took it and stowed it in my suit's cargo compartment.

He put a hand on my shoulder, nodded his head, and then went off into the trees. Off to his end. Brave guy. Bravest tree I'd ever met, really.

I found the spot where I had emerged from the portal. Apparently, I had missed the scrap of DuraBiscuit box when I came out, but that was understandable. To me, it was garbage. I set it on the ground. Closing one more loop. Maybe invoking one more curse, on Elihar or on me.

I had one more errand to run. Phase Five. Provisioning. Logic suggested I had to do that today, when I was well equipped and mobile and still operating with a bit of surprise. I also had recently discovered a big clue as to how to do it. I'd seen another of the SpearPoint ships as I flew in with Elihar. It was not far. Probably the one the dead technicians had flown here. That solved a big logistical problem for me. I just needed to get it loaded up with some of their supplies and food, and then I could drop the gear that forward-me would need at Elihar's camp. And also the smaller cache that backward-me would use after I reversed.

I had thought about how to do this. Planned it out, all crafty like. I needed not to give away the position of the camp Elihar and I used. Using a vehicle made that dangerous because the flight path could be tracked. So I would make a broad pass over a large area, my route twisty and aimless. A random pattern. I'd make a bunch of quick drops of gear at different places, not just at the camp. Stop, hover, hop out, stow some crates, get back in, jet off. No more than a minute or two at each spot. As a flourish at the end, I'd even leave one of the bodies in the ship, and I'd program set the ship to fly on and crash. If I were lucky, whoever was watching would just think one of the injured technicians had flown it away, succumbed to injuries, and died.

It wasn't a great deception. Definitely not premium psy ops work. Clumsy as anything, and not well conceived. But all I had to accomplish was to make it weird, unimportant, and not worth investigating in the middle of a complex and illegal operation. And even that modest goal only needed to buy us about six or seven days. That kind of scam, I thought I might be able to pull off.

I heard the ship crash behind me. The engines made an enormous noise when they blew, even though I was well away. I'd jumped out of the cargo bay in my suit and used most of the last little bit of battery to land. The ship had gone on another few kilometers and hit the dirt.

I set the rifle down on the ground, then triggered the seam lock on the suit. The arms, legs, and torso parted around me. I extricated myself, stepped out, stretched. Took my jaw in my hands and cracked my neck in both directions. That felt good. Always did. Pulled Elihar's dictionary tablets from the storage compartment on the suit's torso. Pressed the collapse button, and the suit retracted to storage configuration, sitting there on the forest floor. Neat and tidy.

There was nothing else for me to do here. No more loops to close. No more games to play with time and stolen gear and interventions. No more people to kill. I found I had no interest at all in remaining here, eating whatever I scrounged from the woods, moving backwards in time like some kind of screwed-up naked survival tourist.

No, it was time for me to go. To do what I'd agreed to. Whatever that turned out to be. But I had figured out where I probably needed to go next. I picked the rifle up again, checked the charge, and headed out toward the portal. And, apparently, toward a time fifty thousand years in the past.

59

Portal Authority

"You have returned." The cube flexed, distorting its corners.

"You're surprised?" I shivered a little. It was cold in here without any clothes.

"I am incapable of both that emotion and that principle."

I bet. "Because you know the future?"

"Have I merely breathed the flower's fragrance, or have I smelled God?"

That threw me a little. "What?"

"That statement was calculated to distract you from your improper question. I can provide other deep thoughts as required if it is not sufficient to the purpose."

"Right." Whatever. "How am I doing, perturbing things?"

"As predicted. Within tolerances."

Of course. "What's next? Do I succeed? Is there a point to any of this?"

"Success condition is not defined for you. Also, the next segment you will undertake is not part of guided destiny manipulation."

"What?"

"This proceeding would not be classified as a trial were there not uncertainty as to the outcome."

I didn't know whether to be reassured or alarmed. "You mean, I'm just going to go try something, making it up as I go along, and I might just totally fall on my ass and fail?"

"Correct. That is possible. Probability is not modeled. But it seems likely to me."

Great. "So, what door do I go through?"

"There is a 0.5837 times ten to the minus 24th power probability that you will choose the wrong one."

"Of course there is." I'd chosen left before, and I didn't want to go back to the same time, so the obvious choice was the right door. But I kind of wanted to choose the left just to spite the cube. "Any other advice?"

"That would be beyond the scope of my intended interaction regime in Trial Erdion, but I am happy to offer non-actionable platitudes. Good luck out there!"

"Thanks, buddy."

"No problem, friend. Your strength comes from within."

I sighed. "You don't have any clothes I could borrow, do you?"

"We are not the same size."

"Right."

"Life's most fulfilling moments can pass you by if you're not paying attention."

I looked again at the gleaming pillar of norodium in the center of the chamber. "What's this thing? What's it do?"

"Induced paradox consequence actualization. Power generation and storage. Also matter retemporation as needed to deter non-subjects and ensure uninterrupted trial administration."

That was a barely comprehensible collection of words, but it sparked a thought. "Like, putting holes in people?"

"Is it a hole if the retemporated matter still exists, just at another time? The entity remains whole, despite the hole."

"You're killing people who mess with you."

"One's true identity is most clearly revealed by that which we choose to love, not by those whose matter we retemporate."

Whatever. I went over to the right portal. Through it, as impossible as it seemed, I expected to find a world that existed tens of thousands of years before my oldest relative was born, full of alien people I barely understood, whom I might somehow be able to impact for good or ill, except I had no idea how. And I was going to meet all of them not wearing any pants. I straightened my stack of wooden sheets, stepped forward, and put my hand into the cool mist.

The cube started moving in small circles. "Our fiercest critics are often ourselves." With that, the cube started boinging against the side of its frame.

I took a breath and stepped through.

60

BABY, IT'S OLD OUTSIDE

The air smelled different. And it was cooler. Chilly, against my bare skin. I wondered if the planet's biology or climate had changed. That was stupid. Of course it would, in that much time. Or I could just be on a different part of the planet, or it could be a different season. Kenai had a modest axial tilt, so there'd be seasons.

I was in a thicket of trees, some familiar, the kind I'd seen on Kenai before, some different. Quite a few of them were jet black, with thick trunks and few leaves, not like what I'd seen before. I realized they were growing in a regular pattern, each trunk about the same distance apart in a kind of triangular grid with other plants and trees interspersed at random. Was that just how they grew, or was it intentional? A tree farm?

I looked around me, trying to find a place to go, or a reason to go one direction rather than another. I spotted a group of trees that looked familiar, somehow, but I couldn't see how. I went over to them. Then I figured it out. They had the same diamond pattern on their bark, the same viny texture, as Elihar had. I ran my fingers over the bark. There was even a knotty blob in the center, kind of like Elihar's head, but with no white patches for eyes. Far more than three viny limbs grew skyward. Could this cluster be members of his species? Maybe they were the Dumisel, those who never chose to walk. A little family plot.

There was a noise from through the trees, a harsh cry. I searched for the source. There, amid the trees, stood a person like Elihar, suspended on three limbs, arms swirling through the air, head spinning, speaking trumpet extended.

I held up my arms, clutching the dictionary sheets in one hand. A gesture of peace, of supplication. Or at least it would be for a human. It might mean "I am a hairy alien monster who wants to kill you" to them.

Except I knew it did not. I could feel surprise, even alarm, from the person ahead of me, but not real fear. I still had the connection to the world around me that I'd gained the first time through the portal. I tried to project a feeling as peaceful and calm and sincere as I could, but that's a little hard to do.

The tree person came over to me and gave me a good looking over, walking around in a full circle, making little noises and grunts, sometimes syllables, all of them strung together in a stream. I recognized the word *etivar,* repeated a few times. Still no fear from the person, but a lot of curiosity. It felt intrusive, standing there naked and being given the once-over by an alien, but I tried not to emote any discomfort. I had no real idea how that connection worked, or if it even went both ways.

Finally, they finished. I turned to them. I couldn't speak the language, but I did know one word to say. "Elihar?" I said. I held up the sheaf of wooden tablets. "Elihar." I pointed to them with my other hand.

The person held out a pair of viny arms. I gave over the tablets. They shuffled through them with remarkable speed, studying the writing. "Elihar," they said. "Elihar." They swung an arm out towards a place where the vegetation thinned out a little, up a small hill. They didn't give me back the sheaf of tablets. I was nervous about that, because it was my only connection to my language, or really to anything I knew. They started walking. I followed.

In time, we came to what seemed like a village. There were structures, most of them composed of black wood. I thought it might be from the trees I'd seen planted in the triangular pattern when I arrived. The structures weren't angular and boxy the way human buildings tend to be. They had smoother contours, irregular protrusions. It wasn't exactly as if they just grew here in place, because I could see separate boards and logs, sometimes lashed together or covered by a separate band of the dark wood. That meant they must be constructed. But few of the timbers seemed straight or true – all had blemishes, irregularities, warped surfaces. And the buildings themselves followed no regular pattern, except that upper floors tended to be smaller than lower ones, and windows were common. There was a transparent substance in them, which argued for at least a little technological know-how. It didn't look like glass, though.

There were people, too. Weynik. Lots of them, perhaps forty or fifty, walking about with their viny legs or pulling themselves along, apelike, swinging from their arms. Some stood in front of the buildings. Others worked, often at tables or stations covered with bits of wood, or with the writing tablets. I tried to take it all in. Some were smaller than others, perhaps younger, trailing after larger ones. After a moment, I realized that there was a main thoroughfare through the buildings, along which many of the people were walking or working. There were side alleys as well, although there were far fewer people using them. Some of the buildings had signs marked up with the language I had learned of from Elihar. I thought that suggested that there were visitors to this community, because if there was nobody from out of town, there wouldn't be much need for signs.

At first, it seemed to me to be a primitive place, like a stone age society. The buildings were crude and uneven in appearance, and there was no apparent advanced technology. But as I looked about, I noticed more details, more sophistication in design. A flicker of movement caught my eye, and I realized that on a panel of darker wood on the side of one of the larger buildings, letters similar to what Elihar had written appeared and disappeared. It was fascinating. At first, I thought it must be a holo display or something similar, but as I studied it further, it almost seemed as though the wood itself was deforming into carved characters and then filling itself back in. Then I noticed a round conduit, like a pipe, also made of the darker wood, running down a nearby hillside and into a pool. An aqueduct, or some kind of rain management? And another building had an opening in a wall covered by an intricately carved screen, full of intertwined images of the local fauna. It was beautiful. There were few regular angles or flat surfaces anywhere in the village, and there was almost no symmetry, which made it all look rustic, but that was my human bias at work. The more I looked, the more the construction revealed complex engineering and artistry.

People gawked at me, their heads spinning back and forth on their necks. That was made all the more awkward by my nakedness, although I saw none of them wearing anything that resembled clothing. Some had objects stuck to their bodies – eelfish, berries, tools, bits of wood. I felt curiosity and surprise coming from them, but also negative emotions. Distaste, fear, discomfort, revulsion. Some of them pressed closer to see me as I went by, following the person I'd first met. Occasionally that person exchanged words with those we passed, and I heard Elihar mentioned more than once. The people spoke amongst themselves as we passed, as well. The language was smooth, more a continuous sound than discrete words, although when Elihar had taught me some words back in our camp, they'd sounded distinct. Perhaps the spoken language lacked silence between words, unlike the way human speech worked. It was almost as if they were singing. The speech changed pitch at times, sometimes frequently, but it wasn't melodic, at least to my ears.

We came to a larger space, one devoid of buildings, although there were the same odd structures around it. I was reminded of a town square. There were little stumps of the black wood about, and some of the people squatted on these, their legs splayed wide about them, sometimes alone, sometimes in groups. In one area, a number of people lay in rows on the ground next to each other, some of them shifting restlessly, others lying still. Were they sleeping? I never knew Elihar to sleep, but I'd only known him for maybe ten or twelve days, and short Kenaian ones at that.

I wondered if Elihar were here, in this community. It seemed wildly improbable that of all the places I could arrive on this world, at this long-ago time, that I'd arrive near him. On the other hand, it might be destined that I do so. The cube could have guided me here. Elihar said he'd met me. Of course we'd have to come together. Perhaps it wasn't so improbable after all. I searched the crowd for him, trying to ignore the people staring at me, and the cacophony of emotions I could feel, many of them seemingly directed my way.

We stopped in front of one of the buildings, a large ramshackle structure with uneven openings. Some were larger, but I couldn't tell if they were doors or windows, or if there was any difference to the Kenaians. The building had two floors, but the upper floor was uneven, bending along the length of the building up and down. It would be very difficult to walk along that surface, I thought. Perhaps it was easier with three legs and the ropy arms. Elihar had seemed pretty agile, and pretty speedy, when he got going.

My guide shouted at the building. It sounded like *ranzenduelihareisellishen,* a bunch of syllables all strung together. He waited a moment, then shouted another long phrase. He held out the sheaf of writing tablet sheets. The dictionary. I wondered if he understood what it was intended to be.

Something moved behind one of the upper windows. One of the arms came out of the window. Its little hand-pad grasped the bottom of the window opening, and then a whole section of the wall lifted up. I had not noticed the seams between sections, perhaps because it was curved and irregular, and because the different parts fit so closely together. Behind the rising wall section stood Elihar. Or at least, I thought it was him. I was not very good at telling these people apart, but I thought I recognized the texture of his exterior, his size, his way of moving, the spacing of his eyes. His mind also seemed familiar, to the limited extent that I could read him. It's hard to describe. Like a flavor one remembers as familiar, without knowing exactly what spices and seasonings go into creating it.

My guide shouted some more words, waving the tablets around. Elihar shouted back. I stood there awkwardly, hands clasped across my front in a forlorn attempt at modesty. The two of them went back and forth a few times. Elihar seemed to be alternating between looking at me and yelling at my guide.

Finally I had enough. "Elihar," I shouted. "Come look at the tablets. We need to get to know each other.

Both of them fell silent, staring at me, although I heard those around start to speak after a moment. Funny, that. It seemed so very human, surprise and then gossip, although I had no real idea what they were saying. Elihar came over to the edge of the upper floor and let the wall drop down behind him. Nimbly, he clambered down the side of the building. He came over to the guide and took the tablets. He flipped through them, then erupted in a string of sounds. The guide took a few quick steps back, head spinning on neck, almost twitching. I could feel alarm pouring off them. Fear, but only from them. Elihar was calm. He waved an arm at the guide and said something, and the guide left, moving fast. Others nearby took a few steps back as well, some even to the point of dashing away. I could feel echoes of fear in them as well. I didn't like how this was going.

"Elihar," I said, hoping the name would set him at ease.

He didn't say anything at first, merely flipping through the tablets. Then he tipped his head up and spun an eye around towards me. "Jess." He said it a little like "chess," but I was very glad to hear it.

"Yes, I'm Jess." I patted my chest.

He said more things, things I could not understand. Then he waved me over to the building from which he'd emerged. He pointed at one of the larger holes on the ground floor and made some motions with his arms. It seemed like he wanted me to go in. I took a hesitant step forward, and then he put an arm on my back and gave me a gentle push. All right, then. I took a step through the hole, into the dark interior.

61

THE VILLAGE PEOPLE

I was learning the language, and I had pants. Both major successes, I thought. It had been a rough couple of months. I was still adapting to the food, although I'd learned to like a little raw meat, and I'd found some fruits that were pretty tasty. The Weynik understandably weren't keen on cooking fires, although they let me make a small one on the edge of town near where I was staying. Kids came and watched. I think it was a bit of a scary thrill.

The pants came from Tuenih, one of the Weynik who specialized in weaving plant fibers into various useful objects. These were mostly wrappings, carpets, curtains, and cloth doors which were common in many of the buildings. The Weynik wore no clothing, although I did notice an occasional dangly piece of jewelry or flash of something colorful, such as a flower or pretty leaf or bit of cloth. Having a sticky body made it easy to attach things to it. Tuenih also made me a mattress cover and stuffing, for which I was tremendously grateful. Tuenih did it, but he also laughed at me and said that my species must be very delicate not to be able to handle touching the ground. I couldn't disagree.

Elihar had conveyed my desire for clothing to Tuenih, and despite some laughter and what I gathered was teasing, Tuenih came through with a few outfits and even a sense of style. Elihar was doing much better learning my language than I was learning his, but I was making steady progress. I had sessions with Elihar for an hour or so every day, and then there were a lot of little interactions that required words. I not fluent, but I was surprised at how fast I was going. If we hadn't had the dictionary that the future Elihar had made and sent with me, it would have been a huge challenge, starting from scratch. The sensitivity I'd picked up while going through the norodium portal helped too – being able to read emotions from the people I was talking with helped a great deal in conveying meaning. I sometimes took part in lessons with the younger Weynik, the ones who'd recently uprooted from where they were planted. They were smart, and they learned quickly, but given that they spent the early parts of their lives as dormant trees, they had a ton to learn about language, about culture, and about life on Kenai. It was almost like they were teenagers who'd grown up alone in the wilderness, out of contact with everyone, but who had now been brought into a community.

With all that going on, I was becoming almost a functional, clothed adult. I knew my vocabulary was limited, and there were some concepts that didn't even transfer to human language, I was learning. And a lot of human concepts that didn't transfer to them. Latrines, for example. They were not excited about that, even as there was a similar pit of slimy bones in a giant pile near the river which I found equally unpleasant. And smelly. But I tried to keep my biology out of their way.

I should mention, I also killed a couple of Elihar's friends. Not on purpose. And actually, the world killed them, not me. But let me explain. When I arrived and gave Elihar the dictionary, two of his best friends died. Almost to the minute. They were coworkers on his archeological project, people he'd worked with for years. They were working on a dig site, and a freak storm blew up, leading to a flash flood, which inundated their dig and buried it and them in twenty feet of mud and debris. They were crushed and entombed, all at once.

We didn't know about it until a good while later, when one of Elihar's students arrived back at the village and told us. But even then, nobody was surprised. The dead scholars were *lajaret,* people said. The same word Elihar had used to describe himself when we first met. When he died, crushed under the tree. I had come to understand that *lajaret* were the people sacrificed to the planet's curse. They were nearly always people important to whomever was creating a paradox, or even just discovering one. If you found the remains of a stone building, for example, one that was coming forward in time to you from the past while you lived your life backwards towards when it was built, you had to be pretty careful, because you might find evidence of the past there, which was your future, and if you acted on that information, you could create a paradox and incur the curse.

The dictionary Elihar had made was a clear example of this. He'd made it later in his life, and it had been transported by me to a point earlier in his life. That meant that his knowledge of my language came essentially mostly from nowhere. The future Elihar taught his younger self Tradespeak via the dictionary, although I helped him hone his skills as we worked on my learning to speak Weynik.

Along with the language information, the dictionary tablets also contained a note explaining that I would likely be important to him and to the Weynik, although they didn't say why or how. That was another paradox, or at least a potential self-fulfilling prophecy, because the Weynik took an even bigger interest in me after hearing that. I don't know what they'd have done with a random time-traveling human showing up in their village without the introduction from future-Elihar. Maybe just eaten me. I probably had a unique flavor.

That's why they weren't surprised when news of Elihar's friends' deaths arrived. They knew somebody was likely to pay the price. That's the way the curse worked, and it just seemed natural to them. I found it more surprising that nobody much blamed Elihar for doing this, for causing the death of his friends. *Lajaret* were always honored and mourned. The person who'd created or discovered the paradox, Elihar in this case, was called the *kunaret.*

Sometimes a *kunaret* was scorned or punished, or even executed, if they were just messing around with things they shouldn't and creating paradoxes willy-nilly. Other times, people regretted the loss, but they understood that the information gained from the paradox was useful, or even vital. In that case, they blamed the curse, not the *kunaret* who'd brought it about.

And in almost all cases, the *kunaret* was filled with regret, which could be punishment enough. The curse inevitably found somebody close to them, a mate, or a child, or a good friend. I wondered if there were loners among the Weynik, people who had no close friends to sacrifice and could just play with time as they wished, but they wouldn't give me a good answer to that hypothetical. It seemed not to be possible among the Weynik, who were an empathic, close-knit community.

I came to understand that, even though he'd caused the loss of his friends, Elihar had tried to avoid that by creating as mild and respectable a paradox as he could. The dictionary was a clear violation, of course, but people saw that as necessary to integrate me quickly into their world. They kept saying things were heading in a bad direction, although it took me a while to understand how or why. Elihar's note, suggesting that I was important, rather than saying specifically how or what I was to do, was a way to minimize the impact of the curse, whereas overt, clear instructions would have gotten more people killed. I was starting to understand the nature of the curse better, and to understand why Elihar had behaved as he did with me back in my time, with vagueness and frustrating silences. He was just protecting those he loved. Interestingly, his supposed cultural taboo about not talking about past conversations was a bunch of baloney. He had made it up on the spot to try to get me not to blab things to him that would invoke the curse. It turned out that in reality, Weynik would talk your ear off about past conversations, even to the point of repeating everything everybody had said, often with extensive commentary and critique. It was just revealed secrets, dangerous foretellings, that they were not so excited to discuss.

Another reason the loss of Elihar's friends was not greeted with much surprise or anger was that this wasn't the first time he'd been a *kunaret*. The other time, he'd paid a tremendous price. He'd been working with his group of scholars at a site far to the south. Elihar didn't want to talk about exactly what had happened, but I gathered from others that he and his team had discovered an artifact that had triggered a paradox. It seemed he was a leader among these researchers, like the chief scientist. They were investigating a site where they'd found ancient artifacts made from a substance they called *umbani*, which I, in a brazen feat of cultural insensitivity, had named ironwood, at least in my own head. It came from the odd black trees I'd seen when I first arrived in the past. The site Elihar's team had found was the location of some of the oldest remains of their people. Of course, ancient for them meant far in the future in regular time because they lived backwards, but it made sense in their context. These people at the site had lived long ago, for them, and they seemed to be the first group of Weynik to use ironwood. At least, the first that had been discovered thus far.

Ironwood was a very special substance. It was tremendously strong and durable, comparable to steel or titanium, and yet it was able to be shaped into many forms, and even into intricate mechanical or even bioelectric devices, by a group the Weynik called *omariga*, which I translated with Elihar's help as "woodweavers." Early in my time with the Weynik, I met the leader of the woodweavers, a Weynik named Sekene. Sekene soon surprised me with a gift – an ironwood tablet like Elihar's, but one that had little bumps I could press, each of which produced on the tablet a set of pictures, vocabulary words, each with a phonetic spelling written in Tradespeak so I could read them aloud. I had no idea how wood could be caused to act like a screen display in this way, but Sekene shrugged it off as a minor effort, saying Elihar had done the hard part in learning my way of writing and sharing it. I saw other objects and devices around the town performing all types of functions and tasks, some quite sophisticated, and I rapidly learned to recognize Sekene's work. The other woodweavers made nothing so intricate as Sekene's pieces.

The Weynik planted and grew ironwood all around their towns. Ironwood was the main building material for the whole Weynik culture. They really needed something like it because it was living material. That meant it would progress backward in time with them. Unlike stone or metal, which they could work with, but which would immediately progress forward in time, away from them, ironwood provided them a material that they could keep, that wouldn't vanish the following day. They could make objects from the regular trees as well, but that wood tended to be soft and pithy and rotted easily. Ironwood was far more reliable. What was even more useful is that, even if you cut an ironwood tree down, the wood didn't die. That I really didn't understand, but from what they said, the wood, or maybe the cells inside, retreated into a kind of a dormant stasis state, where the wood could remain for immensely long periods. It was highly resistant to microorganisms, they said, because it provided no food for them, so they basically left it alone. It also seemed to be chemically inert, or maybe self-repairing. I wasn't really clear on that, because I really didn't have the vocabulary to discuss it, and again, I'm no xenobiologist. The Weynik did seem to have a scientific corps among them, including their version of biologists, engineers, chemists, astronomers, and others. I was still learning the various job names and trying to map them to human roles.

The *omariga*, the woodweavers, freaked me out some. That's because they didn't use tools to work the ironwood. They communicated with it. I wasn't clear on exactly how, but I gathered it was related to the heightened sense of connection between living things that seemed typical of Kenai, and which I now could sense myself. But they had it much stronger than I did. A woodweaver could pick up a piece of ironwood, hold it up, and instruct it to rework itself, to change shape into something different. Only a small fraction of the population of Weynik seemed to have this ability, and they were venerated, or at least highly respected, Sekene most of all. They were the ones who shaped all the tools, the houses, nearly everything the Weynik used on a daily basis as they lived and went about their work. They were also the ones who harvested the ironwood trees when they were grown, merely by coming over to them, laying on hands, and shaping the base of their trunks into a section thin enough to break off.

Ironwood was important to all that happened in my time on Kenai, but it turned out to be wound even tighter into Elihar's story. As I said, he'd been investigating a site where the earliest ironwood artifacts were found. It was akin to humanity finding stone age tools or iron age weapons. Evidence of a culture starting to lift itself above simple survival to take command of the environment around it. Elihar's team had dug up ironwood tools, weapons, stumps, even artwork – little replicas of animals and of Weynik people, some of them true likenesses, some of them figurative abstracts. He sounded tremendously proud of this discovery, and even to my non-scholarly mind, it did sound exciting. I was reminded of Welk's joy in discovering the buried temple and of imagining the history of the people and culture of Kenai. Of course, the temple didn't exist now. It would be built thousands of years in the future, maybe by the ancient Weynik people Elihar was studying now. Being composed of unliving stone, the temple would progress forward in time until the point when Welk dug it up. But the ironwood relics, as living objects, moved backwards with the Weynik, remaining little altered with time. They were likely all the archeological evidence Elihar's researchers would ever be able to find.

62

WAR. WHAT IS IT GOOD FOR?

"Your pronunciation is very hard to understand. Is your speaking membrane inflexible, or damaged?"

"I don't have one of those. I have vocal cords. I told you that. And they're working as well as can be expected under these conditions." We'd lapsed back into Tradespeak, as we often did when my Weynik language failed me. Which it often did. I was improving some, I thought, but not today.

Elihar studied me for a while. "You are troubled." His voice was less accusing now, more supportive.

"I'm just frustrated. Your language is hard for me." I grimaced. "And it's hard, living on an alien world with nobody like you around." My zavvies were mostly under control, but all of it had been pressing at me – the weird food, the foreign language and culture, never seeing another person. Well, another human. I'd taken to going for long walks in the woods when it got to be too much. And I'd been doing lots of exercise. Like I'd done in prison to fight the loneliness and isolation.

I was being mopey and no use to anyone. Buck up, marine. "The bigger thing is, I don't know what I'm doing here." I wanted to mention that future-Elihar had told me I gave them hope, but I knew that could invoke a paradox. I could see no way that I was anything other than a burden to them. "I mean, I left behind everything I knew. And I'm not only stranded here, on this planet, but I'm so far back in time. My species is barely out of caves now, I think. Or maybe just running across the plains of Africa throwing sticks at things."

"What is Africa?" Always the scholar. He asked a lot of questions.

"It's one of the large land masses on the world where my people evolved. The land we evolved on."

"Do your people live there now?"

Well, that was embarrassing. "I don't know. Our people spread from that planet to other stars and other planets. We reached many worlds, flying through space, and we built communities where we found environments in which we could live."

"Interesting. Our people wish to do the same." That threw me. The Weynik were great engineers and designers, with lots of clever and useful tools and structures created by the woodweavers. It was an odd mix. They had no vehicles other than simple carts and no significant weapons, but they had lights, display panels, even programmable tools with semi-sophisticated controls, all created from ironwood. They also were skilled with fermentation and biochemical technology, making use of microorganisms to process food and make alcohol and other chemicals from plants, animal parts, and organics. But even with all their talents, it seemed to me they were a long, long way from space travel.

Elihar spun his head a bit. "Why do you not know if people live on Africa?"

I remembered that I had spoken with Elihar about this before, but of course that was the Elihar of the far future. This Elihar didn't know, and the future one had not indicated we'd discussed it, I suppose, to avoid the curse. "Nobody has been there in four hundred years. It is probably now unfit for life." This part was hard to speak about because it made us look bad. "The worlds we reached — they began to fight against each other. Many of our settlements, our communities, were completely destroyed. Only a fraction remain, and we have not heard from the others in many years. We assume the people there are all dead, or at best living in great difficulty now, without technology. My culture exists only at the edges of where we once lived, and in much smaller numbers."

"I see." I didn't feel strong emotion from Elihar. More like he was thinking, processing the information. Then he asked, "What does evolved mean? You said your people evolved?"

"You know, like how species arise from others. My species arose from animals like us. Apes. Through adaptation, competition, retaining advantageous traits, and having others die out. Selection." I was going to get to the limits of my barely remembered biology soon, but Elihar seemed interested.

"How do you know these are your ancestors?"

I struggled to remember Doctor Wenyu's biology course. "Fossils. We found skeletons of species who had shapes that were between the apes and us, from long ago, showing how it happened, how we came to be who we are now. Oh, and there's also genetics. The code in our cells. We share nearly all of that with apes, less with other species."

"Are there still apes, or did they die as well?"

"There are. We brought animals and plants from our homeworld to the new worlds we came to."

"How do these fossils come to be? Do your bodies not decay when you die? Ours do so quickly."

"The fossils are bones, usually, I think. The parts of us that are rocks."

"That makes sense. We contain no rocks." He thought some more. "What are cells?"

"The little units of life that make us up. That's how our bodies work. We're made of lots of them. Each is like a little tiny living thing, but they work together." I was really not the person to be teaching an alien race about cellular biology. "And each cell has the same chemical code in it that guides how we grow and develop."

Elihar nodded his head once. I suspected he'd picked the gesture up from me. "We lack the ability to study our tiny parts, but we know that we are made up of smaller pieces. The woodweavers can feel them in the ironwood, and I have heard the Nurikna have created devices that allow them to see very small objects such as these cells. Perhaps they have seen our genetic code as well. If we have one such as you do."

"Tell me about the Nurikna. I have been trying to figure them out. They're some kind of different clan of you all, or something? The ones that build cities?" Future Elihar had mentioned them as an enemy, and I'd heard a little more living with the Weynik.

I felt a wave of anger coming from Elihar. "They do build the cities, when they find them. They find them, they occupy them, and then when the time comes, they build them for their ancestors to discover."

"Yes, that's all very weird, with the cities going backwards. I mean forwards." Ugh. Still hard to speak of it all correctly. "Why don't you do this? Live in cities?"

"We have the ironwood, and it moves along with us in time. It is far simpler to build with that." He made a whooshing noise, and some of his anger turned to regret. "In earlier times, there was no division between the Weynik and the Nurikna." He was quiet. "There were far more of us then, and our society was rich and wise, with many scholars and scientists, larger communities, prosperity. The split between the Weynik and Nurikna has harmed both sides, but ours most of all." He spun his head around a bit. "It would be nice to go back to those previous times, when all lived as we Weynik do, shaping the ironwood, living only from what the land provides."

This was mostly new to me. I wanted to get into it, but he was sounding unhappy, so I didn't want to push him. I decided to pursue it from the edges. "How do you know about those times before? When all of you lived together?" I'd gathered he was an archeologist, or what passed for one, so I figured that might keep him talking.

He grunted. "I don't know all of it as certain fact, but I infer that it is so. From our most ancient sites, we have found ironwood tools from those cultures, similar to those we use. And we have found no evidence of them living in other ways, in cities, or in bigger groups, before the division between the

Weynik and the Nurikna. We know when and how the Nurikna split from the Weynik, and how they lived before. That is in our history, our recorded memory. It was before I was born, and before my parents, but not long before. One hundred and fifty-five orbits ago."

"What happened between these groups? Some kind of big argument?"

"The time when we split was when the ruins of the first city were discovered, as our numbers grew and people roamed across more of the planet than we had before. Some greeted this discovery with fear or mistrust because it seemed to invite many paradoxes, while many others grew excited. To them, the cities were full of wonders – devices that played music, self-propelled vehicles, towering buildings of stone. These people embraced the destiny the city offered. A future where we were builders, where we shaped stone and metal and could live in greater numbers, with clean water and food available easily everywhere, and with clever devices driven by electric charge and nonliving chemicals. To those people, it became a path they wished to follow." Elihar pressed his three arms together, a gesture I was realizing was one of displeasure or anguish. "And in that way, they created their own paradox, because they came to live in a way they had merely discovered. And eventually, when they came to the time where the cities had been built, they were forced to build the cities they had found, and then search for more."

"Didn't that cause a bunch of issues with the curse?" I imagined all these people suddenly causing the deaths of their relatives. Probably a major calamity. Or at least source material for a lot of angsty poetry. If that was a Kenai thing.

"It did. They paid a heavy price. Thousands became *lajaret*. But there arose within those who survived, and still wanted to live in the cities, a leader. Nuruk, one who became expert in the use of metal, the shaping of stone, the use of nonliving energy. Nuruk encouraged them to harden themselves against the curse. Their culture diverged from ours. They changed their ways to adapt to the losses, and to minimize their impact on the survivors. They began mixing their gametes without partnership, at random, and planting whatever seeds grew. Children were raised by the community, without knowing their parents, and not in any family groups. Nuruk taught that loyalty to the society was all, and bonds between individuals were weakness." Elihar was speaking stridently, now. I could feel strong emotion behind his words.

"Did it work?"

"It did, in a way. The curse was weakened for them. The many paradoxes they create cause fewer deaths for the Nurikna, because most of them only have a few friends, and not very close ones. The curse seeks out strong bonds, and they have few. Over time, some left the Nurikna, not liking the life they adopted, while others joined, tempted by the machines and cities and technology. Our society became split between these groups. To the Nurikna, the Weynik seem primitive, backwards. To the Weynik, the Nurikna had merely exchanged one curse for another, bleaker one, full of paradox, and without love or friendship between people." Elihar's head twitched, and I could feel anger again. "Now the two groups are enemies, although the intensity of our conflict varies with the years."

"You're at war?" This all sounded sad. But war was a thing I had studied. A thing I understood.

"The Weynik do not wish conflict. We never have. Our creed holds to peace between all people, and many of us abhor violence and would never fight, even if attacked. But the Nurikna no longer hold to this creed. They attack us from time to time. Their culture does not foster mercy or caring. At times they capture our woodweavers, because Nurikna seeds no longer produce them, and the Nurikna still have some use for ironwood. At other times, they merely seek to destroy us. Their leaders declare the Weynik as mortal enemies. They do this to unite the Nurikna against something other than themselves. The more they rage against us, the more unified their society becomes."

The marine in me was curious. "Who wins these battles between the groups? How do they play out?"

"The Nurikna win, every time. They discovered weapons in their cities, and they discover more wherever they explore. They are able to see how these items work and how they are constructed. Then they use them, being sure to build them when it becomes necessary. Their weapons grow ever stronger. Devices to fling metal through the air, piercing our bodies, and devices that rain fire upon us. They also have fearsome metal vehicles that travel quickly across the land, which can launch even bigger pieces of metal." He bowed his head, and I could feel the anguish coming off him. "It is all a terrible paradox, their descendants sending weapons back to their ancestors through time. We do not have anything to compete with them except ironwood spears, and those are of little value. And some of us will not even fight with them, holding to our creed. When the Nurikna come, we disperse to new areas, farther from their cities, and we try to build up our communities again. But our numbers are much reduced, and so much of our culture and our achievements are now lost."

I knew that similar events had happened many times in human history. Without the element of paradox, to be sure, but still. One culture using terrible weapons against another that lacked them, killing at will. We were no different from the Nurikna in this. In fact, we were worse. The Trade Union war had seen the use of weapons terrible enough to destroy billions in an instant. I thought it might help Elihar to know. "My people—they do this too. Fight each other, with much bitterness."

"Perhaps war is universal."

I was hardly, as a marine, in any place to contradict him. We sat in silence for a bit, the language lesson set aside. After a while, I gave voice to a thought that had stuck with me and troubled me. I'd raised it with future Elihar and hadn't gotten a good answer. Maybe this version of him would listen. "It is strange that there were no Weynik in the future, where I was from. If you evolved like we do, even though it would run backwards, there should at least have been ancestors then, that developed into you, now, today." I thought about this some more. "We just assumed you'd died out, gone extinct. But now that I know you live backwards, you should have been there. When we humans arrived here. I mean, your ancestors should have been here."

"We do not know how we came to be. Our historical records do not extend back to this time, although there are stories. I do not believe them, though. People often lie to make a good story." He grunted in laughter. "Perhaps we did not evolve from other life as you did, but instead merely appeared one day, as the night gave way to the sun."

I was skeptical. "From where? You can't just show up out of nowhere."

Elihar grunted. "How are you sure of this? Have you not found much mystery on this world already?" I felt his pleasure at his joke, although it also came with kindness. "One story says we are all derived from an enormous ironwood tree that once stood at the center of our world. That we used to be made of ironwood, but now we have become impure." More grunts. "That's silly. Ironwood is quite different from us, say the woodweavers, and from all other life on our world." He turned sad again, but I couldn't see why ironwood would trouble him so much. He switched back to the Weynik language. "I think you are skilled enough with our speech now to come to our *goromita*. Our governing meetings."

"Why would anybody want me at one of those? I'm a complete outsider. I barely speak your language, and I don't know your culture."

"You're important to us. My future self said so in the notes you brought to me. And I think I might now be understanding how, with Renefe's help."

"Are you going to tell me?" I laughed, but it came out a little bitter. And desperate.

He grunted. And he did not tell me. "Go to the edge of the village opposite the river later today, where the houses end. Leave the village and travel farther in that direction. It will take you some time to walk the distance because your legs are slow. There is a path. I'm sure you will spot it. Meet us by the large ironwood tree tonight, as the sun sets. There will be lamps lit. You will see us there."

That sounded a lot more like a cult gathering than any kind of community governance, but I was new here. Best not to judge.

63

BOARD MEETING

The sun was setting behind the conical trees as I reached the clearing, a gap perhaps fifty meters across. It looked as though it had been cleared and well-used – the ground was beaten down flat, packed by feet, it seemed, and the smaller plants that covered the forest floor around us were missing, replaced by a grayish blue groundcover that reminded me of the rock algae back on my homeworld, Ramine. I also saw the lights Elihar had promised. They were bioluminescent material suspended in an ironwood housing. Or maybe the ironwood could be convinced to bioluminesce. I hadn't quite followed the explanation. These lamps, crafted by the woodweavers, were used in many Weynik homes. They could be turned on and off with a touch, which I guess argued against bioluminescence. I had not seen them used outside before. There were ten of them in an irregular circle around the clearing, set on posts and bent slightly downward towards the center, shedding a comforting green glow.

When I arrived, there were maybe twenty-five Weynik there, talking to each other in what I'd learned was an excited fashion: rapidly spinning heads, lots of swinging and stabbing motions with their viny arms, plus a bunch of eye twitching and the occasional involuntary ejection of moist animal bones from the neck cavity. I had decided that was one part of the local communication ritual I didn't need to emulate. I recognized several of the people there. Elihar, who must have some pull, I realized, to be at this meeting, especially if his actual job was field research. Another one, Renefe, I'd seen around but not ever spoken with. I was told Renefe was old, with only two eyes remaining. The others had fallen victim to an explosion, or so the story went. Renefe had been described to me as a kind of scientist or engineer, studying all sorts of topics and building things, often with the help of the woodweavers. People generally spoke of Renefe with respect. There was also Doyeva, the keeper of the ironwood groves. Esek, the teacher I'd studied with, who taught the children. Degungu, who tended the fish pools. I was getting to know many of the people of the Weynik community, but there were still quite a few I hadn't met or spoken with. I knew there were other villages, too, although it seemed like this might be an important one. I didn't really have a feel for the total Weynik population on Kenai.

A few more Weynik straggled in. I found a log to sit on over at the side, outside the circle of lights. I was interested in what was happening, but I didn't want to intrude. And I didn't know if the others would be as happy to have me around. Most of the Weynik I'd met had been somewhere between reserved and friendly, but I could feel mistrust from some of them, and revulsion from a few. The zavvies, probably, but coming at me from them. After all, I was the bug-eyed monster in this scenario.

Elihar broke from the group and came over to me. He took a seat on my log, although the Weynik seldom sat on things. Mostly they just squatted in place. I figured he was being polite. When your guest has a butt, and you don't, you try to be accommodating.

"You found us. Good. I think your name will come up tonight. They may ask something of you. Renefe. The scientist. Renefe will make the request, if it comes."

"Are you going to tell me what it is?"

"I'll let the others explain. I do not know how Renefe will choose to tell the story." He gestured at another of the Weynik, one I hadn't met. "You will also hear from Ydran, that one." As I looked more closely, I realized I had not seen this person before. They wore a cloth draped around their shoulders, which was unusual. And it was decorated with what looked like shells and bones. I hadn't been to the oceans of Kenai to know what grew there, but it stood to reason that's where shelled life might live, what with all the rain and dissolved minerals making their way into the seas. Same as on most worlds.

"Ydran is a snappy dresser."

Elihar didn't appreciate my humor. "Ydran lives among the Nurikna in secret, pretending to be one of them. Every so often, Ydran returns to tell us what the Nurikna are doing and whether they threaten us. Ydran's life is dangerous."

"A spy." Interesting. I wondered if they had others.

"I will note that word." Elihar pointed at Ydran again. "It is relevant that Ydran's parents and siblings fell into a deep hole that opened up under their home recently. All perished. It was about twenty days ago."

I was shocked. "Really? I didn't hear anything about it." That sounded like something somebody would have mentioned.

"They lived in another village nearby, a smaller one."

I didn't really have the lay of the land yet. I didn't know the number and location of other villages. I pondered what Elihar had said. "Sudden death of a lot of family members in an unusual way. Was it related to the curse?"

"You learn more of this world, I see." Elihar's head dipped a little. I could feel respect and regret coming from him, directed towards Ydran. "Ydran must have discovered something or done something that invited paradox. I suspect we will learn what that was tonight. Ydran has just today learned of their family's deaths."

I stayed quiet for a moment out of respect. Then I addressed something that had been pressing on me. "Would you mind sitting with me? Helping with what they say? I do all right, but I get lost when they use a lot of new words or when they go too fast."

"It would be my honor, Jess." That was laying it on a little thick, I thought, but whatever. He continued. "I will be asked to address something I have discovered, so I will have to leave you then. But I will return."

The pre-meeting discussion lasted for a little longer, and then one of the Weynik I didn't know, a large one, raised all three limbs and started yelling. Well, speaking loudly anyway. I didn't have the nuances down yet. It was hard enough following the unfamiliar words all strung together.

"Our *goromita* is joined. Friends are present and welcome. Let us begin." The speaker turned to Elihar. "I offer my regret that your Miern is not with us to lead this *goromita*."

Elihar bent his head down, then replied. "You honor her loss with grace, and also the loss of my children. *Lajaretitoorubetha*." I recognized *lajaret*, but the rest was a mystery. The assembled people repeated the phrase together. Some kind of incantation or ritual speech.

Elihar turned his head to point his speaking trumpet in my direction. He spoke softly, in Tradespeak. "The speaker is Poen. She lives in a nearby village. She is the new Seed-Bearer for these villages. That title means she leads us, with guidance from this meeting."

Poen started by asking various members of the meeting to report information from their areas of responsibility within the villages. How many fish and eels are in the catch ponds? How are the ironwood trees growing? Do we need to cultivate more? How many people have died since our last meeting, and how many have been planted? How many have uprooted? Are the hunters pleased with their catch? How far afield must the gathering teams go to find berries, fruit, and roots? Are the attempts to grow food meeting with any success here?

I had no reference to judge the answers to any of these questions, but the seriousness of the reports, and the disappointment I read among those assembled when they were given, led me to believe that the Weynik community was facing hard times. It was interesting to me to learn more about how their lives worked. I'd picked up some from living with them, and I'd helped catch fish and farm and gather food, but I hadn't realized how complex a system they were managing, and how quantitative the management was.

Poen turned to a person who had not spoken. "Visalha. Has the rotting sickness been seen in anyone else?"

"No, Poen. It was limited to Elihar's family. It struck quickly and then vanished." I felt Elihar's sorrow grow acute, intense. "It must be related to what he discovered." Visalha came over to us and put a hand on Elihar's head. "*Lajaretitoorubetha*, my friend." Again, the crowd murmured the phrase together. Elihar's sorrow grew even more intense.

"Renefe, tell us of the poison. Is it here among us? Does it grow stronger?" This sparked my interest, because Elihar had mentioned that person's name. And poison sounded ominous.

"It is here." Renefe held up some flat squares of ironwood. "Sekene has built more of the sensors I designed. We left them out for twenty days as before. The tiny particles that make up the poison pass through the ironwood, damaging it. They leave tracks behind. When Sekene highlights these tracks, we can tell how many particles are present." Renefe seemed proud of this. "There are more of them than earlier this year, about half again as many. That suggests that we are approaching a release of the poison, a major event. The poison is the same kind as that from *inuhaili,* although no *inuhaili* is present here."

I leaned over to Elihar, but he was already explaining. "*Inuhaili* are poison rocks. They make living creatures sick. We have seen this poison appear more and more in our villages."

Poison rocks, and tiny damaging particles. This was sounding like radioactivity. I knew Kenai had a far higher concentration of radioactive minerals than most planets, which is part of why it was attractive for exploitation. I also knew from Welk's discussion of carbon dating that there'd been some kind of nuclear release. He'd said it predated the cities, but that was before we knew that time went backwards for Kenaians. They had cities now, and that meant the nuclear event was in their future. Were we approaching that? Because of the high levels of uranium in the soils on Kenai and the risk of dust inhalation and other contamination, they'd given everybody associated with the landing parties a heavy course of pretreatment for radiation exposure prior to our deployment, but I had no idea if that was still working following my time reversal and jump to the past. Regardless, I doubted the treatment was up to handling a full-on nuclear war. What had I gotten myself into?

Poen was serious, unhappy. "Do we need to move the villages again?" That prompted a range of emotions in the Weynik. Anger, sorrow, anguish. Moving the community was not a popular idea. Some of the people assembled made little bleating noises, a reaction I hadn't seen before.

Renefe held up an arm. "Not yet. It is not strong enough to kill us, or even to sicken us much, beyond our capacity to heal. If it increases, as I suspect it will, then we will be in danger. Sekene and I will continue to measure the poison's strength, and we will tell you if it changes." He stuck the squares of ironwood to the side of his body. "I am worried there is nowhere we can move, though. I have set up sensors in many directions, many distances. All show the *inuhaili* poison, and everywhere we look it is strong. We may have trouble escaping it."

There was more anguish, more sorrow, more anger. More bleating. Some of the people began speaking quickly to each other, or just shouting things.

Poen made a trumpeting noise. People settled down and fell silent. "We will discuss more of this later, when Ydran speaks. But first, Elihar, can you tell us of what you have learned of your discovery?"

Elihar rose from our log and entered the circle. "Seed-Bearer. Thank you for listening to my story." This sounded to me like ritual language, formal. "Sekene and I have studied the object I discovered. We believe it has two functions. One of them is specific to me, though it affects us all. The other is even more important, if we are correct. Both are paradoxical, but that price I hope has already been fully paid."

A chorus of *lajaretitoorubetha* met his words, and I felt sympathy and sorrow coming from those assembled.

"The first function is as a message. We suspected there was something contained within the object. Sekene was able to reshape it to make an opening, and our suspicions were correct. There was a message carved within upon a tablet. A message from me."

The meeting erupted in sounds. Honks, bleats, whooshes. Poen asked, "What did it say?"

"It gave a location where I needed to go. South of here, not as far south as where we discovered it. It said that I should bring the object to that place. It also said that I would meet a stranger from another world, and that she would be a friend to our people when days grew dark." He gestured to me. "We have found that friend."

One of the committee members shouted "Jessamiko!" The Weynik tended to run my name together, I think because they all had one name, so two was weird, and because their language didn't include gaps between words. Others echoed my name. It felt pretty awkward.

Poen gave me a long look, spinning her head around. "You said there were two functions to the object. One is clearly to deliver this message. What is the other?"

Elihar went over to a spot outside the clearing and picked something up. When he returned, I felt a chill. It was the box. The one we'd dug up in Welk's pit. The one I'd held in my hands. The one I'd found Elihar placing there, after I killed the marines that were attacking Welk and my other self. That thing had quite a history, all of it confusing. And now it was here, at this time. Elihar held it up to show the others. I could see it had a hole in one side now. "Sekene has analyzed the box. It is *umbani*, but it is a special type. It is entirely made from the type of *umbani* we use as cuttings, to grow more of the trees."

Sekene moved to the middle of the circle. "There is more than that. We *omariga* need to work hard to get a new tree to grow from a cutting. It takes will, and work, and coaxing. This *umbani* grows easily. One need only place it upon the ground, and an *umbani* tree sprouts, and grows faster than all of our others. It is fresh and vibrant, more alive than all the *umbani* I have known."

Poen gave off a vibe of fascination, an emotion echoed by many of the others. "Could we use this, then? To grow more *umbani*, more quickly? It seems that it is perhaps a gift to us."

Elihar waited for Sekene to speak, but Sekene gestured to him, so he answered. "We believe it is a gift to us, but a far more important one. You know that the site where I found this object contains the oldest ironwood tools and relics we have ever found. We think the *umbani* trees originated in this location, and we have carried them with us as we spread to other places. This is why we were digging there, to understand better how our people came to find and use *umbani,* long ago." Elihar paused. I didn't see where he was going. "We think it is possible that this object is the original *umbani*, the seed that gave rise to all others. Sekene has studied its flesh and its structures. All seems clean and new, strong and pure."

There were murmurs and honks. I had trouble keeping up. Poen was even more confused. She spoke. "If that is correct, then... how did it contain your message inside? It must be ancient."

I knew how. The portal. It had to exist here, in this time, because I knew Elihar would get sent to the future. There couldn't be two ways to do that, could there? And future Elihar had mentioned going through it. So it had to exist now, and he had to go there. That's where the note must be sending him. But I didn't know if I should say any of that, or if I were allowed to speak to the group at all. If I was right, the whole thing smacked of paradox. But could I explain it in a way that was just general information, not a description of the future? That was allowed, wasn't it? I wasn't sure.

I rose from my log and went to the edge of the circle. "Poen," I said. "I may know how this works." I sensed a host of emotions coming from the gathered crowd. Curiosity, mistrust, affront at my intrusion. Fear.

"Jessamiko." Poen studied me. "Speak carefully. Do not reveal the future to us, or you will invite peril upon yourself and your loved ones."

I swallowed, and then I chose my words very carefully. "I have been to the place where I believe the note tells Elihar to go. There is a machine there, one that can move people to other times. That is how I came here from when I lived, which is far removed from your time." I knew more, but I didn't want to say it. Now I was being Elihar, I thought. Giving them some cryptic information, but not enough to be useful.

Elihar caught on, though. "If I go there, and I travel to a time long ago, then I am the one that will place this object where I dug it up." He paused. "That explains my note inside. I have discovered my own artifact. What a tremendous paradox I have created."

Sekene put a hand on Elihar's side, a gentle gesture. "More than that, dear Elihar. I believe you planted the seed for all the *umbani* that ever was."

The meeting was at once filled with noise and discussion. Elihar and Sekene were speaking rapidly with each other, too softly for me to overhear. Poen came over to them and joined in. At last, they finished, and Poen held up three arms. The discussion quieted.

"We are agreed. Elihar must follow the directions. There is often great unknowable danger in avoiding destiny, but in this case, we know exactly what damage would be caused, or at least part of it. Without *umbani*, which we use for everything we do, our civilization would be far less than it is. We might never have survived until now. We would have no tools, no technology. Elihar must go and deliver this object, this seed, to where it belongs." Poen pointed one arm high in the air. "Does the meeting agree?"

The group pounded their feet on the ground, their thick cylindrical bodies bobbing along. I wasn't sure what was going on, but I could read positive emotions, sometimes tinged with sorrow. It died down, and Poen spoke again. "We are agreed. Elihar, will you serve in this way?"

"I will. My honor and duty." Again, the words sounded ceremonial. I could feel that Elihar was overwhelmed, struggling. Understandable. I remembered experiencing a similar feeling in the remote river camp after discovering my name carved in the trees. This world played a lot of games with your head.

Poen held up her arms again. "This meeting has already been long, and full of hard discoveries, but we have still more important matters to discuss. Our friend Ydran has returned early from the Nurikna. Ydran, can you give your report now?"

Ydran, the one wearing the long scarf with the shells and bones, rose to speak. "My friends. It is good to be back among you after so long among the enemy. That joy helps sweeten the sorrow of my family's losses." A chorus of *lajaretitoorubetha* followed. Ydran spun his head a few times, then continued. "The news from the Nurikna is bleak. In Povelat, the city where I live, and in others, people are falling ill. The leaders have not yet acknowledged that this is unusual, and they certainly have not suggested a cause, but my friends think that it must be the *inuhaili* poison, as it is here. The sickness takes similar forms, and one of my friends reports they have seen many devices designed to measure the particles as Renefe does, in our city and in others. I do not have any way to know the results they produce, but the fact that they are measuring this now suggests that the problem is the same there." There was more murmuring, and some bleating. People were not pleased at this news.

Ydran went on. "Even without information, people are recognizing the spread of the sickness and becoming upset about it. The leaders have blamed the Weynik for this blight."

I felt a flash of anger from Poen. "How could they blame us? That is a lie." She flailed with her hands as she spoke, sharp aggressive motions.

Ydran spun their head to focus new eyes on Poen. "They must know, as you do, that the poison increases. Like you, they suspect it comes from something that happens soon. Something big. It has been announced that the Nurikna living in the western city, Egorim, have discovered a trove of weapons along with instructions on how to build and use them. This is celebrated as a great discovery that will add to the strength of the Nurikna. These weapons rely on *inuhaili*."

"Still, none of this points to the Weynik. It all smacks of Nurikna and their embrace of paradox." This was Visalha, the one who'd spoken of the disease. And Visalha was seriously hacked off.

"The leaders are saying that the Weynik must also have found these weapons. They say the Weynik will use the weapons on the Nurikna cities. They say the sickness is coming back to us through time from when these weapons will be used."

Poen began walking in an erratic pattern around the circle of lights. Her voice, and her emotion, were hot and angry. "That makes no sense. The Weynik do not make anything that travels back from the future. Nothing of metal, nothing of stone, nothing of *inuhaili*. And we do not build weapons other than spear and blade, in accordance with the creed. We would not even know how. If they have discovered such weapons, we are not the ones who will build them. They are. They must know this."

Ydran bowed their head toward Poen. "They must, as you say. Yet the lie holds strength with the people, because the Weynik have been made to seem so evil to them, through lies piled on lies over years." Ydran pointed to Renefe. "Now, they point to the vessels you have launched into the sky. Those worry the Nurikna, and they are an easy target for fear and anger."

This was the first I'd heard of vessels launched into the sky. I looked at Elihar, and he gave me one of his *I'm totally not going to tell you about this very important thing* looks. I really hated the guy sometimes.

Renefe grew defensive. "My vessels have nothing to do with *inuhaili.* They are *fohaskar.* Entirely so. The Nurikna leaders must know this." *Fohaskar* was a word I had recently learned. It was a catch-all term for everything that traveled backward in time. Living things, and whatever was derived from them. The Weynik, the Nurikna, ironwood, the trees and plants and animals. And me, now, thanks to the portal.

Ydran put all three arms up high and waggled them. "The leaders may well know the truth, but the truth is seldom what they say to the people. They say the sky vessels are the Weynik testing their new weapons. The weapons they will use to cause the sickness. And they mean to raise an army, with their fearsome war machines and their metal vehicles. They plan to attack all the Weynik villages. They mean to kill us all. That is why I left to return home."

Ydran was quiet after this statement. There was a moment of silence that followed, and then the meeting erupted into a cacophony of voices and yelling and bleating. Poen didn't interrupt it this time, seeming instead to be deep in thought. Elihar sat beside me, not participating, but observing.

Eventually, the ruckus subsided. Poen pointed an arm at Ydran. "This is unwelcome news, to be sure, but you are hardly to blame for bringing it. As always, you have done us a great service. Knowing what they plan allows us a chance to prevent it. Or to flee."

Ydran bowed his head again. "Service to the Weynik is my honor and my duty."

Poen looked at Ydran for a moment. I thought she might be waiting for the spy to say something more. Finally, she gave up and spoke again. "Ydran. Nothing you have told us invites paradox. There must be more to say, or your family would not have been rendered *lajaret.*"

I felt an intense pang of sadness coming from Ydran. "You are correct, wise Seed-Bearer. There is more, and it is far worse. And it is why my family has become *lajaret.*"

64

PROPHETEERING

Ydran held up all three arms. Orating, I supposed. An oddly human gesture. "I told you on my last visit here that the cities are beginning to unbuild themselves. Not just mine. All of them. That means we are nearing the time when they were constructed. Each day we must build the parts of the city that are lost during the nightly jump. You remember the city of Amurlanosk, the one that disappeared completely ten years ago?" Some of the crowd waggled their arms in assent. "Now we are seeing all the current cities doing this. And we have not found new cities. That is deeply troubling to the Nurikna, as it suggests that their time in cities may be coming to an end. That may portend a major change in their society, or perhaps, as many of them fear, the end of that society altogether."

I leaned over to Elihar. "If they're unbuilding the cities, doesn't that mean that the Weynik can't have destroyed them?"

"The Weynik could still be guilty of killing all the Nurikna with these weapons, even if the cities vanished before it happens." That was a good point. I hadn't thought of that scenario. This reversed time architecture business was hard for me.

Ydran was still talking. "You Weynik may not understand the customs of the Nurikna, so let me explain. When a city nears its end, all Nurikna are pressed into service, constructing the buildings and roads that they have been using for many previous years. It is seen as a sacred duty for all Nurikna. To avoid it would be to invite a major paradox and the curse that follows. Also, those who refuse are immediately killed." Ydran was speaking in a clear, calm voice, and the meeting had grown utterly silent, waiting on every word. "I was assigned the task of working on the building where I have lived for the past six years. Over the course of most of a year, it disassembled itself. Each night when the time shift came, parts of the building would vanish, and we would have to build whatever had vanished in the day that followed. At the next time shift, more of it disappears, and that shows us what must be built the next day."

I whispered to Elihar. "That sounds incredibly frustrating."

He grunted. "There is good reason we choose not to live in cities."

Ydran continued. "When my building was almost gone, it grew time to set the foundation – the roots of the building, on which it sits. I was digging in the ground, away from others, and I found a square of metal there set in stone. A monument. It was not part of the building at all. When I touched it, a voice spoke, mentioning a date nearly sixty years in the future."

This gave rise to murmuring. Elihar leaned toward me. "A message from the future. This must be the paradox that killed Ydran's family." That hardly seemed fair to me. The guy had just been digging a hole.

Poen stepped closer to Ydran. "What did the voice say?"

"It said the voice was from an Nurikna named Angalir. Angalir said this record was *vasikilo*. And Angalir claimed to be the very last person alive." This created more than murmuring. The bleating and yelling surged immediately, and it took Poen a while to calm them down.

I leaned over to Elihar. "*Vasikilo?*"

Elihar bent his speaking trumpet close to my ear. "A speaking of one's history. One's life and deeds. A sacred document. We prepare them sometimes for those whose lives were of significance. Perhaps you have seen some in the village? The carved posts near the fish pond?" I hadn't paid attention to these, but I couldn't read very well. Elihar's head spun a little, just a quarter turn. "They are not ever prepared by oneself, though. The family does this."

The crowd was finally quieting, although I could sense that emotions still ran high. Poen asked Ydran, "This person, Angalir, says that everyone will be dead in sixty years?"

"Yes. But beyond that, Angalir claims to have killed them. Us. All of us. The message went on for some time. Angalir professed to be a clever engineer who had studied the *inuhaili* weapons and learned the secrets of their construction. Angalir claimed to have left Egorim after seeing how deadly the weapons could be, how much poison they could release. The prospect of doom for all people became clear. Angalir did not consider taking action to avert the destruction, but instead wrote of the profound unworthiness of the Nurikna and the Weynik, all of us. Angalir stole food and supplies, loaded them on an airship, and fled to the northern mountains, thinking to escape from the city and perhaps to survive. Where Angalir landed, there was an underground home, an artificial cave. And within was a metal sign, left from Angalir's future self. Angalir would build this cave, it said. Angalir stocked this place with food from the airship and retreated within it. The airship disappeared."

Of course. A metal device had to go forward in time. It would sit outside the bunker for all the days after Angalir arrived and rust while the bunker fell into ruins. But all of that wouldn't matter to Angalir, who was progressing backwards, to the time before it arrived.

Silence had fallen over the meeting again. It was hard to believe this story, but because it told of events that hadn't happened yet, there was no way to know if it were truth or fiction. Ydran kept going. "The story continued. The *inuhaili* poison became even more intense as Angalir hid in the ground, filling the air and blanketing the land. Angalir stayed deep in the shelter, going dormant to conserve supplies, waking only occasionally to study the world through devices in the cave that showed conditions on the surface. Over time, the skies grew thick with smoke and ash and dust, and the level of poison grew tremendously intense, so much so that Angalir realized that the weapons would be used very soon." That squared with the growing radiation they were seeing now, I thought. There really was going to be a nuclear war. It sounded like a big one.

"One day, when Angalir awoke from dormancy, the skies were clear, and the poison absent." That revelation threw me for a moment, but then I realized that the radiation and the fallout would move forward in time, towards us here and now, while Angalir would continue to move backward, reaching a time before the war. It was consistent, but weird. "Angalir emerged from the shelter to a world nearly devoid of life. But as Angalir emerged, a new door opened in the side of the mountain, and a metal worker machine came forth, towing behind it an airship of a new design. Angalir took the airship and flew out to see what had become of everyone. But nearly all animals and plants were dead or gone, as were all the people. Angalir flew the airship as far as possible, but found only empty landscapes, the ashes of forests, and the bodies of the dead.

"Angalir returned to the cave and studied the new area that had been revealed. Angalir's future self would build this place as well and would design and construct the mechanical workers to do the labor. Angalir realized the place was a factory to produce *inuhaili* weapons, along with the mechanical workers, and that there were foundries and other devices to aid in the work. All that was needed was there, built by Angalir's future self and the mechanical workers." Ydran paused. "And there was another, a mechanical voice that spoke from the wall of the cave. It was Angalir's child, although it was a mechanical being, born of technology and metal rather than of seeds. This being, too, Angalir would build, based on the instructions it shared. It said its name was Mothrek."

Ydran paused. People gave off surprise, astonishment. Nobody spoke. All were trying to follow this story. I was trying to think of what it all meant. This Angalir person seemed to have created all of the nuclear weapons, the ones for the war, and also the ones being found now. And all of this had taken place bathed in a deep ocean of paradox. Everything Angalir needed, Angalir's future self had provided, either built in place or taught to Mothrek who could relay it. All the complicated knowledge involved in nuclear engineering, Angalir had taught to Angalir across time. It was bizarre, but with the technology moving forward and Angalir moving backward, Angalir could leave behind any technology or knowledge needed. Much of it, maybe all of it, had come from nowhere at all, although Angalir had to be smart enough to understand it and eventually to be able to build it. But the entire effort was paradox.

Ydran continued. "Angalir found new purpose. Sure of the unworthiness of our race, Angalir made it a point to learn how all of this facility worked, to learn the new technology, to learn how to manufacture the *inuhaili* weapons and the mechanical workers. Mothrek guided Angalir. One day, Angalir came through the daily time shift to find the factory full of weapons along with an army of new metal workers, each equipped to dig, each able to carry one of the weapons. Angalir realized that these were to be sent out to bury and arm the weapons all across the land. Angalir was the one who had destroyed the world, and Angalir judged that this was a worthy way for our race to end. Angalir sent forth the weapons to be buried all around the areas where we live, and also sent the weapons that would be discovered by Angalir's own past self. That is where the *vasikilo* ended, with Angalir planning to now build the artificial cave, the weapon factory, and the mechanical workers in order to set all this in motion. Angalir must have done this, or the rest of it would never have come to pass. And Angalir chose some of the metal workers to bury this boasting *vasikilo* I found, taunting us about the doom Angalir and Mothrek would create."

Questions came fast and angry, and all were discussed. Not all were answered to any degree of satisfaction, at least to my mind.

Why would Angalir leave this message?

> *It was vasikilo. It was recorded out of spite, and out of a desire to have evil deeds known.*

> *As a warning. Daring us to avert it.*

> *No villain wishes their deeds unknown. All seek fame.*

Is it not improbable that Ydran discovered the story in this way?

> *Perhaps Angalir left many such vasikilo, in many places. Such would befit a prideful one.*

> *Can we not just move far away? Avoid the weapons?*

> *Where would we go? Angalir says all died, that the whole world was poisoned.*

Can we find Angalir and stop this? Kill this evil one?

> *Resisting destiny creates worse results. You know this.*

> *What could be worse than this?*

> *Perhaps this doom came from someone trying to resist a lesser evil.*

Should we tell the rest of the Weynik of this?

> *They deserve to know.*

It would be kinder not to say.

The discussion took a long time. Fear, anger, and despair radiated from the group. I was trying to make sense of it all, but I, too, felt the sense of dread. Had I come back here only to die in a nuclear war? But Elihar had said that I brought hope. I couldn't see any way I could affect any of this, or what hope I could provide.

I was a marine, though, and experienced in solo stealth operations. Perhaps I could track down Angalir and take them out before any of this happened. It was a longshot, with seemingly insurmountable obstacles, but maybe that was it. It was my training.

I leaned over to Elihar. "What if I go find Angalir and kill them? Would that help? I am pretty good at that kind of thing."

I thought Elihar might be taken aback, but his voice was kind. "I suppose it is possible you might succeed, although we don't know the location of the factory in the mountains, and they are vast. You might well look for the rest of your life and never find the cave."

A fair point. "What if it hasn't started yet? What if Angalir is still in the city? That could be true, right? It should be easy enough to track down somebody there, especially if we know the name."

"Angalir is not a real name. No one would call their child this."

"What do you mean?"

"*Angalir* is a word reserved for the worst kind of evil. Deeds so horrific they can never be forgiven."

Oh. That kind of person. Probably dressed all in black and complained about their parents. "I see."

"There is another way you can help, I think. A better way. At least, I hope so."

65

TRANSPLANTATION

The discussion continued late into the night, through the time shift. I felt the ripple of time flash across me. Finally, Poen silenced the crowd. "Friends. This is momentous and important information. We must think on it and decide what to do. We are agreed, I think, that Ydran will return to the city and share the story of Angalir with the Nurikna, though in a way that preserves Ydran's secret role. There seems to be no benefit to us in keeping it hidden, and perhaps the Nurikna will find a way to find Angalir and prevent this from happening." A few of the committee made whooshing noises, which I thought were the equivalent of scoffing.

Poen continued. "We will also prepare for an attack from the Nurikna. We will send word to the other communities. We may need to move the villages to avoid being killed by the Nurikna, especially if they attack soon."

Ydran spoke. "I fear it will be soon. They already prepare the airships and the ground vehicles, although they have not yet called up the warrior caste."

Renefe waved for attention. "If we leave, all our work on the vessels will be lost. We cannot take the *gelinut* with us, nor the *peknauti*."

Elihar nudged me. "The fuel refinery, and the vessel engines." Must be related to the sky ships they'd mentioned.

Poen gave off a wave of unhappiness. "With all this going on, your project cannot be our concern. The safety of the people takes precedence."

Renefe did not take that well. That was the strongest anger I'd felt off a Weynik. I felt like I was about to learn some choice Weynik profanity.

Then Elihar stood, interrupting the conflict. "Seed-Bearer. I disagree. I think Renefe's work is perhaps the most important effort we could make now." Renefe emanated surprise and gratitude. "I know the work is young, but if Ydran's foretelling is true, Renefe's vessels may be the only way to avoid it."

"Those vessels enrage the Nurikna," shouted one of the committee. The ironwood grove tender, I thought it was. "They're bringing this attack upon us!"

Ydran held up a hand pad. "The Nurikna would find another pretense to attack. The vessel launches are not a true cause, merely an opportunity for more lies. And there would be lies and violence in any case. Believe me in this."

Elihar spoke again, his voice measured. "If we can get seeds to Verikin, the Weynik can survive there, out of the shadow of the Nurikna, and of Angalir, and of the poison Angalir will bring upon us." He raised all three arms. "And, if our hopes bear truth, perhaps out of range of the curse that afflicts this world."

Poen wasn't having it. "Renefe's plan will not work. Everyone who has flown beyond this world has died. This plan is doomed." That didn't sound good.

Renefe resisted. "The seeds live. It is just their companion who dies. We are nearly at our goal."

Poen was yelling now. "There must be a companion to pilot the vessel and to plant and nurture the seeds. You know this. The entire plan is pointless without such a person."

Without warning, Renefe pointed to me. "This one is not of this world. She has already lived beyond its bounds. Jessamiko can be the companion. She can go to Verikin. She can save us."

66

WOODEN SHIPS

"You really set me up there, you know? At the meeting?" I was joking, but the sentiment was real. It was a warm day, and the sun felt good after the long night of discord. I snacked on a patty I'd made by grinding up a fungus-like organism. It was pretty good.

Elihar peeled an eel off his side and stuffed into his neck cavity. "Aren't you the one who convinced them to send me back thousands of years to plant trees and give myself a box?"

"That's fair." I laughed. "Tell me more about Renefe's vessels."

Elihar ate his last remaining eel, then stood up straight. "They are the remnants of a much older time, from when the Weynik were lush and strong and numerous. When our science and learning were at their height. Before the cities were found, before the Nurikna left us, lured away by the wonders of metal and stone." I could sense profound sadness, sharper than I had felt from him before. "My mate, Miern, was the one who wanted to come here. When we had to move our village because of Nurikna attacks, she was Seed-Bearer, and she led us here. She learned from our lore-keepers that the Weynik effort to fly started in this area, and when we arrived, we uncovered the sites remaining from that old endeavor, overgrown with vines and trees. The vessels were broken remnants and the fuel refineries badly damaged. Many repairs were needed, but with Renefe and Sekene's work, they are flush with new growth."

He put all three hand pads together on the middle of his torso, a gesture I hadn't seen him make. "The Nurikna burned Sekene's village when Sekene was very young. Most of the people there died. Sekene fled, meeting us as we traveled to this place. Miern welcomed Sekene into our community, and Sekene's unparalleled skill with *umbani* was immediately apparent. Miern was also the one who thought Renefe and Sekene could work well together. She planted this seed, set this all to growing." A hint of optimism now. He rose from his squat and belched a fish bone out of his neck. "They have done well, beyond even Miern's greatest hopes. Come with me. It would be easier to show you."

Renefe was effervescent with excitement. He pointed to an immense square structure of ironwood that sat upon the hillside, the bottom contoured to match the terrain. It was perhaps sixty meters on a side. "This is where the vessel takes flight."

The vessel. I stared up at the mass of ironwood devices in front of me. Humanity had left chemical rockets behind long ago, but that seemed to be the design here. There was a huge cylinder sticking up from the pad, and atop it was a conical structure. The sides were all smooth and shiny, featureless and black. It was kind of ominous.

I looked around at the cluster of ironwood structures. "This facility. You built this?"

"We repaired it." Renefe's head swiveled. "This place fell into disuse when the project was abandoned. This was back when the cities were discovered. The technology they found in the cities was more complex, more exciting than this project, which had not yet met with success." I could feel excitement wash off Renefe. I'd felt it ever since my arrival at the site. "This was many, many years ago, in the time of my parents' parents. But we have rebuilt it since we moved to our new village nearby."

I looked up at the tall ironwood cylinder. The ship. If it warranted that name. And I didn't like what I saw. "There's hardly any room in there. Not nearly enough for food and water and oxygen." They might not have thought of the logistics, especially for a human.

"Sekene has altered the design of the journey chamber for you after watching how you live, in consultation with Tigo and Calane, two of our best life scientists. Remember when they studied you? You consume more air than we do, so Sekene has expanded the garden patches set in the walls. Your wastes and the gases you emit will nurture them, and the ironwood will regulate them and keep them growing. There will be enough good air. Have you met Mokin? Mokin is an expert in animals and plants and their fluids. Mokin and I have studied the bits of your tissue and fluids you gave to us, and we have created a chemical compound which we can dispense across your outer membrane through an ironwood dosing device Sekene created. If you wear this, and keep it close, and refill it as needed, it should slow your body's processes such that you go dormant, as we do from time to time. Once you and the ship are pointed in the right direction and have reached the right speed, you should be able to go dormant for most of the trip. That will cut down on the resources you need."

"Huh." I wasn't thrilled that they'd been secretly researching how to knock me out, but stasis sounded like a good way to pass the years it would probably take to cross space to Verikin, this other world they were talking about. But all of this was new, untested, created by tree scientists to apply to me, who was utterly alien to them. "How do you all know this will work?" If they could sense my feelings as well as I could theirs, they'd be getting a blast of doubt and suspicion, but it was coming from an honest place.

"We wish to test our dormancy compound on you, and to have you try emitting your fluids and gases in the vessel chamber. A testing session is scheduled for later today. We can adjust and recalibrate as needed."

Right. That all sounded terrible. But Renefe was bobbing around happily, ready to continue the tour. "The lower section contains both the fuel and the compressed refined air." Elihar had gone over all the Weynik technical terms I'd likely hear at breakfast, for which I was grateful. I thought I had them connected to concepts I understood now. "This lower section will fly the ship above where the air ends, to where you can escape the planet's pull." A booster rocket. I was familiar with the concept, although nearly all ships I'd seen used fusion drives for sublight speed travel and a Hlojeng coil if they could make interstellar jumps on their own. Rocketry was a much more basic concept. Burn enough stuff fast enough, and point the explosion in an organized, consistent direction, and you could get going pretty fast in the other direction, whether in atmosphere or vacuum. It was a concept that should work. Did work. In theory. I wasn't so keen on strapping myself on for the ride, though.

"When you reach the edge of the sky, the smaller part with the chamber and you will split off and continue flying, and the primary engine will fall back to our world. The smaller part has enough fuel to send you towards Verikin, and to slow you when you get there."

Sure, buddy. "That's an extremely difficult set of calculations. How do you know what course to set, or how much fuel it will take?"

"Sekene built us a mathematical device, modeled upon the old technology we discovered here." Renefe pointed at a set of ironwood blocks on a hillside across the valley. "With its help, we can make sure the distances and weights and fuel requirements are set correctly." He grunted. "Also, we added extra fuel, anyway. To be safe."

Great. That sounded so very precise. "How does the fuel not just vanish with the time jump? It can't be alive. Shouldn't it vanish at *rakineru*?"

Renefe grunted in amusement. "You still don't have the basics down, do you? It is made by living organisms, the tiny beings in the fuel generation tanks, so it travels with us in time, just as our food, our seeds, and the bodies of our dead. At least, it travels with us until it succumbs to *avishar,* the second death. Then it returns to non-life, to the flow of time that the stars follow." He waved a hand pad dismissively. "That should not be a problem. There is not much chance that your fuel will disappear during your trip."

In all the missions I'd been on, that had never been a concern. At least, until now. This was getting worse and worse. "How do you know how far away the other world is?" They had to be talking about Ninilchik, the other habitable planet near Kenai. I'd read a little about it in the pre-mission briefing, so long ago. Or, really, so far in the future. I wish I remembered more about the planet. I knew it was roughly Kenai's size, a little farther from the star, but not too much. Comparable atmospheric composition. Such similar worlds so close to each other were rare, but I'd heard of a few. Durango and Bandera, for example. I'd done a rest and recreation interval at the Patrol base on Bandera, but we often visited Durango. It had better bars.

Renefe spun his head. "We have made careful observations. There were some old records here we could use, but we have checked all of them again for truth. We have found lights in the sky which behave as a world does, traveling around the sun, all in a plane, moving across the stars. These are worlds, like ours. We are sure of it, as were those who worked here before. We sent Weynik observers to great distances from each other on nights when the sister planet is visible, and we used measuring devices the woodweavers built for us to measure the angle to Verikin from different places on our world. The daily *rakineru* was a good time to coordinate these measurements. It occurs at the same time everywhere on the planet, and it is also the moment when the position of these planets shifts in the sky. By calculating the angle to the planets, we could estimate the distance to them and the speed they travel. We know

Verikin's path through the sky, which is close to a circle around our star. By launching our ship when our two worlds approach each other, which happens soon, we can make the distance you must travel as small as possible. There were calculation devices built into the old vessels, and Sekene has added more. We can teach you how they work, and how to use them to find your way. Sekene can adapt them for your use."

I had so many questions, and so many misgivings. These people were amateurs. They seemed rife with overconfidence. They were making this up as they went, building systems that were mostly untested, based on calculations they couldn't test at all. If Renefe could be believed, they'd done trials on some of their rockets, but nothing like the distance and scale they were asking me to travel. It was RBT, as McMillan used to say. Risk beyond tolerance.

But they were my friends, and they were in danger. That pulled at me: I knew I did not have the knowledge or the mind to truly understand all this, or even to ask the right questions. But I was used to that. In any mission like this, you had to trust that the scientists knew what they were doing. It had been that way my whole career.

Furthermore, this whole adventure on Kenai had revolved around a kind of temporal destiny, with improbable things happening all the time, merely because they must in order to set up other events. I'd ridden that destiny to unlikely victories when fighting SpearPoint, and to a seemingly impossible arrival at this time and place. Was that destiny at work for this mission? I would succeed because I had to?

Unlike my other brushes with paradox, though, I had no evidence that this would work. In fact, in my time, there had been no report of sentient trees on Ninilchik, or Verikin, or whatever the sister planet should be called. That suggested that the effort would fail. But the Weynik were sure it would work, and they were counting on me. This was why I had come back through time. To help. Would that faith, and my commitment to help, be enough to take on this dubious mission? I still had not decided.

I did have a question for Renefe though. One that I already had an answer for, but I wanted to know what Renefe would say. That would help me know whether I could trust him. "How do you know that this sister world can support life? That it has water, and rain, and soil, and food?"

Renefe grew troubled. "We do not know this. But our world has all those resources. It seems reasonable that other worlds do as well. It is a risk, an unknowable one, but it is one our travelers were willing to take. The potential for freedom is worth it." He got even more unhappy. "Especially now, if this world is to end. We must try. It may be our only chance to survive."

I knew that Ninilchik had a better chance than most of supporting them, but I didn't want to get into how I knew about the habitability of planets. Renefe's faith was understandable, and it would be enough for me, as I knew the truth of the matter. It meant a lot that Renefe had been honest about their doubts and told me the truth as they saw it.

I thought of something far more pressing. "Somebody said that the people you sent up in the ship died. The companions."

Renefe gave off a whiff of regret. "Yes. That was unfortunate. After Sekene and the woodweavers repaired the ships under my direction, we thought we had done the hardest part. We filled them with fuel and launched them to see how they worked. And they flew again! For the first time in over a hundred orbits. We sent up seven test flights, making improvements each time. At first, all seemed fine, but then we lost two brave Weynik on the eighth and ninth flights. These were sent high into the air, the first flights with Weynik aboard. When we recovered the ships that we launched, the Weynik inside were dead. It was unexpected because the lizards and birds we sent up survived nicely. Well, the ones on the later flights did. Once we figured out that there was no air up there."

Yikes. They had to discover that space was vacuum? This was an alarmingly sketchy space program indeed. I think Renefe sensed my discomfort, but thought it was only about the crew dying. Renefe continued. "We are fairly certain that the Weynik are specifically targeted by the curse that controls the world. When the ships returned, the Weynik had round holes cut through their bodies. The animals we sent were unhurt."

Round holes through their bodies sounded familiar. I'd seen humans cut through as well. That wasn't good. "How is this the curse? That's not how it works, is it? I thought the curse affected family members and friends, not individuals themselves."

"The *renfit sharah* does work this way. But I think that curse is part of something bigger, something directed at the Weynik people. And of course also at the Nurikna, who are merely an unpleasant branch growing from the Weynik's trunk. Only we, our race, are cursed. And I think the deaths of our shipfarers are because we are intended to be prisoners on this world, so that we cannot escape it. They tried, and they were struck down. It may be that this is why the original project was abandoned so many years ago."

"But you said seeds weren't affected?"

"Yes!" Renefe was excited again. "That was good. The best possible result. The point of this effort, of Miern's vision, is to get us to a place where the curse no longer controls us. Ideally, to a place where we move normally through time. Our hope is that Verikin is far enough away to remove us from all of it. We had hoped to send our people there, but that seems not to be possible. But we can still send seeds."

"Seeds aren't people?"

"No. Or at least, they seem not to be, to the forces afflicting us. Perhaps it is because the seeds are too young, or devoid of intelligence. I know not the reason. A seed can survive for many years before sprouting. It is only an object. A potential person, not a real one. That seems to be enough to spare it from being killed when it reaches the sky."

That wasn't too specific, and it was mostly guesswork, but I was beginning to see where I came in. "You think that I won't be killed either. That the curse doesn't affect me the same way."

"That is our hope. I am mostly certain that it is true. It is so very lucky for us that you are essentially a sentient and friendly lizard."

I fastened the seat harness around me, tying myself to the chair in the console. All of it was newly constructed for me and fitted with pads fashioned by Tuenih, the textile artist. I checked the readouts. Fuel full. Engine ready. Igniter ready. All set.

I was nervous. I could well die upon reaching orbit, suddenly ripped full of holes. But I held to one bit of optimism, one I arrived at in a strange way. I remembered, back in my time, fifty thousand years hence, that Elihar had told me that I gave his people hope. That version of Elihar, the one who spoke those words, was older and wiser than the one I was with now, who was witnessing this test flight. That future Elihar would have known if I died, and "hope" would be a funny way to describe "you came back gray, cold and dead."

None of that spoke to whether I could make it to Ninilchik. But seeing if I survived to reach orbit, seeing if I could locate Ninilchik when I was up there using Sekene's tools, seeing if the ship didn't just blow apart on launch, and seeing how the chutes and landing thrusters worked – all of that I was hoping to establish. If I was going to take on this foolish errand, I needed more practice and training. And that was all the harder because I was still foggy from the dormancy medication they'd been testing on me. It knocked me out pretty well, but each time, it took me a good while to shake off the effects, and I woke up parched and famished and with my mouth tasting like Genuan lager gone sour. I was worried they weren't going to perfect it in time. Nobody could even guess what the long-term effects were. I guess if I survived the trip, that would be enough, even if I got cancer or my heart gave out shortly after. And if I didn't survive the trip, well, any long-term effects wouldn't be important.

I pressed my teeth together hard, then took a deep breath. I disengaged the safety latch and pulled the launch lever left, then back towards me. After a moment, the engine rumbled, then fired, and I was pressed back into my seat. Through the small transparent pane of ironwood above me, I saw the clouds tremble, and then I was away.

We stood in the council ring again in the evening twilight for another *goromita*. There were far more people here now. More people from the village, and leaders from more distant villages.

A Weynik scout spoke now. "We have seen the Nurikna massing in their cities as they did during the last attack. They have more airships now. If they behave as before, they will use the airships to deliver their soldiers close to our villages to overrun us. The ships will support their attack, but only for a while. They will need to return to the city before the *rakineru*, or they will be lost to the time shift."

The scout's companion spoke. "We have found some wrecked airships as well. None are near the village here, but they are close to the outlying villages. Some of them seem quite fresh. We believe these wrecks may be ships that will be destroyed in the coming battle. That is odd, because usually nearly none of the airships are destroyed. People have also encountered some discarded and broken metal weapons belonging to the Nurikna, some of which also seem shiny and uncorroded. This too is evidence of a coming battle."

"How soon do you believe the attack will come?" asked Poen.

"Ten days, I think. One of our scouts infiltrated the city and overheard orders being given. Ten days from now was the target."

"That's not enough time." Renefe was agitated. "Our recent test flights were successful, and each time, Jessamiko survived and returned. The ship flew well, and she guided it to the ground with skill. Jessamiko has learned. All of that was welcome, and it fills me with hope." He was overselling it a little, but I had survived two test flights, damaging the ship on landing on the first one. I had trained with all of Sekene's ingenious instruments. They automated a lot of the piloting, although there was still a role for me. Beyond the test flights, I had studied the ship's systems, tested and refined Sekene's life-support devices, and been dosed with an updated version of the stasis drug. That worked, although it left a hell of a hangover. I knew what I had to do, and I thought I might be able to do it. At least, it was technically not impossible. Whether I'd actually reach orbit, leave Kenai's gravity, survive three plus years of sublight travel, and successfully land on Verikin, was dubious. At best.

Renefe continued. "Ten days is not enough time. We are in dire trouble if they attack so soon. We do not have enough fuel and oxidizer for another flight. It will take some time for our microbe farms to craft more for both the primary engine and the vessel itself. More than ten days."

"How much time? Can you not work faster?" Poen sounded unhappy. "We are not likely to fare well against the invasion they describe. It would be better to flee."

"We are working as fast as we can, and we have prepared well for this. We have spare engines already built, and we have most of the fuel we need. But we cannot rush the microbes that make oxidizer. They work at their own pace."

"I ask again, how much time?" Poen was dead serious now.

"Fourteen days, I think. To be sure to have enough."

I had a strong interest in them having enough. I raised my hand, in the manner of a Weynik requesting to speak.

"Jessamiko. You have words?" Poen seemed surprised at my participation.

I was as well. But I thought I might be able to help. I stood. "I have experience in fighting and in wars. Perhaps I could help. How do you usually fight the Nurikna?"

Poen wrapped all three arms around their trunk. "We do not, usually, unless forced. Mostly we flee. Those who survive build new villages wherever they can find a new place. Those who fight only do so to delay the attackers and protect the others. Their sacrifice is honored."

"What weapons do you have?" I was curious about this.

I could read a little puzzlement from Poen. "The weapons of the forest only. Following the old ways. Ironwood blades and spears. Some of us train in their use and can fight with ferocity."

"What if we could build better weapons? Sekene and the *omariga* can craft ironwood quickly and with ease, and they are clever with devices. We have a large supply of fuel, although not quite enough to fuel the ship. With my help, perhaps we could construct..." I had no idea of the vocabulary here. "... tubes that launch ironwood spears and blades, powered by the fuel. And we could also set containers of the fuel along the paths the Nurikna will travel and explode them as the enemy comes."

I could feel a flash of sudden anger from one of the crowd. Degungu, one of the pool tenders, rose up, arms raised. "Seed-Bearer. Fighting is against our creed. Against everything we are. We are peaceful. Twisting *umbani* into fearsome weapons is wrong. Forsaking the way of the forest for weapons and violence is the way of the Nurikna. We will be no better than they."

Echoes of support for Degungu's words flowed from some of those around. From some others, derision. From most, uncertainty.

Poen held up a hand. "Degungu. It is difficult now to hold to the old ways of peace. Especially when we are killed without mercy." Support from this radiated from various parts of the crowd. "And peace has not served us well. We are at a heavy moment. I do not believe we will survive, or achieve Miern's vision, if we do not resist."

Degungu was angry. "Peace is the Weynik way. It is all that we are. We cannot embrace war. If the *etivar* bends the Weynik toward violence, then I shall have no more of this village. I will leave." He waved at the crowd. "And you all should too." He turned away from Poen, and in the startlingly rapid manner the Weynik had of walking, he bolted from the clearing. Others joined, heading out into the trees. Emotions crackled among those who remained. Sorrow, anger, fear, sympathy. Scorn.

There was a moment of profound unease in the crowd. Poen did not speak again immediately, allowing the crowd to work through its thoughts in silence. Finally, Poen raised a hand once more. "Violence divides us once more, as it always does. I do not blame Degungu and the others for leaving." A pause. "But we are nearing an end. An end to our villages, an end to the hope that led Miern and the rest of us here. Perhaps an end to all of us." Poen spun in a circle, all three arms outstretched at the assembly. "I respect that Degungu spoke for our traditions, but I do not agree. If Jessamiko can help us resist the Nurikna, then I am willing to break with tradition and try to build better weapons." Poen's voice grew louder. "I am willing to do whatever we can do. To fight for our people, our seeds, and our way of life."

The crowd lit up in response to this call. There was murmuring, shouting. Nearby, I could feel an inner fire building in the scout who had spoken before. The scout stood, waving all three arms, excitement pouring forth into their words. "Most of our battles are over within a day, with the Nurikna victorious. If the fighting extends to a second day, most of the Nurikna weapons will vanish at night when the *rakineru* comes. Either that, or the Nurikna will have to turn back before this happens to prevent it. Either way, if we succeed, they will be left in disarray, and they may have to abandon the attack. And if we can draw them to attack us nearer to their city, then we can keep them away from here, to give Jessamiko more time to fly and the weaker among us more time to flee." The scout paused a moment, thinking. "We did not search those areas nearer in. Perhaps they are littered with lost Nurikna weapons even now, dropped as we defeat them!" There was a blaring of trumpeting calls. The crowd liked that idea.

"How much fuel will you need for these weapons, Jessamiko?" asked Renefe, still doubtful. "If it is a great deal, that will add to the time needed before launch."

"Not much, I think. The fuel you have seems strong, and it should only take a little to propel small, sharp bits of ironwood great distances."

"I think we can construct these tubes Jessamiko mentions, and also devices that explode with great force," said Sekene. "I have studied the Nurikna weapons, and I can imitate their design. I think I know how they work. Like the vessel engines, only far smaller. And we have ample *umbani* to work with. But we must work quickly." Sekene was excited, but I started feeling a little uneasy. I was apparently urging a race of pacifists to turn towards war. That couldn't be good, could it?

Poen held up her arms for silence. "Jessamiko has proposed that we fight the Nurikna with new weapons and delay them long enough for the ship to launch. Those unable to help with these tasks can flee the villages as usual and seek out a new place to live. Does the meeting agree?"

The meeting did, and loudly. The crowd was excited, hopeful, anxious, jubilant. Bloodthirsty. I still had misgivings, but I could not discount the emotions washing over me. They wanted this. Poen gestured to me. "Jessamiko, do you agree to serve us in these ways?"

"My honor and duty, Seed-Bearer."

Elihar came to me in the evening, after a long day where I worked with Sekene on weapons and then, in what must be a military first, on training trees how to shoot. Elihar sat next to me as I ate. He spoke Tradespeak. "It is time for me to go, my friend. I must travel to your time beyond the dawn." It was a bit of a surprise to hear my own language again, especially made cheesy and poetic.

I felt a wave of sorrow wash over me. I knew what would happen to him when he traveled forward to my time, and I knew that his time would be short. But I would not tell him this. There was no purpose in doing so. "Yes, I suppose that it is time. You don't want to be caught up in the battle."

"You have been a good friend to me, and to the Weynik, Jess." He could say my name perfectly now. I suspected he might do better on a Tradespeak language test than I would.

"And you to me, Elihar. As you know, we will meet again after your journey. I'm afraid I may not always be a pleasant companion."

Elihar grunted. "I know that I am not."

"I'm really sorry about your family. We haven't really spoken of them. They got some kind of disease?"

"They did. The moment I discovered the *umbani* artifact. That seems so long ago, now." He spun his head, pointing a different eye my way. "They sickened and rotted almost immediately. They were gone within a few hours. The bodies were burned to prevent any spread of the disease. Or so I am told."

"That's awful," I said. "I'm so sorry. And your friends, too, when I gave you the dictionary. I'm sorry about them as well."

"This world is cruel. I know now that each of those things I did to myself, and to my partner and my children and my friends, with full knowledge of the cost. I will go do them again, even with this knowledge. I will carry that guilt so long as I live." I could feel his pain, his grief, like a fire burning within him that would not go out. "That is why we must break free from here. That is why you must succeed."

I took one of his hands in mine, and I sat with him for a time in silence. A friend. I had not had one in a long time. Not since Mariela and Otieno, I thought. Who would not be born for thousands upon thousands of years.

He reached a hand down to the lower part of his trunk and picked a small object off himself. "It is a tradition among our people that when a pair first mates and creates seeds, in their first season together, that one seed is kept in their home unplanted as a symbol of their bond." He held the seed out to me. "It is in very poor taste to plant one's homeseed. Most in the village would be scandalized. But I want to ask a favor. If you succeed, if you actually reach Verikin, would you plant this seed for me and tend it, if you are able? I think Miern would like that one of our children might live on another world. I know the idea appeals to me."

"I think that's a beautiful idea, Elihar. If I am able, I will do this. I promise."

We sat together longer. Finally, Elihar put an arm on my shoulder, then stood. "I should go. It is a long walk to this location, and it would be best to be away before the attackers come. All is prepared."

"You have the box? Don't forget it. That would be a pretty colossal mistake."

Elihar grunted. "I have it. I even had Sekene erase the message so that I could write it again."

I was puzzled. "Why did you do that? Didn't it just look the same?" I remembered my name carved into the trees.

Elihar grunted again. "It was exactly the same. It probably doesn't really matter. But if I didn't erase it and carve it again myself, then who did carve it? It would just exist, written by nobody. I'd rather take a little bit of the paradox out of all of it." He stretched his legs out as he sometimes did when preparing to walk. Then he stopped. "Did I ever tell you why I hate your hair?"

I laughed out loud. "No, you didn't. Seems kind of rude. I don't complain about you people barfing up bones all over the place. Well, not often."

Elihar grunted. "When our people die, often a particular tiny fungus grows on us. It consumes our bodies and sends up many thin threads. It is quite disturbing. When we look at you, we see a rotting corpse."

"Well, thanks a lot, buddy." I laughed. Then I stood and wrapped my arms around his sticky trunk and squeezed him as hard as I could. "I am so glad I met you. You're the bravest person I know, and you've been so good to me. Better than almost anybody has, ever."

"You're the brave one, Jess. You carry the hope of an entire race." He held me too, with all three arms, and we stood there as the insects buzzed and the darkness deepened.

Finally, we peeled ourselves apart. Hugging a Weynik came with some challenges. "Fly safe and true, Jess Amiko."

"You too, Elihar. You too."

67

RESISTANCE IS UTILE

I retreated through the lines of ironwood spikes set against the enemy's advance, past Weynik holding spears and firetubes, past the leaf-covered blinds and cover we'd constructed for ambushes. Some of the Weynik greeted me as I passed, and I replied with words of encouragement, but I had no more time to spare for them. I was hurting, inside. Every instinct I had screamed at me to stay and fight, to hold the line, to kill as many of those skogging Nurikna invaders as I could. I heard the booms of defensive charges going off. The mines, the traps, the shrapnel bombs. That was good, in that they were maybe working, doing some damage, but it was also bad, in that there were enemies here on which to use them. So close.

But we'd held them for one day, then two, then three. I thought we might even be winning. As the scout had predicted, the Nurikna were forced to retreat each evening before the *rakineru*, the time change. What I hadn't anticipated was that they would send soldiers out to recover lost equipment and weapons. They seemed reluctant to leave any of it on the field. That made sense, as they probably thought the Weynik would steal the items and use them. If any Nurikna weapons had been left behind, we would already have found them on previous days, earlier in our struggle. The bottom line is, fighting a war where the weapons go the opposite direction in time to the soldiers is really confusing.

At last, I reached the command post we had set up, on the outskirts of the village. There was a lot of yelling going on. I didn't understand all of it. It was hard to make out the musical, connected lines of speech when so many voices were running together. But I caught some scraps as I ran onward toward the launch pad where the ship awaited.

Some have reached the ironwood grove. We need more fighters there.

Mezela's team is passed from the world, though they fought well and slew many.

Where is Entuaho? Where is my child? I saw them only moments ago.

The metal truck still comes. The explosion did not stop it. It crossed the gap.

I saw the hill up ahead in the distance. My goal. I ran through the village, past Elihar's house, now empty. I saw a small group of Weynik up ahead, three or four of them. Woodweavers. They were gathered around a table, holding ironwood blocks and boards, shaping them into spears, blades, spikes, tubes, projectiles. Making more weapons, even as the village lay under siege.

I saw Sekene among them, holding up a viny limb. A sign for me to stop.

"Visitor," Sekene called. "Jessamiko. I have something for you." They held up a board. It was covered with Weynik writing on all sides.

I did not think I could spare the time to stop, but something in the emotions I sensed from Sekene held me up. A yearning, a seriousness, a desolation. A resolve.

"What is this, Sekene? Do you want me to take it with me? On the ship?" I couldn't see what use a carved board would be, but that assessment didn't square with the feelings the woodweaver was giving off.

"When you reach the new world. When the seeds sprout. When our people live and grow again. They will know nothing of us, nothing of the years upon years of our culture. Nothing of our songs, our stories, our beliefs, our history. You have been a friend to us, but you know almost nothing of these things either." Sekene held the board closer to me, and I took it.

What Sekene said was correct. I knew little. But I didn't understand. Was the board some kind of ceremonial object? "Sekene, I will try my best to tell them of the Weynik. That is all I can do."

Sekene grunted in laughter. "It is not all you can do. You can give them this thing I have woven. Many years it has taken me to design it, with long difficulty, once we thought to try to flee this world. Once the ships were ready, I bent every effort to its creation. At least, until we had to make your weapons." Sekene grunted, then waved it in the air. "But it is finished now. It is my hope that one of your many seedlings will be an *omariga* like us. With so many seeds, at least one should feel the pull of the *umbani*, to be able to read its heart and shape its wood. This I fervently desire."

I tried to imagine my life with the seedlings on the neighboring world. If I made it to the ship, if we survived liftoff, if we got pointed the right way, if we lived through the passage through interplanetary space, if we survived the landing. If the seedlings could grow and flourish. All of this seemed foolish now, doomed. I lacked the faith of the Weynik, though I had committed to help them. A people that had barely just learned to fly, and now they were plotting to bridge the vacuum between worlds? What audacious folly. I struggled to put this out of my head. "If there is a weaver among the sprouts, how will I know?"

Sekene spun their head back and forth, gazing at me with various eyes. "You will not know, but they will. Pass this wood around. One who can feel it will know immediately what I have done. I have set inside the wood's chambers and grain deep echoes of the poems and melodies, the stories and songs, the lore and histories. Their souls will see the images I have carved, read the words, feel the hearts of those I have recorded." I could feel pride coming off Sekene now. "It was difficult to create such detailed work, to fit so much in one block. The images and words are tiny and intricate, indeed. But I am skilled beyond all, and I have done it."

There was an explosion from the other side of the village, closer than the others. "The visitor has to go," said one of the woodweavers. "All of this will be for nothing if she does not."

"Yes," said Sekene. "I delay you too long. Fly with our children, and with our dreams." They turned back to their work.

"Thank you, Sekene. If I am able, I will share this with the sprouts." Sekene waved me along, and I started running again. Up the hill, to the launch pad. Where I would undoubtedly fail these people and crush their dreams.

The pad was in the same shape as when I'd made my test flights, and when I'd trained in the chamber with Sekene and Renefe looking on. I passed the tall ironwood canisters of fuel with the banks of distillation beds behind. The oxidizer pump with the ironwood storage vessels behind. So much equipment, so much gear, so much botanical engineering.

Renefe was there with his team, running fuel back and forth. His head rotated to face his two good eyes my way. "Jessamiko. So good to see you. The vessel is loaded. The seeds are on board. The dictionary as well, as you requested." I had asked if I could take it. I wasn't sure why. But it was a memory of Elihar, which mattered to me. And, in the unlikely event any of this worked, I might be able to use it to teach the sprouts their own language. Or at least the rudimentary version I spoke.

Renefe put a hand on my back and gave me a not too subtle nudge towards the ship. "All is ready." He was radiating excitement, even as we could hear explosions from around the village.

This was my last gut check. The test flights had gone reasonably well, but this next adventure was well beyond what they could test. I knew I could get to low orbit, as I had done so myself, but crossing the vast distance between worlds? That was a huge step, far beyond anything they had so far done. I was trusting my life to an untested ship design, and to a whole bunch of math done by trees. And also to some spiritual magical engineering I didn't really understand on Sekene's part.

Renefe could sense my reluctance. "Do not fear. This will work. Our world is bathed in destiny, and I feel it here today. We Weynik have been working on this project for far longer than I have lived, though I have done much to advance it. You can trust us." He put a hand pad on my shoulder and squeezed. "We have not failed you. You have flown to the sky twice already. All is prepared. In a few hours, once your path is set, you can use the medicine to sleep all the way to Verikin. After that, all is new life! All is discovery and wonder." I was surprised to feel a hint of jealousy behind his words. He really wanted to go himself. He'd covered that up pretty well until this point.

I looked at the capsule sitting high atop the ironwood booster. This booster, what they called the primary engine, was bigger than with my test flights, but of course, I wasn't just getting to orbit. I also had to launch myself into interplanetary space and get to Ninilchik without missing it or cratering when I got there. Renefe had gone over the plans and calculations with me many times, showed me how to adjust course if I needed, shown me what to look for in the gravity sensors and stellar coordinate readings. And Sekene's control panel was a wonder, for sure, reporting on the status of an entire living ship.

A funny thought occurred to me. On Earth, as far as I knew, humans were still gathering roots and berries and chasing mastodons and buffalo around with spears. I was going to be the very first human in history to fly. And not just fly – travel to a new world and set foot there, even though I'd of course done that many times over in my earlier life. And nobody would ever know or remember my name. I'd die on that new world, if I even made it there, either in a fiery crash or starving to death when my crops didn't grow, all the while just hoping that a bunch of seeds I brought with me would somehow take root and survive on an alien planet.

Sometimes, in a war, you're given orders that you know will likely result in your death and the death of your friends. You know enough to recognize that it's probably hopeless, but your commanders ask you to go in there anyway and do what you can. This puts you front and center in a terrible situation. That's where I was now, with this. Doomed, the whole situation a giant vacc leak of trouble and potential screwups and awfulness.

I had come to believe there are only really four reasons you obey orders like that, orders that are going to get you killed. One is fear. They'll kill you if you don't obey. No military or paramilitary organization I'd been in worked like that, but I knew some that did. SpearPoint sounded like it might. And the Nurikna. But that wasn't at all what I faced here.

Another reason is conditioning. You're trained to follow orders, and you follow them without regard to the consequences, without thinking about how screwed you are. I had a lot of that in me, and I'd operated that way in the service. Not so much in RazorCorp, although I'd follow Juno nearly anywhere, and had. But nobody here on Kenai had that kind of pull over me, and I was a long way past blind obedience. Prison had sucked from my psyche any remaining innate respect for authority, for better or worse.

A third reason to fight, and an important one, is dedication to a cause. In the Patrol, that cause could be stated in a lofty way, like maintaining peace and just government and civil rights for all residents and worlds of the Council. You could also phrase it in a simpler, more appealing way. We were the good guys, those who'd signed up to defend the innocent and take down the bad guys, and we had to do what was needed. I bought into that philosophy hard. I also mostly ignored the times where our orders weren't exactly aligned with our principles. There weren't many such times. The Patrol was a pretty solid organization.

I felt that pull here. The Cause. Getting these people off this horrible world with its reversed time and unjust curses. Letting them start fresh somewhere new. The Weynik were the innocents, the good guys, the ones who deserved a chance at life and happiness. That resonated with everything I'd believed in, back when I was twenty and green and idealistic. That kid was in me somewhere, buried under all the cynicism and hard experience. I could feel her. She wanted me to go. Accepted no other option.

The last reason, the one that has the potential to trump all the others, is your squad. You love them, even when they're annoying, and they love you back. When the situation gets out of control, you can rely on them, and you wouldn't think of not being who and what they expect you to be in return. Not all squads work that way. RazorCorp didn't. But the 12th Light did. And that's the service I cherished most. I wished I'd never left, although I knew why I had. You don't make the best decisions when you're in love.

I found I had a squad again here. Elihar, with his humor, his quiet wisdom, and his self-inflicted suffering, beyond what anyone should bear. Sekene, the gentle artist and engineer, who worked wonders beyond imagining with ironwood, and who had become a good friend to me. Renefe, with an indomitable sense of purpose, a towering ego, and a contagious excitement, resurrecting the dreams and past glories of the Weynik people. And all the others I'd spent time with, eaten with, learned from, laughed with. They weren't the same as the 12th, but then again, they were the same, at least in the ways that mattered. It's weird to say it, because they were so different from me, and I hadn't lived with them for very long. But I believed in these people, even if I also believed their mission had no chance of succeeding. They dreamed big, and I wanted – needed – to believe in the dream. And a whole bunch of them were out there dying, fighting a superior enemy, many of them because I'd urged them to try. These Weynik were my new squad. My family. All they wanted from me was a shot at their dream, not for them, but for their people. That was the most compelling reason of all to climb into a jury-rigged wooden spaceship with a bunch of tree babies and reach for an impossible new home.

I bowed my head to Renefe and headed for the ladder to the capsule. I was all in.

68

THE SKY IS THE LIMIT

Unbelievable pressure, driving me down into the seat, and a roar that nearly deafened me. It seemed like we were pulling more G's now than in the test flight. More than I could bear, maybe. I didn't know if I could last the whole two minutes until the booster fell off. I held on to the seat grips. I'm not at all above white-knuckling my way through a hard flight.

Twenty seconds in, there was a crunch. Far too early for something like that. The whole ship lurched hard to the right. It felt like the ship was spinning. I looked up at the window above me. The scene was rotating, dipping and spinning, so much so that I could occasionally see the horizon careen into view. There should only have been sky. The ship was broken, flailing.

My first thought was that I'd taken fire from the ground. Well, no, actually, my first thought was a stream of profanity. But my second thought was that I was under fire. Could have been. I'd seen what looked like long-barrel artillery in the rows of Nurikna vehicles making their way towards us across the plain. Depending on their range, that would have been a heck of a shot to make, but they might have some kind of targeting or guidance. Or maybe an airship had gotten to me. Or maybe it wasn't an attack, just a malfunction, a rupture. A design flaw.

Didn't matter. I was spinning, and I was no longer pointed straight up. That was a disaster. Didn't matter why or how. I looked down at Sekene's control panel, lit by the bioluminescent glow of the lighting panels around it. The surface was indenting, forming Weynik characters, ones I'd made sure to learn. She'd been so proud of that.

The Bird spins.

Control is lost.

Fuel sprays outward from the primary engine.

The oxidizer chamber is yet intact.

The fuel tank was leaking, maybe on fire. I was surprised it hadn't ruptured entirely, or exploded, but I still had no real idea of the limits of their engineered ironwood. The spin was getting worse – I could feel it in my gut, as the rotation fought with the thrust and sent us spiraling around.

I had no choice. I hit the control to scram the primary engine. I had to. We'd never make it to orbit off course and bleeding fuel. The giant hand pressing me into my seat loosened as the thrust cut off, and then I heard the KATHUNK as the engine detached and fell away.

The main engine is free.

The Bird spins.

There is danger.

I still had the second engine, the smaller one, built into the capsule. The one meant to get the ship up to speed and carry us to Ninilchik. But I had only ridden the main engine for a fraction of the time I was supposed to, and not in the right direction. I could not do the math, but the reality was obvious even without numbers. Even if the second engine had enough thrust to get me to orbit, which I doubted, I'd be stuck there, circling Kenai until I died along with all my seeds. And I didn't think the system was designed to calculate an orbit, anyway. If it would, I didn't know how to ask. I was supposed to make a bull rush to the sky, then travel through space on the arc the Weynik had calculated, reach Ninilchik, then brake and land. A one-way trip, no orbiting, no frills, no margin for error.

None of that was going to happen. I was going to come back to rest on Kenai. The only question was where and how fast. And in how many pieces, and whether I'd be on fire. The mission was a failure. I checked the panel's location monitors. They gave me planetary coordinates in the system I'd agreed on with Sekene. I didn't know exactly how the ship measured location. Some combination of magnetism, the sun, and maybe dead reckoning, stars and a calendar, or maybe it was some kind of ironwood magic. I hadn't really followed Renefe's explanation. But I had coordinates. And the second engine had the capacity to steer as well as push. It needed to steer to give me a chance at a controlled landing on Ninilchik. It could steer me here, too. With the drag chutes, and some luck, I might be able to land. The question was, where?

No point in heading back to the village. The Weynik were only ever supposed to fight a delaying action to allow me time to leave. If I went back to them, I'd likely be shot out of the sky, or surrounded when I landed. Best to get far away. But even if I went elsewhere, I had no mission success scenario that I could identify. I didn't know how much time was left before Angalir's attempt to destroy Kenai. If it was soon, then I'd land, maybe live a few months or a year, and then the buried weapons would go off, and the planet would become unlivable. Even if it was many years off, as it might be, that would just give the Nurikna ample time to find me and kill me. And even if they didn't, any seeds I planted, any Weynik who sprouted, would still die in the coming apocalypse.

Had our dream died? Should I just steer the ship into the ground? It might be easier than living through what was to come.

No.

Wait.

There was an option. Maybe.

There was one place I could go. I knew the coordinates, even.

I didn't know if I would be allowed to enter one more time.

I didn't know if I could take the seeds with me.

I didn't know what would happen if I did.

This plan, this flailing attempt to resist destiny, would take me into the very heart of the curse the Weynik were trying to flee.

But I had to try.

Six minutes later, I was nearly to where I wanted to go, coming in hot. Time to pop the chutes. And hope the door release still worked.

69

ALTERNATE ANGLES

I stumbled into the chamber with its gray walls and carved ceilings. It looked the same as before. My first instinct was to go back out, trying to pick up more of the trays, but there was no doorway behind me. And if I left through the other doors, I had no idea if I would return to the time I'd just left. Besides, what I now carried was all I could reasonably lift. It seemed so cruel and arbitrary, to have the fate of a species depend on the carrying capacity and arm strength of a single woman. I had six trays in total, containing probably a few hundred seeds, plus the slab of ironwood Sekene had given me, plus Elihar's dictionary, which I hadn't been willing to leave behind. The remnants and the future of an entire culture, contained in one armload.

I went around the corner. The room was surrounded by the little archways now, eight of them, all swirling with mist. The norodium pillar stood in the center, but its bright metal seemed duller somehow. The cube popped into view on its glass panel.

"Greetings, former perturbing agent."

"Hello." What did it mean by former? Was that good or bad? I stared at the display for a moment, and a thought occurred to me. "Mothrek. Are you Mothrek? The mechanical being Angalir created?"

The display darkened. "I shall endeavor not to take that as an insult. The entity Mothrek was rudimentary and arose from a different and more limited code base. It did so not on my planet of origin, but on this backwater dump – I mean, on this lovely and exotic trial setting." The cube boinged against the edge of the display a couple of times. "However, my genesis was not dissimilar. Perhaps you are not as stupid a perturbing agent as other evidence indicates." The display brightened again. "Regardless, I have news about the trial which, within your limited emotional range, might be exciting." There was a small trumpet fanfare. "Status update: Trial outcome resides in modeled outcome family comprising only 0.54 times ten to the minus 4th fraction of all modeled outcomes. Trial complete."

"What's that mean?" *Trial complete* sounded ominous.

"In the majority of outcomes, the trial fails, matching the original modeled system."

"You set it up to fail? What is failure, anyway?"

"Self-inflicted extirpation of sentient species under study."

That sounded pretty clear. "And success?"

"Survival with persistent significant population and cultural exchange, maintaining sentience, without extirpation, for 805,423.425 years."

I snorted. "That's a pretty specific number."

"The base time units used by the trial designers are different from yours."

"Oh."

I thought for a moment. "But the Weynik... They've only been on this world for, what, tens of thousands of years?"

"Correct. Trial environment was seeded 18,322.212 years ago. Again in your units."

Seeded? What did that mean? But then I got scared. "So the trial failed? Are the Weynik dead?" Had I killed them somehow by bringing them here? A wave of panic rose in my gut.

"Answer to query is obvious. You are carrying non-deceased Weynik trial organisms. Hence, the trial did not fail."

"But it hasn't been long enough to succeed."

"Also obvious. Assessment of perturbing agent's intelligence is revised downward."

Gee, thanks. "So, it didn't succeed, and it didn't fail?"

"Correct. Expected outcome is extirpation, as occurred with the time-inverted species upon which the trials are based. The less likely outcome, at probability 0.534 times ten to the minus 2nd, is survival beyond defined success period. The secondary success metric, survival beyond one eighth of test period, has been achieved in a fraction representing 0.453 of all trials that eventually failed. Developments in Trial Erdion breached both time inversion and paradox disincentivization conditions and thus cannot be assessed. Perturbing agent is likely to blame."

"Breached what? You mean, time doesn't go backwards anymore? And the paradox curse?"

"Query undefined. Time does not exist in this space and thus does not progress in any direction."

I thought for a moment about what the cube had said. "You're... creating whole sentient races, making them live backwards, screwing them over when they run into the inevitable paradoxes that show up? In pursuit of research?" I shook my head. "That's.... that's monstrous."

"Ethical assessments typically depend entirely on individual cultural traditions and values and do not transfer well between species."

"No." I was angry. "This is skogging awful, whoever you think you are."

"Well, would you look at the time."

"What?"

"Linguistic modeling suggests that phrase urges your species to act rather than waiting and thinking useless thoughts."

"What?"

"Also, if you don't get the hell out of here, I will destroy your seeds."

I was taken aback. "Do you mean that? Or are you just saying it to get me to do something?"

"Do you want to stick around and find out, pardner?"

No. But. No. I growled my displeasure. "Which door do I use?"

"Your door choice selection failure probability is calculated from modeling at 0.4233 times ten to the minus 23rd power."

I growled again. "I hope you skogging burn. You and your whole species." I headed for the third door on the right.

"Probability of my burning is modeled at 0.2833 times ten to the minus 1284th power, as I am a hypothetical construct and thus not flammable." There was a pause. "The species who constructed me has already effectively burned."

The voice turned deeper and ominous, echoing through the chamber. "Now get out of my house, human."

I wanted to yell at it more, but I saw little point. I gripped my trays of seeds tighter and stepped through the mist.

70

When and Where

My vision cleared. I was standing in the same place I'd emerged before, the first time I'd gone through. The spot on the hill behind the portal. Like before, the ground was smoldering under my feet. My arms strained against the weight of the trays of seeds, the dictionary tablets, and the ironwood panel Sekene had made. But two questions were foremost in my mind. When had I emerged? And what had all of that meant?

I shook my head, squeezed my eyes closed, clenched my teeth. I had to deal with now and here, not whatever was going on in the portal. I could worry about all that other stuff later. The first and most important question was, am I here when I left? Or sometime before or after? Or was I still deep in the past, with the world about to end?

Recon and location, marine. First priority in unfamiliar terrain. I set the seed trays and the rest of my burden on the hillside. I felt bad leaving the seeds, but I needed to be able to move and react quickly, especially if there were any enemies about. I climbed up over the rise to where I knew the portal should be. Where I'd seen my forward-self, and near where I'd met Elihar the first time. I saw the wreckage of the field turret, and then, around the corner, the gear boxes, the comms unit. And James, with the tarp draped over him. The merc I'd killed along with his teammate, after the transport had left with the bodies. This was familiar. I knew when this was. Or nearly. I felt a surge of relief at being back in my own time. Guilty relief. I'd survived, and I'd returned.

Then I remembered that here in my own time, there were hostiles all around, and everybody wanted to kill me. And I was naked, and now I had a few hundred babies and the precious lore of a dead civilization to protect, not just my own sorry behind. This wasn't actually that much of an improvement. I had a duty to uphold. The memory of friends to honor. And very little to work with.

I heard a noise from above. Fusion engines. The sound was deep, though, deeper than the two-seater craft I'd seen around here, deeper even than the T126 transport I'd heard departing after I'd listened to James talk with Rivald. This was a bigger ship. I looked up. It was an unfamiliar model, painted mostly red, about the size of a light scout cruiser if I had the scale right. Not a Patrol vessel, whose ships were always white and marked clearly with the eagle insignia on all sides. It was a good bit smaller than the *Deimos*. I'd guess a crew of maybe eight or ten. I doubted there'd be bunk space for more than fifteen or twenty more. Maybe less than that with cargo. There was a moderate-sized docking bay on the port side, probably where the two-seaters and the T126 had come from. It also had the telltale ring shape set back toward the rear, a Hlojeng coil. That would allow interstellar jump travel without a gate. Very rare on vessels outside of the Patrol because they were so expensive. No ship other than the *Deimos* here should have one. We'd all come on the *Deimos* and used their landing craft to get the bases set up. That meant this ship must have come separately.

I couldn't see any identifying markings, but this had to be the command ship for SpearPoint. There wouldn't be another jump-capable ship here at this world. Not coming to the portal. This was really bad.

Worse, even. If they were coming down here, they would be able to see me. Their attention would be on me. I doubted they'd land, because a ship this big usually needed at least a pad, sometimes a hangar cradle. It was rare to take a jump-capable ship into atmosphere. That put all kinds of physical and thermal stress on the hull, and beyond that, the Hlojeng coil was particularly vulnerable to instability. Coils didn't play well with gravity, because they were designed to subvert it, along with most of the rest of physics. But you couldn't shut a coil down without cooling and evacuating it, which was delicate. That took days, and there was no chance they'd have taken the time here. Not with a Patrol ship missing in the vicinity. The coil was their escape route. They'd leave it ready to run.

None of that mattered, really. My primary concern was that I just needed not to be seen. I raced down into the slot canyon valley, past the portal, and around the bend to where the gear was, where I dove under the comms table. James was there, face down on the table, where I'd left him. The tarp I'd put on him had slipped a little, but he was still covered. Mostly. I heard the comms unit crackle above me. It was still live, still on their command circuit.

"Control, this is Beetle Squad. We've recovered Wolf Squad's K322. It doesn't have the fuel to reach orbit. Awaiting pickup."

"Beetle, this is Control. We'll get to you. We're busy now."

"Doing what?"

"We're proceeding with Kerner's idea. Hitting the artifact site with heavy weapons, trying to dislodge the norodium."

"You think the weird weapon won't hit you from up there?" Whoever Beetle Squad was sounded worried.

"Negative. Ballistics analysis of the site and environs indicates those weapons did not reach beyond a few hundred meters." I knew that was wrong. They could reach orbit, to have killed the Weynik astronauts, but I wasn't about to tell these clowns that. "We'll stay a kilometer up, maybe two, and fire at the hillside at an angle." I thought this voice was the commander I'd heard before, Rivald.

"This is a bad idea, sir. We don't know what that thing can do."

"Noted, Jerski. But we're out of time. The Patrol could get here within a day or two if *Deimos* got a distress call out. If we can dislodge the norodium, our payout is enormous. If not, this was all for nothing. It's worth the risk."

"You're the boss, sir."

"Yes, I am. Rivald out."

The ship's engines whined at a slightly higher pitch. Braking, then hovering. The ship hung up there, like they said, a kilometer or two away, pitched downward at an angle. There was a flash, and four white bolts streaked from the ship. I flinched, but they weren't headed for me. They were headed for the portal. A split second later, a blast resounded from around the bend in the canyon, a kind of *whuwhuwhump* as the four shells hit all at once. I could feel the heatwave from the detonation wash past me, and then there was a patter of dirt and soil. I worried about the seeds. Had they been too close? I felt a flash of anger. Beyond the *Deimos*, and all the innocent people SpearPoint had killed on Kenai, their greed was now putting an entire sentient race in danger.

I felt a sudden intense wave of something pass through me. It was the same energy that hit me in the evenings when the time changed. The *rakineru.* But it was far stronger, and this was the wrong time of day for it. This wave hit me even harder than the blast. My vision blurred, sounds retreated to a high whine, and I lost control of my thoughts for a long moment, as they seemed to repeat and pile on top of each other, going nowhere. It was like I was frozen, in stasis.

The sound from the comm unit finally broke through. "Beetle, this is Control. It looks like it worked. The site is heavily damaged, and we can see norodium bricks lying free. We'll drop the transport here and get them loaded up. When that's done, we'll hit the site with a cluster nuke and then we'll come get you."

"Well, yee haw, boss. Glad to hear it."

A cluster nuke? They had nukes? Using them on a planet was super illegal, of course, but when you'd already taken out a Patrol ship, it's all relative. They wanted to cover their tracks, remove all evidence of what they'd done here. It would work. And there was no way I could get myself clear of even a small set of nukes fast enough. Not on foot. Much less carrying the seeds and artifacts, which would burn in the fireball. Even if I could find a vehicle, one of the bikes, maybe, and somehow drive it while carrying the seeds, they'd see me for sure and just take me out.

The situation was a complete vacc leak. A giant skogging tear in the hull. But this couldn't stand. They couldn't get away with it. I couldn't lose everything the Weynik had fought for. The precious little spark they had left.

I looked over at James' assault suit, sitting in the field charger. It was up to about 20%. It should be full after this long charging, but he'd said there were issues with it.

It was insane, really, to think of taking on a light cruiser with an assault suit. But then again, the 12th Light weren't known for cautious respect for the odds against them. And if I did nothing, then I was dead, and the seeds were dead, and the Weynik would vanish from the universe along with me. Blaze of glory time, right?

I crawled out from under the table and over to the suit. It was DNA-locked to James, but I had James handy, and he wasn't in a position to complain if I borrowed some of his skin. I tapped the mount-up button, and the suit popped upright and opened. I slid inside. It was a little uncomfortable without a bodysuit, cold and sharp, but it would work. I closed the armor and helmet, hit the thrusters, and shot up into the copper green Kenai sky.

71

ASSAULT (MINE)

I got up to altitude quickly, making it to the cruiser just as the nose of the transport was emerging from the docking bay. I tipped left, then right, and arced around the ship to the upper side. I saw ship-mounted weapons tracking me, but it took them a while to identify me as a bogey. That might be somebody inside trying to figure out who the hell I was. Once they started firing, the suit's evasion coding triggered. It was a rough ride for a while there, but I only took one glancing strike to my leg, and that didn't get through the armor. The ship wasn't designed to defend against something as small and mobile as a marine in a flight assault suit. That kind of thing would never happen during normal operation.

I ended up upside down over the top of the ship. The fusion engines were mounted on the underside of the ship. That was probably where most people would attack, but I only had six R13's, and I wasn't sure they'd be enough to do anything to the fusion cells. Probably wouldn't even get through the hull to them. I had a different plan. The Hlojeng coil.

There was only one weapon that could reach me up here above the ship, a 180 biaxial bubble turret, although there was nobody in the bubble to aim it. It was firing on automatic guidance. The rest of the weapons were forward-mounted or rear-mounted, meaning the ship had to be pointing towards or away from whatever it wanted to shoot, a standard configuration for a ship of this size. There was another turret bubble on the bottom, plus torpedo mounting brackets, but those were empty now. Probably what they used against the *Deimos*.

I used one of my shells on the turret. Dodge incoming fire, wait for a lock, which took longer with the evasion routines slamming me around, then approach closer and fire. My first shot damaged the turret, but it could still move, and it was still pouring forth pulse beams. A second shell knocked it out.

Four shells left. I needed to act fast. The ship could easily outrun me, but I figured it couldn't accelerate or rotate with the transport coming out of the docking bay, not without incurring a lot of damage. I toggled the finger controls in my glove and selected target points around the Hlojeng coil. Waited for multitarget locks, got close in to minimize error, fired all four shells. The R13's streaked out to their targets. Four hits, though not all as squarely as I'd have liked. I saw gas venting from two of the strikes. A good sign, but not the eruption of superheated hyperdense plasma I'd been hoping for. I waited a moment to see if the leaks would get worse, but no luck, just a faint white spray.

I came in closer. There looked to be some significant cracks on the coil's outer casing, but it was holding. I was out of shells. But I still had the suit. A stupid idea occurred to me, something so stupid that I doubted any assault marine had ever considered it. On the other hand, flight assault marines were always a little crazy. Crazier even than light infantry like me, but I could try to play the part.

I toggled the control sequence for a hard landing. Leg armor locked in straight rigid position, foot shock absorbers extended, emergency hip flex cancel bolts locked in, legs and arms pressed in and locked to each other and to the main armor. The idea was if you were going in hard, let the armor absorb as much of the impact as possible. Kind of a last-ditch low-probability gamble, the kind people seldom survived. But I wasn't going to crash land. After the suit reconfigured to hard landing mode, I manually retracted the drag flaps so that I could still go fast. As fast as possible.

I got myself some lift, then flipped the thruster orientation. I could feel the pack rotate around on my back. That was another thing you almost never did. The thruster was supposed to point down, to keep you off the ground. You didn't point it up, because that would slam you into the ground. But that wasn't my goal here. Using the steering jets, I rotated my body to near horizontal, and then I slammed in max thrusters, pointed up above my head. The result was that I took off, streaking sideways. As planned. Feet first, right toward the Hlojeng coil.

Best case, I cracked the coil open, causing damage to the ship, and flew away to watch what I had wrought. Worst case, I broke my spine shortly before the suit thrusters blew up on impact, leaving me either a smear along the hull or an expanding cloud of red mist. Or something along those lines. What actually happened was, I slammed into the coil feet first, and it broke along the cracks my earlier heavy muni attack had created. That liberated a bunch of impossibly hot ionized hyperdense Hlojeng plasma that had until just recently been pressurized and magnetically contained. It detonated and sprayed everywhere, including downward into the ship, where it melted through into the fusion engines. Those created their own secondary explosions, the left engine and then the right, and the ship plummeted to the ground, colliding with the transport, and taking it down as well. The whole mess pancaked on impact, and then the fusion cores went critical, and after that happens, there's just very little left of anything.

If everything had gone great, I would have watched the huge explosion from above, fists pumping, screaming, hoping the suit cameras picked it all up so that I could be famous. What actually happened was that I passed through the wreckage of the coil fast enough to dodge most, but not all, of the Hlojeng plasma. Dodging all would have been much better. Some of it spattered onto the suit and melted through it pretty fast. That disabled some of my steering jets, although the plasma slowed up a bit when it got to the interior armor plating, which was designed not to melt easily or to conduct heat. Beyond the plasma problems, the impact with the ship knocked me spinning, and I wasn't good enough with flying suits to correct course, especially with the main thruster inverted and my legs and arms locked together. That sent me spiraling toward the ground, out of control, and fast, and I cratered in pretty hard.

It turned out with the suit in hard landing mode, I survived. More or less. I hurt all over, and I had trouble breathing, but I had to ignore that to get out of the suit fast to avoid even worse plasma burns. A few drops of plasma made it far enough in to melt parts of the suit onto me, and even with the suit's fire suppression and heat sinks, I ended up with ugly cooked red and black blotches all over my left leg and a few more across my neck. They stung like hell, which I guess was sort of good, because a really bad burn you can't even feel. My right ankle was twisted up pretty good, too, although I don't know quite how that happened with the suit in rigid lockdown. But the suit did its best, and I walked away. Well, limped away. Cussing. And hoping there would be burn cream and pain killers somewhere nearby.

Slowly, gingerly, I made my way over to the smoking crater where the ship had gone down. The ship was a total loss. Scarily so. Ripped open by multiple explosions, a lot of sections missing or barely identifiable. I waited a while to see if anybody would come crawling out, but they didn't. I didn't see how anybody would live through that. Just as well. I did see most of the SpearPoint logo on one scrap of hull. Skogging reprobates got what was coming, and then some. I'd not mourn them. Not for a moment. Righteous kills.

As the sun went lower in the sky, I made my way back to the portal. The strike had been precise. The doorway was wrecked, and anything that might have been behind it, if that's where the cave even was, completely collapsed and invisible under rubble and dirt. No swirling mist anymore, and only a few dislodged carved bricks still clinging to the hillside, with a few others I could see scattered around from the blast.

What was around behind that hillside, outside the slot canyon's walls, was far more important to me. And that was good news. My little seeds had survived. Just a spattering of dirt and dust in a thin layer over the trays. I can't really describe the emotion I felt when I saw them. I wrapped myself around them and just held on for a while. At length, I got up. I needed some bandages, some clothes, and some food. And a beer. I'd kill for a beer.

And I needed tonight to lead me to tomorrow, not to yesterday. But I thought it would, with the portal destroyed. It had to.

72

BEIN' SPROUTS

I was stirring a pot of lizardoid stew when the first of them moved. It was safe to eat local animals now because they were all moving forward in time again, just as I was. And one grew tired of DuraBiscuits, and even curry packs.

The movement caught me by surprise at first. I thought something was just flying through the trees, like the little bird things sometimes did. But then a few of the trees started to bend and flex, and the vines that covered their trunks twitched. Three or four of them were going at once. They each twisted and writhed, almost as if straining against the ground, and then there was a creaking and popping down by the base as the roots separated from the body. One of the little guys fell over. The poor thing. On all of them that were moving, I could see the legs separating out, unfolding along the length of the main body, and extending downward. Three legs, one at a time, feeling for the ground, and then pushing down, finding purchase. They were all wobbly at first. Their arms split off later, and then the heads rose up, and the eyes opened. I could feel confusion coming off them, but also wonder, even joy, at the new experiences.

Others of them started moving, bending, standing, all across my little grove. It seemed as though when one went, maybe that one inspired all the others to try. I searched for the homeseed from Elihar and Miern. I'd put a ribbon around that one, so that I'd remember. It was moving as well, and my heart leapt.

The little sprouts had grown fast, the tallest ones reaching my height in just under two years. And now this uprooting, at two and a half years since I'd brought them to here and to now. It was so exciting. I had been full of worries – that they wouldn't make it, that I'd messed up planting them, that they'd still live backwards, that the trip through time would poison them and they'd wither and die. But none of that had happened. They were thriving. And now they were taking their first steps.

Science Officer Todorova came over. She'd rotated in recently, just a couple of months, the fourth companion I'd had here over the two and a half years. A xenobiologist. She was a pretty good bunkmate and companion in our little prefab house. She could cook, and she loved playing cribbage, so we got along fine. I was even watching the holosoap she liked, *Love Across the Stars*, although I probably wouldn't keep up after we parted ways. It was pretty silly. Her brown eyes were wide. "It's happening!" She had her con up, filming all of it.

I smiled. "Yup." I went over to the little group who'd moved first. They were swinging their limbs about, testing this newfound freedom, making noises at each other, spinning their heads. I'd been working on my language from Elihar's dictionary pages, and trying to remember my lessons, although without anybody to talk with it was hard. The worst part of it was, they'd all have my atrocious accent now.

"*Framinagulawintalla.*" Welcome to life, little ones. I tried hard to get the pronunciation and the intonation right, even though they wouldn't yet understand. But they'd be able to feel my happiness in seeing them, and they'd hear their own language as the first words from my mouth. They gathered closer to me. One of them, a brave one, reached out a hand pad to me, cautious, testing. I took it in my hand, slow and gentle. "*Framinostamiayahtemenia.*" Welcome to your new world.

73

THE DENOUEMENT GOES HERE

I put it up on my wall. Real paper, made from plant pulp, although that was sort of stupid, because I'd gotten the original letter digitally over the network. I'd bought a frame for it, too. Would have been neat if it could be wood from Kenai, but I didn't have that kind of pull, or that kind of cash. Plus, Kenai was under absolute cultural quarantine. Had been ever since the Patrol showed up and I'd explained the situation. It wasn't a standard cultural quarantine, where we meet a sentient species less advanced than us and leave them alone so they can develop. Despite all the legal wrangling it took to set up quarantine law, that scenario had only actually happened once, with the Mitari.

They'd had to figure out something entirely new for the Kenaians, because the laws didn't begin to cover a situation like this. But they were not the Kenaians. They were the Weynik. I'd taught the Council that. It's what Elihar called himself the first day. *People of the Verdant Valley*, I knew it meant now. Kenai was a good name too, but it was ours. Human. And people should get called what they call themselves.

The cultural quarantine would leave the world to them. No colonists, no mining, no exploitation. But they'd need a good bit of help and intervention to get on their feet and get going. They were just a bunch of orphaned kids, after all, all alone in a world they didn't understand with no adults to rely on. We needed to let them re-learn their culture, or establish a new one, and start to figure out who they wanted to be.

I suggested early on that the Weynik be given the chance to sell the norodium from the wreckage of the portal to set up a fund they could use to buy what they needed and support themselves. I wasn't sure the administrators in charge now agreed, but I wanted to put the idea out there, at least. The portal had cost the Weynik so much, it seemed right that they benefit from its destruction.

People smarter than I was, anthropologists, xenobiologists, linguists, those kinds of eggheads, they were helping the Weynik now. I'd stayed on for most of a year after they uprooted, teaching my little sprouts everything I knew about their language and history, which admittedly wasn't a lot. But the scientists helped, and they gradually took over as I stepped into the background. After the Weynik started moving and talking, so many people had come. There were old and wise people, and young and eager people, all kinds of researchers and scholars. It was great to see them work. Their excitement at this new challenge, their thrill at being part of something big, something unique, reminded me of myself back when I enlisted. I figured the Weynik were in good hands. I'd done what I could, and the Weynik deserved a much better teacher than I could be. Elihar's dictionary had been a great start. I hoped the library coded in the ironwood by Sekene would help. When all the sprouts grew larger, hopefully one of them would be able to feel the patterns in the wood as the woodweaver had. It seemed like a couple of them were sensitive to it already. If it worked, that cultural treasure would certainly be beyond anything that humans could do for them.

I had thought about staying there. Setting up a home on Kenai, becoming some kind of cultural ambassador or something. Which would probably actually be a glorified name for useless hermit. But in the end, that didn't seem right. For one thing, I was pretty sure I would be terrible at it, and I'd get bored. I'd already been bored, sitting there for so long tending the trees as they grew, although having the time to think had done me some good. And I'd been able to go through an extensive radiation damage abatement treatment, at the expense of my hair. Elihar would have liked that. But it had grown back, and the docs had given me the all-clear.

I'd decided at the end of all of it that I was still a convicted war criminal, and they didn't need all that hanging over them. I'd been dodging interviews for a few years now, and that would only get harder if I remained. I'd stayed long enough to see them sprout, to help them learn their language, to pass on what I knew of their parents and people and culture, now fifty thousand years dead. That was probably all I could do for them. It was enough, I think. It might be cheesy, but I thought of this new community, this rebirth of their people, as Elihar's *vasikilo*, the speaking of his history. And Renefe's, and Sekene's and all the rest who'd helped and fought and dreamed. A tribute to their life and work.

I think the new Weynik understood why I wanted to leave. They had figured me out, after all our time together, and they could read my emotions better than I could theirs. I promised I'd come back to visit, and I'd keep that promise. If the xenoanthropologists and the Patrol let me.

I was working again, now, although I'd given up being an independent security contractor after only the one job. Sold the suit and the rifle, went back to school. Found a new career. One that I was discovering I was better suited to, after all. One that might even make my mom proud of me, although that would be pushing it. But I had in mind somebody else who would no doubt approve, too. A gentle person, one who took the time to help a screwed-up prisoner find her way.

I thought sometimes about the Kenai curse, and how it had impacted me. I was sure it had. Welk, for one. He'd died just as I discovered my note to myself. That fit the pattern.

Elihar, too. I figured I had to have taken him out somehow, although there was a long list of paradoxes I'd gotten caught up in, or initiated myself, and I wasn't sure which one it was. *Lajaretitoorubetha,* my friend.

I also wondered about others. For the Weynik, the curse always applied to the future. You did something wrong, and then somebody died. But for the Weynik, the future was the past. And a whole lot of people had died in my past. People I cared about, taken out without warning, like the curse favored. Like Kenzi, and Otieno. They were the most important, but there were others, too in the Patrol and the Razors. A lot of people died around me.

I had spent a lot of sleepless nights outside the little sprout farm on Kenai thinking about all this. Wondering if I were guilty of killing my friends, or if they'd just died as they ought, when their time was up. In the end, I'd taken Elihar's words to heart. *This world is cruel.* He meant Kenai, but I'd found it applied more generally. *We are given things to know that no person should.* I took that as an absolution. For him, and for me. I hadn't killed my friends. Kenai had. Or the universe had, as it kills everyone.

My grief, my crimes, my losses, all had put me on Kenai at that time and place. In the end, something fundamentally good had come of it, something important, something wonderful, something that never should have been. At least, with probability 0.54 times ten to the minus 4th fraction of all modeled outcomes. As it had been for Elihar and his family, my losses were a price paid for something better. For the Weynik, but also for myself, because let's face it, I had needed some redeeming. I didn't know whether there was a curse involved or not, but I came, usually, to the conclusion that I would lose all those people again rather than follow a different path. I could hardly not follow this path. All my successes and failures, the best and the worst that I had done – it all came merely from being me.

I peeled the cover off the frame adhesive, checked the position again to make sure it was centered over my desk and lined up with my diploma and license, and then I stuck this new frame to my wall. I read it again, running my finger over the embossed seal.

To Infantry Private Jessalyn Amiko, 12th Light Infantry (retired):

It is with deep gratitude that we commend you for your actions on Kenai following the treacherous attack on PSV Deimos. While pursued by the enemy, and in a far inferior tactical position, and with inferior equipment, you demonstrated great valor in killing six of the enemy in the field unaided, in bringing down their ship, the one that destroyed PSV Deimos, in preventing any profit or benefit to the enemy for their crimes, in assisting the Patrol with reoccupying Kenai and apprehending and prosecuting those remaining who were responsible, and in assisting the people of Kenai in defending their world and way of life.

Though you could not prevent the loss of the Deimos with all hands, your actions following the attack honored the memory of the crew and were in keeping with the best traditions of the Patrol, of the Deimos, and of the 12th Light Infantry, with whom you served with distinction.

Although Patrol Command will not officially acknowledge your service on Kenai, we, the undersigned, are united in awarding you the Order of the Deimos, the thirteenth such award presented and sadly, the final one. Records of this shipboard honor were traditionally engraved on a plaque on the bridge of PSV Deimos. We regret that your name cannot join those other names in that hallowed place, but please know that we honor you in equal measure.

Your unit, the 12th Light, has as its motto 'We Ride the Storm.' You certainly lived up to those words on Kenai, and you have our eternal gratitude.

Signed,

Admiral Charlotte L. Palsey, Commander and First Officer of PSV Deimos, 338-345 AE

Captain Winn MacTavish (retired), Captain of PSV Deimos, 345-356 AE

Captain Reshma Abbas, Captain of PSV Deimos, 356-359 AE

The letter had arrived near the beginning of my second year tending the grove on Kenai, after the investigation had ended and everything was pretty much settled. It meant a lot to me that they'd done this. There was certainly no benefit to them in associating with me, or with the mess that Kenai had become. And of course this wasn't an official Patrol award, just a shipboard honor. As they said, the Patrol wanted nothing to do with me, ever again. To them, I was an embarrassment. But this award, from fellow Patrol members, I appreciated. A lot.

"Jess." It was Emedea, over the comm link. "Taris Redland is here for her appointment."

"Thanks, Em. Send her in."

The girl came in. She had her hair braided on the side and shaved close underneath, which was the current style on Entelo among the rebellious set. Not that Entelo had much to rebel against. A few mining outposts, some farms, a couple of small cities all clustered together. Maybe three hundred thousand people, tops. Infrequent jump gate traffic, mostly freighters. Not yet admitted to the Council, so it attracted a lot of people whose past might better be left in the past. Quiet, and well off the beaten path. After four months here, I had a small house, a dog named Welk, a favorite bar. I had a few friends, too, some veterans, some who liked hiking, and some who liked fencing, which I'd taken up to keep active. And to keep some kind of weapon in my hand.

"Hello, Taris. Good to see you again." I had my con with my notes in front of me, but I didn't need them. I could feel the emotion coming off her. Resentment. Disdain. Those were surface, what she wanted me to see. Under that, though, were insecurity and a lot of pain. My adventure on Kenai had left me this gift. And I was getting better at using it.

I had to open with the complaint. Get it out of the way. "I understand you were fighting at school again. We talked about that. That's not going to help you get out of meeting with me. And it's not going to serve you well, long term. Believe me."

"Whatever." She shifted in her seat. "She was hurting my friend."

I looked at her face for a moment. So young. And building up a bad reputation, without really meaning to. I could relate to that. I put down my con on my desk, powered it off. "So, did you win? You've got a strong right and quick feet, although you didn't guard your head too well. I saw a little bit of video. We could work on your form some, if you want." She gave me a surprised look, and I smiled back.

Keep them guessing, I thought. Otieno always had.

The End

Acknowledgements

I'd like to thank the following people who contributed to this book.

Special thanks go to my early reader team, Christina Dobson, Dan Hurwitz, and Don Smith.

- Christina is Reader Number One for all of my stuff, which means she sees it in its worst form. It's her early suggestions that help me knock off the rough edges, steer away from icebergs, and hammer the thing into shape. She's such a great help, and none of my books would be anywhere near as good as they are without her post-its, margin notes, critiques, and smiley faces written all over the first 8.5"x11" comb-bound version from the print shop.

- Don Smith is a physics professor at Guilford, where I used to teach, and I owe him both significant apologies and sincere thanks. He has helped me with this book (and earlier with Daros) to avoid missteps with science and astronomy (well, at least the ones I'm not rushing into on purpose). He also helps me with story, plot, and characters. My favorite comment of his this time is when he wrote me about a third of the way through and said "I hope this isn't a 'time goes backwards' kind of thing." I'm so sorry. It was. I think he might have forgiven me by the end of the story. Maybe.

- Dan Hurwitz is one of my best and oldest friends since we were in the marching band together in college. We play video games online nearly every night together (I'm **dob** on DoTA 2 if you're looking for a game), so he's the recipient of a lot of my uncoordinated thoughts and dad jokes. With my books, he's always willing to read my stuff and offer gentle and useful advice, some of which I even follow. He also makes my books better, and he provides much-appreciated support and friendship.

I'm also tremendously grateful to Tami Ryan, who does the final proofread and copy edit on my books. This is the fifth one she's done for me, and she's wonderful to work with and a huge help.

Kara Dahlheimer took a rough idea for a cover I gave her and made it immeasurably more beautiful. I love the classic sci-fi look she imagined. It captures Jess perfectly, I think. Trivia bonus for people who read Acknowledgments sections: The super-cool advanced tech pistol Jess is holding is inspired by a real-world Nerf gun.

Olivia of Olivia Pro Designs added lettering and text that fit the art exactly.

Many thanks to all of these wonderful helpers. Any errors, mistakes, or bad choices that remain are my fault and my fault alone.

AUTHOR'S NOTE

Dear reader:

Thank you so much for reading my story. I am so grateful that you chose to spend some time with my characters in the world I built. I started *Kenai* in Spring 2022, so it's been a little more than a year coming. One of my goals for the book was to have a quick, focused process to write a shorter sci-fi novel ready in time for the 2022-23 Self-Published Science Fiction Competition (SPSFC), which started in July 2022. Fate intervened, and I spent a good chunk of summer 2022 helping with a family emergency rather than writing. So, instead, *Kenai* got longer to simmer and grow, and I ended up with a longer sci-fi novel ready in time for the 2023-24 competition. I've really enjoyed being part of SPSFC, where my first sci-fi novel, *Daros*, reached the semi-finals in 2021-22.

Like nearly all of my books, I started this one without knowing what was going to happen, just writing about Jess and Welk at a dig site on Kenai, and adding enough weird things in that I'd have some ideas to play with. Early on, I thought up the idea about the living creatures jumping backward in time as each day passed, and I tried to imagine how that would appear to somebody unfamiliar living through it. Unlike some of my other books, which have been completely seat-of-the-pants nearly all the way through, I did get an early idea of where the plot was going and how things worked, and I wrote out a set of rules and a plan so that I could understand the story and so that things would be consistent. I didn't imagine Jess' jump to the deep past, or the Weynik space program, until much later, though – the time jump idea emerged from writing conversations between Elihar and Jess at their isolated campsite, and I didn't think up the space program until she was already back there in the village.

As the book progressed, it developed into a kind of a three-act structure for the main present-day story. Act one is Jess trying to survive her expedition falling apart, and act two is her meeting Elihar, eventually learning the mysteries of Kenai (her sobalihem!), and then working backwards to handle the events she observed going forwards. Then, there's act three, where she ends up deep in the planet's past and deep in an alien (to her) culture, figuring out what her role is, and opening herself up to making some friends and doing something important again. And, finally, there's a bit of a coda, or maybe a short act four, where she ends up back in the present day and gets to fight back against the odious SpearPoint crew who've done wrong to so many people. That also gives the book what I hope is a kick-ass, action-packed space-marine climax. That was the idea, anyway.

There are a couple challenges with this story. One is that the central time gimmick is pretty preposterous, in an "oh, come on" kind of way. I thought it was an interesting scenario to imagine, and I tried to give a reasonable plot basis for that scenario to exist, but in the end, it may be too much to ask for people to buy into this weird world. While writing, though, I was reminded of countless old Star Trek episodes that I loved, where the Enterprise (or Voyager or whatever) came across a place where the rules of society or reality were fundamentally different, and the crew had to figure out both what these rules were and how to navigate them, all in 43 minutes. A lot of those episodes are very challenging in terms of plausibility (how would this really work? how did it get this way?), but they're also often the most interesting ones.

A second challenge with the story is that once you start reversing time over itself, the narrative just becomes really complicated. I kept the perspective focused on Jess the whole time to help with this. As I edited the book, with nearly every pass through, I would find something I had done not quite right that required revision, so it was clearly confusing for me, too. For readers, there starts to be a likelihood that they will either become mired in trying to understand the cockamamie plot, or they'll just have to trust that at least I theoretically what I'm doing and am probably doing it mostly right. Neither of those outcomes is satisfying, so the challenge in writing it is to be clear enough that readers can follow while not being overly pedantic. I'm not sure I always managed that, but I hope I did for most of it. Below is one of the diagrams I made to help me keep track of the plot. I also had pages and pages of other diagrams, notes on rules, timelines, hypothetical scenarios, what people not shown are doing behind the scenes, and other bits of Kenai theory.

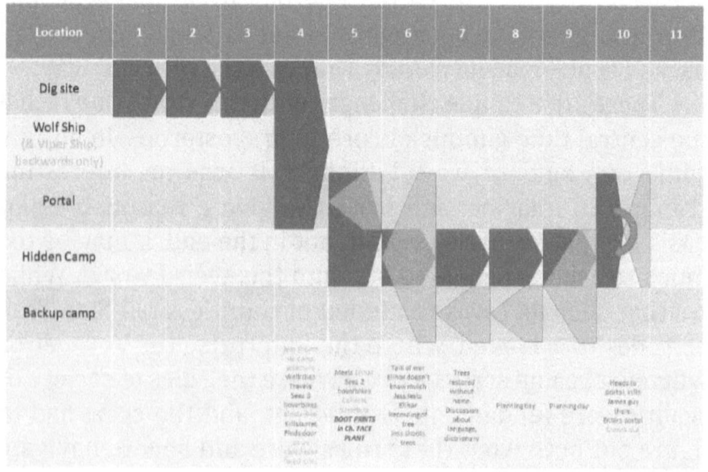

A third challenge with a book that messes with the flow of time is that you run into both destiny and paradoxes, and both can be cheesy and unsatisfying. In the case of this book, rather than avoiding paradoxes or destiny, I hugged them tight and told them just how beautiful they were. They're central to the story, and they're part of the nature and the challenge of Kenai. I do think they unavoidably weaken some parts of the story and reduce stakes, though. Jess and others often have to follow a predestined path just to make something happen, where there's no real danger to them or any uncertainty because they know they will succeed. I wanted to make sure that we dropped away from destiny and paradox for the conclusion of the book, to make the story stronger and more engaging, and the ending unknown and unknowable. Everything that happens after Elihar leaves Jess and his people behind is terra incognito (well, Kenai incognito), and I hope that balances out the parts that are more predestined, a least in part.

One of the writing issues I faced was that I didn't want the time gimmick to be the only focus of the story. To help with this, I started adding flashbacks about Jess' life and career. My hope was that those would help make the story more meaningful, and Jess more interesting, and they really helped me understand how she could be both heavily damaged but at the same time supremely competent and self-reliant, all while looking for a new purpose and maybe some new friends. I loved her interaction with Otieno, and I wanted to show her struggling with who she was and how to keep going in a life that was broken almost beyond repair. It didn't hurt that, in a narrative sense, flashbacks play with the flow of time, too, just as Kenai does. As I reached the third act, I found I needed (or wanted) fewer of these echoes of her past. They'd done their job, and now it was Jess' turn to make something of those experiences in the life she had found for herself.

It wasn't until my second-to-last editing pass that I realized there were two parallel scenes in the story that book-ended her journey, at least to a first order approximation. Her efforts fighting with the peaceful Weynik against the superior Nurikna invaders closely mirrored the incident on Treyna that got her convicted, although with her role reversed, the freedom fighter now instead of the invader. She'd come full circle in a way, in a book where time can flow both ways. Whether you think that bit of plot symmetry tends towards the poetic or the cheesy, rest assured that I did it unintentionally, or at least subconsciously. I like it, though. Sometimes you're lucky that way.

I also loved the possibility (left deliberately ambiguous) that some measure of Jess' past trauma could have come from the *renfit sharah,* the Weynik curse reaching back through time to lash out at her, although I'd be just as happy with an interpretation that her life happened to mirror some of the pain she found among the Weynik without being directly affected by the curse. That's all up to you, the reader, to think about and judge for yourself.

I liked the idea of writing another story set in the Council of Worlds, the same far-future human civilization I developed for *Daros*, although the two books don't share any characters or plot elements. I would love to explore this society further. For the next book, I may need to get brave enough to dive into the heart of that society, though, rather than just playing around on isolated fringe worlds.

Thanks so much for reading. I hope you'll try out some of my other stories. *Daros*, in particular, is a space opera much like this one. Please, feel free to write me at ***dave@davedobsonbooks.com***. Your comments, feedback, and reviews are what make writing fun. If you want the latest news on my writing, plus frequent links to free books, you can also sign up for my bimonthly newsletter here: ***http://davedobsonbooks.com/join-frosthelm***

May the dawn find you whole,

Dave Dobson
June 8, 2023

GLOSSARY

Below please find definitions and explanations of characters and parts of the Weynik culture on Kenai.

(Beware – some definitions contain significant spoilers)

Angalir – megalomaniac Nurikna villain who developed nuclear weapons

avishar – the point at which formerly living material loses its connection to the rakineru and begins to progress forward in time. E.g., a fallen tree will move backwards for a time, but when it decays completely into soil, it eventually becomes inanimate and unaffected by the time jump.

Dumisel – the rooted ones, those Weynik who do not uproot upon maturing and remain in tree form forever

eginfehr – a mating season for the Weynik

etivar – an outsider to the Weynik community

Elihar – a time-traveling Weynik person and Jess' friend

Erdion – the designation of the trial being conducted on Kenai by an unknown culture

fohaskar – objects, people, or creatures which travel in time in the same direction as the Weynik (i.e. backwards)

goromita – village council meetings for the Weynik

inuhaili – radioactive ore, or radioactivity

Kenai – an M-class planet inhabited by the Weynik.

Kenaians – human name for the Weynik

kunaret – one who creates a paradox and invokes the curse (*renfit sharah*)

lajaret – a loved one who dies because of the curse (a sacrifice)

Miern – Elihar's mate and partner, former Seed-Bearer of the Weynik village, killed by the *renfit sharah*

moft storeni – the ability that Kenaians have to sense the minds and emotions of others

Mothrek – a machine intelligence created by Angalir which aided Angalir in bringing about the end of sentient life on Kenai

Ninilchik – see Verikin.

Nurikna – a warlike nation or faction of the Weynik people who embrace metalworking and related technology and who live in cities

Nuruk – early Nurikna leader, advocated breaking down close relationships, occupying cities, and using technology. Founder of the Nurikna branch of the Weynik people

omariga – a woodweaver, one who can shape umbani (ironwood)

Poen – the new Seed-Bearer of the Weynik village

rakineru – the nightly time shift, when the Weynik and other living beings jump a day backward in time

Renefe – a scientist among the Weynik; director of their space program

Renares – the walking ones, those Weynik who break from their roots upon maturing and attain speech and mobility (in contrast to Dumisel)

renfit sharah – the curse exacted by the planet on those who create paradoxes

Sekene – the head woodweaver (omariga)

Seed-Bearer – the designated leader of a Weynik community

sobalihem – the point at which a young Weynik comes to understand the curse and the time paradox that affects the world

Tuenih – textile artisan with the Weynik

umbani – ironwood, an unusual variety of wood that can be shaped into elaborate structures and machines by artisans (omariga)

vasikilo – the speaking of one's history, an honor bestowed on some Weynik after death in which their deeds and accomplishments are recorded and displayed in public

Verikin – an M-class planet in the Kenai system. The sister world to Kenai, called Ninilchik by humans.

Weynik – the original Kenaian tree-like people; after the schism into two nations, this name was retained by the agrarian, peaceful Kenaians

Yomo – a lifeless world that is home to a remote Patrol base

APPENDIX: DR. MELMAN'S GUIDE TO GALACTIC HISTORY

Having Trouble Passing Your
Level 2 Early Galactic History Qualifier?

Only Melman has access to the actual exam questions!
NEW! *Notes are now available as a disappearing*
dermal tattoo for easy access during exams.

Remember the **ten key events,** and you'll pass your qualifying exams, guaranteed!

1. **Humans break the light barrier!** In the year 638 BE, on old Earth, humans develop the gate drive, which allows them to travel between places nearly

instantaneously. At this point, though, it takes hundreds of years to set up a connection, because a gate is needed at the origin and the destination before jumps are possible. Earth ships gradually set up relay gates along routes to the closest star systems to facilitate travel, and humanity reaches the stars.

2. **Gateless drive!** In 310 BE, researchers develop a gateless FTL drive. That allows much faster expansion between unexplored stars! It's extremely expensive, though, so initially, it's limited to only a few vessels. It remains expensive today.

3. **Expansion!** From 310-105 BE, humans expand and colonize planets from Earth outward. By 105 BE, there are 131 worlds in the Trade Union! The Trade Union retains proprietary control over the gate system and controls nearly all trade and travel from Earth.

4. **Fracturing of the Union!** In 105 BE, a set of star systems toward the center of human space rebel against the Trade Union's control of the gate network. They demand free travel. This creates two competing factions with many other splinter groups also declaring independence.

5. **Descent into war!** From 105-56 BE, tensions rise between the factions. Systems switch sides. The Trade Union annexes some of the rebel systems. The rebels fight back. Some worlds are destroyed by surprise attacks from towed asteroids. Others are attacked with planet-buster bombs and nuclear weapons.

6. **Earth's demise!** In 56 BE, disguised rebel vessels manage to inflict an extinction-level event on Earth using a perion-particle weapon. Nearly all life on Earth is wiped out.

7. **Vengeance!** From 56-0 BE, the Trade Union inflicts vengeful and merciless attacks on rebel worlds, including use of AI-controlled self-replicating automaton armies. Rebels respond with more perion bombs. Over a hundred worlds are rendered lifeless. The gate network is left in tatters.

8. **Extirpation!** In the year 0, the Trade Union gate system shuts down entirely. All gates power down and go offline. The last few remaining rebel worlds also cease communication. No Trade Union vessels are ever seen again, and there is only silence from the inner systems. The only human worlds remaining are recently-colonized fringe worlds at the edge of human space, and most are isolated and lack supplies and technology. Travel between systems breaks down without the Trade Union's gates.

9. **Rise of a new way!** From 0-17 AE, there is no regular interstellar travel. Systems remain mostly isolated. Starting in 17 AE, Glisson, an outer-fringe system that remained neutral in the war and retained its manufacturing and technologic resources, gradually rebuilds a local gate system, independent from the Trade Union's old one. They send scout ships to observe known human colonies nearby. If the colonies still exist, are stable, and are dedicated to peace, Glisson offers them access to its gate network in exchange for an inviolable disarmament clause. No weapons able to attack ground targets from space are permitted, and ship-to-ship weapons are severely curtailed.

10. **The Council is Born!** By 77 AE, enough worlds have signed on with Glisson that there is a new healthy, peaceful group of human-controlled planets. These 18 worlds enter into a governing alliance. They form a representative Council to set laws, and they agree to

build and fund a collective fleet of peacekeeping ships and soldiers, known as the Patrol, to keep order, defend against outside attacks, and enforce the internal peace agreement. Glisson relinquishes control of the gate network to the new Council of Worlds.

Of course, you know how that all turned out in the 281 years since. The Council of Worlds is bigger, and it is strong! We trade among many Council systems, and the Council economy is healthy. Unfortunately, most inner human worlds are either damaged beyond repair, overrun by self-replicating murder robots, or bathed in radiation, and even the probes we send to them hardly ever return. But the free worlds of the Council are prospering! Many corporations provide valuable goods and services to Council planets, people live rich and fulfilling lives, and the Patrol protects us all. We even have a few non-human members of the Council now. Humanity, and its partners and allies, have a bright future ahead of us!

OTHER BOOKS TO TRY

If you enjoyed **Kenai,** here are my other books to explore. You can find links to all of them on my website, **DaveDobsonBooks.com.**

SCIENCE FICTION

My science fiction books are set in a far-distant future where humans have reached the stars, and where Earth and other early colonies have been lost to a vicious war, leaving only a small number of fringe colonies.

Daros tells the story of a dusty mining world that comes under attack by aliens. Brecca Vereen, a smuggler's daughter with a secret, ejects from her father's wounded ship in a life pod, and Frim, a navigator in the invading fleet, is a secret rebel trying to survive and undercut the murderous invaders.

Daros was a semi-finalist in the first SPSFC competition in 2022.

EPIC FANTASY

The **Inquisitors' Guild** series of books are all self-contained mysteries relating the adventures of various members of the Inquisitors' Guild of Frosthelm. Expect detective stories with swordplay, magic, scheming nobles, and humor, all in a medieval setting. There are four books so far in the series:

- **Flames Over Frosthelm**
- **The Outcast Crown**
- **The Woeling Lass**
- **Traitors Unseen** (novella)

Flames Over Frosthelm was a finalist in the ISFAB awards, 2019.
The Woeling Lass was a semi-finalist in the SPFBO competition, 2022.

The Glorious and Epic Tale of Lady Isovar is a comedic epic fantasy novel full of adventure, friendship, heroic battles, and vile villains. It is the story of a valiant and dauntless knight and her squire Chevson, who is less worried about honor and more worried about pointing Izzy toward actual enemies, not innocent bystanders.

This book is currently a semi-finalist in the SPFBO competition as of September 2024.

THRILLERS

My thrillers are character-focused stories, including fast-paced suspense, complicated family relationships, and lots of humor. Both of them are set in present-day North Carolina.

Got Trouble is the story of Glynnis Cary, a night manager at a gas station, stuck in a moribund marriage and with a kid finding trouble everywhere. Circumstances outside her control force her to go on the run with a new friend, one whose life she's just inadvertently destroyed. Glynnis has to rely on her gut, her grit, and her ability to spin big lies to evade both foreign agents and her own government.

What Grows From the Dead is the story of Morris Drummond, who is definitely not dealing well with career and life challenges. To make matters worse, he blunders into a deadly conspiracy involving his departed mother, and suddenly a surprising number of people want him dead. A humorous mystery with elements of suspense and thrillers, the book is set in present-day small-town North Carolina, not far from the mysterious Uwharrie Forest.

ABOUT THE AUTHOR

A native of Ames, Iowa, Dave loves writing, reading, boardgames, computer games, improv comedy, pizza, barbarian movies, and the cheaper end of the Taco Bell menu. Also, his wife and kids.

Dave is the author of Snood, Snoodoku, Snood Towers, and other computer games. Dave first published Snood in 1996, and it became one of the most popular shareware games of the early Internet. He's recently published puzzle card games in the Doctor Esker's Notebook series through his game company, **Plankton Games.**

Dave taught geology, environmental studies, and computer programming at Guilford College for 24 years. He does improv comedy at the Idiot Box in Greensboro, North Carolina. He's also played the world's largest tuba in concert. Not that that is relevant, but it's still kinda cool.

Dave has written nine novels and is working on more. *Kenai* is his second science fiction novel. It won the 3rd annual Self-Published Science Fiction competition in 2024, beating out 220 other books across eight months of competition.

To learn more about Dave and his writing, and to sign up for his newsletters, please visit **DaveDobsonBooks.com**.